Myrdden

by

Robert Haseltine

PublishAmerica
Baltimore

First printing

At the specific preference of the author, PublishAmerica allowed this work to remain exactly as the author intended, verbatim, without editorial input.

ISBN: 1-4137-7023-1
PUBLISHED BY PUBLISHAMERICA, LLLP
www.publishamerica.com
Baltimore

Printed in the United States of America

chapter 1
Avalon

Daylight no longer hid the oncoming menace as it made its way through space toward its impact with Earth. The bright dot of light belied both its size and the speed of its approach. At first it was only a pinpoint, but each passing day it became a little larger until now it was had become nearly the size of the head of the pin. It was like a firefly in the daytime sky: a firefly whose light was on perpetually as a warning of what was to come.

On a mountain twenty miles east of Salistar a young man in his teens stood near the telescope his father was using to observe an approaching asteroid. The observatory was on the highest peak in the country; safe, it was hoped, from the devastation that was coming. "Father" he said looking up at the platform on which his father stood. "Father." He continued when he had the older man's attention. "We have powerful weapons don't we?"

Murdo Emres looked down at the youth and smiled. "Aye, Myrdden, we have powerful weapons." He was proud of this son; a son who stood near six feet tall, broad of shoulder and narrow of hip, his blond hair a complement to the blue eyes; eyes that showed the intelligence of the mind behind it. His son, now seventeen and taller than his father, was already well versed in the lore of Atlantis.

"Well then. Why not use one of these weapons on the asteroid? Break it into bits so it will not make such a large *lan mara* when it hits, or turn it so it won't hit?"

Murdo smiled ruefully. "Because," he sighed, "the asteroid is just too large. This one isn't like the others that have passed us by. We've seen the damage they did when they hit the moon. Neither are they like the comets we see once in a while. Those are mostly ice that leaves a trail of crystal behind.

Though some have called this a meteor, we know it isn't a meteor; it's actually an asteroid; and a very large one at that.

"In the time of your grandfather, many years ago," he came down from the viewing platform to the floor where Myrdden was standing, "another even larger mass approached the planet Agnor, then the fifth planet from the sun. Many believe it was a stray planet, a rogue that happened to enter our area of space. It grazed the atmosphere, and its stronger gravity field disrupted Agnor's. Some believe it may have even hit Agnor. Either way, Agnor broke into the smaller pieces we call asteroids. The total mass of those asteroids is at least equal to the mass of Agnor when it was whole. Most of the asteroids achieved an orbit similar to that of Agnor's; some did not. This," Murdo looked up at the sky, "is one that did not. It took an orbit, but the orbit was a decreasing spiral."

"Decreasing spiral? So every time it orbits it moves closer to the sun?" Myrdden asked.

"Yes. As it orbits, every revolution brings it slightly closer to the sun. Eventually it would have died by burying itself in the sun. Unfortunately Talab has gotten in its way. Now, rather than dying in the sun, it will hit in the ocean somewhere between Atlantis and Lemur. If it skips through the atmosphere and skims the water, it may bounce back into space. The effects of that would be bad. There would be a huge *lan mara* if it skips off the ocean, a dense cloud of steam would hide the sun for a long period of time, and there would be devastating earthquakes. Depending on the angle and depth Atlantis and Lemur would be badly hurt, but possibly not destroyed. The worst case is if it hits at an acute angle. If that is what happens the resultant *lan mara* could destroy Atlantis, Lemur, and the land masses bordering the ocean." He sighed and gazed out over the piedmont lying between the mountain and Salistar. Shaking his head he murmured. "That being the case, the geography of most of the other continents would be altered as well.

"We may be safe on this mountain." He continued. "Then again, we may not. We don't know the angle of impact as yet, so we don't know how high the *lan mara* will be, nor how powerful will be the contact of the asteroid. We do know from our measurements it is almost as large as this vast island on which we live." He sighed again, his eyes still looking over the area below. He was quiet as he gazed at the beauty of the forests on the side of the mountain, the fenced fields of the farms, the white towers of Salistar, and the sparkle of the waves reflecting the light of the sun. "Perhaps that asteroid was once as lovely as what we see from here. Perhaps it comes from the interior of Agnor. Now it is just a mass of rock large enough to destroy us."

"What are we going to do when it hits, Da?"

"Your mother and I have purchased a means of escape, we think. Soon they will deliver an escape capsule. There was no time to have a boat made. I have calculated the dimensions of this capsule to make it seaworthy. We hadn't time to make it with a motor, so it will have no means of propulsion. That being the case it needs no bow or stern. It will float, and it will go where the wind and the tides take it. We will be safe within. I will place food, water, books, and important state papers within it so we can survive the onslaught. Once the seas calm down again we may be able to land here on Atlantis. If Atlantis is destroyed we may be able to land on one of the other continents. We will put our trust in the Creator and he will take us where we are to go."

Myrdden stood by Murdo and looked out over the lush greenery that was the large island/continent called Atlantis. He nodded slowly. "I see. There is then no hope. When will the impact be?"

"From my calculations we have another ten days."

"What of all the others in Salistar," he paused, "or Atlantis?"

Murdo shook his head sadly. "Most will perish by one means or another. Some will escape and find refuge elsewhere. As you know, many are buying passage on some of the larger ships; others are being frozen in order to preserve themselves against a time when they believe they can be thawed and resume their lives. In any event our way of life will be altered drastically."

Myrdden lifted an eyebrow, his lips pursed in thought. "But if they are frozen don't they realize they will really be dead? Once everything stops and the brain has no oxygen it won't survive. Besides, the water in the body will expand as it freezes rupturing every organ. Even I know that."

Murdo nodded. "You are right, of course, but people will believe what they want to believe, no matter what the facts are."

Myrdden shook his head in disbelief. "It doesn't matter what you want to believe, truth is truth whether you believe it or not."

"Aye, but many don't want their beliefs clouded by facts. Meanwhile, my son, make sure you remember what we have taught you here. Atlantis is more advanced than the other countries we know. What you are able to do with your mind will seem like magic to them, though it is common knowledge among our people. Be careful how you use what you know if worse comes to worse and you are in a foreign land. I speak this way because I know not what will happen to us, and I believe we should be prepared for the worst event that can happen. You do understand, do you not?"

Myrdden nodded. "I understand. I understand all too well. You do not believe Atlantis will survive this blow."

Murdo's smile was proud, but sad. "Your powers of interpreting other's emotions are well developed. I didn't believe I was showing that much pessimism. Be careful using the power you have, it can get you into trouble in other lands. They may look on you as a wizard or magician, even though you are only using the powers of the mind and nature we of Atlantis have cultivated over the centuries."

"You don't believe you and mother will survive, do you?"

Murdo paused and shrugged his shoulders as he sighed. "I do not know." He said slowly. "We will try. When the time comes, however, do not wait for us to join you in the capsule. Affairs of state may take us away from here. We may be where we cannot return in time. Make sure you get in the capsule and close it tightly. It will have food and water so you will neither starve nor thirst. Even if we die we wish to assure ourselves that you will survive. Promise me that, son, for I would not have all of us perish in this coming *lan mara*."

There was a long silence as the two looked at each other. Then Myrdden slowly nodded. "I promise, Da. If you are not able to be with me I will go alone. But what makes you believe you will not be here?"

"My perceptions are more advanced than yours are right now. You will later acquire more of the extra senses, but it will take a few more years. I can sense a bit of the future, and I see neither your mother nor myself in it. As their ruler I may be where I can give our people inner strength. I fear your mother and I will be away when the asteroid hits, and unable to make it here in time. You must survive, for I see you having great influence in the future; where and with whom I know not."

The two were silent as they again stood side-by-side and gazed at the bucolic scene stretching from their mountaintop to the sea. A golden sun was slowly sinking into the ocean, as the clouds took on the color of crimson and orange against the deep blue of the sky. Murdo put his hand on his son's shoulder as they watched the burning globe sink out of sight and the shadows creep in from the sea to cover the land leading to their mountain to finally cover their position as well. "Come." Murdo said. "Let's go in and have our supper. It is late and I fear your mother might be wondering what is detaining us."

* * *

For hundreds of years the island continent of Atlantis had been a lamp that shed its light on other continents of darkness. It held a people devoted to research and education; sharing bits and pieces of what they had found with others willing to be enlightened. Though the large island was somewhat hidden in the middle of a large ocean, a young man named Solon the Hellene had found it. He had heard of it and come for education. Atlantis welcomed those willing to learn, and Solon had been sent back to Hellas to bring a new idea of law and governance in a world dominated by despotic rulers. Five hundred years had passed and the people of Hellas were now foremost in philosophy, oratory, and literature. Only recently the young Plato had returned to his home country to lead them toward a new and glorious future: it was hoped.

Reluctantly the people of Atlantis withheld many of their findings from the rest of the world. On a continent devoted to peaceful pursuits and discovery the constant warfare of the other lands was seen as a detriment. Thus, while Atlantis enjoyed the use of vehicles powered by energy from the sun, a means of communication that was almost instantaneous in transmission, and lighting that did not depend upon candles these advances were withheld from the other civilizations on the larger continents. Discoveries meant for peace had too often been turned to destruction when previously offered to those on other continents.

Unfortunately, a new method of destruction was looming on the horizon: a destruction they could do nothing about. From the normally peaceful sky they watched as an asteroid sped through space, growing larger with every passing day. They had seen it coming for months. With their telescopes focused on the asteroid, the astronomers had plotted its path, and warnings had been transmitted to all parts of the continent. While the impact would be far from their shores, the very size of the object would create a wave of such proportions the major coastal cities of the island continent of Atlantis would be wiped out. Depending on whether it struck earth or sea a thick cloud could blot out the sun for weeks. Under either circumstance earthquakes would follow the flood. It was hoped these phenomena would not cause such damage that could not be repaired.

Forewarned, the people had been moving inland for the past few months. All on the coast were moving to avoid the sure death that would be theirs when the *lan mara* would sweep in. Many, unwilling to accept the fact of the *lan mara*, still refused to leave the capitol city of Salistar, on the southwestern coast, so business to a lesser degree was being carried on as usual.

* * *

Myrdden glanced up from his book, a puzzled look on his face. Everything was still. It was a silence unlike any he had ever known. It was as though all nature was holding its breath in anticipation. The birds had stopped singing, the dogs weren't barking, the air seemed to become dead, the wind chimes were silent; and then the dogs began whining. It was not their usual warning bark, but a voice of fear. He put the book down and went to the door. In the distance he could see a gigantic ball of fire falling from the sky. Though it was far away it appeared huge against the dark sky; it seemed to be so close he almost expected it to hit in the bay outside the town. A cold fear gripped his heart as he watched it fall. The asteroid seemed to fall in slow motion, though he knew it was traveling thousands of miles per hour. Murdo and Naomi, his mother, had gone to town to give heart to the people in the hour of peril. During the past week the capsule had been delivered and now sat in the yard behind the house, loaded with the provisions Murdo had put in it.

Myrdden watched as the falling mass of superheated rock plummeted toward the ocean beyond the horizon. Almost immediately both steam and a wave rose. The wave continued rising until it seemed to be a mile high. At that distance and at that height Myrdden knew the wave was already higher than the mountaintop on which he stood. As he watched it began to spread out from the impact area as the cloud of steam rose skyward to rapidly fill the atmosphere and cover the sun. He stood quietly, heart feeling as though it would pound through his chest, and watched the *lan mara* wave as it gave the impression of standing still, it was so far distant. He knew, however, it was traveling more rapidly than sound while it grew even higher as the asteroid displaced more of the ocean's water. Then he saw a dark speck against the sky. The asteroid had hit a glancing blow and was headed out of the atmosphere. Even the glancing blow was enough to cause untold damage from the huge wave it had raised.

He stood still, binoculars at his eyes as he watched the road for the vehicle his father would be driving. He knew his parents would leave the city and head home as fast as they could. The guards would make sure he left the hall as rapidly as possible. Then, too, the other citizens would also be headed away from the sea. The traffic jam would be massive. He could only watch as the gigantic wave hit land. The tallest of the buildings were as toys against its height. As it rolled inland the buildings disintegrated in its path.

Far below he could see the tiny specks of racing vehicles, frantically attempting to outrace a wave that was moving a hundred times faster than they could. When the wave overshadowed the last of the vehicles he knew he was alone. His mouth tightened as he stood for a second longer, watching where the vehicles had been, wondering which had been his parents'. Then he rushed to the capsule, climbed inside, dogged the door tight, strapped himself into a seat, and waited for the wave to reach him.

With a lurch the capsule was flung skyward as the wave rolling up and over the mountain impelled the capsule upward as though it was a shell shot from a cannon. The capsule somersaulted, twisted, and rolled as it was buffeted by the strong currents set up by the *lan mara*. As it did he was thrown against the straps holding him in the padded chair. He could hear an almost constant thud as other objects bounced against the outer wall, but his father had made sure the capsule would be strong enough to withstand such impacts. Myrdden knew he was traveling rapidly through the water because he was being flung one way and another against the straps as the capsule tumbled and rolled in the turbulence created by the impact of the asteroid. He lost consciousness as his head struck the back of the chair. Even its padding couldn't protect against that blow.

When he woke he was no longer being thrown about. Now it seemed he was riding the crest of the *lan mara* wave even as it began to slow. The friction of the land and water over which it surged was causing it to diminish its fierceness. Much later he found himself floating calmly on the sea. Beneath the capsule he could sense the gentle waves of a relatively calm sea. He dared to undo the straps that had held him in place. They had saved his life he was sure, though he could feel every bruise and abrasion where they had been. Standing up he unlatched the cover of the window and slid it back. Outside was the blue of the sky against the aqua of a sea covered with the flotsam and jetsam of the land in which he had lived.

For the first time since the wave hit he had a chance to look at the interior of the capsule. The entire family had checked it out when it arrived, had sat in their specially built seats, strapped themselves in and tested the webbed straps for strength and comfort. Murdo had stored things well. The interior of the cabin was relatively clear of debris. A few idle scraps of paper littered the floor but anything that could cause harm was still safely in the various compartments.

Myrdden looked at the two empty seats, straps still waiting their occupants, turned and slammed his fist into the padded side of the bulkhead. He hit it again and again until finally exhausted he sat in his own seat. He stared sadly at the other seats, put his head in his hands, and wept. He had been warned, but the reality of the truth was now apparent. His father, called away on state business with his mother, had perished with millions of others when the island of Atlantis had been overwhelmed by a *lan mara* the size of which no one had ever dreamed possible.

As the days passed he found himself in the straps during storms, or gazing out the window at the never-ending sea on all sides. While there was much reading material, a great deal of it was papers of state his father had stowed in case Atlantis could be rebuilt. Along with these were his schoolbooks, and some works of fiction by writers from Atlantis, Greece and Egypt. Still, inactivity leads to boredom, and Myrdden became bored.

As days grew into weeks the cache of food and water dwindled. He put himself on short rations, wondering when he might expect landfall. Perhaps his father had been wrong and he would perish at sea, killed by the same disaster that had taken his parents and the people on what had once been Atlantis. Finally his food ran out, then the water. When the capsule eventually washed up on a small beach it contained an unconscious, dehydrated, and famished body.

* * *

Seanard Maire, second in rank of the Sisterhood of Avalon tapped on the door of the Beanard. "Lilith," she said on entering. "A capsule washed up on the beach. We broached it and found a youth emaciated and dehydrated. He is in cottage C being nursed back to health. I have Moira with him at the moment."

Lilith nodded. "Yes. The *Sidhe* have informed me of the arrival of the capsule. What did you find in it other than the boy?"

"Papers indicate this was the private escape capsule of Murdo Emres and his family. Most of the papers were state papers of Atlantis, some were of familial importance. The youth is most likely his son, Myrdden. Apparently it was only he who was able to be near enough to the capsule when the tidal wave hit the island. I assume his family perished in the tragedy."

Lilith nodded again. "That is my understanding as well." She paused. "The *Sidhe* are very interested in this lad for they were friends of Murdo, and helped the peaceful people of Atlantis. In fact, some of the *Sidhe* intermarried, so it is possible young Myrdden has some of the blood of the *Sidhe* in his veins." Her face became even more thoughtful. "So, that makes three who may have escaped the wave." She looked up. "Make sure we do our best by him. I will inform Kings Lir and Brian he is in our care."

Maire nodded understanding. "Lilith. You know anyone in this shape would get exactly the same care this youth will get. It is always our best."

Lilith's laugh was like silver bells in the room. "You are right, Maire. It is the way of the Order. I was just speaking without thought apparently. Still, watch over him well."

"As always." Maire laughed as well, "As always."

* * *

The first sensations he had were those of a relatively soft substance under his back. He couldn't open his eyes, though he could hear voices, women's voices, as they discussed his condition.

"I believe he is gaining consciousness." The voice was soft, seemed to be from a young female, and came from his right side.

"I believe you are right, Moira. Thank goodness. When we found him I was afraid we might not be able to save him. He was barely alive after the terrible ordeal he must have faced."

"Yes. The other survivor, the one that landed in Lyonesse, came through much better. Then too, she had not been so long without provisions." He felt the touch of a soft cloth as it wiped his forehead. "I wonder if they knew each other."

"Doubtful. Atlantis was a large island; a continent really. It would be unusual for them to have known each other, though Morrigan may even have come from the same city."

"I've heard of Atlantis, but have never been able to visit." Moira said thoughtfully. "I've heard the people were special, but never understood why."

The voice of the older woman was soft and kind in his ears. "The people were special and had powers many others do not have. Their powers are, were, similar to ours, but much better developed. They have an ability to use their minds to make normal people believe they have done things impossible to understand. Normal people call it magic, though it is merely the use of natural law to produce an effect others cannot. It is much the same as some of our powers here in Avalon. We are able to do certain things others cannot because of our use of natural law. Those others do not understand and often fear us, or try to kill us. That is why we live on Avalon, and why we hide the island from those we do not wish to see. Then too, our close ties with Tir na nOg are often misunderstood as well."

"Oh, Maire, but Tir na nOg is a land of magic."

"Not of magic, dear. It is a place that time didn't touch, and where they know even more than we do how to use natural law to obtain what they want.

Even to us it seems a place of magic, but what to one person is magic or a miracle is another's use of natural law to accomplish a natural end. Oh, your young man is coming to."

Myrdden's eyelids fluttered as he tried to open them. At first the room was blurred, dim in the light of the candles burning in the sconces on the wall. He had been right; the young voice had come from a lovely young girl clad in the robes of an acolyte. He knew not an acolyte of what order, but the robes of the novitiate are similar in many orders. The older woman was obviously one of the senior orders. She looked down at him and smiled. "Welcome back, young man. I will give you a bit of time to organize your thoughts then, when you recognize your hunger, let us know and we will bring you food to help bring you back even further." She smiled kindly, "Oh, it won't be meat yet for your body will not tolerate much at the moment. However, broth is a good start. After that, as you gain strength, on to the heartier foods. Never fear, we will bring you back. Now, can you tell us who you are?"

Myrdden's mouth was dry, and he found it difficult to form words, but was finally able to whisper, "Myrdden Emres."

Maire nodded her head as she caught the name. "Ah. You are the son of Murdo Emres?" She asked. Myrdden nodded. He tried to say 'yes', but no words came. "Moira. Give Prince Myrdden water. Then we will let him rest and gather more strength. We will leave you now, young Myrdden. Rest well."

Moira looked up at Maire. "Might I stay, Maire? He is still weak. He may need more than just water."

Maire smiled knowingly. She nodded. "All right. Stay and tend him. Call me or one of the other sisters if you need help."

"I will." Moira answered as she tenderly used the cloth on Myrdden's forehead. "He has a little fever yet. If it becomes worse I will call."

"You do that." Maire said dryly as she left.

* * *

"What is the news from Lyonesse regarding the girl who survived the tidal wave?" Lilith, leader of the Sisterhood on Avalon asked Maire as they walked along the seashore of Avalon. The path they followed was a circular one that ran from the small community through groves of beech trees to the shore. It followed the shoreline before curving back into the trees and finally to the buildings that comprised the village. The capsule that had washed on shore was now resting in a hut in the compound. Maire, second in the leadership, was in communion with others of the sisterhood in other lands.

"She says she is called Morrigan, the Queen of Air and Darkness. She also says she is the daughter of King Murdo Emres of Atlantis. She believes she is the sole survivor of the tragedy that took Atlantis to the bottom of the sea. We have told no one of the boy Myrdden as yet. We received the word from you, while you were yet in Tir na nOg, that King Lir, King Brian, and Queen Mabd wished it kept secret for a little while."

Lilith nodded. "Aye: as well as the one whose capsule landed in Tir na nOg itself. You say this girl calls herself Morrigan. Yet Morrigan was a city on the northeastern coast of Atlantis. We know Myrdden is son of Murdo because of the books and records stowed away in the capsule. Apparently Murdo wished to assure anyone who found the capsule, if he were unable to reach it, that the occupant was truly his son. Salistar, the capitol of Atlantis was on the southern coast, thus it received the brunt of the tidal wave when it hit. While still strong when it reached Morrigan, much of its force had dissipated as it went over land. Thus this girl who calls herself Morrigan was able to escape in a much weaker capsule than Myrdden." She paused as they continued to slowly walk the white sands. The susurration of the waves was the only sound as they gently lapped at the sandy beach.

"When he is able we must question him on his knowledge of this girl, though I suspect they had no knowledge of each other. We really need to know if she is his sister, though to the best of my knowledge Murdo had no other offspring than Myrdden." Lilith continued as they turned up the path.

"Myrdden is young, and his body is healing rapidly. The lack of food and water, especially the latter, did drain him." She smiled gently. "Moira is watching over him, and I suspect she has certain feelings for him. She seldom leaves his side, and makes sure he eats and drinks what we give him."

Lilith's laugh was like a tinkling bell. "Moira is young, as is Myrdden. I find it not strange she is attracted to him. With her ministrations it would not be strange for them to be attracted to each other." She laughed. "Knowing the way of a young man with a maid I deem it wise if we watch them both lest our young acolyte present us with a younger present."

Maire laughed along with Lilith. "Aye. I have already made sure they are not alone too long at a time. Naila and Morag are to check on his well being, and I have staggered the interruptions so neither knows when they will enter. Though I suspect there has been an exchange of kisses already when they are sure they are alone."

Lilith nodded. "No doubt. Leave us make sure it goes no further. Moira is to be the queen of Beltaine, and the bride of the High Priest. The time is not yet ripe for her to conceive."

They continued in silence until they reached the small temple. Pausing outside Lilith turned to Maire. "I have been told by King Lir they wish to meet with Prince Myrdden once he has regained his health and strength. Keep me informed of his progress. Meanwhile, find out if there is any knowledge of this…Morrigan." She paused in thought. "I would have you send word to our sister in Lyonesse to ascertain if the girl is completely in control of her mind. The tragedy may have addled her a bit, especially if this idea of being Queen of Air and Darkness is something she believes to be true. Such beliefs, if beliefs they are, would lead one to suspect something is amiss. Of course it could be a design to gain power over others." She nodded to Maire, then turned and entered the temple.

* * *

His youth and good health brought Myrdden's strength back in short order. Once on his feet he and Moira would walk on the beach, watching the fishermen ply their trade in the waters between Avalon and Cymru. On the first walk, as he was still attempting to handle himself in an upright position, he asked Moira, "Why don't they land their boats on the beach? It would save them going all the way to the other shore, and I'm sure we could use what they catch."

Moira smiled. "They cannot see us. Avalon is hidden from the eyes of mortals so the Sisterhood will not be disturbed in their work. While we know the island is here, and those of Faerie and Tir na nOg know of it, mortal man does not. Only if the Sisterhood approves will any mortal see this land, and then only when they call for them to come."

"So the Sisterhood has powers over nature that they are able to hide such a large island as this?"

Moira shrugged. "I am only an acolyte training to be a Sister. I do not yet know all the ways of the order."

Myrdden's brow furrowed in thought. "You are mortal, as are the Sisters I've seen. How did you come to be here?"

"My mother was the seventh daughter of a seventh daughter. I am her seventh daughter. There is magic in that number, or so I'm told, and those who are born such have mind powers other mortals do not have. Because the people of the village were afraid of me, they tried to kill me as a child. Mother Lilith knew of it and rescued me from them, along with my mother. I have been here ever since, and am training to enter the order at Beltaine."

Myrdden nodded understanding. "And your mother?"

Moira smiled, "Oh, you know her. She is Maire, now second only to Lilith in the Sisterhood."

A week passed, with daily walks, and new strength. On the seventh day, as the two were again walking on the beach, Maire came to them. "Mother Lilith wishes to see you, Myrdden. You will come with me, please."

When he entered the study Lilith motioned him to a chair. "I am happy to see you have regained your strength Prince Myrdden."

"Thank you. I appreciate all you have done for me. Still, in the time I've been here I have heard no mention of the fate of Atlantis."

Lilith nodded, her face a study in sadness. "I'm afraid Atlantis is no more. The wave the asteroid raised created an undersea earthquake and the entire continent of Atlantis has sunk below the waves. The sinking still progresses for Lyonesse is now slowly sinking as well. In a few years it will no longer exist as it joins your country in the nations lost in history."

Myrdden sat quietly, the silence hanging in the room like black crepe. Finally he looked up. He smiled sadly. "Then, Mother, I am no longer Prince Myrdden for I have no land that I am destined to rule. From this time forward I am merely Myrdden, the man without a father, or a country."

Lilith sighed and nodded. "I understand, Myrdden, and it shall be so. While you will always be Myrdden Emres, you will also be sung about as the man who has no father. While those in this age will remember Atlantis and its people, those in the future will lose any knowledge of all trace of its ever existing. The only mention might be in the writing of the philosophers of Hellas, and they will be accused of making it out of the whole cloth."

Myrdden smiled impishly, one eyebrow raised, "As it will with Avalon? If no one can see it, or come to it unless you call, it will become a myth; a legend."

Lilith chuckled. "Aye, Myrdden, as will Lemur and Atlantis, and the two of us."

She paused and fixed her gaze on him. "For one so young you already seem to have the ability to perceive the emotions and thoughts of others. I can already see you as more mature than many of your age. Now, tell me, do you know a young girl who calls herself Morrigan, the Queen of Air and Darkness?"

Myrdden sat back in the chair, thinking. Finally he looked up. "I heard my father speak of someone in Morrigan City the officials were having trouble with: though she didn't call herself the Queen of Air and Darkness. She was trying to use her mind powers to manipulate others. Since she was young, and older people were mentally stronger, she could only manipulate those younger than she. But where did you hear of her?"

"It seems you are not the only one who survived the *lan mara* that wiped out Atlantis. A young lady who calls herself by this name was washed up in Lyonesse. She is under the care of the Sisters there. They are stronger than she so she has not been able to manipulate them. If her goal is power over others, then we may have trouble down through the years, for the normal mortals are easily manipulated."

"I understand. Moira has told me the island is invisible to them. No one comes unless they are called."

Lilith smiled wryly. "Or unless they have mental powers and are unconscious when they arrive. We help heal those who are unconscious, cloud their memories of us, and transport them to the mainland. I believe you forget that we didn't call you. You are here because King Lir, Lord of the Seas, ordered his selkies to hunt for your capsule and bring you to our shore. It took them longer than he expected, for the capsule was not that large in the vastness of a sea covered with the detritus of your civilization. You were near death when they finally brought you here."

"King Lir." Myrdden mused. "Da talked of him. I believe he knew him."

"He did. That is one reason for him to want you safe. Now King Lir wishes to see you at your convenience."

Myrdden laughed humorlessly. "At my convenience, eh?" He shook his head. "No. It should be at his convenience. He is a king. I am merely Myrdden, an orphan from Atlantis. I will be happy to meet him whenever he wishes."

"I will arrange it. I am sorry for your loss. I hope you are not bitter about it."

"Bitter?" Myrdden paused in self examination. Finally he shook his head. "No. Not bitter. Sad, I guess would be the best description. How can one be bitter about an act of nature over which no one on this planet had any control? I will remember it, though, and hope to make other's lives better because of what I have inherited from my father." He smiled ruefully. "Atlantis was a peaceful nation for the most part. That is one reason it was able to achieve the technology it did. If I can help other nations achieve a way of looking to a more peaceful future I will do so. I do thank you for watching over me, and helping me back to health."

"I also knew your parents, Myrdden. It is the least I could do for them. Leave now and I will let you know when you will meet with the rulers of Tir na nOg."

* * *

"I think," Lilith said as she and Maire took their daily walk, "we should bring this Morrigan person here to meet Myrdden. From the message you received last it would seem her delusions and ambitions have grown over the past few weeks."

"True." Maire said. "Naomi has indicated the girl seems to have more than one name, and perhaps more than one personality. She now calls herself by a number of other names, seemingly depending on the phase of the moon. She has called herself Morgana, Morgana le Fae, Lilith," At this Lilith lifted an eyebrow in surprise, but did not interrupt. "and she claims to be daughter to Murdo and sister to his son, though she seems not to know Myrdden's name. She still claims she is Queen of Air and Darkness, and vows to become the ruler of the mortals. She has told Naomi only she knows the direction they should go, and she is the only one who can lead them in that direction."

"Morgana le Fae, eh? She believes she is a part of Faerie? I doubt Queen Titania has heard of her." Lilith smiled. "After all, she is a bit large to be one of the Trooping *Sidhe*, now isn't she?"

Maire nodded and smiled. "Aye. That she is. She is a full grown mortal, though she doesn't wish to recognize who she is at that time of the month. I do believe the loss of her parents, city, and kingdom have unsettled her. There is, I hope, some way of bringing her back to her right mind. Perhaps, as you point out, confronting Myrdden will help in her healing. Her body is healed, but her mind seems to need to be healed now."

Lilith sighed. "Yes, you are right. She is mentally unstable, yet from what I have seen in the reports she is stable enough to make others believe her to be sane when she talks with them about things other than this delusion of being a queen." There was a long silence as they continued to walk the sands of the beach. As they turned up the walk toward the temple she said, "Aye. It may be the best medicine to have her come here to meet with Myrdden before he goes to Tir na nOg. See this is done within the week, please."

* * *

At sixteen Morrigan already possessed the endowments of a woman in her twenties. Her auburn hair, what some would describe as red/gold, seemed to reflect light onto the very walls of the room, though the only illumination was from the sunlight shining through the two windows onto the top of the table. Her eyes were the deep aqua of the Irish Sea; large and guileless in a face that reflected the innocence of a child. The green of her dress brought out both the color of her eyes and that of her hair. In all, Morrigan was a girl any male would desire, a fact she had already used to her advantage in her home city.

She looked around with keen interest as she waited for the coming interview. The library of the temple was not large, but hand copied and embellished books on foolscap lined the walls. Only the two windows and a door interrupted the shelves. A table and two chairs were the only furnishings. The essence of the room spoke of a sheltered place of contemplation and study.

After a quick glance to make sure she was alone Morrigan picked up one of the books. Her lip curled in disgust as she found it was copied in the old Ogham form. She shelved it and opened another. A smile touched her face as she found it was in a more modern Gael script. It was a history of the Forbirg race that had inhabited the area more than two centuries before. The noise of someone approaching caused her to quickly reshelf the book and turn toward the doorway, her face again a mask of complete innocence.

"Ah, Morrigan, happy I am to see you. I am Lilith, Beanard of this group of the Sisterhood. I believe you were treated well with our friends on Lyonesse."

Morrigan made a sign of obeisance to Lilith. "Aye, Beanard, I was treated well, but wonder why I was brought to your island."

"You were not the only survivor of the *lan mara*, though you were the one who was least harmed by its violence. Apparently it had lost much of its force when it hit your part of Atlantis. I would like you to meet Myrdden. He lived near Salistar, so received the brunt of the force of the wave. I believe you two have much in common, so will leave you to discuss your futures in the quiet safety of this library. Please seat yourself at the table so you will not grow too weary from standing." Lilith smiled sweetly, though her eyes were hidden in shadow, motioned toward the table, then left the room.

Morrigan smiled at Myrdden. "Hello, my brother." She said.

Myrdden frowned and shook his head in bewilderment. "I am not your brother."

"In a sense I will always look on you as my brother because we are the only two who are alive from Atlantis. I think that makes us kin." Her smile was winsome, aimed at melting the hardest of hearts.

Myrdden was silent as he gazed at the vision of loveliness before him. Her eyes sparkled like diamonds, and her long auburn hair hung over her shoulder held together with a black velvet band. Finally he said, "Please be seated." as he took a chair on one side of the table. "I will accept your statement for the moment." He paused as she seated herself opposite him. "I believe they told me you lived on the northwestern edge of Atlantis, and were able to survive in a similar capsule. How was your ordeal?"

Morrigan looked at her hands as they rested on the table. She bit her lip, sighed, and began her story. "Mum, Da, and I got into our capsule when the news came that the *lan mara* had crossed the Reeks of Montour. Da strapped me into the seat he had prepared for me while Mum closed the hatch. They had not estimated the speed of the *lan mara* correctly. They were still standing when it hit. I could only watch helplessly as they were tossed about, thrown about actually, in the capsule unable to protect themselves. It was terrible to watch as they were battered into unconsciousness. That occurred early, but their bodies were still thrown around until they were dead. There was nothing I could do but watch since the force was so great I couldn't get my hands down to the catches on my straps. I couldn't release myself. But even if I could I would have been able to do nothing.

"When the violence stopped and we were floating calmly I was able to release myself. It was too late. They were dead. I cried for help. But who could help me? Then there appeared in the capsule a… I don't know what to call him, spirit, god?" She shook her head, and then shrugged, a half smile on her face. "Anyway, he told me not to fear. He was there to help me. He said he was the King of Earth and Light and his name was Solas, though sometimes he was called Lucifer. He told me he had selected me to be his queen, and from now on I was to be the Queen of Air and Darkness, his counterpart. I was in the capsule for another two days. I didn't want to throw my parents into the sea, I wished them to be buried on land. When I washed up at Lyonesse my desire was granted."

"I am so sorry. " Myrdden said. "I understand your grief. I lost my parents in the *lan mara* as they were trying to get to me and our capsule. It was a violent ride, and I ran out of food and water before I was washed up here on Avalon's shores. We are both orphans now, but we have our memories of our parents and Atlantis."

“Yes.” She leaned forward and lowered her voice. “Now I am Queen of Air and Darkness, and have the powers of the mind I inherited from my parents, I can do many wonderful things. You have the powers as well. Together we could make a mighty team. We know the secrets of Atlantis and can lead these mortals to greatness. The rulers of Atlantis kept our secrets from the other continents because they were not civilized enough to use them properly.” She drew a deep breath, her breasts rising in response to her intense emotion.

Pausing, she got to her feet and moved to Myrdden’s side of the table. Caressing his cheek she whispered, “Together we could rule this world. We could be the most benevolent rulers they ever had, and lead them into peaceful times because the world would be united under a single head. As Queen of this world I would lead them on the paths only I know to be the best for them. If anyone did not follow, of course, they would have to be dealt with. If you come with me I could give you many of the treasures of Darkness, and riches that have been hidden for ages.”

Myrdden frowned as he heard the last part of her story. He shook his head. “No. I don’t believe we should try to lead them into paths we feel,” he emphasized the word, “are best for them. We are too young to know what is best. We are not all knowing. We could be wrong. That would make them worse off than they had been before. Besides, being greedy for these riches and treasures would only make us venal. Greed was something our fathers were trying to do away with. “

”But you don’t understand.” Morrigan’s eyes narrowed as her face hardened into a grotesque mask of the innocent girl. “I have the help of the King of the Earth and Ruler of Light. He knows where these treasures are, and the direction all the earth should take. All I have to do is listen to him and everything will be perfect. But I need a human male to be my consort. Since we are both Atlanteans, and both possess the powers of the mind that we have inherited, we would make a beautiful, and strong, team. I could love you dearly, and show you many of the pleasures that come with that love. Join me, and we can rule together.”

“Morrigan, you are very beautiful, and will lead many men to their doom because of it. This is one man you will not sway to be your consort. I believe you are a sick person to hold ideas such as these. Our people were always looking for the benefit of the other continents. They released their secrets slowly, as people became ready for them,” Myrdden smiled ruefully, “and see how many of them have been turned to evil.”

He shook his head firmly. "No. I could never allow either of us to attempt to take over their world. I believe we should help from behind the scenes, to sway their leaders to better the lot of their people, not lead them into the future. I do not believe your plan is feasible."

Morrigan stood, her eyes mere slits in a face that was twisted with the scorn she felt. "Then, Myrdden, we see things differently. We are on opposite sides." She smiled sweetly, her face again that of the innocent girl. "We could have made such good partners. I know I am beautiful, and you are a handsome man, it would have been so much fun for both of us."

" Now." She shrugged. "Now I must find someone else, someone who will work with me and be my companion. I will fight you until you come to my way of thinking. When you do, please look me up. I will always be ready to accept you as my consort." She rose and strode to the door. "Beanard." She called. "I am ready to leave." She turned back to Myrdden in a final gesture. "I am going to try to see King Lir and have him help find someone to be my consort." She left as Lilith escorted her to the boat to take her back to Lyonnesse.

Later Lilith came to the library where Myrdden was still seated, deep in thought. "What is your opinion?" She asked.

Myrdden looked up. "Watching her parents die, and then having to be in the capsule with them for as long as it took, has unsettled her. She is unsound of mind, but believes she is sane." He answered. "She wishes to become ruler of the world, feels she is in the service of some being from the spirit world whose power will help her become that ruler, and is searching for male consort so the two can gain power over the world. I believe we have an adversary of enormous mental strength, at least when it comes to the balance of humanity. She tried that strength on me, but luckily my will was stronger and I was able to fend her off. No one of the people on other continents will be so lucky. She is strong and strong willed."

Lilith nodded agreement. "Aye. What is the name of that spirit she talked of?"

"She called him Solas, or Lucifer."

Lilith drew a deep breath, her lips set in a thin line. "That is too bad." She muttered. "He is evil, and will mislead her as long as she follows him."

Myrdden's lip curled into a half smile as he lifted one eyebrow. "At least she will only live out her life in Lyonnesse. What harm can she do if she is there?"

Lilith shook her head. "You don't understand. Lyonnesse is a part of Avalon, and Avalon is a part of Tir na nOg, the land of eternal youth. Because you are here you will live a much longer life than you would in the land of the mortals. Like you and me, she will have a long lifespan because of the effects of the timelessness of Tir na nOg."

Now Myrdden frowned. "The effects of Tir na nOg? I don't understand."

"We are a part of the Land of Eternal Youth." Lilith explained. "While there, or here, a year is like a hundred years in places outside Tir na nOg. Lyonesse is a part of Tir na nOg as well. You have been here many weeks, and will travel into Tir na nOg tomorrow, for King Lir has called for you. The time you have spent has already increased your normal life span by many, many years. Though not immortal we are of extremely long life spans. Morrigan has begun the journey back to Lyonesse, though I fear she will not stay there long. I suggest you rest now, for tomorrow may be a stressful time. There are many in Tir na nOg who wish to greet you."

chapter 2
Tir na nOg

Myrdden stood at the brink of the cliff as he looked down at the waves beating against the base. The seemingly slow rise and fall of the sea, the white horses topping the waves as they found the hidden reefs, and their tumbling approach as they finally dashed against the steep walls sending a spray of white into the air to fall back into the sea recalled similar scenes in Atlantis. The sight calmed him as he was reminded of his home.

It had been, as Lilith had predicted, a long and stressful day. They had left Avalon to travel to the west. The land changed as they traveled. For one thing it became brighter, and at the same time softer. The harshness of the normal landscape took on a brighter and cleaner look: one which seemed to have a light of its own as it glowed in the light of a warm sun.

As they approached Hags Head the castle itself was difficult to distinguish. Rather than being built of wood, as the other castles of the mortals were, this was built of stone. Yet it was a stone with which Myrdden was unfamiliar. It was of a light blue that seemed, like everything in Tir na nOg, to radiate its own cool light. From the castle a song was coming: a melody that was almost unheard, yet one that soothed as it permeated the whole body. The walls of the castle were part of the mound on which it stood, or into which it was built, he couldn't tell which was the more accurate. One couldn't tell where the walls ended and the mound of grass began. The gates opened as they approached, and the singers and pipers began to herald the approach of the group from Avalon.

Colorful streamers and flags decked out the entryway and hung from the walls to give him the honorable welcome as a prince. The high vaulted ceiling seemed to be hundreds of feet above his head, yet the appearance of the castle from the outside was no higher than the mound in which it was built. From the rafters above came the harmonious sound of a choir singing a song with which he was unfamiliar, yet seemed to be one he had known all his life. The party approached the dais at the far end by walking along a runner that seemed to be made of the waves of the sea, yet was as solid as the earth under their feet. On both sides of the aisle were crowds of nobles and citizens of Tir na nOg applauding as they approached the dais.

Five thrones were on the dais. Four were occupied by the rulers of the various tribes living in Tir na nOg. King Lir, ruler of the sea, sat in the center. On one side was King Brian Connor, ruler of the Leprechauns, on the other were Queen Titania and King Oberon of the Fae. The empty throne was one he would occupy as the welcome continued.

It was his first full greeting as one who rules, and he was both excited and awed at first. As the morning grew longer the plaudits grew tedious, and his smile began to lose its sparkle. Finally it was over. The festivities began as long tables were brought into the hall; tables soon covered with a wide variety of the foods that had been prepared throughout the morning. Vats of ale and mead were set at the end of each table so the tankards could be filled quickly with the foaming brew.

The revelry had continued for the balance of the afternoon as many a tankard was lifted in his direction accompanied by a shouted '*Slainte*'. It was finally over and he was able to escape from the crowds in the castle. Now, as the sun began to sink in the west casting a long stripe of bright orange across the face of the relatively calm sea, he was able to relax. The sky was a riot of color as the setting sun painted the clouds a mixture of colors ranging from a pale violet to bright reds and oranges. The lighter blue of the sky added to the contrast wherever the clouds were rifted.

"Lovely, isn't it?" The voice startled him for he hadn't heard anyone approaching. This was not surprising for the area atop the cliffs was covered with lush green grass. Then King Brian was standing beside him. "Lir has returned to his castle undersea." Brian continued without waiting for Myrdden's answer. "Oberon and Titania have returned to Tara and their castle, so I guess you're going to have to put up with me. Here have a drink." He smiled as he handed Myrdden a small jug.

Myrdden, thirsty, put it up to his lips and filled his mouth with the fluid. He swallowed before he had a chance to think. His face turned red as he coughed and sputtered while the fiery liquid seemed to burn his throat all the way down to where it set fire to his stomach. It seemed to bounce and return to expel flame through his nostrils as he fought to catch his breath. After recovering he handed the jug to Brian. “What is that stuff?” he asked. “I expected the clear liquid I had in the castle: the one that takes away fatigue and pain.”

Brian smiled. “Sorry. I forgot you are so young. This is called poteen, and it is a home grown liquor made in the valley behind us. We Leprechauns are quite attached to it.”

“I would say it’s an acquired taste.” Myrdden said dryly as he cleared his throat once again. He looked closely at Brian who was dressed in a green vest and green breeks. Around his neck was a gold torc that seemed to be made from a single filament of gold and woven into the unending knot of the Celts. The man appeared to be the same height as Myrdden. “I thought all Leprechauns were only about two feet high.” He said. “Yet you appear to be my height.”

Brian smiled broadly. “Aye, lad, it would appear that, wouldn’t it? My appearance is because I am able to make it seem to you I am taller than I am.”

Myrdden nodded toward the torc. “That is a beautiful torc. I’ve never seen one like it before.”

Brian raised a hand to touch it, and nodded. “One of our goldsmiths fashioned it for me. You know, you are also allowed to wear a gold torc since you are a king.”

Myrdden smiled ruefully. “A king of a kingdom that no longer exists. No, sir, I believe my father was the last king of Atlantis.”

Brian shook his head. “Just because the kingdom lies buried under the sea doesn’t mean you are no longer a king.” He nodded forecefully. “I will have my goldsmith make you a torc similar to this that all may know your heritage.”

He paused to take a drink from the jug. After wiping his mouth with the back of his hand he continued. “I was sent out to fill you in on the plans. Tomorrow your education will begin. Your father was going to send you to us when you reached the age of eighteen: it had all been arranged.” Brian shrugged, his face showing his sadness. “But your father died when the wave wiped Atlantis off the face of Talab.” He smiled slyly, “But you still have someone to rule. Now you and Nimue are the only two from Atlantis to survive.”

“Nimue?” Myrdden’s face echoed his puzzlement. “I thought Morrigan was the only other survivor.”

Brian pursed his lips. “Morrigan? I believe I heard her mentioned, but only in passing. You know for sure she is a survivor?”

“Aye. I had a talk with her two days ago.”

"Then we should invite her to be trained as we will train you and Nimue."

Myrdden shook his head. "I wouldn't do that. She calls herself the Queen of Air and Darkness, and claims a spirit named Lucifer came to her before she washed up in Lyonesse telling her she would rule the world. She plans on trying to see King Lir to ask for a consort so she will have a male counterpart to help her rule the world."

Brian drew a deep breath and released it slowly. "Lucifer, eh?" He nodded. "Things are worse than I thought, then."

"What do you mean? You have heard of this Lucifer?"

Brian nodded. "Aye, much to my dismay, I know him personally. He was pretty high up in the hierarch of the Creator when he rebelled. He swayed many of us. He has persuasive ways, you know. When we Leprechauns finally realized his plans we couldn't follow him, but we couldn't go back because we had followed him. Now we are condemned to be here as long as this Talab lasts."

"You are immortal?"

Brian nodded. "Aye." He sighed. "For what it's worth we are immortal. At one time we were the rulers of Eire. We were called Tuatha de Danaan. Then the Fomorians came. We were a peaceful people: they were not. They conquered us. We love this land and asked if we could stay. They said we would only have the places they could not occupy. So we moved to this plane, the land of Faerie, or Tir na nOg, and became what mortals call the *Sidhe*. The Fomorians were later conquered by the Milesians, and then by the Celts who stayed in the land. We *Sidhe* identify closely with the Celts, though they often cannot see us. Now we try to help mortals when we can, tease them a great deal more than we help them, and wait anxiously for the time when we will face our end."

He perked up. "But that is beside the point. If this Morrigan is under the influence of Lucifer she is very dangerous. There are a number of things we must do. One of the first is to inform Lir of her plans, though I hope Lilith would have already done so. Then we must make sure you and Nimue are well trained in all the arts, mental, martial, and physical. You will have to use all three if she is to be defeated."

"All the arts? I thought it was only mental arts we needed."

Brian shook his head. "No, though that is a large part of the training. You are now, or will be, in a world that is far from peaceful. You need to know how to use the sword, the spear, and the use of the bow. Tomorrow we will begin your training. Now, with the sun no longer visible, we should go to the castle and get a good night's rest. It's been a long, and sometimes boring, day."

"You found it boring?"

Brian nodded as he smiled. They began walking toward the castle. "Aye. All that panoply and foofooraw we have to put on to satisfy the citizens of Tir na nOg. If it were me I would have shook your hand, given you the jug, and we could have sat down to a good game of chess. That would have been far more interesting."

* * *

The early rays of the sun came through the open window of Myrdden's room, rested on his face, and wrestled him from slumber. He looked around the room, oriented himself, and smiled as he remembered where he was. He arose and walked to the window. It had been dark when he finally went to his room and he had not been able to orient himself to this part of the keep. Hags Head was situated on a premonitory with cliffs leading down to the sea some four hundred feet below. No need for a wall on that side of the castle. His room, it appeared, was on a corner of the keep with a window facing east and another south. He looked out at the grassy lea below him. Further away the surging breakers crashed against the towering cliff as though trying to break through a barricade. The flung spray and blowing spume rose skyward, only to drop back into the sea, their attack a failure.

The entrance of a servant interrupted his reverie. "Ah, I see you are awake. King Brian sent these clothes for you. If you need help in dressing I will assist you. Otherwise you may break your fast in the dining area on the third floor. Go down the stairs and follow the hallway. The dining area is two doors down on the right."

"Thank you." Myrdden nodded. "I will dress myself." After the servant departed Myrdden looked over the clothing. There was nothing of splendor there. Rather, it was the clothing common to any of the working members of the household. The only thing setting it apart were the number of colors it contained. A jerkin of soft, multicolored, cloth, loose breecs belted under a short kilt, a long leather strap to wrap around the legs of the breecs, and a pair of sturdy leather buskins that, to his surprise, fit as though they were molded to his feet. *Interesting*, he thought as he began to don the garments, *I guess this means we now start to work*. Dressed, he headed down the hallway.

Myrdden stopped short at the doorway. His heart seemed to jump in his chest. The girl at the window was gazing out at the land, the sun hidden by her head. He had a good look at her profile against the deep auburn gold of her hair as it shone with the reflected rays of the sun behind it. The sight fair took his breath away. She sighed, her sadness shone through. Myrdden finally said, "I'm sorry. I didn't know there was anyone here."

She looked at him, a sad smile on her face. "Oh no." She said. "Please come in. I was just looking out toward where my country used to be. I found out I'm not the only survivor of the *lan mara* that destroyed my land. Now I find I must wait for another of the survivors who will train with me. I got the impression he was one of the rulers of the country. I suppose he's one of the old men who governed." She sighed again. "Oh, my name is Nimue. Why don't you sit down and we can wait for the old one together."

Now she was facing him he felt he could drown in the deep green of her eyes. Morrigan was beautiful, but there was a hardness to her that detracted from that beauty. The girl before him had a gentle look. Suddenly Myrdden believed in love at first sight. "Thank you." He said. "I am truly sorry you are so sad, and that you have lost your country. How did you manage to survive?"

"My folks were scientists living in Condan. Da was a mathematician. He knew of the asteroid and what it would do so he built this vessel so we would not die in the aftermath. He was away when it hit, so I was alone. I washed up on the shore of a bay to the south and was brought to this castle. They have been very kind to me, and say I must now begin training because there is another girl who is going to be formidable in her attempt to gain power. I don't know how well this governor will be able to learn the mind tricks they say we must have. I only hope he is a nice person." She tilted her head and Myrdden lost the rest of his heart. "Oh. I am Nimue. You haven't told me your name." She said.

At that moment the servants entered, bringing their breakfast. When they had departed he looked across the table. "My name is Myrdden."

"Are you from around here?"

"I am now, though I really only arrived yesterday. Were you here yesterday?"

She shook her head. "No. The lady in waiting they gave me had to go to Lahinch and wanted me to go with her. I did because I heard there was to be a long, boring, ceremony to welcome this other person. She told me he was the king of Atlantis, though Atlantis is no more. Not wishing to be bored I went with Lady Sheila. It was fun."

"I assure you, you didn't miss a thing. I had to be there and it was very long, and very boring. I was happy when it was over and I could get outside. The sea air was invigorating after the stuffiness of the ceremonials."

Ronan entered the room where Nimue and Myrdden were finishing breakfast. “Ah.” He said. “I see you two have met. If you are finished breaking your fast we can get on with the lessons.”

“But you said the other person training with me would be the Ruler of Atlantis.” She said to Ronan. “I’m waiting for him to come.”

A puzzled look crossed Ronan’s face. “But he is here. You had breakfast together. I thought you knew.”

Nimue looked across the table at Myrdden. “You are the ruler of Atlantis? And you let me make a fool of myself talking of the old man who would come. You are despicable.”

“I’m sorry. I didn’t mean to mislead you. When I saw you by the window your beauty overcame me. Besides, despite what they say I am not the ruler of Atlantis. I am merely another survivor, like you and Morrigan, who no longer has a homeland. As such we are equals. Now we must work together if we are to win this battle.”

“You make it sound like it is a serious thing.”

“Believe me. It is. Morrigan has enlisted the aid of the Dark Lord. Our aid will come from those who are of the light. She is very beautiful, and will use her beauty against us. We must learn how to defend ourselves in all aspects or we may not make it, and if we don’t, we give Talab over to the legions of darkness.”

Nimue was thoughtful. “You say she is very beautiful?” Myrdden nodded. “Did you fall in love with her beauty?”

Myrdden shook his head. “No. Her beauty is a cold beauty that she uses to trap men. Thank goodness I was able to withstand her, though I believe it angered her that I did not succumb to her charms. You are more beautiful and desirable than she.”

Nimue’s smile was bright as she bent her head to acknowledge the compliment. “Then we must use our minds if we are to win.”

“You are not angry with me, then?”

“Of course I’m angry with you. But we are going to have to work together, and if you are really nice I may forgive you for playing such a nasty trick on me.” Her smile seemed to light up the room, and the twinkle in her eye belied her anger. “Now let’s get to work: equal.”

“Thank you, Rua (Red). I will work to earn your forgiveness.”

Ronan had been silent through the dialogue. “Now that you two are finished, let’s get to work. If we are to make the two of you into adepts at the use of controlling another person’s mind, and the use of the *geis* to bring others to us, as well as other *geis* to make them do what we wish there is about three years of work ahead of us. We also have to learn the means of viewing the various roads the future might take. That is one of the most difficult to learn. We will, however, begin with some of the easier things to conquer. Our first lesson is that of making others believe we are not in their presence. To do so you must be able to subdue a portion of their minds. Here is how it is done...."

* * *

"Beanard." Maire blurted out as she entered the office in the temple. "I have just received word Morrigan has left the community on Lyonesse. They fear she has taken the land bridge to Cymru."

Lilith looked up from the table. Her face was impassive. After a few moments silence she nodded. "After her discussion with Myrdden I wondered how long she would be content there. As you know, Myrdden found she feels she has a power no one else has, and it may well be true in the world of the humans. She has had discussion with Lucifer, and he promised her much."

Maire sank into the other chair. "Oh, no!" She cried. "Not Lucifer. Nothing good will come of that."

"True. Therefore I sent a messenger to Tir na nOg with the information along with Myrdden. I fear it is up to Myrdden to try to control her now." She sighed deeply. "Now we must place a psychic wall of force around our community for I feel she will attempt to take revenge on us. We gave succor to Myrdden, and he is stronger than she as well as being her lawful ruler. He refused her advances, and that cut her deeply. It is indeed unfortunate that the tragedy has caused her to become unstable. That, her mental powers, and her beauty make her a dangerous foe. She tried to use her physical charms to sway Myrdden. The fact he was able to resist her feminine wiles humiliated and angered her." Lilith paused to think.

"She knows Myrdden was to go to Tir na nOg. She also wishes to go there, but unless she is invited she will never enter. I believe she understands, but does not accept the truth, that only those who rule Tir na nOg are allowed to invite outlanders in. She may wait until Myrdden emerges before she tries anything, but she may attempt to practice her abilities on us in the meantime. It's difficult to figure her out because of her instability. She just doesn't think like a normal person." She sighed deeply and shook her head, her face echoing her mental distress.

"Aye, that asteroid has caused far more problems than a mere *lan mara*. I fear these islands are going to be her playground as she matures to her true strength. Assemble the sisters, we must prepare for the worst."

* * *

The sessions for Myrdden and Nimue were not all held indoors. As had been told to him they had to learn more than the honing of their mental facilities. After a morning's classes with Ronan they were turned over to Aengus to learn the gentle art of handling a sword, lance, and quarterstaff. At least that was what was being taught Myrdden. Nimue was sent to Siobhan to learn the art of using a short sword and scian. Since the scian was a small knife most women carried at their waist and men carried in a sheath on their back, it would be one of the most usable weapons for her to learn. After a few hours with weapons they were sent to the stables to learn horsemanship. By nightfall the first night both were exhausted mentally and physically.

The following day the first hour before breaking their fast was spent in various forms of calisthentics: to toughen them up for what was to come they were told. Once breakfast was over they began the usual mental calisthentics with horsemanship immediately after lunch to be followed by weapons training. The days went by slowly at first as they dropped wearily into bed. By the second month they were not so weary, and the third month found them ready to take part in the festivities of the caer even after a heavy day of study and practice. Their bodies hardened as did their minds under the tutelage of the skillful teachers of the caer at Hags Head.

chapter 3
The Walker Between the Worlds

We sing of the men of old,
Finn McCool and Fenians bold
Of their strength and their daring
As they fought for old Eirrein
And of stories that still are untold.

Another story I now will unfold
Of a child both young and yet old.
He's a boy with no father
Though he did have a mother
And Queen Mabd was the reason, I hold.

Oh Queen Mabd is not of this land
For her castle is over the strand
Where Avalon does exist
An isle lost in mist
Where strange things are always at hand.

Queen Mabd had a sad lonely life
For evil will always find strife.
She wished for a son
For she really had none
Who would ever take her to wife?

She found a young maid in a ville
Where she sent her hordes for to kill.
The young girl was so sweet
Yet Mabd forced her to eat
Of a seed that Mabd's wish could fulfill.

When forty weeks were passed and done
The young maiden delivered a son
That Mabd did adore
As never before
Though the maiden had died and was gone.

It was Myrdden Mabd named her new boy
And it was Myrdden who became Mabd's joy
And as he grew older
He also grew bolder
And no longer would be Mabd's boy toy.

So Myrdden peace he is seeking
That none will know what I'm leaking.
He is out of Mabd's land
And is now on this strand
And into your lives he'll be peeking.

Morrigan was strolling around the Great Hall of An Tinbhear Mor as she accompanied herself on a lute. As she walked along the table she would give each man a smile, bending over to display her charms. No man in the room could resist her, and with her mental abilities she made sure they would remember the words of the song. As yet she didn't know how she could use the idea behind it, but she was sure there would be some way in the future. At the moment it was to create distrust between the warriors, the king, and Myrdden should he come that way. As she sang her song she knew she had every male in the palm of her hand.

The group of bards and jongleurs had found her shortly after she had crossed the land bridge from Lyonesse. They couldn't understand why they had not had their way with her, but for some strange reason they accepted her as one of their own. Now she was their main attraction. Her beauty was the key to getting in to the various castles of the kings of the small baronies at which they entertained. Her beauty was also the reason they were now getting wealthy. Once inside she would captivate every male in the castle from the youngest page to the oldest dotard.

She finished the song in front of the king's chair. It was larger than the others in the room, and gave an indication of his rank in this town. He looked at the sight she offered as she bent forward as she curtsied. His eyes were not on her face as he said, "And is this song true or merely one of the legends of Queen Mabd?"

"Oh, your highness, it is very true. I know Myrdden personally and know he is well trained in arts the average person knows little of. He is a man to be wary of, for if you allow him he will give advice. But that advice could well cost you your kingdom. After all, can a man with no father be one you could trust?"

King Aengus thought this over as he admired the charms Morrigan presented him. "No, I suppose not. For what other man has ever been born without a father?"

"What other man indeed, Sire." Morrigan retired to the group she was with as the jugglers and acrobats took over. It would not be long before she would again sing one of the songs, but this time it would be one of the old battle songs of this kingdom. It had taken her hardly any time at all to memorize the songs of Finn McCool and the Fennians, of Bran of the Thousand Wounds, and of the other heroes of the old country. Tonight she would sleep with the king, of that she had no doubt, and she had found out with the others of the troupe the one who slept with her was forever under her spell. Power was there, and she was not afraid to use that power, for it was well known the Celtic women were hot blooded, and the Celtic men were willing to take advantage of it.

* * *

Ronan was a taskmaster. He demanded nothing less than perfection from his two students. "Once more." was heard more often than the slight nod, and "That's good. Now try it again." When Myrdden and Nimue protested Ronan merely shook his head and said, "You must perfect your abilities. Your lives will depend on your being able to blend into wherever you find yourselves. Now try it again." So it went as the two spent the days that turned into weeks, then months, and finally a year.

"You are doing well, so far." Ronan said dryly. "Now is the time for a little test. I've had Brigid fix us a bait of food. We are going for a walk, and a picnic. While we are there we will see how well you have learned some of the arts I've been trying to stuff into your heads this past year."

Nimue smiled gratefully. "You mean we're going to have a rest from the work we've been doing this past year?"

Ronan shrugged and grinned. "You might say that, if you think a test is a rest from what we've done."

"At least we'll get out from behind the walls of this caer and see what this part of Tir na nOg looks like." Myrdden exclaimed. "I feel I've been cooped up so long I've forgotten what a forest looks like, and what is that thing called that has water running in it?" He affected a puzzled look as he thought. Finally his face lit up and he said, "Oh yes! I remember. It's called a river."

"All right you two," Ronan said, a dour look on his face, "enough of this farce. Get your hiking buskins on and we'll take a walk." Two hours later the three were in a small clearing just off the well-worn path and next to the river Lee. Ronan was watching a small pot of stew boiling over an open fire as Myrdden and Nimue talked nearby. Without looking up Ronan said in a low voice. "Someone is coming. Remember. I am the only one they see." Both his students nodded as he continued to stir the stew. They watched in silence.

Daire, a warrior who had helped teach the art of the sword, came around the bend, saw Ronan, and moved from the path to where Ronan was seated. He looked around the clearing, but his eyes passed over Myrdden and Nimue as they leaned against the trees under which they were seated. Daire's eyes fastened on the pot. "You're alone, I see." He said. "I was told that Myrdden and Nimue were with you, but they obviously aren't. Do you have any idea where they might be?"

Ronan smiled and turned his head nonchalantly so his gaze rested on the two as they sat in plain sight. He looked back to Daire. "I know they aren't too far away. Why don't you wait with me? They could appear at any minute."

Daire hunkered down near the fire and looked at the stew pot. "That's much too much stew for one person, Ronan. Do you mind if I join you? It is almost lunch time." He undid the package he was carrying. "Here. I can help with the meal. Brigid fixed me a packet of bread, cheese, and some of last night's cold hock. It's no fun to eat alone." As he did so Myrdden and Nimue walked to the fire, took two bowls, and after filling them with stew returned to their former positions. Ronan smiled as they did so as Daire sat and watched the stew bubbling merrily in the pot.

Ronan smiled and nodded assent. "Sure and we'll have enough to feed the four of us with no trouble."

"Four of us?" Daire said, a puzzled look on his face. His eyes searched the clearing. "But I see only the two of us."

"Good." Ronan said. "That's all you were supposed to see. All right you two, you've done well and the stew is done. Join us."

Daire's eyes grew larger as Myrdden and Nimue seemed to come out of the trees they were under. He looked at the dishes of stew they brought to the fire. Then he shook his head and chuckled. "Arra, I see. So this was a test. Ronan has a closed mouth when it comes to his students so I hadn't heard how you have been doing. You did well. I never saw you at all, and I was looking right at you I'm sure. I can see you are good students." He reached under his jerkin and brought out a parchment. "Your student days may be over. I was sent to find you and give you this. I see I've found you so I can now give it to you." He handed the scroll to Myrdden.

Myrdden broke the seal and read. "We've been invited to Lough Dorca two days hence." Myrdden said as he finished. He handed the scroll to Nimue. "It seems there is to be a meeting of the leaders of the country to figure out how to handle the problem of Morrigan."

Ronan nodded. "I heard she left the sisters of Lyonesse." He said. "The rumor is she is somewhere in Cymru." He thought for a moment then shook his head. "I don't see how she can cause much trouble there. It is a country of small kingships where no one king has much power because their area is so small." He shrugged. "But a visit to Lough Dorca is always welcome. Both King Lir and King Lugh always have the best entertainment and food. Now you've passed this test we have to get to work and move on to other things you will need: if we have time."

"Actually," Daire added, "they have both done very well in the arts of weapons and horses. In my estimation they don't need any more of my instruction. I think they are ready to go on."

Ronan smiled approval. "I agree. They have done very well in my training as well. Let's finish our meal and get back to Hags Head. We have to leave tomorrow morning if we're going to get to Lough Dorca two days hence."

The four joked about things that were going on, and the way in which Daire was fooled. With the meal finished Daire rose to his feet. "I found you so I carried out that duty. Now I must return to finish my other duties." He nodded to them all. "I'll see you back at the castle."

When they were alone Ronan turned to Myrdden. "You did well with Daire. I was concerned when you got the stew, but you brought that off very nicely. Congratulations to both of you. You have done in a year what I thought might take three when first I saw you arguing. I think most of your lessons are a thing of the past."

He paused. "This Morrigan seems to be causing King Lir some problem. Because you are actually her sovereign Morrigan must come under your will. There is a *geis* you will need to learn if you are to be able to summon her to you wherever you are. I hadn't mentioned it because I wasn't sure you would need it. I believe now you will have to have it as a control."

He turned to Myrdden. "This is for you alone. Sorry Nimue. Go to the stream and select sixteen small white stones and five more that are larger." He watched as Myrdden waded into the stream and found the stones he had mentioned.

"Good. Now lay them out with the four large ones pointing to the four major points of the compass. The headstone must point in the direction the sun rises on the summer solstice. The others will lie between those four, and they must be equidistant from each other. The fifth must be placed in the center of the circle." This done he added. "Now stand in the circle." Myrdden did so. "You have now created a stone henge. When you are within that circle of stones, and have done the other runes I will show you at the castle, she cannot reach you. In the true *geis* you will need a candle on the stone in the center of that circle. We will not repeat the words of the incantation now for that would call her to you, and we do not wish her to join us as yet. Besides, I know not if she can enter Tir na nOg without the knowledge or permission of King Lir or King Brian.

"What we call this *geis* the Leprechauns call a 'come hither', for that is what it does. This particular geis will force her to come to you even if she does not wish to. Remember, by standing in the protective aura of those white stones you will be safe from anything she can do. She can neither enter herself nor cast a spell that can pass through the barrier, though she can speak to you and you to her. Because of the *geis* she must answer your questions truthfully. When we get back to the castle I'll write the words down. To speak them would invoke the spell without the protection. Memorize them. I am sure you will need them in the future. Now, let's go back to the castle."

* * *

As the small caravan rode toward Lough Dorca Myrdden turned to Ronan, a puzzled look on his face. "We have been so busy studying I never had a chance to ask. Just what is Tir na nOg, and why is King Lir so interested in the two of us?"

Ronan rode on in silence for a minute. Brian Connor, now his normal size, was riding on the back of the horse behind Ronan's saddle. "You may as well tell him. It's in his best interest to know." He said as Ronan's silence grew.

"Do you think King Lir will mind?"

"I believe Lir would wish it so. It will help their understanding of themselves, of Morrigan, and of the reasons they are here." He paused. "If you don't tell then I will."

Ronan sighed. "Eons ago there was a rebellion against the High King, the Creator. One of the chief captains revolted and took a third of the population with him." Ronan snorted without humor. "He was very charismatic, and his silver tongue won many over. When some of us found out what he was really up to we rebelled against him, but it was too late to return to our true king. We were banished from the Upper Realm, and unwelcome in the lower, so after some searching found the island of Eirrean. There were some small bands of people already there, but they accepted us as neighbors. The land was good, the people few, and space was plentiful. We became known as the Tuatha de Danaan because our leader was named Danae.

"Many years later another group of humans came to the island. They were the Formorians. They were allowed to defeat us for it was in their destiny to occupy the island. Since we had lost our place in Eirrean, as well as the land of the Creator, we were allowed to find a way to move ourselves into this place we call Tir na nOg. It is in a universe parallel to that of the humans, though there are places like Avalon where bridges allow access across that divide. While we were living on that side many of our people found the people of Atlantis desirable. Unions were created and with the heritage we had those of Atlantis were able to rise above the level of other humans. They became more intelligent, had longer lives, were more inventive, and wound up being more peaceful. For over two thousand years Atlantis lived in peace with all they met. They were not quite of us, yet they were not quite of the other humans either. Since they were part of us we took great interest in them.

"Tir na nOg is the Land of Eternal Youth, and seems to have a different time sense that the other. A year here is a hundred years over there, though this is not quite so in Avalon, so you have already been here the equivalent of their century of years. Because of your background and your residence in Avalon and here the two of you have acquired near immortality. You will age, but it will be at a very slow rate. The same applies to Morrigan. Her lineage is similar to yours and she has been in Avalon, or Lyonesse, so she has also acquired that curse. If she were merely human she would be elderly now, for the life span there is about forty of their years, though there are those of the ruling class who live longer.

"When we came here we became gods and goddesses to the Milesians," he smiled cynically, "we became the *Sidhe*, and this also became the land of Faerie. So there are many stories that are told, some good, some bad. We will probably hear more when we reach Lough Dorca for those at Lough Dorca have eyes and ears on the other side. Do they not King Brian?"

Brian chuckled. "Aye, that they do. Those of us that are small, and know how to make ourselves unseen, can see and hear much of what is going on. Those of my people who go there report to Lir and Lugh, and to me. From what I have heard lately from a *bean Sidhe* that lately returned, things are not going too well at the moment." He paused. "But that is a secret that only Lir can impart to others, something he may well do when we get to Lough Dorca."

They topped a small rise and surveyed the scene below. Off to their left was a small town. The harbor was busy with a variety of boats tied to the moorings. Between town and the road, and off to their right, the golden heads of wheat and barley swayed gently in the breeze. In some fields the men were scything the wheat while the women collected the mown stalks and made them into stooks that could later be loaded on the wains and taken to the mill for grinding.

Ahead of them the castle rose solid and strong as though just rising from the lake. Sunlight glinting on the slight waves glittered like the sparks from diamonds as they watched. Here too were moorings for the boats that servants used to catch fish for meals.

Unlike the castles on the other side of the passages between the two worlds that were still constructed of wood, the castle on Lough Dorca was of a light blue stone. The stone itself seemed to have light emanating from it, a light that reminded one of the look of the sea on a peaceful day. Now it loomed before them; a large stone edifice of six stories sitting on a *crannog*, a man made island in the lake. A long causeway led from the land to the entrance. Since Tir na nOg was peaceful, and the castle was a *crannog* with the lake surrounding it, there was no need for battlements. The castle was merely an enormous structure that would later be called a palace rather than a castle.

"Ah, and there it is now. Soon our questions will be answered, I hope." Brian said as they started down the slope toward the open gate.

As they dismounted the Castellan met them. "Welcome." He turned to a servant. "Nealle! Show our guests to their rooms, make sure they have fresh clothing, and then bring them to the main hall." He turned back to the foursome. "Nealle will see to your needs. There will be scented water to wash the dust of your travels, and clothing to refresh you. Please hurry as they wait you in the Main Hall."

Recognizing from the Castellan's demeanor important things were transpiring below, they wasted no time. After washing the dust of the journey from their hands and faces they changed into the clothing that had been laid out for them. Tunics of a light blue that seemed to change color as it reflected the light, breecs that reached to the ankles and long leather straps to wrap around them, a short kilt of sea green, soft leather buskins, and a light cape of a darker shade of blue topped off the ensemble. In a few minutes Nealle appeared, smiled at their being ready so quickly, and said, "Follow me, if you will."

The hall was decked in colorful flags, bunting and hangings. Candles burned in the large candelabra hanging from the ceiling as well as in the wall sconces. The room was bright, though the mood of the occupants seemed to be quite somber. This was readily apparent for there was little of the normal laughter, jostling, joking, or conversations going on. The tables were filled with a cross section of the folk of Tir na nOg. Leprechauns sat near Trooping Fairies, *Bean Sidhe*, and other of the various people inhabiting the island. Lir and Lugh sat in their chairs at the head their faces somber and unsmiling. King Oberon and Queen Titania flanked them, and there were three empty seats next to them. Ronan, while a teacher, would sit further down the table. Lir waved the four to seats saved for them. "Eat." He said. "When you have broken your fast we will discuss things that are transpiring in the world of the humans."

The dour mood was contagious, though the food was elegant and well served. Three different soups, haunches of beef, rotisserie chicken, mashed turnips with fresh butter, fresh baked bread, rashers of bacon, hearty ale, and apple pies were a part of the meal. Without a word the four began to take of the food the servants placed before them, casting sideways glances at the rulers sitting at the center of the table as they ate. The journey, plus the savory viands, gave them excellent appetites. On the balcony above the entranceway three musicians played softly as an accompaniment to the meal. They played softly yet were easily heard in the solemn silence of the room. Nimue felt she could hear the breathing of the two kings even above the gentle voices of the harp, whistle and bodhram.

"Now you have finished," Lir said as his guests leaned back from their empty plates, "join us in the Room of Seeing." He rose, followed by the other rulers, and led the way to the stairs. On the floor above the Great Hall he led the way down an aisle, pushed on an ornately carved door, and ushered them into a small room. In the center was a pillar. On the pillar was a stone. Myrdden examined it as they formed a circle around the pillar. It was of purple hue with lavender and pink veins that seemed to wreath like smoke as he watched.

"This is the Stone of Seeing. It is one of the articles we have been allowed to have, and use, even in our exile. I helps us see what the plans of the Creator will be, and what might occur if his plans do not come to fruition." Lir explained.

Myrdden shook his head in wonder. "I thought the plans of the Creator could never be changed." He said.

Lir gave a half smile. "The overall plans will not be altered." He said. "It is the plans in the short-run that are able to be altered. Man has been created to have his own will, and even if he knows the plan he is to follow, may choose to go another direction. When that occurs there is a change in strategy if the overall plan is to succeed.

"Morrigan claims to have been recruited by the King of the Earth and Ruler of Light. He is ever trying to alter the plans of the Creator because he wishes to usurp his place. This we know for once we followed him, to our great dismay."

"Yes. She told me she had been made his queen. She also said she needs a consort in order to be made whole and tried to recruit me in that position."

"Because of her time in Lyonesse, or that part of Lyonesse in which members of the Sisterhood reside, she not only has obtained longevity of life, but also no longer needs a single consort. She has been traveling the islands as a member of a troop of bards, and has been singing of a young man named Myrdden who has no father. She has found she outlives any male she has been with so changes from troop to troop so no one will be suspicious of her not aging. She has also found once she has lain with a man she can control him even from afar. Her abilities and talents have become great." Myrdden nodded understanding. "Concentrate on the Stone and think of the future." Lir ordered.

As Myrdden did so the lines swirling in the stone seemed to come together and, in the air above the stone, a picture formed. As he watched it seemed to solidify and come to life. He watched as a small fleet sailed from a far shore, crossed a narrow channel and landed on the eastern shores of the larger island. The warriors that disembarked then began to fight their way inland following a flag showing a white dragon, destroying villages, killing the peasants, burning crops, and setting themselves in the place of the existing rulers. They continued until they had crossed the body of the island and were staring across another channel at a smaller island blue in the mists to the west.

As he watched the scene changed and another man rose from Lyonesse. Gathering an army about him he moved north through the southwestern corner of the island. At the head of this army was a flag with a red dragon. The two armies met, and as they stared at each other from two hilltops, the vision faded and disappeared.

Myrdden waited for Lir to explain the vision. Silence seemed to hold the room in thrall as he waited. Finally Lir asked. "What did you see?"

"Why. The same thing you saw I suppose." Myrdden answered. "I was just waiting to see what you thought it might mean."

"I saw nothing." Lir paused a moment. "The Stone of Seeing shows a vision to only one person at a time. I knew you were seeing something due to the attention you gave the air above the stone, so I did not interrupt. The vision and the interpretation are yours, Myrdden. No one else was privy to what you saw. If you wish to tell us it is well. If not, that too is well."

"Is all Lyonesse like Avalon and Tir na nOg? That is, does all of it have the ability to give longevity to those who are there?"

Lir shook his head. "No. The majority of Lyonesse is merely another part of the human's world. The portion in which the Sisterhood dwells, like Avalon, is not available to normal humans unless invited."

Myrdden nodded. "Then why could Morrigan find her way there?"

Lir smiled sadly, "Because Morrigan, like you and Nimue, as well as some others we have found to be survivors, have the blood of Faerie in their veins. That makes places like Avalon, where you washed up, and the Sisterhood portion of Lyonesse, where Morrigan washed up, available to you."

"I saw a foreign peoples invading a large island. They were a cruel people who burned crops and killed the citizens as they subdued them. At their head was an ensign showing a white dragon. I saw another army coming from the direction of Lyonesse led by a commanding figure under the ensign of a red dragon. The two met where a river flows through a valley. One on one side of the river, the other on the opposite hill. At that point the vision disappeared. I know not the outcome."

Lir nodded. "While the vision is for your interpretation I can tell you the meaning of the end. There will be a war between these two dragons. The outcome is in doubt. Whichever one wins the future will be guided by their governance. That means the outcome of that battle will decide the future history of that country, and possibly of the world to follow. I suspect you will have a hand in the outcome of the battle. Which side you will favor I know not, nor do I know which side will win." He shrugged his shoulder. "From the looks of it the future depends on your decision."

Myrdden drew a deep breath and glanced at Nimue. He shook his head. "Thanks a lot." He said dryly. "The future of humans depends on which side I wish to be on. It's certainly nice not to have to be concerned about where one's feet take one."

Lir nodded. "We are done here. Let us go to the library to discuss this further."

In the library Lir beckoned his guests to sit around a table in the center of the room. He was thoughtful for a long moment as the others watched him. Finally he spoke. "Before I asked you to come I used the Stone of Seeing. In it I saw things regarding the future of the island of Eirrein and of Breton. Ronan." At the mention of his name Ronan nodded to indicate he was listening closely. "I am going to send you to Eirrein to King Dairmot Murrough. You will present him with an idea of building a new castle. Instead of using wooden palisades and a wooden keep you will present the idea of using stone.

"This will make a more permanent building, one that will last for hundreds of their years. I have had Brady working on plans you will present. He is fashioning it after this building, but the one you present will be built on a hill overlooking the ocean to the south rather than on a crannog. There will be a long island half a league off the coast. There will also be an outcrop of stone nearby that will be a ready supply for the caer. I would you leave on that errand now." Ronan rose, bowed, and left the room.

"Nimue. I am going to have you stay here while Myrdden goes to Cymru. There will be an invasion there and he will be needed if my ideas regarding his vision are true. I know Morrigan has been at work there for many of their years as she instills her lies in the people. Later, when the time is ripe, you will join him." Nimue nodded her understanding as her hand moved to hold Myrdden's.

"Myrdden. I am going to entrust the sword of Nuala of the Silver Hand to your care. It is an enchanted sword that can only be used by you." Lir smiled cynically. "In your hands any slight cut on an enemy will cause his death, so use it wisely and sparingly. At the same time, I want you to remain alive to carry out the plans King Brian, Lugh, and I are working on. You will know later what they are. Meanwhile, you have had your vision and must act on it.

While you are there you will find Brian's and Oberon's people will help you when need be. Your own powers gained under Ronan's tutelage will be ample to take care under most circumstances. Are you ready?"

Myrdden nodded. "Aye. From what I saw above the Stone I believe I know what my duty will be. I will meet with he of the red dragon and help him prepare for the battles he must face."

"Good!" Lir said. He glanced at the other rulers of Tir na nOg and shrugged. "I wish we could do more, but as you know we are not allowed to directly affect the lives of mortals. We can help you, but only through advice, not action."

"I understand. I will appreciate the assistance though, since it will keep me informed regarding what the other side might be doing."

"And you know how to make Morrigan come to you?"

Again Myrdden nodded as he smiled wryly. "I know how to make her come to me, but not how to make her tell all the truth. I know she will dissemble and make me try to second guess her actions."

"Good." Lir rose to his feet. "Then we all know what we are to do." He smiled at Nimue. "You may stay here or go back to Hags Head, as you wish." He said. "If you stay here you will hear the news of what is happening earlier, though."

"Thank you, Sire. I wish to remain here." She caught Myrdden's arm in her hand. "After all, I have to make sure he doesn't succumb to Morrigan's seductive ways."

"After seeing you no other woman will ever appeal to me." Myrdden said.

* * *

"Ah, Willm, you are a man of strength. You have pleased me greatly tonight."

Willm turned his head toward the naked form of the lady at his side. He smiled with pride. "Thank you, Lady Morrigan. I am happy to have been of service to you."

Morrigan turned on her side, pressing herself against Willm. "You can be of even greater service, my lord Willm." She whispered softly as her hands caressed his chest.

Willm breathed deeply. "And how may that be, my lovely wood nymph?"

"Remember the person I sang of tonight? Myrdden of no father?"

"I remember well." He whispered as his hands groped across her body.

"He is very evil. I believe you may find him one day. He would be a lovely sacrifice to the Druid gods, would he not?"

"That he would, my princess, that he would." Willm murmured as his lips found hers once again. There was no further conversation, nor was there any need, for Morrigan had made her point.

chapter 4
The Two Dragons

Harol of Tyne gazed with understandable pride at the magnificent edifice the artisans under his command were building. Sitting at the top of a rocky crag, with the sea as a backdrop, the fortress that was a castle was rising toward the cloudy sky. Two sides of the castle were at the edge of the four hundred foot cliffs. There was a steady, though faint, roar as the waves crashed against the base of the cliffs. Before the fortress was a grassy plain over twenty fathoms long. Once done the fortress would be impregnable. Harol's eyes gleamed as he watched workmen lift yet another log to be seated in the wall that would hold a battlement. At his side stood Vertigorm the Saecsen, king of the area, whose castle this was to be. He nodded his head with approval. "Good, Master Harol, the caer seems to be sturdy enough."

Harol turned to him. "Sturdy? Why, my lord, situated as it is on this rocky mount there is no army that can bring it down. Why, only the gods themselves are able to touch it, and I doubt even they could tear it log from log. When I build a caer I build it to last forever." He turned back to smile with pride at the massive walls above them; thick log backed by thick log. Moments later his smile turned to amazement, then to fear, as the ground trembled, the walls shook, swayed, and began falling apart as the crag itself seemed to shake. The workmen who were not caught in the tumbling logs ran toward safety as rapidly as possible as the massive tree trunks bounced along the hillside into the valley below, breaking and splintering as they went.

Vertigorm, his face as stony as the crag he faced, stared at the ruins of what had been his future caer. "This is the third time this has happened." His words fell flat from gritted teeth. "Can you explain to me, Master Harol, why your permanent caer is no longer so permanent?"

Harol stammered, trying to find the words to say, knowing he had to be quick if he was to save his life. "There has to be a curse on this place, or magic, to cause the caer to fall. It was built as strong as the caer at Pembroke, and in similar location. Did you not feel the ground tremble before it fell? Did not the ground tremble when the other caers fell as well? If it did the cause of the fall was not my building but of some other's desire that you not build here. Have you incurred the wrath of those of the other world?"

Vertigorm paused as he thought of the destruction of the other caers. He nodded thoughtfully, "You are quite correct, Master Harol. The ground did shake, the walls sway, before the others fell. We will see about this." He turned to his castellan. "Bring the Druid priest before me at once."

Granoch, the castellan, turned and beckoned a guard. "Bring Daemon to us at once. Tell him King Vertigorm is wroth."

When Daemon arrived Vertigorm pointed to the craggy knoll. "As you see, Your Eminence, the caer has once again fallen. Master Harol points out it may be because of some curse or magic that is in this area. Have you or your fellows placed a curse on me or on this crag?"

Daemon was quick to shake his head. "Nay, my lord Vertigorm, we have not. Yet it may be there is a *geis* on it. Allow me to consult with my fellow priests. Allow us to conduct a ceremony to find out if such a thing exists; and if so how to cancel it."

"And how long might such a search take?"

Daemon sighed as he thought of an answer. "I will let you know our findings tomorrow at this time."

Vertigorm nodded. "All right. Begone and do your ceremony. I will expect your answer tomorrow." He turned to the guard. "Take Master Harol to his tent. Do not allow him to leave. If he disappears I will have you roasted over a slow fire." The guard bowed and left with the master builder in a firm grip.

* * *

The practices of the Druid priesthood were secret. No one who did not belong to the order was allowed anywhere near where they were held. That evening the four priests Vertigorm had in his retinue to ward off dangers and curses, went to an oak opening a mile from the camp. There they had set up an altar where they were to perform their ceremony. The site was far enough from camp the men could see their fire, but too far for them to see what they might be doing, if they were inclined to do so.

"Vertigorm is wroth." Daemon stated as he placed a sacrificial chicken on the altar. "We must find something to tell him, else we might join Master Harol and the other two builders whose caers fell before this one." A fire burned to the left of the stone altar, throwing flickering shadows on the trunks of the oaks surrounding them. It was such that the shadows filled Daemon's eye sockets making his head more a skull with a beard than a human face.

"Aye. The first builder merely had his head separated from his body. The second was skinned alive. I would not wish to join either of them. What we say must be a word that makes us seem to have a vision of the future." Willm commented as he sharpened the knife. "It must be a prophecy that will seem to be impossible, yet plausible."

As the rites continued the four discussed the manner in which they would tell Vertigorm of the problem of building the caer. Each suggestion seemed to have a flaw in it. Finally Wambla spoke. "This new sect, the Christians talk of a child born without a human father. Why not tell him the only way the curse might be lifted is by sacrificing a child born with no human father?"

"What of the one the Christians talk of?" Daemon asked. "Might he still be found?"

Wambla smiled. "No. There is no chance of that. They say he was killed over four hundred years ago."

Willm face screwed up in thought. "I remember talk of someone who might answer, though." He finally said.

Daemon turned to him. "And who might that be?"

"A lovely young lady named Morrigan was singing a song of just such a person. It was at the castle of King Ronal a few weeks ago. She said she knows him personally and she is a lady of truth. He calls himself the boy of no father. She called him by the name Myrdden." He spoke as though the thoughts and memories were coming even as he spoke. "There is talk he is the creature of Mabd. It is said she created him because she wanted a man child to do her will, but did not want anything to do with a man. Others say he was found by the Lady of the Lake, floating up river to her lake from the sea. She is said to have him taken to either Tir na nOg or to Avalon and the Sisterhood for training. In either case it is said he is one who has no father."

"A child." Mused Daemon. "It is perfect. A child can say nothing in its defense, and yet we can be saved from death at the hand of one who does not really believe our powers." He nodded his head. "Yes. We will tell him to find this Myrdden, bring him to us, and we will sacrifice him on this altar."

Parfon spoke up. "But if he has been to Tir na nOg, the land of eternal youth, it is all the better. He would still be young enough to have no ability to say anything in his own defense."

"True." Willm thought out loud, "But if he is the creation of Mabd he will be under her protection, and she has powers greater than ours. Too, if he has been to Avalon he may already have acquired their abilities to contact the spirits of nature. If he has them, those attributes might make him a formidable foe. His ability to find the truth of what is wrong might be greater than ours."

"You say the truth." Daemon paused as he thought of the possibilities. Finally he nodded. Perhaps we can persuade Vertigorm to make certain he is never allowed to utter a word in his presence." "We must take the chance. We will inform Vertigorm of our findings tomorrow. We must persuade him to make certain this Myrdden is never allowed to utter a word in his presence if, and there is that possibility, he is no longer a babe."

* * *

Ronan laid the plans for the castle on a table in the Great Hall. "As you can see King Dermot, this is a new concept for the building of a caer. Unlike the one in which we find ourselves this will be built of stone. I presume you have people who work in stone in Leinster."

Dermot Murrough studied the plan before him. It was a simple drawing of a palisade of stone surrounding a stone keep that would stand five to six stories high. Unlike the wooden caer other kings would have, this would not be able to be burned, and would be far more difficult to win if a foe came against it. He leaned back in his chair and looked at Ronan. "And where might we build such a caer as this?"

Ronan smiled. "Let us take a tour of the area, Sire, and pick a good spot for its building."

"Excellent." He turned to his aides. "Sean, Neal, Ryan, let's find a good place to build a new caer."

The group left on horseback to study the land and pick a spot. Dermot turned to Ronan. "What should we consider when we look at a site?"

"One thing would be the necessity of being near enough to a large mass of rock that the masons would be able to cut and shape quickly. The other, as you already would know, is the position of defense. It must be able to be defended so it will not be easily conquered."

Dermot thought for a moment, and then half smiled as he nodded. "I don't think we have to tour the area. I believe I know a place that is just what you want." He said. "Come. I'll take you there." He turned his horse and headed toward the south.

They rode over a rise and Dermot brought the small band to a halt. They looked toward the sea over green fields with sheep grazing contentedly. Beyond the dry stone fences enclosing the fields were forests of mixed hardwoods. Nearby, standing by themselves, was a small group of rowan trees. Below the pastures an outcrop of the base rock of the island jutted out of the soil. Half a league out in the ocean a wooded island appeared almost blue through the haze of water evaporating under the hot sun.

Ronan surveyed the area. He turned to Dermot. "You were right. This would be an ideal place for such a caer, Sire. The long, open, fields would give good defense from any invading force, it is near a good source of stone, and there is plenty of wood for the furnishings of the keep."

Dermot looked out over the expanse and nodded approval. "Aye, Sir Ronan, you are certainly right. This is a good spot." He pointed to the rowan trees, "Do not cut those but include them in the bailey. I know the rowan trees are places the Leprechauns enjoy. I would not wish to be on their bad side. We will call this caer Dun Rowans, and it will become the seat of my government."

"Good, Sire. With your permission I shall assemble workmen and begin work immediately."

"And how long do you expect this to take, Sir Ronan?"

"With the help of the men of your province, I would estimate about three years."

Dermot was silent as he thought of the plans and the work involved in cutting and fitting the stone. Finally he nodded. "All right. It will be worth the wait to have such a strong place in which to live. Give my castellan the orders for men and material and he will see they are filled." He smiled a broad smile. "I look forward to enjoying such a caer as no man has had before."

* * *

Myrdden was older than the Druid priests imagined, and his powers had already matured, though his body appeared to be that of a stripling His thirst for adventure, and insatiable desire for knowledge, coupled with the desire of the rulers of Tir na nOg, had led Myrdden to the shores of Cymru (now known as Wales).

Morrigan, riding in the enclosed caravan of the troop of entertainers spied him as they passed him on the road. Her eyes widened as she recognized him, and noted the direction in which he was traveling. At the next town she found a group of Saecsen soldiers in the pub where the troop was relaxing after their meal.

"Who is in charge of your cohort?" She asked one of them.

"Graham, lovely lady," he bent his head in the direction of another table, "but I am as good a man as he, if a man is what you need."

Morrigan raised one eyebrow as she half smiled. "Your desire is noted." She said, but I must speak to your leader." She walked to the table where Graham sat. "Has anyone told you of a man who has no father?" She asked.

Graham looked into her serious face. He lifted one eyebrow in inquiry. "A man with no father?" He shook his head. "No, but we are looking for a boy of that description."

"Boy he was, man he is now."

"Boy, man, what's the difference when I have twenty men with me. What does this person call himself?"

"Myrdden."

"Merlin?" Graham nodded. "Aye. We are trying to find him for King Vertigorm. He has sent scouting parties throughout the land in hopes of finding this person."

"For what purpose does he wish him?"

"Our liege is building a caer that continually falls before it is erected. The Druid priest has told him that only the sacrifice of one with no earthly father will satisfy the curse on the land."

"And what would it be worth to you to bring this man to your liege?"

Graham smiled. "If I bring him in I may be given command over a larger group, and that would mean a promotion and more money. I would gladly pay ten pieces of silver for knowledge of where he might be."

Morrigan smiled slyly as she held out her hand, palm up. "Then place ten pieces of silver here, for I can tell you where to find him." She watched closely as he counted the coins into her hand. "If you take the road to Pembroke you will find a young man walking toward that town. He is the one you want. He will be only half a morning's walk down the road. Be careful with him, for he is wily."

"There may be many men walking on that road with fields to tend. How might I be assured of capturing the right one?"

Morrigan's smile was on her mouth though not in her eyes as she said, "He will have a cloak of midnight blue, a gold torc around his neck, and beneath the cloak will be dressed in motley, for with Mabd as mother he is of high degree."

"Ah! Thank you kind lady. You have given me my promotion." Turning to the rest of the room he shouted. "Men. Assemble outside. We have found our prey." They left the town doing double time as they ran down the road.

An unsuspecting Myrdden heard them as they approached from behind and moved to one side to let them pass. Quickly and easily surrounded, he was overpowered. He rapidly ascertained the leader of the group, and began concentrating on him. Orders would be followed so, using the skills honed by Ronan, he gained control of the mind of Graham. Though he was trussed he was able to keep Graham from gagging him or taking his sword.

Once he was thoroughly tied Graham grinned at the sight of his captive. "So, Master Merlin," he said, "we now take you to King Vertigorm. He has need of you for a sacrifice that his caer might be safely built." He admired the gold torc around Myrdden's neck. "I believe you won't need the torc any more, nor will you need the sword." He reached out to take his plunder

"You really don't want them." Myrdden said gently. "You will find a greater reward when we reach your king." Graham thought for a moment, then nodded as he put his hands down. "But," Myrdden continued, "you do desire to tell me the story of why I am wanted as we walk. It will help while away the tedious hours it will take to reach your lord."

"Yes." Graham replied, "That is an excellent idea." He recounted the story as he knew it as he marched his prisoner back to where Vertigorm waited. When they finally reached the place of the caer, and before coming into the presence of Vertigorm, Graham whispered, "It is too bad you are to die, Master Merlin, for I found your conversation interesting."

* * *

When Myrdden was ushered in the presence of Vertigorm the Druid priests were aghast. This was not the babe they expected, and his mouth was free to speak. Myrdden, hands tied behind him, looked directly into Vertigorm's eyes, something no other man dared to do. "To what do I owe this honor, King Vertigorm?" He inquired.

Vertigorm waved at the ruins of the caer and the craggy knoll on which it had stood. "Three times I have tried to have a strong caer built on that knoll. Three times it has tumbled in ruins before it was finished. These Druid priests say only the sacrifice of a man with no human father will satisfy the gods to allow me to finish the castle. They say you are that man, so you will be sacrificed."

Myrdden sneered. "So you always listen to the advice of old men who have no idea of what they speak?"

"What do you mean?"

"It is not the death of a man with no human father that will allow the caer to be built. There is far more here than their meager magic can reckon." Myrdden's voice dripped with sarcasm.

Daemon motioned to a guard. "Shut him up!"

"Stay!" Vertigorm commanded, then looked at the priests who were trying to make a good show of their arrogance. Daemon's eyes dropped as he could no longer meet Vertigorm's stare. Turning back to Myrdden he said, "Explain yourself."

"Take me to the table with the plans." Myrdden said. At the table he pointed to the knoll's outline. "What you see here is a knoll covering an underground lake. The sea has created a large cavern and lake beneath this hill. In that lake live two strong dragons. One is red, the other white. There is a limited amount of food for them because they are too large to go through the small hole leading to the sea. When they become hungry they fight for the few morsels the sea brings to them. When they fight the land trembles with their battle. Whatever is made by the hand of man cannot withstand the violent movement. Your three caers have each been destroyed when they were fighting. If you have your men dig down to the lake you will find what I say is true.

Vertigorm turned to look at the knoll, smiled wryly and then shook his head. "And how deep must they dig?"

Myrdden had a half smile on his face as he answered. "The lake is twenty fathoms below the level of the sea."

Vertigorm smiled cynically as he looked at the four hundred feet of cliff below where he stood and another fifty feet to the top of the knoll where the ruined caer lay." He nodded. "Aye, and it would take these men months to work their way down to that lake. I fear I have to take your word for it, though you may be lying."

"I lie not." Myrdden said. "I am not like the Druid priests who make up their wise words to fit the situation in which they find themselves."

Vertigorm frowned. "What do you mean by that?"

"They told you to find a boy who had no father. You found me. If these are so wise why did they not inform you to look for a man instead of a callow youth?"

Vertigorm nodded and glared at Daemon who was putting on a brave show of anger.

"There is more." Myrdden added. Vertigorm nodded for him to continue. "These dragons represent far more than the destruction of your caer. As I said, one is red and the other white. I see by the ensign before your tent that your symbol is that of the white dragon. There is another coming from another part of Cymru whose symbol is that of the red dragon. The fact your three caers have been destroyed is also a sign of what is to come. There will be three battles between you and the other. In the first two neither will win, but you will be killed in the last battle, and these lands will be taken by the Cymru."

Vertigorm's face fell as he stared at Myrdden, with a suspicious look on it. "And who might this king be?" Vertigorm asked.

"As yet I know not his name for it was not told me as I looked on the knoll. But beware of the Red Dragon, for he is preparing his armies at this moment to come against you."

Vertigorm nodded his acceptance of Myrdden's statement. "Then I will attack him first and defeat him before he has a chance to assemble his full army."

Myrdden shook his head. "Aye, you will try. And what is foretold can be altered by the actions of man. Even so, his reign must begin and yours must cease. It has been written for some time that this be true. The one God is displeased with the cruelty you have shown to friend, foe, and to the peasants under your authority. You use your power to harm, not help. This is not acceptable to him. You will cease."

Vertigorm frowned. "And who might this one God be?"

"It is the God of the Christians, brought here by the Romans, and who is taking over the island from the pagan gods that have been worshipped here before. In Eirrein a man named Patrick has introduced him to the people, and he is now the first one worshipped there."

"I could have you killed for those statements."

Myrdden nodded. "Aye. That you could." He shook his head. "But you will not, for it is not yet my destiny to die. That too is written."

"Then I may have you thrown into a dungeon."

Myrdden shook his head. "No. That you will not do either. In a dungeon I could do you no good for I would languish to nothing in such a place. I am a man of the outdoors, the wind, the sun, the rain are my friends and allies. It is they, and my powers of observation, as well as the gift of othersight that allows me to see a short time into the future. I would be useless to you unless I am in a place where I can hear the voices I must hear."

Vertigorm stared at the mound of ruble, then back to Myrdden. "Then what must I do?"

"You must let me go."

Vertigorm nodded slowly, his voice thickened as he said. "Aye. I must let you go." He motioned Graham. "Untie him and allow him his freedom."

Daemon stepped forward, arm outstretched. "Nay, My King. He has put you in thrall to his voice. He is evil. Do not release him."

Myrdden said in a soothing voice. "You have no need of the Druids, Vertigorm. They have misled you before, they will do so again."

Vertigorm nodded. "You speak truth. Guards. Seize the Druid priests and throw them over the edge of the cliff." He turned back to Myrdden. "What other advice do you have for me?"

"Do not try to build another caer in that place. It will fall. Go back to your wooden caer and wait. Soon you will hear of the army of the Red Dragon, but you will not remember this conversation." With that Myrdden turned and strode through the ranks of the guards assembled behind him. With no word from Vertigorm, they allowed him free passage.

Turning his face to the southeast Myrdden began walking. Lyonesse was attached to the place the Cornish people lived, and it was from here the one with the Red Dragon would come. "I should have had Vertigorm give me a horse." He muttered to himself as he walked.

* * *

"Come on Tim." Kevin MacMurrough, son of Dermot Murrough beckoned Tim Mac Egan, his friend and companion down the hall. He held a small clay jar with his hand held over the opening. Tim looked back to see they weren't being followed. Kevin peeked around the corner of the door to make sure the room was empty, then entered. The room, much like the large dining room used by the adults, was similarly situated. The table was already set for the evening meal with plates, knives and spoons. "Now, let's turn all the plates upside down."

"Why?" Tim asked.

Kevin smiled slyly, "You'll see." He walked down one side of the table turning plates upside down. Once all were turned he went to the center where he would sit. Because he was son of the King of Leinster he would have the central place at table as his father did at the table in the Great Hall. Tim would sit on his right. His sister, Fiona ni Murrough would sit on his left and her lady in waiting and companion, Maeve ni Grady would sit on her left. Kevin lifted Maeve's plate and slid the salamander he had in the jar under it. "Now." He grinned broadly, "When Maeve turns her plate over she is going to get a real surprise. It should be a lot of fun to watch. Hurry! Let's get out of here before we're caught."

"Maybe she will be so frightened she won't eat."

"Why? There's no harm in a little salamander. She can always get another plate."

They hurried down the hallway and outside. "Why do you always tease Maeve?" Tim finally asked. "She hasn't done you any harm."

Kevin thought for a moment. "No she hasn't." He smiled with glee. "But I love the way she reacts when she sees the things I've done. I have fun scaring her."

"What if she or Fiona tells your father?"

After a pause Kevin said. "I don't think they will. I guess they don't think father will do anything about it."

"I don't think Maeve likes you very much."

"That's all right. There are plenty other girls around. She's just my way of having fun. After all, she's just a lady in waiting, or maybe I should say, a girl in waiting. Anyway, with all that red hair she's not that pretty."

chapter 5
Uther Pendragon

Vertigorm stared down at the field of battle. The ground was littered with the wounded and dead of both armies. "These cursed Celts," he muttered through clenched teeth, "and that cursed Uther Pendragon that leads them. They fight like madmen. They seem to care not whether they live or die, but wade in with sword and pike killing until they are killed. And if one falls it seems two more come to take his place. Call back what remains of our army. We will return to Londinium, regroup, and meet this Uther again. Under better conditions, it is to be hoped."

On the opposite hillside Uther also stared down at the battlefield. A bitter smile covered his face. "Well." He sighed. "They are withdrawing with no victory. Unfortunately we also have no victory. Call back our men. We will return to Caer Gaofar. We will meet this Saecsen who calls himself king again; and again if need be. "He turned to a lieutenant, "Lane. Call all the kings in my domain together a fortnight from now. We will have a meeting of the chiefs to prepare for the next battle." He smiled thoughtfully. "Have them bring their families with them as well. We will have a grand party."

Myrdden glanced over sharply at the last words. "That may not be a good idea, my lord." He said.

Uther lifted an eyebrow and asked, "And why do you say that, seer?"

"'Tis but a feeling I have. Something evil will come of it I fear."

Uther laughed heartily. "You fear? I need more of a reason than 'I fear'. I need a stronger reason than your sensitive feelings give me. No. We will have a grand party for all of the kings of the region. It is important their families also be behind our wars against the Saecsens. I appreciate your vision regarding the battle, Myrdden. You told me true what would be the outcome. I believe your have better vision for the future of battle than for the future of the gathering of the kings." His hand clapped onto Myrdden's shoulder as a gesture of his good will. "Keep me informed of battles and I will take care of the kingdom, eh?"

Myrdden drew a deep breath and released it as a long sigh. What was to happen would happen, and there was nothing he could do to prevent it now. "Oh, my lord Uther." He said as an afterthought.

"Yes."

"I would have a boon of you, if you would grant it."

"What sort of a boon?"

"It is that warrior there. The one wounded as he protected you from the pike of a Saecsen. He saved your life."

"Aye. That he did."

"It would appear his wound is one that will render him unable to fight again. I believe a reward would be as a watchman at the pass north of Cardiff. It would be through that pass the Saecsen would come if they were to invade Cymru. Since Ector is wounded and unable to fight more, and as a reward for your life, such a position would take care of him for his life, and he would be of service to us."

"Good idea, Myrdden. I will do it." He looked at the man limping ahead of him as they marched back to Caer Gaofar. "Ector! Come to me." Ector walked back to the group. "Ector, I am retiring you from my army and giving you a post and land in Cymru. Take a horse so you might ride there. There is a pass above Cardiff that needs a watch kept. I give you that and land surrounding it and the town below the hill as yours for good service."

Ector's smile was huge on his face. "Oh, thank you Sire. I do appreciate your generosity, and I will keep a good watch."

"I am sure you will. Because such a post needs a noble in command, I name you baron of that area." Uther answered. "But you must thank Myrdden for your position. It is he who suggested it as a reward for your faithful service."

Ector turned to Myrdden. "I thank you, my lord. And if I can ever do anything for you, you have but to ask and it shall be done." Myrdden nodded, a secret smile on his face.

* * *

Caer Gaofar was full to overflowing with the aristocracy of the people of Cornwall and Cymru. Uther sat on the throne in the great hall. Torches guttered in their holders along the wooden wall, battle shields and swords interspersed between them, as the various kings and their wives were presented to Uther. It was the first time many of them had met this man who had pushed the Saecsens from their land, and they had come to enjoy as well as to swear fealty to him as High King. Myrdden stood behind the throne, watching as the nobles lined up to be presented to Uther.

The line had been long and Uther had become somewhat bored with the entire proceedings. He was slumped on his throne as the servant announced, "King Gorlois of Tintagel and Queen Ygraine."

Myrdden watched as Uther took notice and sat bolt upright from his slouching position. He hardly glanced at Gorlois for his eyes were on Ygraine. There was no denying she was very beautiful. "Yes. Gorlois and Ygraine, eh? I must talk more with you Gorlois. You will sit with me at meat tonight, you and your wife."

"An honor, Sire." Gorlois bowed as he took Ygraine's hand and moved to depart. Uther's eyes had not left Ygraine since he first saw her, and he took little notice of the next lord to be presented as his eyes followed her around the hall.

When Gorlois and she disappeared into the next room he turned to Myrdden. "Did you see her, Myrdden? She is the most beautiful woman I have ever seen in my life. I must have her."

"My lord, she is the wife of Gorlois. It would be suicide for you to take her, especially here as you are being accepted as High King. No one would accept you if such a thing happened."

Uther nodded, as he frowned. "True. This is not the place. You will find a way for me to have her. I will not rest until I have bedded her. I leave it in your hands." He turned his attention back to the reception line, slouching once again on the throne.

Dinner that night was a fiasco for Uther paid little attention to Gorlois. Rather, he talked around him to Ygraine, his desire written plainly on his face. As the flirting continued Gorlois became more and more upset until, before the final serving, he took Ygraine by the hand. "Come. We are leaving." He said as he pulled her to her feet and out of the room. The clatter of dinnerware and talk suddenly became silenced as all eyes turned to his retreating form. Minutes later they heard the sound of horses hoofs as Gorlois and Ygraine departed the Caer. The unthinkable had happened. No one could leave the king's presence without his giving permission. What Gorlois had done was an act of war, and all realized it.

Uther rose to his feet. "You have seen me insulted in my own Great Hall." He announced. "A state of war now exists between Gorlois of Tintagel and myself. We shall repair our army to fight. Leigh and Bryan will lead my men into battle against Gorlois. Prepare your men."

Two of the men rose from the table, bowed to Uther, and left the hall as the sound of voices now rose to fill the room with gossip about what had been seen.

* * *

Colm an Dubh watched through narrowed eyes as Kevin and Tim began putting together another trick to play on Maeve. Kevin had found a puppy with the same markings as Maeve's pet. Now he and Tim were busily skinning the puppy they had killed as they chuckled to themselves. "I can't wait to see Maeve's face when she pulls back the cover and finds this skin in her bed." Kevin whispered. "What did you do with her real puppy?"

"I hid him under a tub until tomorrow." Tim answered. "We can bring him back from the dead, and see what she thinks of that."

Colm was Kevin's older half brother. Before his marriage Dermot had been with a village maid. She had born Colm and he had acknowledged him as his son. Colm Murroughs-garsun early had dreams of becoming Dermot's heir. Then he had married and his first born was Kevin. A year later Fiona was born and shortly after that their mother died as she miscarried a third baby. Colm's dream died when Kevin was born. Now he watched Kevin and Tim at play.

He turned to his friend and confidant, Boyle, as he pointed with his chin to the two. "There must be some way to rid myself of that spawn." He muttered. "With him out of the way I would stand to gain the throne."

"You forget, Colm. Fiona would inherit. There have been many daughters who inherited from their fathers, and were good queens."

"True. That means I must rid myself of both of them." Colm continued to watch as his rage seethed inside. "We must figure a way to do this." He said.

"Och. A way so that none will know it is you who did it." Boyle added as they turned away from the scene.

"That's easily done. I will hire someone to make sure both of them die."

* * *

"My men are fighting Gorlois men near Borleigh." Uther said to Myrdden. "I have sent orders that Gorlois must not be killed. I would not want to murder him. I just wish to have him out of the way while I bed Ygraine. Can you help me?"

"You say he is at Borleigh? That is to our north. Tintagel is to our south. I can make you appear to be Gorlois, I would be Barne, and Lane could appear as Lunde. We could appear to be coming home from battle for a few hours. You could be with her through the night and we would leave in the early morn. You would have your way with her and the war could end."

Uther's smile seemed to light up the room. "Capital! Let us go now. We should arrive at Tintagel at dusk. I will then have the entire night with Ygraine while Gorlois is fighting at Bobleigh."

"I will do this on one condition." Myrdden said. "If you do not agree we will not go."

Uther stopped in his tracks. "You are making conditions on me?" He asked in a stern voice.

"Aye. That I am. You forget. Without me you will never have the lady Ygraine and your war will have been for nothing. You will have lost a friend in the process. You will remember a few weeks ago I told you not to invite the families. You laughed because of my fear of what would happen. You see what has happened. My fears were justified. Now. You will grant me a condition or we will not embark on this venture. If you do not do as I ask the consequences will be dire. If you do the future might be saved."

"What is the condition?"

"You grant it?"

"Grant it without hearing it?" Myrdden nodded solemnly. "Oh, all right." Uther finally said. "I will grant your condition."

"From this union a boy child will be born. You will take that child from Ygraine and give it to me immediately that I may do what I wish with him."

"A boy child, eh? And why do you wish to take him? Do you not believe I will raise him properly?"

"If I were sure you would be there to raise the boy I might leave him with you. I see two roads in the future. In one you are there. In the other you are not. I know not which road that will be taken; therefore I must take the boy and assure his safety. On him the future of these islands lie."

Uther glanced around nervously. "Two roads, you say, and I am not on one of them." He nodded. "Yes. I will keep my word. When the boy is born you shall have him to raise." He smiled crookedly, "Now, since I am to die later, let me die happy having had Ygraine in my bed. When Gorlois returns she will never know it was not he who was with her tonight."

Unfortunately the statement would prove to be false, for Gorlois was to be accidentally killed in battle that very night. Ygraine would then know who was with her, and would never forget.

* * *

Uther was true to his word. When the young lad was born he gave the infant to Myrdden. Myrdden left Tintagel as Uther was preparing for another battle with the Saecsens under Vertigorm. Traveling north he moved into the country of Cymru, past Cardiff, through the valleys to the north until he came to a small wooden caer set near a pass. He pulled the horse to a stop in the courtyard as a warrior came from the wooden keep to greet him. "Ah, Merlin. 'Tis an age since I saw you last. It is welcome you are to Caer Garda. But what is that you have bundled in your arm?"

Myrdden slid off his horse as a lackey came to take it to the stable. "This, my friend, is a babe, and I believe him to be an important babe. I place him in your care to raise as though he were your own son, though I see your own son is a bit older. I will return for him one day. What day I cannot tell. Say you will take care of him for me."

"After what you have done for me, getting me a barony, setting me up in this caer as watcher of the pass, what can I say? Of course I will take care of him and raise him as one of my own."

Mheare," he called, and waited as a young woman came from the building behind him. "come and take this babe." He took the bundle from Myrdden and handed it to her. "I know you lost your babe," he said tenderly, "and I am truly sorry. Would you suckle this babe and tend him in place of your own? Perhaps it will make the loss less tragic."

Mheare took the bundle and lifted a corner of the blanket off the baby's face. Her own face brightened at the sight of the blue eyes looking trustingly into her own. She smiled at the tiny face and said, without looking up, "Gladly Sire. Thank you. He is a braw boy, is he not?" The young boy began to cry, "Oh, and he is hungry, too. There now, little one, we will make sure you're well fed." And she left them to take care of her new duties.

"Come in, my friend, come in. I still am in your debt for this fief I have because of you. I have kept good watch, but so far nothing has happened. You will stay, will you not?"

"Overnight only. I must go on an important duty before I return to Uther."

Ector knew enough not to ask further. Myrdden already had a reputation as a seer, *seanachie*, and bard. Ask too much and you might regret the answer you found. True to his word Myrdden left the following morning.

* * *

Nimue was in his arms before the servant could lead his horse to the stable. "Ah, m'acushla. This past week has seemed like a year without you." She lifted her head to be kissed. "I missed you terribly."

Myrdden chuckled. "It was two years for me, acushla. You forget, time is different here than there." He looked into her green eyes. "Then you have forgiven me for the first time we met?"

She buried her head in his chest. "I'm working on it. But I am glad to have you back with me. You must tell me all about your adventures. I only wish I could have been with you."

Myrdden shook his head. "I'm afraid if Uther saw you he'd want you even more than he wanted Ygraine. No. I'm glad you weren't with me. Though I did miss you." He kissed her again. "Now, let us go and see King Lir."

In the Great Hall Lir motioned them to chairs. "I have been to the Stone of Seeing." He said without preamble. "Brian's people have reported events to us. What you have done with the babe is good. He will be safe. Still, the future is uncertain. I wish you to use the Stone and see if your vision agrees with mine. If it does we must do something unprecedented. I'll let you know after you have used the stone." Lir and Nimue waited as Myrdden left to go to the upper hall.

Some time later Myrdden returned to the Hall. "I saw a bad future and I saw a good future. It depended on the decisions that will be made by the new king after he achieves his throne. In one the Saecsens won and there was a long and bitter period of time in which they conquered and destroyed people and nations as they forced them under their thumb. In the other I saw a long time of peace as a Celtic people were able to make their own way on these islands and in the world. I also saw the future depended on advisers to this king who knew his future and the pitfalls that would face him."

Lir nodded. "That is what Lugh and I felt also. I have called Brian, Oberon and Titania also. We all have to talk to the Creator to get permission to use the upper dimensions to bring back the minds of two men from the future to become advisers to this king. It all depends on if it fits into his plans, for his plans are the ones that will be accomplished, not ours."

"Two men from the future, Sire?"

"Aye. While Kevin MacMurrough and Tim Mac Egan are only eighteen, and these two men are in their fifties, we believe it will work. They are both warriors in their age, and direct descendants of the two whose bodies we wish to use. I will keep you informed as to what the Creator says about our desire."

* * *

Cdr. Kevin Murray and Lt. Cdr. Tim Keegan watched their SEAL battalion parade before them. As they returned the salute of the men Tim commented, "After thirty-five years in this outfit I'm just a little reluctant to leave."

"I know what you mean." Kevin said. "We joined when we were just seventeen, and it's really been the only life we've known since we were kids. Now…well the Navy says it's been nice, but the time has come to part. At least we get a good pension, and we're still young enough to get other jobs."

"Yeah." Tim sighed as he watched the last men in the battalion march past. "Fifty-two isn't too bad an age. We've still got a lot of life in us." He stopped talking as the other officers in the command came forward to shake their hands and wish them good luck. As they left the stands and headed for their car he added. "I just wish I knew what we were going to be doing."

"Well." Kevin answered. "I know one thing we'll do if you want to come with me."

"What's that?"

"I just got notified I've inherited a broken down castle in Ireland, along with some land to go with it. I thought I'd go over and take a look at it. Maybe spend a bit of time looking Ireland over. I guess this castle is the one that my family used to own back in the old days. Care to come along? After all, you're Irish, and it would be nice to get a good look at the auld sod, as my grandmother used to call it."

"That sounds like a good idea. We could use a vacation, and I know my people came from Ireland. I'd like to see the place myself. You're on. I'll go with you."

* * *

The late afternoon sun shone through a window on the fourth floor of the keep of Dun Rowans as Kevin MacMurrough and Timothy Mac Egan walked along the carpeted hall. After they passed the open door of a bedroom two young men snuck quietly up behind them. Each held a knife and a rock. As they struck each of the two on the head they plunged a knife into the back of both the boys. Hearing someone approaching from the opposite direction they turned and fled.

part two
Leinster

chapter 1
Dun Rowans

"So that's the place, eh?" Tim Keegan said as they rounded the curve on the bumpy grass covered lane. Ahead of them, at the end of what had turned out to be not much more than two long ruts between the wild rhododendron hedges, lay the ruins of what had once been a tower keep. Now the outer wall was a heap of large stones while the keep itself had only four of the original stories left. While the wall on the fourth level was standing it was in bad disrepair. The floor now served as a roof over the third floor that had held the Great Hall, still stood, and much of its walls were still in place. The second floor housing the men at arms rooms was still intact, as was the first floor.

Kevin Murray slowed the rental car down a bit to maneuver around a large pothole. Once safely on the other side without blowing a tire he nodded. "I suppose they'd call this a 'borreen green'. Yep, that's the ancestral palace." He chuckled sadly, "Doesn't look like much now, does it? Once it was a rather lovely place, or so I've heard from my grandmother. She told tales of the bards, seanachies, and poets old Donal MacMurrough used to have there. There was always music, and stories, and poetry that rang through the halls of Dun Rowans. That was its name, you know, Dun Rowans." He fell silent as he maneuvered through another water filled hole.

"A couple questions," Tim said as he held onto the side of the seat so he didn't get thrown completely out of the car. "Done sounds like it's finished, and what's a shanaky?"

Kevin laughed, "I thought you'd know, being of Irish ancestry and all. Dun is the old Gaelic word for fort, and the seanachie was, and is, the teller of the old tales. He or she remembers the old stories, myths and folklore and tells them to keep them alive. Grandma was the seanachie of our family. She could tell the tale so you felt you were living it yourself. You could see the people, see how they dressed, how they fought, how they lived the stories she told." He smiled wryly. "I used to sit at her feet and be enthralled at the tales she told; not only of our family, understand, but of Brian Boru, or Finn Mac Cool and the Fenians, the little people. Oh, she had a way of telling them that put you right into the story so you were living it yourself. She knew all the tales of the Irish heroes; and some of them probably came about before the Celts were even on this island."

"Sorry if I'm so dumb about my ancestry, but where were they before they came here?"

"In central Europe, what's now Germany. The Romans had many a battle with them and since they wrote the histories gave the Celts a name of a primitive and cruel people. As it turns out the Celts were far more civilized and honest than the Romans. Anyway, somewhere in the B. C. period some of them moved through what's now Spain, and found their way over here. When is lost in the veil of antiquity. The Murroughs became kings of the area called Leinster somewhere before even Patrick came over here. This is one of the castles they built to protect this part of their barony from invaders. Grandma thought it was built well before the year 1000, but wasn't sure."

"So when you inherited this piece of land you decided to come over and have a look, eh?"

Kevin pulled the car to a stop before what was left of the main gate. The wooden doors had long since rotted, and parts of the lintel had fallen in. After picking their way over the rubble they began walking through the tangle of bushes and gorse toward the main entrance. Kevin stood, hands on hips, and looked up at the grey walls towering above them. "Yep. I figured my people hadn't been here since the late 1700's when the English forced the aristocracy to leave, and since it was still owned by the family the government wouldn't fix it up like they did Bunratty and The Ferns, or turn it into a tourist attraction as they did with Blarney." He smiled ruefully. "I thought it would be in disrepair, but didn't think it would be this well preserved."

"This well preserved? It sure looks run down to me."

"Aye, it does that. But look at some of the other places that have been abandoned. Some of the round towers and old castles are nothing more than heaps of rock. You can hardly tell they were once stately castles in which people lived, and loved, and had banquets and song. Here there's a lot left standing. Look up. Grandma said it was six levels high when it was built. The living quarters for the family were on the fourth level. The chapel and private rooms on the fifth floor. The sixth was a library of books copied by the monks from Kilkenny. The third was the Great Hall where all the banquets were held. The second was for the men at arms, and the ground floor was where the cooking was done and where most of the servants lived. There was a small village outside the walls where other servants lived. A smithy, the local fisherman, shepherds, and the like would live there as well."

The two approached the front of the keep where Kevin pointed at an opening above them. "See how this whole entrance area is set in from the rest of the wall? Look where the main door is located, it must be twelve feet off the ground. It's inset, too. Look up. They could pour boiling oil through those grates on anyone trying to get up to the door. Too bad they didn't consider cannon when they built it, but cannon hadn't really been invented yet I guess."

* * *

"I see the main door, but how are we going to get up to it. There's no stairs."

"No, and the wooden stairs they used have pretty much rotted away. That's why I brought the rope and grappling hook along. I figured, from Grandma's description of the place, it might be inaccessible. Stand back a bit." Kevin swung the hook around and threw it at the sill of the main door. It hit and, as he pulled, bit into the rough stone. He leaned back to test its ability to hold him. No stones came loose, so he put his feet on the wall and walked up as he pulled himself hand over hand along the rope. Once Kevin was in Tim followed him in the same way. The oak door, once thick and strong, hung askew off one rusted hinge. Kevin shook his head sadly as he looked at it, then turned toward an inner door still attached to its hinges.

"This is where the men at arms lived and slept." Kevin said as he walked through the doorway into a large hall that occupied most of the entire second floor. "Grandma said there were a couple hundred men at arms when the castle was a living thing. You can see where their arms were stored, and there are still the remnants of some banners on the walls. They're so old and thin you could read a newspaper through them. Imagine their being here after all these years. Let's go upstairs."

The two men continued their tour of the ruins. They ascended the narrow circular stairs at the corner of the keep. Kevin looked out of an embrasure, a narrow slit on the outside that widened to a large opening on the inside. "What's the point?" Tim asked as he examined the opening.

"An archer could stand here and command a wide range of the inner bailey, but an enemy archer would have a hard time getting an arrow through that opening from the outside." Kevin answered. "Just as this stairway is so narrow only one can walk up at a time. One man at the top with a pike could keep an army at bay if they tried to come up. Let's go on to the next floor." They looked over the Great Hall; then went to the overseers and house servants area on that level.

"It sort of gives you a creepy feeling looking at these empty rooms. It almost seems as though their spirits should be here. When was it built, do you think?" Tim said as they wandered through the halls and rooms of that floor.

Kevin shook his head as he ran his hand over some relatively smooth stone that formed the wall. "Grandma didn't know. She did know it was before the Vikings invaded, and they first came during the ninth century. A long time ago, really. I guess that's why the place is in such disrepair, it must be over a thousand years old."

"I wonder if any ghosts still hang around here. I know I've seen some TV programs and read of some rather angry spirits at some of the other old castles in Ireland."

"I don't know. I've never much believed in ghosts, but it does give one goosebumps to wander these empty halls. Just think of the events these halls would recount if only they could talk. Let's go upstairs and see what's left of the family quarters." They found a narrow stairs located behind a statue at one corner of the Great Hall and finally walked out in the remnants of the fourth level. Above them the sky was a lovely cerulean blue with wispy clouds scattered over the wide expanse. While they explored the castle the winds had blown the clouds away, and now a bright sun shone down on them. In the distance were the dark clouds of the rainstorm as it moved east over the Irish Sea, and the wind was blowing it further away as they watched. "Grandma said there was never a day it didn't rain in Ireland." Kevin commented as he walked to the remnants of a window. "Look!" He pointed toward the sea, "What a lovely picture that makes."

Tim stood beside him to look out at the expanse of dry stone walls encasing small pieces of land, sheep grazing contentedly in the small fields, and the blue-green of the Irish Sea beyond. About a mile out was an island with the ruins of a round tower at its base, and the green of its trees hazy in the distance. The dark gray clouds served as a background to the white of the sunlit cottages, and the ruined tower, enhancing the beauty of the scene. As they leaned over the sill of the remnants of the window the movement of the stone, or rotten cement, caused a block in the lintel over their heads to dislodge and fall. The rock struck them before tumbling the rest of the four stories to the ground. Both men fell back into the castle to lie as though dead on the rough stone floor.

"Sure you boys certainly do get yourselves in a spot of trouble faster than pig can find a mud hole." The voice was soft, spoken with good humor, and contained a bit of affection in its tone as well.

Kevin shook his head to clear the cobwebs and looked up. Through the blur of his vision he saw a very attractive face framed in auburn hair, and a pair of deep blue eyes gazing into his own. He shook his head again as he thought, *We're alone. Where did she come from*? He tried to focus his eyes, and as the fuzziness disappeared he noticed she was dressed in a green gown of a style he knew predated medieval times. The green of that gown and the auburn hair presented a picture that almost took his breath away again. As he tried to sit up she helped him, smiling as she did so.

"There now. Are you awake?" Her words struck him, she wasn't speaking English she was speaking Gaeilge, the old Irish language, and he understood it. He looked down at the recumbent form of Tim lying on the carpeted floor, who was just opening his own eyes to join the living world again. He shook his head for it wasn't the Tim he knew, but a very young man of about eighteen. A second young lady, blonde hair falling loosely over her shoulders, was bending over him, a look of consternation on her face. It turned to a smile of relief as Tim opened his eyes. Good! Kevin thought. Maybe we'll figure something out together. Tim pushed himself to a sitting position on the carpet.

Kevin leaned against the window sill, still somewhat dizzy, as things began to come into sharper focus. Surprised by the carpet where none had been before, he examined his surroundings. The fourth floor was no longer open to the sky. There was a roof over his head, a carpet covered the floor of the hallway in which he was standing, and pennants and embroidered tapestries with scenes of harvest and planting hung on the wall. The walls were whitewashed to hide the gray of the stone. He turned to the window. It was whole, and the scene outside no longer looked out on dry stone fences and small fields, but on a sweep of majestic trees leading down to the shore.

To one side were large cleared fields where sheep did graze, and he could see the thatched roofs and whitewashed walls of a number of houses clustered outside the bailey. The bailey walls were whole, and inside the bailey grew rowan trees. On an island about a mile offshore stood what appeared to be half finished round tower. He turned back to the girl and felt his heart skip a beat. Eyes as blue as the ocean deeps, a slightly turned up nose, lips that needed no color to make them desirable, and all this framed in a tousle of auburn hair. The lovely face wore a puzzled look, and Kevin knew his was just as puzzled.

"I don't understand." Kevin was finally able to get some words out. "Where are we?"

The young lady shook her head; her lips curling into a smile that made Kevin feel the sun had just come out from under a cloud. "Well now, always the tease, eh Kevin? And it's I'll play along with ye. It's in Dun Rowans ye are, silly boy. What happened to you? When I came along you and Timothy seemed to be sleeping. How could you fall asleep on the hallway floor?" Her face took on a conspiratorial look, "A wee drop too much?"

"We didn't fall asleep, and it wasn't wine for we haven't been drinking." From habit Kevin looked at his wrist, but there was no watch there. He felt the back of his head where a lump the size of a goose egg had formed. "Something hit me on the back of my head, and I feel as though something else jabbed me in the ribs." He felt the lump recede under the touch of his fingers. "I don't understand, there's no lump." He felt his ribcage, and shook his head. "Not even a bruise. I don't understand it."

"Now that is a fine story. And what of you Sir Timothy Mac Egan, have you a non-lump also?"

Tim felt his own head, winced, and nodded. "Well, there's no lump, but it feels as though someone with metal boots is tromping through my head."

The girl turned to the other maiden. "Fiona, come feel the lumps they don't have on their heads. Now who would have done such a thing here in Dun Rowans?"

Kevin shook his head. "I'm sorry, *colleen deas*, but I have no memories of what has happened until I looked at you a moment ago. For that matter, I'm not sure I know who I am, who he is, or who the two of you are. This blow to my head has addled me for certain."

The girl gave a slight curtsy, "Thank you, sir, for the compliment. *Colleen deas* is more than you've ever called me before. As you well know, I am Maeve Ni Grady, maidservant to your sister, Fiona Ni Murrough, and the other gentleman is your manservant, Timothy Mac Egan. You are the son of Dermot Murrough who is Baron of Dun Rowans and King of Leinster. Now, does that satisfy you, or are you going to try to fool me more?"

Kevin shook his head, a painful expression on his face. "I am sorry, Maeve Ni Grady, but I am certainly not trying to fool you. I have absolutely no idea of who I am, how I came here, or who you are. My memories are not of this place, perhaps they are of a dream, or maybe this is a dream, but I feel completely lost."

Maeve narrowed her eyes to look at him. Then she nodded. "All right, Kevin Mac Murrough, I believe you because even you are not actor enough to pretend this well. Though you have teased me and fooled me so much in the past I find it hard to do so. Come. We will take you to your quarters where you might rest and recover." She helped him steady himself and with her arm around his waist and his around her; they began to walk down the hallway. She turned her face up to his, "If I do find this to be another of your bad jests I shall have my revenge."

The two girls led them to a corner room. "Here you are, Sir Kevin, your room, your bed, Timothy's bed, and your clothing. I hope you feel better soon."

Kevin turned to her. "Thank you, Maeve, I appreciate it. Will I see more of you?"

Her green eyes flashed sparks, it seemed, as she gave him a cold look. "I live in Dun Rowans. I am lady in waiting to your sister, so I am here. As to seeing more of me, the only man who will see more of me is the man who will some day be my husband, and I have yet to greet him. Now rest yourself until you feel better." With that she turned at walked away. Fiona stood for a moment or so and gave Kevin a wink as she smiled, and then followed Maeve.

Kevin stood dumbfounded as he watched them down the hall. Finally he muttered, "That wasn't the way I meant it at all."

Tim nodded. "Sure she's got a fine Irish temper on her, that one. She doesn't have that shock of red hair for nothing, it seems. Now the one she says is your sister is a right lovely colleen herself. If we are here for a while I might do a bit of courtin' of her."

Kevin turned back into the room, crossed over and sat on the edge of the bed Maeve had indicated. He gingerly felt the back of his head. "I wish I had an ice pack. From the looks of things they have no idea what in ice pack is. On top of that I have no idea who you are. You're certainly not the Tim Keegan I know."

"And you aren't the Kevin Murray I know. You seem to be about eighteen or nineteen, and you aren't speaking English."

Kevin nodded. "And neither are you. You're speaking Gaelge, the old Irish tongue, and doing it rather well, I might add."

Tim sat on the edge of the other bed. "So are you." He shook his head as if to shake the cobwebs out. "I don't understand this. One minute we're admiring the view of the Irish Sea and that island off in the distance; the next thing we know we're here in the newer/old castle, and you've already got a girl mad at you. Quick work, if I do say so myself." He paused, a puzzled look crossing his face, "You say we're speaking Irish?"

"I think we're speaking a form of Gaelic. I suspect it's Irish because of where we are."

"That's another question I have. Where are we?"

Kevin frowned as he went to the window and looked at the countryside. "A better question would be 'When are we?' I know where we are. This castle hasn't moved since we entered it. From the looks of things, the place being completed, the walls now standing when they had been knocked down, the changes in the fields, and the dress of the two girls, we've gone back in time. How? I wish I knew. Why? I wish I knew that too. Right now I'm more curious about the When than the other questions."

He turned from the window and waved his hand to take in the room. "Look around this room. I guess those are our swords and shields kept handy for our use. I recognize the coat of arms on the right. It belongs to my family, so I know I'm in the old family castle. I presume that's your coat of arms on the other shield. Beds, chairs, closets, tapestries on the wall, candles in sconces: man, do we have a lot of learning to do. As far as I'm concerned we've got amnesia, though they may not know the word they probably have run into the symptoms before, and it's up to us to learn the traditions, customs, and habits of these people and this time period."

He walked to his bed, sat down, and stared at the floor for a long moment. "One thing I'm going to do is to make up to Maeve Ni Grady. Before this situation is over she's going to change her mind about me. I don't know what sort of person the other Kevin was, but he certainly wasn't the type of person he's going to be."

"A couple questions." Tim said. "The first is: what is it with this Ni Murrough and Mac Murrough? Fiona is your sister. Shouldn't she be called Mac Murrough too?" His face showed his puzzlement. "Then she called me Mac Egan, and the baron was just plain Murrough. I don't get it."

Kevin grinned. "It's the Irish." He said. "Fiona is an unmarried woman, so she is the daughter of Murrough yet and the Ni in front of that indicates feminine and not wed. I'm the son of Murrough, so I get the Mac in front of it. If I was the grandson it would wind up O'Murrough. My father is just Murrough, though if he wished he could have either the Mac or the O before it to indicate his forebears. As for you, apparently Mac Egan got changed to Keegan when your people came over to America."

"Okay. Second question. Do you think we're stuck here permanently?" Not receiving an answer Tim rose, walked over to the window, leaned on the sill, and gazed out. Finally he said, "It's funny, isn't it? Here my ancestors left Ireland to escape the persecution they were getting from the English. They came to America and made a good life for themselves. Now, the first time I get a chance to come to the 'auld sod' as my grandfather used to say, I find myself in some sort of a dream world in an Ireland I know nothing about. I wish I knew what year it's supposed to be." He paused then, after a long look out the window, he turned with a thoughtful look on his face. "Do you think someone is playing a joke on us? You know, they knock us out and set up an elaborate situation to see how we react?"

Kevin rose and strode to the window. Standing by Tim he waved his hand to take in the whole scene. "If they did they've certainly done a grand job of it. They've rebuilt the castle, rebuilt the walls, took down the stone fences, grew stands of oaks and rowans, and even worked on that round tower on the island. No. I don't think this is some grand joke, but I remember where we are and the stories my grandmother told of the strange things that happen on this island. I never believed in the fae or in Leprechauns, ore the land of Faerie. I never have seen any of them, but maybe they didn't move to America with our forefathers. Maybe they have something to do with this."

"Hold it. Now you've got me again. What's this about the 'fae' and Leprechauns?"

Kevin shook his head. "You are pathetic. Somehow your folks neglected to tell you the least little thing about your roots. Fae is what a lot of people call fairies. They're known as the 'little people' as well. Rie is one of the old words for 'land of', so Faerie is the Land of the Fae. The word Fairyland is sort of redundant, but it's the one most people know. Another word for 'land of' is 'Tir' as in Tir na nOg."

At that moment they were interrupted as a servant stuck his head in the door. "Sir Kevin, Sir Timothy." He said. "They are awaiting your presence in the Great Hall. The evening meal is being served."

* * *

The two young women walked down the hall after leaving Kevin and Tim. After turning the corner, and being out of earshot, Fiona looked at Maeve, "Why don't you like my brother? Has he been that mean to you?"

Maeve stopped and looked back the way they had come. She shook her head and half smiled, "It's not that he's mean, it's a tease he is, and he tries to hurt with his teasing words. Whenever we're together it's always a mean joke he has at my expense." She thought for a moment, "Not like him? I do like him, and if he would be nicer I could love him." She paused, "Perhaps I do love him. I know I have feelings for him, but he'll never know until he changes his ways."

As they continued down the passageway Fiona said in a thoughtful tone, "Perhaps it's because he has feelings for you he teases. He's young, and may not know how to show a girl his true feelings."

"He seems to have no trouble with the wenches in the public house. From what I hear with them he jokes pleasantly."

Fiona's mouth curled up, "Aye, but they are not his equal. You are a lady in your own right, they are his subjects. That might make a difference."

Maeve thought for a moment, and nodded. "You may be right, Fiona." She drew a deep breath and exhaled slowly. "I can only hope you're right. Sure I don't know what I'd do if he wed some other lady."

At that moment a servant came toward them, stopped, and said, "Lady Fiona, Lady Maeve. They are carving the meat and would appreciate your presence. His Lordship said Sean O'Casey, the great bard, has come to visit and will recite news and poetry this evening."

Fiona nodded acknowledgment. "Thank you, Donal. Will you tell my brother and Sir Timothy?"

"Aye, my lady. I'm on my way at this moment."

* * *

Kevin and Tim sat at the head table. The plates were of pewter with a large wooden spoon at the side. The mugs were also of pewter. They watched carefully how the others at table approached the meal. At various places on each table were bowls with rutabagas, turnips, and other vegetables. Large platters held haunches of meat. As the bowls were passed the diners used their wooden spoons to take a portion of the vegetables and put them on the plate. As the meat came they used the small knife each carried, the scian, to cut off a portion before passing it on. They would then spear that piece on the scian and bite off what they could chew. If the piece had a bone, they would take the meat and toss the bone over their shoulder to the ever present dogs that waited with impatience for the leavings that found their way to the straw covered floor.

The table was well occupied. The head of the table where Dermot sat, with family and other nobles on each side covered the entire head of the room. Two other tables jutted off it at right angles. A large candelabrum made of iron hung from the ceiling, all candles were lit. Above the fireplace a green flag with a gold harp as its escutcheon hung across the wall. In the fireplace a turf fire gave heat and some light to the room. The whole expanse of the center of the Great Hall was open. Above the large door opposite the head table was a balcony on which a quartet was playing music to accompany the meal. The servants brought the food in through the main doors and served from the open floor in front of the tables.

Kevin cut a slab of meat from the roast and passed it on. "Obviously, we're in a time before forks were invented." He commented sotto voce to Tim. "I'm think one of us should find the blacksmith and invent the fork before the week is out."

"Good idea." Tim commented as he tenderly felt his mouth. "I just cut myself on my knife. It's razor sharp. This method of eating may be romantic, but it takes a bit of practice." His eyes roved the U-shape of the table as he spoke. "Don't look now but that fellow with the black stubble of beard, just beyond the curve of the table on the right, certainly seems interested in us."

"What makes you think so?"

"I have good peripheral vision, and I could see him eyeing us for quite some time. It was almost as though he was surprised to see us. Then, when I began looking in his direction he quickly, too quickly for my taste, looked down at his meat. When I turned my head away he was quick to look up again. I don't know what's up, but I think there is something rotten in the state of...well, not Denmark, but wherever we are."

"Sure and maybe your Irish imagination is working a bit overtime."

"I don't think so. I think it's my SEAL training. All I know is I'm going to do a bit of watching of that one."

As the meal was cleared from the table Sean O'Casey took the center of the hall and began reciting poetry he had recently written. The clothing he wore had many colors in it, and his poem recounted tales of valor that had happened in other parts of the country during its history. Then he turned to poems regarding current events throughout the other parts of the island. With no other means of learning of events, the bard and the poet were two of the means of getting news.

After Sean finished his part of that evening's entertainment a small group of musicians in the balcony above the hall began to play. As they played various couples repaired to the floor and began to dance.

Kevin watched for a moment; then glanced down the table to where

Maeve was seated. She too was watching the dancers. She started when he bent over her shoulder and asked, "*Colleen deas*, would you care to dance?"

"You startled me." She commented in a cool voice as she looked up at him.

"I'm sorry. I didn't mean to. I only wanted to know if you would like to dance."

She rose, and as he led her to the floor, said, "None of your teasin' tricks now."

He was surprised as they danced, for he knew the steps though it was an unfamiliar tune and the dance was ancient. As he felt himself turn and step in concert with her movements he wondered if the body he now wore had a habitual memory for the dances as it seemed it had for the language.

They had danced without comment as Kevin kept his eyes on her face when Maeve glanced at him. "Why do you stare at me?"

Kevin smiled sheepishly. "I'm sorry if I offend you. I was just trying to memorize your face. I drink in your beauty."

"Now you're teasin' me again."

"No." He shook his head in denial. "I'm not teasing. I mean what I say."

Maeve was silent as she looked at him as though seeing him for the first time. Her brow puckered as she said in a puzzled voice. "You do seem different somehow."

"Different? How do you mean, different?"

"I don't know." She tilted her head to one side as she studied him. "There seems to be a different air about you. You seem more settled, less the tease and more the gentle man. Usually you are tormenting me with your bad jests and teasing to make me feel bad, but this evening you are acting as though you think I'm a real person. You even apologized for startling me. And you called me '*colleen deas*'."

"You are a lovely, kind, girl, so colleen deas seems to be the right words to say. Should I feel shame or pride for not teasing you? Tell me, so I will feel the way you wish, for your desire is my command."

She laughed softly and shook her head at that, and he felt as though the room had grown lighter with sparkles flying from her whirling hair. "Now you jest, but I don't mind. I just hope you stay this way."

"Maeve Ni Grady, I may have only come to my senses this afternoon, but I believe you are the most beautiful girl I have ever seen in my life."

She bent her head and looked intently into his eyes, her own narrowed to study him better. "Now don't you be giving me any of your nonsense talk,

Kevin MacMurrough, or I'll be leaving you standin' right where you are and go back to my seat."

"No. Truly. I mean what I say. I may not remember very much of what happened before you roused me in the hallway. I do believe I was hit in the head. But when I heard your soft voice and saw your face I thought I was seeing one of the angels sent to help me. Please, I'm not jesting. I truly feel this way."

The tone of his voice and the look on his face calmed her trepidation. "All right, Kevin, I'll believe you for now, though I will be watchin' sharp to make sure this lasts. Though you dance very well, and butter wouldn't melt in your mouth, I remember the Kevin I know. If you've changed, all the better. If not…well, we'll see."

They continued the dance, and every time they turned Kevin noticed the dark bearded man's eyes were fixed on him. He felt there was a puzzled look on his face, though it was hard to tell given the full black beard covering most of it. Perhaps Tim was right in his assumption, he thought. Aloud, he asked. "Who is the fellow with the extremely black hair? He's sitting down the table from where I was seated."

"Above the salt?"

Kevin looked, and then nodded, "Aye. Above the salt."

Maeve kept on dancing, but the look she gave Kevin was one of complete bewilderment. "Sure you're either teasin' me again, or there is something wrong with your memory. Now you can't remember your own half-brother?"

Kevin shook his head, a concerned look on his face. "I'm not teasing you, honest. I have no idea who he is. The only one I knew when I woke up was Tim, and I wasn't really sure it was him. What is my brother's name?"

"He is Colm an Dubh. He's not really noble born. Your father recognized an Dubh as his son when a maid in town gave him birth. Since he was not legitimate, and had such black hair, he was called 'an Dubh.'"

"An Dubh, eh? Well, it fits. I suspect the black beard and hair make that a natural name for him. The Black Dove. Colm an Dubh." He mused. "Interesting name. There is something about his eyes I don't like." He thought for a moment, "And what do they call me?"

"You won't like it."

"Tell me anyway."

"An Clap."

Kevin was silent for a moment. His face was sad as he slowly said, "Kevin the Nasty Tease, eh? Does the name fit?"

Maeve was sober as she nodded. "Aye. At least it has in the past, though tonight it would seem it doesn't." Then she smiled. "But let us talk of more pleasant things. Why do you show so much interest in an Dubh when you should be payin' attention to me? Is he so much prettier?"

"They say beauty is in the eye of the beholder, and when I behold you I have eyes for nothing else. Your beauty outshines the sun, but I'm interested in him for other reasons." His face held a bemused smile, "I don't know what all those other reasons are as yet. I do know he was paying particular attention to Tim and me, yet every time I glanced his way he quickly turned his head as though he weren't watching. For some reason he seemed very surprised to see us at table." He half smiled, his face reflecting his curiosity and frustration. "This has certainly been a day I'll remember for a long time."

The music ended and they went back to the table. Kevin seated himself next to Maeve. "How long will the feast last?" he inquired.

"Why, with a great Seanachie and poet such as Sean O'Casey as our guest, this celebration will last for the next fortnight, at least."

"What about sleep? Doesn't anyone get tired?"

Maeve shot him a sidelong glance, a bemused smile on her face. "Sure now they get tired. They go to their rooms to rest, then come back hopin' they missed nothing in their absence. Of course, the scribes record the words of the poet so they can read them later, but it isn't the same as hearin' them direct."

Kevin nodded. "That being the case I believe I will go up to rest. I feel the need to do a bit of thinking, and my head is ringing that loud and beggin' me to lie down." Impulsively he took her hand. "Maeve Ni Grady, I will certainly be seeing more of you when I return." He held up his hand as she opened her mouth, "I didn't mean it that way. I merely wish to be in your presence, for to me it is enjoyable."

Her laughter was like tinkling bells in his ears, "Sure if 'tis my presence you wish, you shall have it and welcome. Anything more," She tilted her head and smiled impishly, "well, we'll see how much you've changed since you received the non-lump on your head."

Now it was his turn to smile. "It may be a non-lump, but it hurts as bad as if it was the size of a base…er…a rock. I will see you later."

"Of that there's no doubt. Since we both live in Dun Rowans we will see each other more."

chapter 2
Swift Justice

The single candle in its sconce cast a flickering light in his room. He lay on the bed, hands under his head, and stared at the ceiling. Talking to himself he muttered, “What sort of a dream is this?”

“‘Tis no dream Kevin Murray, now Kevin Mac Murrough.” The answer came in a low baritone. Kevin sat bolt upright in bed and looked all about the room. He was alone.

“Now I know I’m going crazy. I’m hearing voices.”

“Aye, you’re hearing voices, but you’re not going crazy.”

“Who are you and where are you?” Kevin’s gaze searched the room and could find nothing.

“I am Brian Connors. I am seated on the chair in the corner of the room.”

“But I can’t see you.”

The laugh that greeted that statement was hearty. “Aye. ‘Tis true. You can’t see me because I’m not letting you see me. Now, lay back and let me talk. ‘Tis glad I am you came up alone. I wished to tell you the story, though I know your friend would also love to hear it. You have my permission to tell him later.

“The reason you are here is because young Kevin MacMurrough of this time was murdered this afternoon along with his man Tim. Luckily, at the same time that happened, you and your man Tim were in almost the same spot in the castle. You were looking out the broken window of Dun Rowans when a rather large piece fell from the lintel above. It hit both of your heads rendering you unconscious. It almost killed you, which was fortunate for both of us.”

“Why do you say that?”

"Because if you had control of your senses we never could have brought you here. However, your lack of consciousness gave Myrdden the ability to transport your essence back to this time into the body of our Kevin."

"But that is impossible. Only God could perform a miracle such as that."

"True. We had to ask his permission, but the circumstances were desperate, so he granted our wish."

"Now I'm even more confused. You can travel in time?" By this time Kevin was again sitting up and staring about the room.

"Travel? No. Lay back and let me explain. You will agree with me God is the creator. Well, he is the creator of more than you realize for he created many more dimensions than those you know of. You and your kind are living in four dimensions; well, three and a half really. You know the normal three dimensions of height, width, and length that make you solid. The other dimension is time, but you can only go one way in it so I will call it half a dimension. Because you are caught in only these dimensions you cannot see the other dimensions that exist. There are eleven dimensions in all, though even my people live in only six of them. We think the Creator lives in an infinite number of them, though we only know of the eleven. It is through these other two in which we live we were able to accomplish what we did, and then only with permission."

"You call this person Myrdden. I've heard of Merlin, but not Myrdden."

"The Celtic name for this seer is Myrdden. Many names get changed when someone in another country hears it wrong, or mispronounces it. Think of it. Brian, John, Ian, Ivan or Juan depending on the country. Over in Britain they call him Merlin."

"Then there really was a Merlin? I thought he was only a myth."

"Of course there was a Myrdden." Brian's voice betrayed his scorn of Kevin's seeming ignorance. "I believe if you really examine stories called myths and legends you will find there is a core of truth in them; truth that has been embellished to make the story better, but truth nonetheless."

"All right. I accept Merlin and the other dimensions. I may as well for otherwise I am crazy and talking to myself. If Merlin is real, then are you also a sorcerer?"

Again the hearty laughter. "No. Nothing of that ilk, and neither is Myrdden. He is a seer of visions of future events. Some call it sorcery, but he has no real powers of magic. He does have an ability to cloud men's minds; to have them believe he has done things through magic, but it is just he is good with his hands, that's all.

"As for me, well, if you've heard much of the tales of other lands, as well as this, you ken most of them have stories of the so-called little people. Did you never wonder if these stories have a basis in fact, rather than being made of the pure wool of the Seanachie? I am what these people call a Leprechaun, though I am one of what others call fae or faeries. As with the human race there are many different types, though all are fae. We live in Faerie, a land your grandmother may have called Tir na nOg, the land of eternal youth. Yet, though we live there we are able to come into this dimension as well. After all, you can see, and have an effect on, those beings and events in lesser dimensions than you. We can see and affect lesser dimensions also, and do it without being seen or known to those who live in those lesser dimensions.

"Some of those in Faerie perform duties connected with various families or types of people on this side of the door. Certain of them have ties to certain of the families on this side. There is a banshee, for example, who is especially associated with your family, as others are with the Mac Egan, Grady, Kennedy, and Kinsella clans. The Dullahan, the banshee, the pooka, are often feared by those on this side, though they live very peaceful lives in Faerie. But there are those on this side who have done them wrong, or in some cases helped them, in one way or another. They come over every once in a while to teach certain of these people a lesson, or to give warning to others, if you will."

"And I'm going to be taught a lesson?"

There was a pleasant chuckle at Kevin's words. "No, not you. There are others, such as an Dubh and his friends, who have been in contact with those who would bring the downfall of this barony and kingdom. The ones they are in league with are allied with other immortals who are not on the side of the righteous. You and your friends have been brought here because Myrdden discovered you two might be instrumental in leading to their downfall."

"Might be, eh? And if Tim and I don't wish to do this, can we be sent back to our own time and our own bodies?"

There was a long pause before the answer came. As he began to rise to try to figure out why there was no answer Brian said. "Sorry for the delay but I had to consult with Myrdden. He says it is impossible."

"Why?"

Brian sighed. "You won't like the answer. As I said, your essence, or soul, was transported back here while you were unconscious. At the same time theirs was sent to inhabit your bodies' moments before they would have died here. The transfer was too late for them, for even in your bodies they had gone too far toward death to turn back. Since their essence no longer lived here, and you two were also close to death, we were unable to keep your future bodies alive. It was an unfortunate accident we did not anticipate.

"Your bodies in the future lie on the floor of the castle, and won't be found for a week when the owner of the carriage comes looking for it. They will bury your future bodies in the burial grounds near the castle, but you and your friend will remain here and continue on in this century in the bodies of your ancestors." His voice sounded as though he shrugged, "We're sorry it happened, but there's naught we can do about it any more."

Kevin stared at the ceiling for a minute as he thought through what the Leprechaun told him. Finally he asked, "And what century do we find ourselves in?"

"Tis the sixth century after the birth of the Christ."

"Sixth Century, eh?" He sighed. With a puzzled look on his face he asked, "Is it the early part of the century, or the last part?"

"That's a good question. It shows you are the type of man we looked for. It is the first part: Five hundred five to be exact."

"Can you tell me something of what's going on so I can get my thoughts straight on what this world is going through?"

"Certainly. You need to have that knowledge, though Myrdden will tell you more. On the other side of the Irish Sea Uther Pendragon will shortly be on his way to be killed in a major battle. I got this bit of lore from a banshee connected with his family. His son Arthur, who is being raised by friends of Myrdden, will eventually acquire the throne.

"The Saecsens will attempt to dethrone him and set themselves up as rulers of that kingdom. They occupy the southeastern portion of that land, a land called Sasona. To their north are the Angles, whom they wish to conquer as well. Arthur is in the southwestern part of that island in a land we call Cymru, or Bheig, but you know as Wales. Like you he is Celtic, as are those who occupy Alba, that the Romans called the land of the Scots. Dun Rowans is, as you know, in the southeastern corner of Eire, not that far from Wales across the Irish Sea.

"Your father is the ruler of Leinster, the eastern side of our island. There are three other kings in the other sectors, plus the High King at Tara. You are the heir to this kingdom, though an Dubh is plotting your death so he will be king when your father dies. His attempt to kill you this morning succeeded, though he doesn't know it. That's why he was so surprised to see you at the feast."

"You were there?"

"Aye. I was there, and so were some of my people. It is interested we are in the events that are to come."

"And what am I to do in all this?"

"That is really up to you. The choices you make will be important, as will the choices made by an Dubh, Arthur, and the rulers in Alba. An Dubh is in contact with the Saecsens. What they want is to take this shore so they can attack Bheig from both the sea and land. If they can get the Angles to attack from the north at the same time they could take over that throne and gain control of all of Sasona. That would allow them to move north against the Albaion and move north and west from here against the kings of Munster, Connagh, and Ulster. Your choices will have much to do with what happens with Arthur, and the other kings of Eire. That is why we brought you back, or your soul back, if you will."

"But that history has already been written, hasn't it. I remember the story of Arthur, Guinevere, Lancelot, and all of them. Camelot decayed after Arthur was killed."

There was a touch of humor in the disembodied voice. "Caer Maellot? Well now, my boy, you are here before Arthur takes the throne, are you not? So if you are here and there is no Caer Maellot as yet, that history has not been written. In fact, what you know as history can be changed if the right choices are made. We thought you and your friend, with the knowledge you have from your time, might be able to hold these invasions in check. Myrdden feels you and Timothy would be good counselors to help Arthur gain control of Sasona as well as Bheig, and form an alliance of the Celtic people that would keep what is happening on the continent from spreading to these islands. He also felt your knowledge that Galahad and not Lancelot was the one meant to be chosen by Arthur as his right hand man would be helpful."

"If I remember it right, Galahad was Lancelot's son, was he not?"

"Aye. That he is."

"But he would be a mere boy also."

"True, but he could also be Arthur's page, and being of a younger age, his friend. Galahad will have no claim on Guinevere, you see, for he is known as the pure one. We hope to keep the wars of the continent from engulfing these islands. Will you be willing to help?"

Kevin thought for a moment. What was happening on the continent? Oh yes, the Roman Empire was disintegrating and they were on the threshold of the so-called dark ages. If the islands could be held for those who valued education and information they might be able to withstand the forces of darkness that would come as the Roman Empire fragmented into small principalities and baronies. Brian was silent as Kevin thought things over.

Finally, Kevin said, "Well. We don't have a big choice, do we? You can't send us back because we're dead there, so we're caught here; like it or not. I don't especially care for what you and Merlin have done, but there's nothing I can do about it. I'm going to have to watch my back with my half brother, that's for sure. I expect you will give me advice on which way to go as this thing moves forward."

Brian's voice was sad. "I wish I could. We aren't allowed to meddle too much in the affairs of this dimension except under certain circumstances. We were only allowed to do this because of the great stresses being exerted on this time period, and the future because of it. You and Tim will be on your own, though Myrdden will be there to help in many instances, but the two of you will have to use your knowledge of history, and your good sense, to figure out what choices to make. Myrdden will contact you and may be able to help you more than I, for he has more power. We are sorry for what has happened, but it was beyond our foreknowledge."

Kevin nodded, accepting the fate he had been dealt. "Well." He said, "At least there is a lovely young lady I can get better acquainted with."

Brian chuckled, "Aye. Maeve Ni Grady certainly is lovely. I will tell you this in confidence, for we are sorry and this may help, the lass has an eye for you and if you do things right you will see more of her, and it's well worth the seeing.

"Mind you also, she is a formidable foe in battle. Havin' her at your side wielding her sword is well worth the knowin' of her. And, by the way, your sister Fiona wields an excellent sword as well. That, me boy, is all I can say. Our good wishes go with you. Myrdden will contact you soon."

"And will I hear from you again?" Kevin asked. He was answered only by the silence of the room and the guttering candle in the sconce. "Welcome to the Sixth Century, Kevin. May you live long and prosper, to coin a phrase." He settled back on the cot with his thoughts.

* * *

"Here." Tim thrust a newly forged fork in Kevin's hand. "I made it to the blacksmith this afternoon while you were resting and had five of these made. It took a bit of doing, but the smith and I finally got together on the design.

After having made these he said he thought they should be done from the metal used for swords. Here's one for Maeve, one for your father, and one for you. I think you'll have fun teaching them how to use it."

"Thanks. This will be a big help." He turned to go to Maeve, then turned back. "Oh yes, I have something to tell you when we are alone."

Puzzled, Tim asked. "What is it?"

Kevin shook his head. "I can't tell you here. It concerns the two of us, and what happened when we woke up in the hallway."

Tim nodded. "All right. When bedtime rolls around I'll be all ears."

Kevin turned to the head table and saw Dermot Murrough just seating himself in the huge chair in the center. He looked at the fork in his hand, grinned, and headed toward the man who was supposed to be his father. He stood respectfully by the chair until Dermot finished a conversation with the Lord Chamberlain on his right. Dermot then looked at him and smiled. "Well son, what can I do for you?"

Kevin showed him the fork. "Tim and I came up with this, Da."

Dermot lifted an eyebrow as he looked at the tines of the fork. "And what use will such a small pitchfork be to me. It is much too small to fork hay to the beasts in the barns."

"Aye, that it is." Kevin said, "But this isn't for the beasts, it's for us. Here, allow me to show you." So saying he pulled his scian from its sheath and cut a piece of meat off the loin before Dermot. Placing it on his father's plate he proceeded to cut a smaller piece using both fork and knife. Spearing that piece on the fork he brought it to his mouth and pulled it off the fork. He father watched, lifting an eyebrow as he went through the process. Kevin repeated the show, eating another small piece.

Dermot nodded approval. "Very interesting. Allow me to try." He took the fork Kevin gave him and, as Kevin guided his hands, proceeded to cut a bite size piece and eat it. He smiled broadly, turned, and clapped Kevin on the shoulder. "Now that is useful. I'll have the smith make one for each of our people. You have done well." He turned back and gleefully began cutting bite sized pieces of meat for his meal.

Maeve had been watching him as he demonstrated the fork to his father. Now Kevin went to where she was seated. "T'is a funny thing you gave your father, Kevin. Though it does seem useful."

"It's very useful." Kevin said as he pulled another from where he had stored it in his belt. "This one is for you." He handed it to her. "Now, shall I show you how to use it?"

"Please." Her eyes shone as he stood behind her one arm on each side, her hands in his as he led her through the process of cutting a piece of the meat.

Kevin was so engrossed with Maeve he hadn't noticed a rather anomalous action. Tim, however, saw a man dressed as a servant move around the table and come up from behind the diners. In his hand he held a large salver with a loin roast. He seemed different to Tim as he watched, then he figured it out. The man was holding the salver wrong. The other servants were holding onto theirs by the handles on either end. This man was balancing it on one hand and holding the back edge with the other. Too, he didn't seem to be as intelligent as his fellow servants. Then Tim noticed the poniard the man held beneath the salver. He turned the corner and came behind the diners at the head table. Stopping behind Kevin he slowly moved so the poniard was pointed at Kevins back.

"Watch out!" Tim's voice was heard above the din of the room as he leaped from his chair and pushed Kevin aside just as the knife was about to enter his side. As Kevin, caught unawares, fell to one side the knife slashed through his jerkin. He stumbled over a chair and, as he fell to the floor, struck his head on another knocking him unconscious.

The server, caught off balance, continued his lunge to fall over Maeve and sprawl across the table. The poniard caught another server in the hand as he was placing a platter in front of the diners. His eyes widened as he stared at the poniard pinning his hand to the table. Then he raised his head to look at the one who had caused the wound, and lashed out at him with his other fist.

"Seize that man." Dermot had seen all the action. He had been smiling inwardly at his son's obvious desire for the maid, Maeve, a union of which he was entirely in favor. Now his son lay on the floor and Maeve was cradling his head in her lap. "Take that man to the dungeon for interrogation, and make sure Kevin is not wounded."

"There is no wound, Sire. He hit his head on the chair." Maeve said, and turned back to Kevin.

Dermot clapped Tim on his back. "Thank you Sir Timothy. You saved my son's life. You shall be rewarded."

Tim knew better than to turn down the king when he offered a reward. "Thank you, Sire. Though my reward is the life of my friend."

"True. But sometimes other things can be of great help as well. You will not find me ungenerous." He turned and left the table, his face angry and set. "Now to attend to the miscreant who tried to kill my son."

"*Acushla, gra mo cre me*." Were the soft words Kevin heard as he fought his way to consciousness. He looked into a pair of worried blue eyes as his own opened. Then relief flooded across Maeve's face as he looked at her.

"Would you repeat that?" he whispered.

"What?" She asked innocently.

"You said 'Dearest, I love you'." He said. "I liked the sound of your voice when I heard it. I'd like to hear it again."

"Why now, I don't know what you're talking about." She blushed as she said it.

Then his hand was behind her head and he pulled her down to kiss her. "That's all right." He said. "I know I heard it, *colleen deas*, and I know I'll hear it again."

"Well now, you're certainly an impertinent one, aren't you? Just for that I'm going to drop your head on the floor and see if it makes a dent." But she was smiling tenderly as she said it. Kevin pushed himself to a sitting position. "What did happen? The last thing I remember was trying to teach you how to cut meat and use the fork."

The hall came back to a semblance of order as Kevin, sitting next to Maeve, was filled in on what had happened. The bards took up from where they had left off before the excitement. The servers returned to their duties, and Kevin listened intently as he heard of Tim's saving his life. "Looks like I owe him one." He muttered as he took Maeve's hand in his. "And thank you for the soft pillow for my head while I was unconscious, and for the words I shall remember always."

She looked at him haughtily, "Well, now, Sir Kevin. Words uttered in the stress of the moment are not always to be trusted."

"I disagree, *colleen deas*, words uttered under stress are the one's we should trust, for they come from the heart without thought. One day I'll hear them when it isn't a stressful event, but for the moment I'll accept them for what they are. I have decided that one day you will be my wife."

Maeve's face became stern as she turned to face him. "Oh you did, did you? Well you may have another thought comin', for when that time comes I will make up my own mind." She nodded forcefully, "And it may not be you, Kevin Mac Murrough, who will be the one to put the ring on my finger."

Kevin smiled at her anger. "You're really beautiful when you're angry. It makes me want to kiss you all over again to take the anger out and put the love back."

"Oh, you make me so—, so…"

"Desirable." Kevin finished for her. "I think that is a much better word. Come now, *acushla*, let's get back to the lesson on how to use this fork."

As he took her hands in his her face melted and a warm smile appeared. She shook her head in exasperation. "Aye, you have changed, Kevin Mac Murrough, and I must say I like the change very much." She allowed him to guide her hands as she used the new utensil.

* * *

Kevin stood in the doorway to make sure no one was near to overhear his conversation. When he finished telling Tim the story Tim leaned back against the wall of the room. "So." He said, finality in his voice. "That's the way it stands, eh? We're here to do a job, and, no matter what happens, there is no way we can get out of this time or go back home. Sure it's a blow, but there's a lovely lady I think I'll try to win. You might consider doing the same with another rather lovely young lady. In our other lives we never had time for marriage, moving around the world so much."

"If we have time here we may well be able to wed these ladies." Kevin said as he checked the hall once more then moved to the bed to sit down. "Brian said Merlin would get in touch with us. I don't know if he can help us figure things out, or if it is just to fill us in a bit more on what's going on."

"You mean with Uther and the war over there?"

Kevin nodded. "Yes. We have to watch for when Arthur rises to the throne and go to him as advisors. I have no idea how old the lad is yet."

Brian's voice came from the corner of the room. "Careful, me boys, someone's comin' down the hall."

The two men were silent as the footsteps came toward the room, passed it and continued on down the hallway. The door had been open a crack and Tim could see into the hall through the crack. "Castle guard on his rounds." He commented. Then, "I presume you're Brian?"

"Aye lad. That I am." Sounded the good humored voice. "I didn't mean to pry, but began thinkin' after me talk with Kevin, and especially after the latest attempt to kill him. The two of ye are strangers in a strange land, and someone has to watch over you, at least until Myrdden shows up. Already ye have the two young ladies discussin' yer strange behavior. Maeve is surprised at the change in you, Kevin, and is wonderin' if the blow on the head was enough to cause it.

"Then the attempted killing of you tonight added a bit to the stew. You now know her true feelings for you. But you will have to be careful. There's no need to tell her where you came from. Learning the customs is goin' to be difficult enough. Besides, she would believe you mad and that would be t'end o' it."

"I had no intention of telling her who we really are or where we come from." Kevin retorted. "I know what might happen to those considered to be in league with Satan in this time period. I really don't relish being burned at the stake, or stoned to death, or to have my head chopped off. I'll keep my silence, believe me."

"Good. Now when you have a problem tell it to me and I'll try to help you." He chuckled, "After all, Leprechauns are supposed to be immortal you ken. Little do they know it is only because we dwell in Tir na nOg that it appears to be so. But over the course o' the last couple thousand years I've learned a few things; things I'll gladly impart to you as we get on."

"I suspect this attempt was by an Dubh as well?"

"You would suspect correctly, though the hireling was not supposed to do the deed in full view of the entire room. An Dubh had a bit of trouble finding someone both dumb enough and greedy enough to assassinate his master. An Dubh wanted it done tonight, the servant saw what he thought was his chance, and took it. As it turns out it will be close to the last thing he did in this life."

"What will happen to him?"

"He was interrogated tonight. He told your father about an Dubh's hiring him to kill you. An Dubh has, of course, fled the castle; and without your father's permission. Now, I suspect, he will flee the kingdom. It would be wiser if he did, for leaving without the permission of the king is a major insult, no matter who does it. The hireling was beheaded earlier and his head now tops a pole outside the gate as a warning. So that part is over. The next thing will be for Myrdden to arrive."

"When should I expect Merlin?" Kevin asked, but was greeted with silence. He half grinned as he shook his head and looked at Tim. "One thing about invisible people," he said, "you never know whether they are there or not." He shrugged with good humor at Tim's returned rueful grin.

"The trouble with all this excitement is that it makes you little uneasy about sleeping. What if someone tries to kill us while we're asleep?"

"Well, I have a hunch we would be warned. Besides, there is a guard walking these halls at all times. There's no use trying to second guess at this early stage." Kevin sighed. "Anyway, all this thinking about what might happen gives me a headache. I move we get a bit of sleep. We might need to be rested for whatever comes next." It was some time before both men fell asleep, for their thoughts were on the information Brian had given them.

* * *

Kevin awoke with a clear head and eyed the rough rafters of the ceiling. Sitting up he gazed at the rest of the room. The white shield on the wall with the rampant lion in red on the upper half and two red crescents, their ends pointed up, on the lower half. Beneath them hung two crossed broadswords. There were two well made chairs, another cot with what appeared to be a feather tick on it, the one he was sitting on, and brocaded hangings on the wall. One showed a battle scene with some of the warriors painted with blue coloring, another was a scene of a scholar copying a book in a library, while yet another was a hunting scene with a wild stag racing before a group of horsemen. A woven carpet covered the stone floor. He sat in silence as he grinned ruefully.

Heaving a sigh he thought, So it wasn't a bad dream after all. Leprechauns apparently exist, he was somewhere in the Sixth Century, five hundred five, and perhaps Merlin could tell him more about King Arthur. It was very apparent from the two attempts on his life that he had to watch his back to prevent an Dubh from killing him. He also had to go to Wales and find a young Arthur, work his way into his confidence and act as some sort of advisor to him so Caer Maellot wouldn't disappear in the dust of the ages. Then what? Quite an assignment, he thought. He rose to his feet, looked in the closet against the wall, found some clean clothes, and changed. Tim had apparently risen earlier and gone downstairs.

He entered the great hall. While he slept it had been decked out with new banners and streamers to celebrate the visit of Sean O'Casey. A group of jongleurs were performing juggling and acrobatics in the center of the hall while the never ending feast progressed. The hall was merry with the sound of music as two harpists on the balcony played lively tunes to accompany the troupe on the floor.

Tim noticed Kevin enter the hall, rose from his seat next to Fiona at the long table and went to meet him. "Feeling any better?" he asked.

Kevin nodded. "Much better, thanks. Have I missed much?"

"Not too much. This traveling troupe of entertainers arrived earlier. They have a couple of bards with them. I guess they sing, recite poetry, and give the news of what's happening in other places. Like the newspapers of the day, I guess.

"Brian said, that assassin told the interrogators an Dubh was behind his attempt on your life. He thought with all the activity in the hall no one would notice him when he killed you. Not too intelligent a flunky. Now there's a search on for an Dubh, but he seems to have disappeared, just as Brian said he had. I'm not sure Brian will discuss things with me; he seems to feel you're the main person for this adventure, but he might have some idea of where an Dubh is. Seeing as the Leprechauns are all over the place and invisible they should have an idea of where he is and what he's doing. What do you think we should do next?"

"First, we have to wait for Merlin, and while we do that we should learn more of the customs and traditions without being too obvious about our ignorance. The amnesia bit seems to be working so far." As he searched the hall for Maeve he asked absently, "Do you remember how to make gunpowder?"

Tim recognized what he was doing. "She went up to rest." He said. Then, "Gunpowder? Sure. Saltpeter, carbon and sulfur make a simple gunpowder. Why do you ask?"

"Well, it struck me that Marco Polo won't make that trip to China for a few hundred years, so all fighting in this time is hand to hand, man to man, sword to sword, whatever way you want to look at it. Oh, they also use archers, but arrows are only good at up to about a couple hundred yards, beyond that the distance is too great. By the time an army gets up to the hand to hand bit archers have to use their own swords. Now, if we could figure a way to make powder we might be able to introduce it in Arthur's war against the Saecsens and, in that way, assure his victory."

"You mean bring modern warfare into play three or four hundred years before it really started."

"Well, we're here to make sure Arthur wins this war against the Saecsens in England. I figure powder might be a way of doing it."

"And how are you going to deliver it? Guns haven't been invented yet."

"I suspect guns would be a natural thing once powder is discovered. Bombs of one type or another would be first though, I guess. Imagine using arrows to deliver a small bomb. It would be devastating. Or seed a field with dynamite and blow it up as the invaders march toward you. It would simplify things immensely."

"I think we'd better run this one by Brian and Merlin before we make plans about bringing gunpowder into play. Maybe a more powerful bow would be better. The one's I've seen around here wouldn't throw an arrow as far as you say. Didn't the English in Richard's time have a long bow? None of these are that long. The swords are longer than their bows."

"You're probably right about the gunpowder. I guess it's better we use the weapons of the time and try to improve on them. What's for whatever meal we're eating now?"

Tim laughed. "Well, we have roast boar, bacon, chickens, geese, beef, and mutton, and we have both a black beer and a regular to wash it down with. Take your pick. Oh yes, there's the regular lineup of vegetables. No breakfast cereal for these folk. When they eat they plan on eating."

"Well, to coin a phrase, when in Ireland do as the Irish do. I'm really hungry. I'm going to have a good breakfast, then go out and enjoy this lovely autumn day." With that he found a place at the table and joined in the merriment.

chapter 3
Myrdden

The month had passed quickly, and the days were getting shorter. Still, Brian had told Kevin the night before to take Tim, Fiona, Maeve, and a lunch for five, to a copse by the River Slaney. Though the day was raw with a hint of snow in the offing, the clearing was pleasant as the four led their horses from the road. Kevin spread his bratt on the ground to serve as protection for the food they brought. That done they unloaded the basket from the horses and laid it out while the horses, saddles still in place, first drank of the water, then began grazing on the lush grass. Maeve, her hand on her sword, surveyed the area, checking all sides of the clearing to assure herself no one could come close without ample warning. Satisfied, she turned to Kevin. "Would you tell me why we've come here? The castle is warm, and the feast at Dun Rowans is in its final days. Sean O'Casey will be leaving soon, and we're missing much of the singing and story telling."

Kevin shrugged. "All I can tell you is we were told to come here. It was going to be very important."

"And from whom came these wonderful words of import?"

Kevin gave her a half hearted grin, "And if I told you you'd probably not believe me."

"Try me. I might be easily convinced."

He chuckled self-consciously as he said, "An invisible Leprechaun named Brian Connors said we were to meet a very important person in this clearing. He was emphatic about having just the four of us on this adventure, and was very emphatic that Tim and I make sure Fiona and you were with us. He said the two of you were excellent with the sword. He wasn't that sure about Tim and me."

Maeve laughed. "Sure he's right about Fiona and me being good fighters, but I don't know why he worried about you two. You've had as much training as we have, and I've noticed your skills are as good as mine. Still, I wonder if you've been dreaming about your talks with this wee one. Why the king of the Leprechauns would converse with you is beyond me. Yet, stranger things have happened, though it might be one of his nasty tricks. They are noted for that, you know."

This opened up a bit of information Kevin hadn't remembered. He knew the Leprechauns had a king and had read his name somewhere, but hadn't realized it was the person who had been talking to him. As he and Maeve were discussing these ideas a young man with a blonde beard and hair was suddenly in the clearing with them. Maeve turned quickly, her sword in her hand before she was fully rotated. Then she paused.

The stranger held up a hand to calm her, but she had already taken in all she needed to know. He had no weapon other than an oaken staff, and beneath the cloak was a coat of seven colors. Around his neck was a braided gold torc on which was engraved the never ending knot of the Celts. Only the kings, high nobles, poets, and Seanachies were allowed to wear seven colors, and only kings wore gold torcs. She and Tim were held to six colors and a bronze torc because of their own ranks, while Kevin and Fiona were allowed the seven colors and silver torcs. Some servants were allowed three colors, but field workers were only allowed to wear the gray clothing of servitude. Maeve held her sword still, though it was in the air above her head ready to strike, as the stranger continued in.

"You may put your sword away, Maeve." He said. "I am the reason Brian Connors had you four brought here."

Slowly Maeve lowered her sword, and then sheathed it. She looked at the man. "You are a seanachie?" She asked tentatively.

"Aye. And more. I am Myrdden." He moved to the where the food was laid out. "I am glad Brian told you to bring food. I've not eaten for the past day. Let us dine as I tell you the story you must hear before you can begin the journey that lies ahead." He sat on the ground where Kevin had spread his cloak and beckoned the others to sit as well. "No need to worry, there will be no interruptions while we are here." He noticed Kevin's odd look as he gazed at him. "Sure now, what is it about me that bothers you?"

Kevin smiled sheepishly. "It is a strange thing, but I always pictured you as an old man with a white beard."

"In your years I am very old, but since one year in Tir na nOg is as a hundred years in this world, I don't show my age well." Myrdden answered as he tore a piece from the loaf, cut a slice of meat, and began eating. "There is much trouble in Britain." He began. "Trouble that could cause much future harm to Eire if it continues on the course it is now taking. Uther Pendragon has been attempting to become High King of Britain. There are sixteen other kings he had to win to his side if this was to be accomplished. Uther would make a good High King but for one thing: that is his inability to temper his actions or his tongue.

Once he became king over Cymru he turned his attention to the south. He was able to win four of the kingdoms in the south to him through diplomacy. I was able to help him in this, for while he is a good fighter he is not one to curb his tongue. Unfortunately, I couldn't do all of his talking for him." Myrdden sighed as he picked up a tankard of ale to wash down the bread.

"To win over the south he invited Gorlois, the king of Cornwall to his castle along with the other kings of that area. To get to know their high king better all these nobles brought their wives to present to Uther. Now Gorlois wife, Ygraine, is one of the loveliest ladies on that island." He turned to the two girls, "Though nowhere near the beauty I see here today."

He sighed, a rueful smile on his face. "Uther became enamored of Ygraine. He was so enthralled with her he had her seated next to him at the meal, and shamelessly flirted with her while he ignored Gorlois, who he placed further down table, as they sat at meat. Gorlois became so enraged at Uther's attention to Ygraine, and the snub he believed Uther gave him; he left the castle without Uther's permission that same night, taking Ygraine with him. As you well know, it is a direct insult to leave the castle of the king without his permission.

"Knowing his actions meant war Gorlois asked for help from the King of Munster, to the west of this kingdom in which we sit, and prepared his men for battle. To protect Ygraine he placed her in his castle at Tintagel. Tintagel is situated on a large rock just off the rugged seacoast of Cornwall, and is impenetrable. The only access to the castle is a narrow causeway from the mainland to the main gate. It is very narrow, so narrow that two war horses riding abreast barely fit on its width. It is about fifty yards long so three men at the gate could hold that castle against an army. To protect Ygraine from the battle scenes he knew would arise, Gorlois then went to his other castle, Dimilioc.

"Uther laid siege to Dimilioc, but his heart was with Ygraine." Myrdden shrugged as he drank from the cup. "Lust or love, and I suspect the former, he was in torment so even as the battle raged he called for me. With the help of Titania, the queen of Faerie in Britain, and me, Uther was transformed to look like Gorlois. At the same time Uther's captain and I were likened unto his captains. Along with Uther, we rode to Tintagel that evening.

"Uther lay with Ygraine that night, at the same hour Gorlois was killed at Dimilioc. She conceived a son from that liaison. Three months later Uther married her. However, before he went to Ygraine, as a condition for my help, I had made a bargain with Uther. I knew a son would be born, so I made him swear he would give that child to me to raise. When the child was born he kept his word and handed me the boy. I named him Arthur and placed him with a good warrior and his wife to raise, not telling them from which parentage he came. This was eight years ago.

"During Uther's attempt to gain power over the other kings to the east he was tactless enough to insult a brother of King Pelles. Mandred was foolish enough to challenge Uther to a duel. Though he didn't have to answer the challenge his pride caused Uther to accept the duel. In the duel Uther killed Mandred. Pelles did not take this well, so he rallied four other kings to make war on Uther. Uther, desperate because he had not enough men to battle the armies of these five kings, sent an emissary to the continent and induced Vertigorm, one of the Saecsen kings to help him.

The Saecsens are a cruel and warlike race, far worse than any we have here. Like the Romans they give no quarter, killing children as easily as they kill a dog. They aided Uther in the overthrow of his enemies, then helped keep the kingdoms in check with a reign of terror Uther wasn't able to control. It wasn't long before Vertigorm decided he wanted the whole of the island for himself, so he began making war on the separate kingdoms. By the time Uther heard the news in his castle in Cardiff Vertigorm had control of Londinium, and the whole of southeastern Britain.

"Vertigorm has now turned his attention to the west. Because of Uther's high-handed attitude toward the other kings he has only their half-hearted support. He will have some allies in this battle for the others prefer the lesser of the two evils, and don't wish to be under the thumb of the Saecsens. Vertigorm is planning to make war on Uther as soon as he believes he has the support of more of these lesser kings. He will use the armies of the kings he has conquered in this war. In the battle Uther will be killed, but so will Vertigorm, and the country will be even more divided.

Uther's kingdom will fall apart and many small kingdoms will be in its place. With no high king to consolidate power each of those kingdoms will be left in a position of weakness. It will be a time of chaos, and they will be looking for someone to unite them. The Saecsens will be decimated in this war, but they will rebuild their armies over time for they still control Londinium and its environs.

"Meanwhile, Uther's son, Arthur, is in the family of this good warrior, Sir Ector. Once Uther is dead there will be much argument over who has the right to be king. The Lady of the Lake, sister to Queen Mabd, has caused a certain sword to be enchanted. She has thrust this sword through an anvil and into a stone on which the anvil rests. Once Uther is dead and the kings are trying to find a new high king the sword in the stone will be placed before the cathedral in Swansea. This will not occur until Arthur is mature enough to take hold of the kingdom. Since he will still be a youth he will need guidance if he is to become wise enough to rule as High King. The spell is such that no one may pull the sword from the stone and anvil but the one who is the true king of the land."

Kevin interrupted the story. "When will this battle take place: the one that kills both Uther and Vertigorm?"

Myrdden's smile was sad. "The battle will be fought in the dead of winter on the plains of the Avon River. Since Vertigorm is still trying to woo the kings of Llogress and Gwdyion that battle won't happen for at least three years, and perhaps a bit longer. These kings are rather hard headed Celts and will not be easy to persuade."

Kevin nodded. "That means we have some time before Uther dies. But you talk of Arthur's being able to pull the sword from the anvil. How long do we have before that happens?"

Myrdden nodded his approval of the question. "I see we were right in selecting you for this work. Arthur will be sixteen years of age, he will pull the sword, but he will yet be a stripling. That will be eight years hence. There will be controversy and argument when he does this, so there will have to be wise heads to calm the troubled waters between the small kings and him.

"We, that is Kings Lir, Lugh, Brian, Oberon, and me, felt we must find someone young enough to befriend him, yet old enough to offer him the necessary wisdom he will need. These people he will come to trust and will accept their counsel. He will need wise advisors if he is to make proper decisions for the future of his kingdom. If he makes correct decisions there will be a long period of peace and plenty throughout both of these islands. If, however, he makes certain unwise decisions there will be eventual war between him and the other kings of the island. This strife will carry over to Aquataine and Paris on the continent. Because of the bad decisions there will be later trouble, death, and destruction for all on this island. If this future is to be changed you must be the ones who become the advisors to assure the right decisions are made."

The four had listened intently as Myrdden told the story (in much more detail than has been recounted above). It was Fiona who asked, "And why will we know what these proper decisions are? We are unschooled in the ways of the Celtic people of Britain, and I believe there are others there also of which we have little knowledge."

Myrdden nodded. "I know. You asked if I were a Seanachie. I am, but I am also a seer, and my vision of the future is clouded. There are decisions to be made, and these decisions, depending on the choice of Arthur, lead in more than one direction. If the proper one is made the future will move in one direction, and that will bring much good. If the wrong one is made it will move in a different direction, and that will bring much evil and darkness. Unfortunately, I see two different futures. Each is clouded, but only one of them will actually happen, and as it does that one will become clear and bright."

"But how will we know what the proper decision is, and even if we know how can we convince Arthur to follow our advise?" Maeve asked.

"You have been chosen because of your wisdom, your strength, and your ability to fight." Then he smiled as though he had a secret, "Kevin is also a seer when it comes to Arthur. He will know when the time comes what will be the right decision. Yet the four of you must gain Arthur's confidence. To do this you must convince him that you are his friends. People will listen to those they know are friends, those they can trust. They will seldom listen to strangers, for one doesn't know if a stranger has one's best interests at heart. You must become his friends. You must teach him to trust you. It is imperative you do so. I will be there to help at some points, but I will also have to be in other places where people trust me, for it is not only Arthur's decisions that have import."

"Since you are a seer, Sir, perhaps you could tell us of an Dubh." Fiona asked.

"An Dubh." Myrdden nodded. "Yes. He plays an important part in this whole thing. I saw him yesterday at Loch Garman. He was there trying to hire a boat to cross the Irish Sea to Britain. His was a slow journey from here to Loch Garman, for he knows he is a hunted man. I believe he hopes to join with the Saecsens to wrest Britain from Uther. If he is able to accomplish this he will then come back here to take over Leinster."

"Over my dead body." Kevin blurted.

Myrdden looked at him coolly and nodded. “Yes, that’s the general idea. He hates you because you are the legitimate heir to Leinster. Next in line is Fiona. He has tried to kill you twice. With you dead he would turn his attention to Fiona. That accomplished he would have Dermot killed, and as the bastard son he would take over the throne. Yes, he must be stopped. That is part of your problem, for you will have to be on your guard constantly. He is very devious in his designs. Fortunately, he chose unwisely in the last attempt.”

Myrdden drank deeply of the ale they had brought. “You must keep what I have told you to yourselves. That’s the reason I had you come to this secluded grove. The water babbling over the rocks makes it difficult for eavesdroppers to understand our conversation if they could overhear us. Though with the distance between us and the trees, no one should be able to hear.

“Now, let us adjourn to Dun Rowans where I will join Sean O’Casey and become one of the Seanachie. I have news from the west that will be of interest to others in the castle.”

* * *

The little fishing village of Loch Garman was dark as the stocky man pushed open the door of the rustic pub, followed by a flurry of snow and cold air. The rough seamen lining the plank that served as a bar, or sitting at the crude tables, eyed his black beard and hair, the sword carried in a sheath at his waist, and the tailored cut of his clothes, then returned their attention to the important items of the day. The swarthy man threw the edges of his bratt back from his shoulders and edged his way to a spot at the bar. “Porter.” He muttered, and threw a gold coin on the bar as payment, “for everyone.” He added. Slowly the loud discussions ceased as his largesse was passed from mouth to mouth. The publican bit the coin, nodded, and carefully placed it in the pouch at his belt. He filled up glasses as the swarthy stranger smiled crookedly, “and keep the balance for another round.”

He turned from the bar to survey the men crowded into the pub. They were mostly fishermen, though there were a few who looked like ruffians. A number of the fishermen raised their glasses in salute, “Slainte.” They muttered as they took their first sip. The small beer they had been drinking sat to one side. The stronger, more expensive porter, was slowly making its way across their tongues as they savored the sharp taste of the black brew. The one who bought raised his glass also, "Slainte!" he answered as he sipped his own drink. His sharp eyes moved across the men assembled there. Yes, they were mainly innocent fishermen, though there were among them some who were obviously more swordsmen than the peaceful fishermen. These men were watching him from the corners of their eyes, gauging him, the size of his purse, and the ease with which they could obtain it. This he knew without a second thought. These were the men he was after.

A glance down the room showed him a table occupied by only two men. He moved to it. The men, recognizing his desire, rose and moved to the bar. The dark man sat. This time as his glance swept the room it rested on the men he had selected. A slight nod of his head and three of them rose from their table to join him. He signaled for another glass for each of them, waited until it appeared, then leaned forward. "I have a job for you." He spoke quietly.

The rusty bearded man across from him drank again from his glass. The other two looked at him, waiting. He was, apparently, the leader of the group. He put his glass on the table and nodded. "I'm waiting." He said.

"My name is Kevin Mac Murrough." He opened the conversation. "You all look like fighting men; men able to use a sword and use it well."

"I am Aione an Rua. We are good with the sword. These are my lieutenants, Kyle Yellowhand and Finbar an Greine." He nodded at three others still seated at another table. Those are my men also." He turned back to the dark haired man, "What do you want with us?" He grinned wickedly, as if he knew the man was lying about his name. "Kevin Mac Murrough?" he said the last in a sarcastic tone.

An Dubh stared at him, eye to eye, until the man lowered his glance to his porter. He raised it for another drink. "To you I am Kevin Mac Murrough." He said at last. "The work I have for you is to make sure a young man we shall call Colm an Dubh is killed. You will find him in the environs of Dun Rowans near Enniscorthy. He will have reddish hair and beard. There will be three others nearby. One is man with dark yellow hair they will call Timothy. Two women will also be there. Be careful, for all are good warriors. The one is called Fiona, the other Maeve. If all four are killed it would please me mightily."

Aione gazed at him, his face expressionless. "This is a dangerous job." He finally said. "The one you call an Dubh is the bastard son of King Dermot. Fiona is his daughter. The others, Sir Timothy and Lady Maeve are also known to us, and known to be members of the court. Such an assignment is very dangerous, even with six against four. I might ask will the pay equal the danger? You see, we heard of the attempt on this 'an Dubh's' life last week, and the justice meted to the attempted assassin. None of us desire to have our heads on top of a pike at the entrance to Dun Rowans."

An Dubh sneered. "Am I dealing with men or little girls?" he asked. "However, to assuage your cowardice and appeal to your greed..." he brought out his purse and counted out seven gold pieces. "There." He said as he pushed them across the table. "Two for you, one each for your men."

Aione looked at the money lying on the table. The purse was still heavy as an Dubh placed it back on his lap. "A year's wages for the men, two for me. A king's ransom. This must be very powerful desire to pay so much for their deaths."

Silence hung over the table like a pall at a burial. Finally an Dubh nodded. "Yes. They are a danger to me. A king's ransom should be enough to buy your loyalty, your bravery, and your silence."

Aione glanced at his men. "Well?" He asked. "Shall we do as 'our Lord Kevin Mac Murrough' asks? After all, he will be next king of Leinster if these people are eliminated."

Kyle and Finbar eyed the gold, looked first at an Dubh, then at Aione. They nodded. "We can do the job. It should be an easy task to kill these, especially if two are women." Both grinned widely, "But before we kill them we can have our sport with them, agreed?"

An Dubh laughed heartily. "Sport? Yes! You may have them as you please. When you have finished you may kill what is left." He rose. "Now I must find one willing to take me to Britain." He looked around the room. "Who is willing to take a passenger to Britain?" He shouted.

"'Tis night." One of the fishermen intoned. "'Tis too dark to launch, and the tide is in. I go there tomorrow. Wait for the dawn and we can sail with the tide. I will lose two full day's fishing, for the trip over will take the day and I cannot return until the following morning."

An Dubh took a gold coin from his purse and tossed it to the man. "Enough?" He asked sarcastically, knowing it was more than the man would make in a year's fishing. The man caught the coin, swallowed hard, put it in his own purse and nodded. "Enough." He said dryly, "Be ready at dawn."

"I need a bed, landlord." An Dubh announced to the publican.

"Yes sire. You shall have our best. Moira, take our guest to his room." He bowed to the man who was willing to spend so much money in his humble pub. "I will make sure personally you are awakened before dawn, sire."

"Good!" He tossed another coin to the man, "For your trouble." He followed the man's wife upstairs.

Aione watched an Dubh's form disappear up the stairs. When he was out of sight Aione turned to his lieutenants. "What do you think?"

"It should be an easy job to kill the four." Colm commented as he sipped his porter.

Aione smiled sarcastically. "Of that I wouldn't be too sure." He said, and leaned back in his chair, draping one arm over the back rest as he eyed the stairs again. His face had the set of one thinking deeply, as if trying to remember something at the edges of his thought. Finally he nodded sharply and turned back to his men.

"I was in Cill Daire two weeks ago." Aione leaned forward, resting his elbows on the table. His lieutenants leaned forward to hear his words. "While there King Dermot, his son Kevin, his daughter Fiona, and their companions were with him. I didn't pay too much attention to them, but did get a good look as they rode to the abbey for services." His face twisted to a thoughtful half smile.

"Then you have seen this Kevin Mac Murrough before!" Kyle exclaimed.

Aione nodded. "Aye. I've seen Kevin Mac Murrough," He looked back at the stairs as he paused, his eyes thoughtful. He shook his head, "and this is not Kevin Mac Murrough."

Kyle turned a puzzled face to him. "But he said he was Kevin Mac Murrough, and he gave us money to kill Colm an Dubh, and the others. How do you know for sure he isn't Kevin?"

"I told you, I've seen Kevin with his father. Kevin Mac Murrough is red of hair and red of beard. The man he described for us to kill is Kevin, the prince and future king of Leinster."

"Then who is this black beard if he isn't Kevin?"

Aione paused and drew a deep breath. "I couldn't prove it, but I believe he is Colm an Dubh. When I was in Enniscorthy I heard tell of this half brother, the bastard son of King Dermot, who would be next in line for the throne if both Kevin and Fiona were dead. They said he had very black hair. That is why they call him an Dubh. Those I heard it from didn't seem to think too highly of him, they said he is not to be trusted. It would seem we've been hired to kill our next king, or queen, or both by the one who wants the throne."

"But he wants to go to Britain."

Aione nodded, and smoothed his beard as he though. "The news from there has the Saecsens trying to get control of that country. Eamon Dunn," He nodded toward one of the seamen at another table, "came from there today. He says the army of Pendragon is preparing for a coming battle between them and the Saecsens. He thinks it will be soon, and probably east of Cymru." He paused again. "If the Saecsens win they might try to invade us by calling more of their fellows from the continent. I heard they had tried to get the king of Munster to help them, but he refused." He jerked his head toward the stairs. "If he is going to Britain I doubt it would be to give aid to Pendragon. If he lied to us about who he is, he could be willing to sell out this kingdom to gain power for himself."

"So what should we do?"

"We have been hired by one calling himself Kevin Mac Murrough to kill Colm an Dubh. If I was assured this man is an Dubh pretending to be Mac Murrough, I would say 'we have been hired by Mac Murrough to kill an Dubh'. That being true we could go upstairs and kill an Dubh as we've been hired to do. As it is I know this man has hired us to be assassins, probably to help him get power in this country." He turned to the others. "Do you want to kill your next king?"

The two looked at each other, and shook their heads. "No. We may not always follow the law, but we are loyal to the king. I don't mind if we bend a law once in a while, but Dermot has been a good leader." Finbar said, he took a swallow of the porter, "Still, we don't really know about Kevin or Fiona and the way they would treat us."

"Fruit doesn't fall far from the tree it grows on. Both have been under the teaching of the monks at Cill Daire." Aione murmured. "I think we should go to Dun Rowans and find out for ourselves. I know I saw those four later, after services were over. They were by themselves as they walked through the streets. All four carried their swords as warriors, in a sheath slung between their shoulders so they could more easily draw and be ready for combat. They had their scians at their waist ready to fight. I asked one of the citizens of Cill Daire if he knew of their fighting ability. He said they had been trained by the best swordsmen in Leinster, and all were able warriors."

He nodded again toward the stairs. "This man knows that, and knew he might be sending us to our deaths for, while we are good warriors, these four could well be able to best we six." He paused. "Yes, I believe we should go to Dun Rowans and discuss this matter with Kevin Mac Murrough himself. Agreed?"

"Do you mean tell this Kevin Mac Murrough we have been hired to kill him?" Kyle asked. "That might sign our own death warrants."

"I doubt that. In fact, as I look at the way things might go we could well become legitimate. We could join him as part of his retinue. He might find he needs able men to help him. I would rather be on his side, and keep my head on my neck, then be on the other side and find my head on the point of a pike. Killing these four would probably be the last things we ever did."

Finbar nodded thoughtfully. "If what you say is true we would never live to enjoy this gold. If we killed the prince the entire army would give chase until they caught us, and I don't fancy having my head parted from my shoulders, and my body parts sent to the four corners of Leinster. I have more fun when they're attached to each other."

"Good. Let's away to camp. Fetch Eamon, Bran and Duff. Tomorrow we go to Dun Rowans."

* * *

A morning squall had cleared the air and now it was a soft afternoon as Kevin and Tim strolled through the fair. Behind them, somewhat unnoticed, were a group of guards from the castle. As the four looked over the offerings at some of the booths, crafts and other goods made by the citizens of the surrounding counties six men, dusty from walking the byways they had traveled, approached them. The guards immediately perked up for each of the six were obviously fighting men.

"Lord Kevin?" Aione asked as he approached. Kevin's guardsmen moved closer to the group.

Kevin nodded. "Yes."

Aione turned to Kyle and nodded emphatically. "I knew it! Strike me down for a fool! I must have been too deep in my cups."

"What do you mean?" Kyle asked.

"I didn't notice that the one who hired us wore no torc." He nodded at Kevin and Fiona. "They wear silver torcs. He wore none. Pity we didn't carry out our work back at Loch Garman."

Kevin's face had a quizzical look as he asked, "How can I help you?" As he did the guards quietly surrounded the small group, ready for any exigency.

Aione glanced around his men at those of Kevin's. He smiled and shook his head. "No need to worry, sir. We mean you no harm. Though I have a story I believe will interest you. If you don't mind, though, we are that thirsty."

Kevin chuckled as he looked over the road weary men. "All right." He nodded toward a tent where ale was being served. "Let's go and have some refreshment while you tell me your story. You and your men look as if you could use it." He glanced at his own guards, "I believe my men could also use a bit of ale as well."

Aione nodded his head and laughed. "You're right there, sir. It was a long and dusty road we traveled today, though a part of it was more mud and rain for awhile. We could certainly use a bit of the black."

"Come then," Kevin smiled, then pointed his chin at the castle guards, "you too. You look as though something wet would sit well." The small group headed toward the tent. Kevin, Tim, Aione and his two lieutenants sat at one table. The guards sat nearby, watching warily while Aione's other men sat at a third table. Aione began the story as he drank from the tankard.

When the story was finished Kevin looked at Tim. "Too bad Aione didn't finish off the task he was given."

"I think it would have saved us a lot of grief." Tim answered. "We'll have to see what Myrdden says about this."

"If we had known for sure it was an Dubh we would have gone up to the room." Aione shook his head in frustration. "There was just too much doubt in my mind at the time, and it was only afterward I remembered seeing you, though I wasn't sure it was you, at Cill Daire." He slammed his hand on the table. "Damme for a missed opportunity."

"If you don't know, you don't know." Kevin told him. "I don't hold you to blame for not killing him. Perhaps your chance will come later. I'm more interested in his lying about his identity, and trying to have me killed; for the third time." He paused, and thoughtfully looked at Aione. "What are your plans now?" He waited for his answer.

Aione thought for a long moment. He looked at the table where the other three of his group were drinking and jesting among themselves. He turned his attention to Kyle and Finbar who waited for his answer. Finally he turned back to Kevin. "I can't answer for my men. I'd have to ask them each in turn, but I'm heartily tired of the ups and downs of being a wild rover. I'd like to have a regular place to sleep, a regular meal and, if needs be a good fight once in a while. Right now I've a good deal of money because of what an Dubh gave me but," He chuckled, "it won't last long if I know me. So I'd appreciate it if you'd take me on as one of your guardsmen." Kyle and Finbar will have to answer for themselves."

The two looked at each other, then nodded. "We're with you, chief." Kyle said as he gestured for the other three to come over. After explaining their decision to the others, they also agreed. "One thing though." Finbar said, "We want to be with Aione. Over the years we've become friends, and we don't want to give that up."

"I have no problem with that." Kevin said. He called to the group of guards. "Niall. Would you come here a moment."

The chief guard came to the table. “Yes sir.”

“These men want to become part of the guard. They also want to stay together as a group. I know their final duties are up to Cormac, but what is your opinion of the idea?”

Niall was pleased to be singled out, especially in front of his men, and asked his opinion by his lord. He glanced over to his own table to assure himself the others had heard Kevin. He smiled broadly, and stuck his thumbs under his belt as he answered. “Why sir, I see no problem with that. Cormac was just saying he would really appreciate having more men in the guard. As to their being together? Well, sir, if you don’t mind my saying so, if you say they stay together Cormac will make sure they stay together. After all, you’re the lord.”

“Good. I thought as much. Why don’t you or one of your men take Aione and his men to see Cormac? Tell Cormac I would like this group to remain together rather than be spread out among the others. It’s always best to have friends fighting with friends.”

“Yes sir. I’ll see to it right away. Come with me fellows and we’ll get you fitted out properly. Lord Kevin wants all of his men to wear the same clothing when we’re on duty so we can be recognized when we’re needed.” He turned back to Kevin. “I’ll take them up personally sir.” He turned to his own men. “Jamie. You’re in charge until I get back. Be alert.” He started toward the castle as Aione and his men followed.

Cormac looked up as Niall brought his group into the guardroom. “Prisoners? You should have disarmed them.”

Niall shook his head. “These men came and asked Sir Kevin for employment. Sir Kevin told me to bring them to you. He said they should remain together.”

Cormac nodded. “All right. Take them back to supply and get them outfitted. Have Liam write them up and swear them in. Then take them to the practice area so we can see how good they are. I’ve got to find Sir Kevin and Sir Timothy. The king has said they are to get more practice in, seeing as how there have been two attempts to kill them. Perhaps they can show these men how to fight.” He smiled sardonically as he looked at Aione and his men.

“We’ll tell Kevin and Timothy they need practice.” The soft voice of Maeve came from behind Cormac as she entered the room. “Lady Fiona and I need a bit of practice ourselves. We’ll fetch Kevin and Timothy and meet you in the back bailey.”

Cormac rose to his feet as he bowed to them. “Yes, my lady.” He nodded at the six new men. “These men have just joined us. I was going to see how well they fight before you came in.”

Maeve and Fiona surveyed Aione and his men. She lifted one eyebrow as she smiled thoughtfully. “Well. Perhaps we can all find out how well they fight. We will meet you in back. I presume Sir Kevin and Sir Timothy will have to change clothes, and I hope they haven’t enjoyed themselves too well at the fair.” She nudged Fiona. “I wonder how well they will fight if they’ve had a bit too much to drink.”

* * *

Colm an Dubh landed at Fishguard in Cymru just as the sun was setting over the Irish Sea. The small pub at the head of the pier held the usual numbers of fishermen, farmers, and rovers. As he ate the pub grub he had ordered he surveyed the inhabitants of the room. There were two, sitting in a far corner, who attempted to remain anonymous among all of the others. Colm nodded to himself. When he finished his own meal he made his way through the crowded room, edging between the rough tables until he stood before the table occupied by the men he had selected. Without invitation he pulled a rough bench to the table and sat. The two men eyed him warily, but finally lowered their eyes.

“You want something?” one of them finally asked.

“Yes, but I also think you want something.” Colm answered.

The eyebrows of the taller of the two lifted as the man looked up from the table to eye Colm once again. “And what might we want?”

Colm smiled grimly, “Money.” He answered. “Money that looks like this.” He placed two gold coins on the table. As the man reached for them he lifted his hand to stop the movement. “No. Not yet. To get these there is a job you must promise to accomplish.”

The shorter of the two raised one eyebrow as he tilted his head to one side and gazed at Colm. “Job? What kind of a job do you have to pay this much for?”

Colm’s grim smile hadn’t left his face. “A job I believe you are well suited for. I need a man killed, and possibly his sister as well.”

Both men’s eyes were on the two glittering coins in the middle of the table. “Easily said, perhaps not so easily done.” The taller said. “Who did you have in mind?”

“I’ll pay your passage to Ireland with that captain.” he pointed his chin at the owner of the boat that had brought him to Cymru. Once there you will go to Enniscorthy and kill a young man named Kevin Mac Murrough. If his sister Fiona is with him you may kill her also. You must be very cautious, however, as they may be well guarded." He shrugged his shoulders, "At the same time they may already be dead by the hand of another assassin. If that is the case the money is still yours." He leaned back and waited.

The two men looked at each other, then at the two coins, then at Colm. The shorter one licked his lips. Colm smiled, turned, and called to the landlord, "Ale here, my man." and turned his attention back to his companions. He paid for the ale and waited for their answer.

Finally the taller reached out and took one of the coins. "You will pay our passage to Ireland?" He asked. Colm nodded his answer as the shorter man reached for the other coin. The taller man nodded, "All right, we leave for Ireland in the morning. You will arrange our passage." Colm went to the captain, pointed to the two men, and passed some coins over the table. He nodded to the two and left the pub.

When he was gone the captain walked to the two men. "You will be prepared to leave on the tide tomorrow morning. I will not wait for you. If you aren't here you lose your passage, and I keep the money." With that he went to his own table, sat down, and eyed the glass of ale with a sour look on his face

* * *

The day's work over the people of the countryside began to stream to the area where the fair was being held. Many came to join the members of the family who had arrived earlier to set up the booths where they would sell their surplus, or crafts, to their neighbors. The young men came to look over the crop of maidens who were there to see if an eligible young man might be caught in their snare. All were dressed in their finest clothes as they came to enjoy the annual event.

Kevin, Maeve, Tim, and Fiona meandered slowly through the crowd as they looked over the wares being offered. The enticing aroma of a rich stew filled the air at one of the booths. Kevin looked at Maeve who was dressed in a green dress that complemented the reddish sheen of her hair. "Ah, my Lady Greensleeves, would you care to test the viands at this rustic booth?" He asked, his grin conveying his good humor.

She looked at him from the corner of her eye. "Lady Greensleeves, eh? Yes, my Lord Kevin an Rua, some of these viands would sit well right now."

Tim looked at the two of them and shook his head as he smiled at their playful attitude.

As they approached the table Kevin looked at her, an impish grin on his face, "Kevin the Red, eh? When did it change from the Tease?"

"During the past month, an Rua, but it can change back just as quickly if you don't watch yourself." Maeve answered as she smiled up at his face.

"Then, acushla, I will be very careful when I'm with you. I prefer an Rua and *gra mo cre me*."

"And you'll get an Rua, but not *gra mo cre me*."

"One day, *colleen deas*, one day."

The four of them sat and the proprietor of the booth hurried over. "My Lords. You honor me. What might I bring you?"

"Four bowls of that enticing stew, and four tankards of ale."

"Immediately. Thank you, Sir." And the man hurried to get the foodstuffs.

"Aha!" Myrdden's voice came from the crowd. "I knew I would find you somewhere at the fair." He pulled a chair from another rude table and sat. A motion of his hand to the proprietor let him know to bring a fifth order to the table. He turned his attention back to the others.

At a nearby booth Aione, Kyle, and Finbar were having a pint. Though they were not on duty, and not dressed in the orange kilt and green blouse of Kevin's men, they were watching the group at the table, as well as others in the crowd around the booths. Kyle's eyes moved to where four men in orange and green sat at another table. They were the men set to guard Kevin and Fiona. He snorted his displeasure and said, "Look at those guards. They guard their ale better than they guard Sir Kevin."

Finbar looked at them. "You're right." He said, then leaned closer to Aione and murmured, "Off to the left of Sir Kevin. Two men in grey and brown. They look a bit suspicious to me."

Aione nudged Kyle and nodded his head in their direction. "Are you thinking what I'm thinking?" He asked after a moment's observation.

Kyle watched for a moment as the two slowly sidled toward Kevin's table while looking off in another direction. He chuckled without mirth. "I think they're being very obvious about not being obvious. It might pay us to move a bit closer ourselves. I think our friend of the alehouse is trying to make sure someone, anyone, kills these people."

"I agree. Let's not be as obvious as they are, eh?" The three men, holding their pints in their left hands moved inconspicuously to a closer position. As they watched the other two moved to within a few paces of the table, then drew their scians. It was the last thing they had a chance to do. Without spilling a drop from their pints Aione and his men drew and threw the knives they had hanging down the back of their necks. A quick flick and the knives were buried in the backs of the two would be assassins.

Those at the table turned as the bodies dropped behind them to see Aione and his men kneel and draw their knives from their victims. Aione smiled at the group. "My lords, my ladies. Sorry for the interruption." Then to Kevin, "We weren't on duty, Sir, but thought you might appreciate our watchfulness anyway. I'm sure you wouldn't mind."

Kevin looked at the two bodies lying behind him, knives still in their hands, then at his guards sitting at another table. He shook his head, "I don't mind at all, Aione. In fact, I think I might have you and your men made our personal guard. You seem to have appointed yourself to that position anyway."

Aione brightened and touched the back of his hand to his forehead. "We would appreciate that, Sir. I assure you, we will do a good job."

Kevin glanced at the men on the ground again, smiled, and said, "I believe you, and I thank you for all of us. If you are hungry let us buy you a meal. Meanwhile, you might tell my men at that table to take these bodies away, if you would."

"Thank you sir. We'll eat as soon as we've carried out you orders." He turned to the table where the other men were just noticing what had happened.

"And while you're at it you might tell the others to go back to the castle with the bodies, they won't be needed here any more." Kevin called after him.

"Aye, Sir, I'll do just that."

Kevin sat down again just as the landlord brought the bowls of stew to the table. "I'm sorry for this, Sir Kevin." He said as he placed the stew before them. "I had no idea they were nearby."

"It's not your fault, landlord, but when my men come back make sure they are well fed. They deserve a good meal for being so watchful." He turned his attention to Myrdden. "What do you suggest we do? I'm somewhat at a loss over these attempts on my life. It is obvious Colm is trying to make sure Fiona and I are dead."

Myrdden began eating as he thought. "I believe we should go to Tir na nOg." He answered.

Kevin laughed. "I'm afraid I don't know the way there."

"No, but I do. We'll obtain permission from your father to leave for Glendalough Monastery tomorrow morning."

"Glendalough Monastery?" Kevin asked. "Why there?"

"Two reasons." Merlin replied. "First, it was founded by your great uncle, so it wouldn't appear out of the way for you and your friends to go there. Second," he smiled broadly, "it is there that a thin spot exists between this world and Tir na nOg. Some believe it is a way into the next world, but it isn't that. It is a way into the land of eternal youth," he paused and nodded thoughtfully, 'which I suppose many would take to be Heaven."

"And what will we do in Tir na nOg?"

"We must get to Britain, but we want it to be done so those in Britain aren't aware of our voyage until later. If we take passage with a vessel going to Pembroke or Swansea the news of our arrival would spread rapidly. We will spend a few days in Tir na nOg where we may obtain the help of Queen Mabd and King Lir. He can have the selkies give us help in getting across the Irish Sea. That way we can use one or two of her curraghs, leave at night so the selkies can move us to a hidden shore, and arrive in secret. Our presence will be known soon enough, but by then we will be well on our way toward our goal."

Tim's face showed his puzzled thoughts. "Selkies?" He asked. "I don't think I've ever heard of them."

Myrdden laughed. "Not unusual for one who spends time inland. Sailors are more familiar with them. They belong to Lir's realm, actually, for they are of the sea. They're half seal, half human. Sometimes they crawl up on a rock, wriggle out of their seal skin and rest there to let the sun warm their human form. Sailors who've seen them come back with tales of what some have called mermaids trying to entice them to their deaths. They weren't, of course. They were just enjoying their human aspect for a while. The thing is, they are excellent swimmers, and can pull our curraghs to a hidden landing in Cymru, and no one will know of our arrival for awhile. I think it's important to keep Kevin's half brother ignorant of our doings. He'll find out soon enough."

"What of Aione and his men?"

"They come with us, of course. They seem to have their wits about them, more so than the usual soldier in your household, and we will probably need their expertise before this venture is over. Now, let's wait until they finish their meal, then get back to the castle and talk to your father. I'm sure he'll give us permission to leave. I can be quite persuasive, you know."

chapter 4
Tír na nÓg

The small group of horsemen rode, single file, through the gates of Glendalough to be met by a monk at the gatehouse. "God Bless all here." Myrdden said. "We look for Brother Aengus, and ask for lodging for ourselves and our mounts."

"God bless you kindly." The monk answered. "Lodging is yours in our guest house," He pointed to a building just behind the gatehouse, "and you shall join our humble repast. The stable is there," He pointed to a small building adjoining the guest house, "and there are both oats and hay for your mounts. Brother Aengus is saying Mass in the church. Ronan!" He called and an acolyte ran from the gatehouse. "Be so kind as to show our guests to their rooms, then stable their horses." He turned to the travelers. "After you have found your rooms please return here and I will have one of our acolytes take you to dinner. There you will find Brother Aengus. Enjoy your stay, Brother Myrdden."

"You seem to be known wherever you go." Kevin observed as they followed Ronan to the guest house.

"Yes. I've been here quite often, and have known Brother Aengus for many years. He is your grand uncle, you know."

Kevin frowned. "That Aengus? But you said he founded this monastery many years ago. I would have thought he'd be dead by now."

"Apparently his superior feels he is still needed." Myrdden said dryly as he grinned in his beard.

"Who's his superior?" Kevin asked innocently.

"God." Was the succinct answer.

* * *

"Ah, welcome Brother Myrdden. It is good to see you once again. And who do you have with you?" Brother Aengus welcomed the travelers to the evening meal.

"God Bless this place and all in it." Myrdden said. "This is your nephew, Kevin Mac Murrough, your niece, Fiona Ni Murrough, Sir Timothy Mac Egan, and Lady Maeve Ni Grady. We beg your hospitality until the morrow when we will go to Tir na nOg."

Brother Aengus smiled broadly, "So you do not come to join our happy group, Kevin. 'Tis a pity. You would enjoy it here. So instead you go to Tir na nOg," He nodded understanding. "That, too, is a major undertaking. I wish you well. Come. Join us at our simple meal." With that he led them all, travelers and monks, in a prayer of grace for the meal.

"I understand your going to Tir na nOg, Myrdden, but I've not seen you take others to that land. Might I inquire what has caused this change?" He listened silently as Myrdden told of the troubles on the island of Britain. He was silent for a moment, a thoughtful look on his face, and then he nodded. "What you hope to do is alter this bifurcated future you see, am I correct?"

Myrdden nodded. "Yes. I see two possibilities for this future. In one the Saecsens defeat Arthur. In the other Arthur defeats the Saecsens. If the former happens I can see great problems in a not too distant future for both the people of Britain and the people of Ireland. If Arthur wins I see a long and peaceful time for both islands, a growing accord between the Celtic people of Alba, Eire, and Britain, and a long-lived Pax Eirrean. The Romans are on the wane on the continent, and it will be up to the Celtic people, because of our love of knowledge, to assure the lore of the ancient world is not lost. Neither the Saecsens nor the Vikings have a great love of knowledge, or of books, and seem not to wish to preserve the traditions of their ancestors. I see your nephew and his friends as a means of assuring Arthur's success."

"I know you have a talent for seeing future events, though not all come true. If what you see is correct, I ask God's blessing on your venture. Meanwhile, we of this humble place will continue to copy the ancient texts, and distribute them to other monasteries that the knowledge not be lost. I presume you expect aid from the people of Tir na nOg?"

"Yes. As you know the Fenians and the Danae have left this realm and are now in Tir na nOg. I hope to enlist them in this venture as well."

"Let us hope you are correct in your desire." Brother Aengus said, and turned the conversation to other topics.

The following morning the travelers took their leave of Glendalough and moved through the gateway through which they had entered the monastery. "Few know this ordinary gateway also is a gateway to the other world." Myrdden said as they approached. "The ordinary traveler passing through the gate merely finds himself on the other side in this world. There are some who are given the gift of traveling through to the other world, and bringing companions with them. This is not done often, for it is forbidden by Queen Mabd for this to occur. It is only due to the intensity of the problem as they see it that I am allowed to bring you through."

When you are on the other side the country will seem the same, for it is. You will have entered another dimension, however, and in that dimension is Tir na nOg. Follow me for we must circle the dolman on which the gate is placed three times." Myrddn led the group around the knoll, going sunwise, three times. Once the circuits were completed he faced the open gate, spurred his horse and disappeared from their sight.

"Well." Kevin muttered as he looked at the empty gate. "That is certainly a sight to behold." He moved his horse forward slowly, looked back at the others with a nervous grin that showed he was not entirely sure of what was to happen, looked back at the gate, sighed, and spurred the horse forward. The land was even lusher than the one he had just left. Though it was the same view as the one he had seen from the other side of the gate, everything seemed brighter. It was almost as though it had just been made. Timothy followed him through followed by the rest of the small band.

Aione came through, and as his other men appeared one by one, looked around him and murmured, "Now that is certainly an adventure." He looked at his body, felt it all over, and said, "It appears to be all here, thank goodness."

"Come, then. Follow me. We go to the castle of Queen Mabd." Myrdden commanded as he spurred his horse forward.

"And where is this castle located?" Kevin asked.

"Why, at the same place the High King sits in Erin." Myrdden answered. "Tara, of course."

* * *

Leprechauns and the fae are the eyes and ears of the rulers of Tir na nOg, so Mabd knew of Myrdden's arrival, and of his guests. Because of this she had asked Lir, king of the ocean deeps, to attend their arrival. While they had been apprised by their messengers of the desire of Myrdden, they asked for the full story from him. When the story, and desires, had been unfolded, Lir stood. "And are these the two you brought from their own country to this to accomplish these ends?"

"Yes, Sire. These are the ones who have the necessary knowledge to be able to advise the future King Arthur what his actions should be."

"And the two ladies from this country; they have important roles as well?"

Myrdden nodded. "Aye. They are important for the project's success. Arthur will trust their feminine instincts in many ways he may not trust the advice of a male. The four, working together, will make a coordinated whole to give bring good cess to the venture."

At these words Maeve's face showed her puzzlement. It was obvious Lir was talking of Kevin and Timothy, but what did he mean about their being brought from their own country, and Fiona and she were talked of as being from this country. Her thoughts were on this as Lir and Myrdden worked out the details of their trip across the Irish Sea.

Later that afternoon she stood on the battlements looking over the green fields and groves of Tir na nOg. She heard the approaching footsteps but didn't turn her head. From her peripheral vision she saw Kevin lean on the balustrade next to her. Without turning she asked. "What did Lir mean about bringing you from your country to this one? He then said Fiona and I were from this country, as if you and Timothy aren't. What did he mean?"

Kevin remained silent as gazed at the fields without seeing them; his thoughts being on her question. Finally he said, "I would love to tell you, but I'm sworn to keep it a secret."

"A secret that you are not what you seem to be?" She asked, turning to him. "And what sort of secret might that be? If I am to be a part of this group, and do what Myrdden wants us to do, I think I should know something of the people I'm with. Don't you agree?"

"Yes. I agree wholeheartedly. I only wish I could tell you, but I swore to Brian I'd keep it a secret."

Maeve didn't have red hair for nothing, and her Irish temper brought her to the boiling point. "Well!" She huffed. "If I'm not good enough to know the people I'm with I'm certainly not good enough to go on this venture with you, or anyone else." She turned and started to leave.

"Please stop, Lady Maeve." A pleasant baritone voice came from around the corner. "Sir Kevin, I believe you have spent enough time with the good Lady to tell her the story. I think by now she might believe it."

“Show yourself, you knave. I like to know who it is that is talking to me.” Maeve said between clenched teeth.

King Brian came around the corner, a broad smile on his face. “Ah, my lady, ‘tis certain sure you’re Irish to the core.” He bowed. “Brian Connors at your service, my lady.” He straightened up and looked at her, the good humored grin still in place, “And I would appreciate it if you’d listen to the story Sir Kevin will tell you. It will explain many things you have been wondering about. Good day to both of you.” With that he vanished.

Maeve stood for a moment looking at the spot where he had stood. She turned back to Kevin, all the air spilled from her sails at the unexpected visit of Brian Connors. “That was…” She looked at the empty spot, then back to Kevin, “that was the king of the Leprechauns, wasn’t it?”

Kevin smiled and nodded. “It was. And he has given me permission to tell the story. I wish he would tell it, but,” and he sighed, “I guess it has to come from me.” He leaned back against the parapet. “When you and Fiona found us in the corridor six months ago it was the first time we’d ever been in the castle.”

“But you were born there, and lived all your life there.” Maeve interjected.

Kevin shook his head. “No, and here you will think I am lying, but King Brian will bear me out. I was born about fifteen hundred years from now on the other side of the ocean.” He raised his hand to stop Maeve’s question. “The morning you came across us lying in the corridor an Dubh and his man tried to kill the Kevin and Tim you knew. At the same time my Tim and I were in the ruins of the castle of the future. I had inherited it and was examining it with Tim. A stone fell and hit us on the head.”

He stopped and shook his head. “This is difficult because it sounds so bizarre. Anyway, at that same time Myrdden, Lir, Brian, and others with great power transferred your Kevin and Tim’s life essence to our future bodies. As they did that they transferred mine and my Tim’s essence to the bodies of your Kevin and Tim. They brought us back for this express purpose.” Maeve shook her head as she tried to absorb what he was saying.

“So when you and Fiona came across us it was really the first time we had been here in this time period. That is why I was so ignorant of the customs of this land. They have changed greatly in the future. Thank goodness this body’s knowledge remained with it, so I remember the language, how to fight, and all that, even though I didn’t remember all the little things that go with this time.”

Maeve walked to the parapet and looked out over the land. Finally she said. “You and Tim are not from here at all?”

"No." Kevin stood near the parapet a little ways from her and waited.

"And when this job is done you and Tim will return to the world you came from." There was a note of sadness in her voice as she made the flat statement.

"No. King Brian told me our future bodies died because your Kevin and Tim were too far gone for them to recover. No, he and I are here, for good or ill, until we have lived our lives out."

Maeve was silent for a long time as she absorbed this information, then she turned to look at him. "I knew there was something I couldn't understand about you from that first day. Suddenly it was as if you were a different person." She smiled thoughtfully. "Maybe it's because you are a different person." She paused, thinking. "All at once you were no longer the nasty trickster. Instead you were a man trying to get me to enjoy myself in your company." She tilted her head to one side as she looked at him through narrowed eyes, a slight smile on her lips. "And you succeeded. All of a sudden you were treating me like a precious lady. You weren't going to the pubs and seeing the wenches of the town, but you were taking me to the fair, having fun with me, and dancing with me, making me feel very special, and trying to win my heart."

Kevin shrugged his shoulders, "You won mine, so I was hoping I could win yours. I didn't want to be the only one in love."

"That's why you've been trying to get me to say '*gra mo cre me*', isn't it?" Kevin nodded. "And I would call you Kevin an Rua, but not say '*gra mo cre me*' yet." Kevin half grinned and looked at his feet.

Maeve stood staring at him, getting her thoughts in order, then walked over to him. She put her arms around his neck and pressed herself against him. "Well now, Kevin Mac Murrough the new, you've certainly done a good job of it. For these six months I've wondered if I was losing my senses because my heart was going to you against my will. I remembered what Kevin Mac Murrough the old was, and though I found him handsome I didn't wish to be that near him. Then, after I found you in the corridor, I wanted to be near you, and didn't know why. Now I know why, Kevin an Rua, and I am happy you cannot return to your own body." She smiled, "Now I will say '*gra mo cre me*' to you. And I mean it, for you do have my heart. Now kiss me, because we are going to be wed."

As they ended the kiss she said, "Oh, it is so good to know I have not gone crazy. I thought I was losing my mind because of the way I was feeling about you. I knew you were different, and I liked the difference, but didn't know why."

"Different? How?"

"The way you treated Fiona and me, but more the way you behaved toward your guardsmen, and especially Aione and his men. The old Kevin would never have treated his men the way you do. You make them feel special. You make me feel special." She kissed him again, and whispered, "*Acushla, gra mo cre me*. Remember what I said to you so long ago? Only the man I chose to wed would ever see more of me? Well, I've chosen, so you will see more of me." She laid her head on his shoulder. "When we are wed." She added. Kevin could only grin.

* * *

Colm an Dubh traveled the byways of Cymru by night, moving off the roads when he heard anyone coming, and finding shelter in the forests on either side while he slept during the day. Recognizing someone approaching Londinium on foot would be taken as a common soldier he purchased a horse and the necessary tack in the small town of Salisbury. The following day he rode across the Thames on the bridge built by the Romans. The castle occupied by Vertigorm was located near the northern bank, a wooden building surrounded by a palisade of logs that had been sharpened at the top.

He rode through the gate, eyed suspiciously by two guards as he did so. They did not deem one man with only a sword and small knife as a threat, so allowed him entry. He alit in front of the building, handed the reins to a vassal, and strode to the guard at the gate. "Announce to King Vertigorm that Colm an Dubh, heir to the throne of Leinster in Eire, desires audience with him."

The guard nodded, motioned a second guard to take his place, and entered the building. Minutes later he came back and said, "Follow me."

The hall in which Vertigorm had his throne was long, the ceiling supported by peeled logs on each side, near each of which stood a guard. The guard who had taken Colm to the door returned to his post the minute Colm passed through. He stood at the end of the long hall looking at the large man sitting on the throne at the other end. The man had long blonde hair, beard, and moustache. His robes were opened to show a barrel chest and well defined muscles. He apprised Colm through narrowed eyes, and then motioned for him to come forward. Colm approached with a trepidation he didn't allow to show in his demeanor. This was much different than back at Dun Rowan where the king welcomed people into his castle and treated them as guests. When he stood before the throne Colm bowed to Vertigorm.

"You say you are Colm an Dubh, heir to the throne of Leinster?" Vertigorm's voice was cold, his eyes like two chips of ice as he held Colm in his gaze.

"I am, Sire."

"And what does an Irishman possibly have that could concern me?" he asked with a dry laugh.

"Ireland, and possibly Alba." Was Colm's succinct answer.

The only change to Vertigorm's face was the lifting of his left eyebrow. "Ireland? And Alba? You think you can deliver Ireland to me? Why?"

"Kevin Mac Murrough and his sister Fiona are both dead. The only one left is the King, Dermot Murrough. With him dead I am the heir to the throne, and I can deliver all of Leinster, the eastern province to you. From Leinster you would have a place to conquer Ulster, Connagh, and Munster. These three kings meet only once every three years at Tara, and while there are minor tiffs between them, they haven't had a battle for over a hundred years. You could take them, one by one, for since they have had no real warfare for such a long time they have become soft."

Vertigorm motioned to a spot on the top step in front of the throne. "Sit, Colm an Dubh, and tell me more."

* * *

On a lonely beach south of the fishing village of Wicklow two large curraghs pushed off. On a flat raft, the deck raised to protect the animals from the waves, were the horses for those in the curraghs. The night was dark, the sea darker, as they began the journey across the forty miles of the Irish Sea. Alongside and ahead of each of the crafts the selkies swam and moved them eastward. The sea was calm with only the slight lapping of the small waves adding a soft sound to the night. King Lir had promised safe passage, and as the King of the Sea he was fulfilling his promise.

The passengers slept in the gently rocking boats as they moved steadily toward the shores of Cymru. It was in the early morning hours, before dawn broke, the prow of the boats scraped the sandy bottom. The men jumped into the shallows and pulled them ashore for unloading. Once that was accomplished the boats were pushed back into the sea and the selkies began the trip back to Ireland. The travelers were now on their own.

"Let's move inland as soon as possible. We are merely travelers at the moment, and will be until we reach Swansea. Uther's battle against

Vertigorm will take place in two weeks, and I must be there for that battle. You will be safe in Swansea. When I return we will seek out Sir Ector and you can begin making friends with young Arthur. Our stay in Tir na nOg was two weeks, which means we were there for almost four years time as counted on this side. Arthur has now three years before he becomes king. You have your work ahead of you, as do I. Let us be on our way."

book two
Cymru

part one
Swansea

chapter 1
A Sword and a Stone

The eastern sky was showing a band of white when the group debarked from the curraghs. The trip across the Irish Sea had been restful for the sea was tranquil and the selkies had done the work while the group was able to sleep. Now, horses loaded with the provisions they had brought, they rode across the beach to the line of trees that bordered it. Beyond the trees they found a country lane and followed it to the southeast. They rode the lane that divided the strips of land farmed by the peasants. As in most fiefs the lands of the Lord of the Manor were divided into strips. Each peasant family would be assigned strips in various directions from the center where they lived. Each morning they would walk to a different strip to take care of the crop growing there. A larger piece of land, called 'the commons', was set aside for the grazing of their animals and was shared by all.

The traveling group attracted no little interest from the peasants as they passed them on the road. It was obvious these were not the normal travelers of this road. Nine men and two women, all dressed as warriors, was something they would talk about for the rest of the day. They stopped, bowed, and knuckled their foreheads in recognition of the rank of the riders. Kevin and Tim were both clad in hard leather cuirasses studded with small bronze plates, and the short kilt of the warrior. Their legs were covered with wound cloth up to the knee, and all wore boots of soft buckskin with rawhide soles. The only difference between them was the torc of beaten silver Kevin and Fiona wore at their necks. The torc gave evidence of their being in line for the throne. Tim and Maeve wore torcs of bronze.

Maeve was thoughtful as she rode. She turned her head to look at Kevin. His reddish blonde hair was in a braid on one side of his head, she had done that while they were carried across the Irish Sea. Now she remembered the Kevin she had known, the one with the sneer on his lips and the tinge of cruelty in his eyes. This Kevin's lips held a slight smile, and his eyes were clear and watchful of danger. Tim, too, was different. His long blonde hair was tied back with a band of blue cloth. It was his face that was different. No more the innocent eyes and open face of the one who emulated an idol. Now his face, like Kevin's, was set with a strong jaw line and eyes alert for danger. It was the face of a warrior.

Myrdden. She tilted her head to look at him. Myrdden of the young/old face. Myrdden of the blonde beard and hair, but whose eyes seemed to hold the wisdom and memories of time beyond knowing. His robe was woven of the feathers of the raven and covered him completely. Yet, beneath it, Maeve knew he also wore the short kilt of a warrior, and carried a sharp sword. In his hand, however, was an oaken staff topped with an intricately carved Celtic symbol, a symbol of power. At his neck was a braided torc of gold, an endless knot of Celtic design carved on its face. Like Kevin's and Fiona's it gave evidence of his status as a ruler.

Fiona and Maeve also wore cuirasses of leather, but theirs were covered with chain links as a protection in fighting. They too wore the short warrior's kilt, and legs wound with cloth. Fiona also had the metal circlet to keep her blonde hair in place while Maeve's, like Tim's, was a strip of cloth, green to complement her auburn hair.

Aione and his lieutenants rode before the party, while the other three rode behind. These warriors were also dressed in leather cuirass with iron links covering the chest and abdomen. It was obvious to the peasants this was not merely another group of nobility traveling to visit another noble. They stood and watched as the procession moved by them and into the forest beyond. Then they continued on to their fields, discussing the sight excitedly.

That night the group made camp on the greensward. There was an open copse of oak near a stream that chuckled merrily as it flowed over a small rapids on its way to the sea. Aione and his men built two fires, one for themselves and one for their masters. They then prepared the necessary food for both groups, set up the small shelters, and took up station nearby to watch for possible trouble.

It was not unknown for a group to be attacked by robbers, just as they had once done before taking service with Kevin. This knowledge was useful, for they knew what they were looking for. Still, few brigands would be willing to attack a group of eleven armed warriors, no matter how much gold they wore around their necks. While the meal was being prepared the companions strolled around the area to get a bit of exercise after the long day's ride.

"We will go to Swansea first." Myrdden commented as they sat around the fire eating their meal. "The kingdom was Uther's seat before the battle. I know not who has taken over its kingship, but have half a notion it will be Ethelbert." He grinned without humor. "Ethelbert is not known for his hospitality. He was one of Uther's captains, but had a tendency to hang back when battle came. If anyone would come out alive it would be him. While Swansea is not one of the major kingdoms, it was the seat of the High King, though with no High King it is now just another of the small, and rather poor, kingdoms. We will see what Ethelbert has to say about the other kings. Since he is a gossip it should be interesting. At least we will be brought up to date on what has happened in the past four years."

Kevin lifted an eyebrow. "Four years. It seems strange that while we were in Tir na nOg for only two weeks four years passed here."

Myrdden smiled. "Aye. Two weeks in Tir na nOg is very close to four years in this world. Believe me when I say much has transpired in the meantime." He thought for a moment, and then continued. "I believe now is a good time to give you news imparted me by King Lir. Aione, would you and your men join us? You need to know what I am about to tell as well as these lords." Aione and his men rose as Myrdden waved them to the fire.

"Shortly before we left Tir na nOg King Lir warned me. He had heard my old nemesis, Morrigan, had decided to join in this fray in an attempt to make sure our goal is never reached. Like me she has great power in this world because she also is of the old Atlantis and a part of Tir na nOg. Because she was jealous of her sister, who she thought more beautiful than she, she killed her in what looked like an accident. She is a hater of that which is good. She escaped the tidal wave that buried Atlantis, but watched as both parents were killed in the capsule she was in. She lived with their bodies for some time before washing up on the shores of Lyonnesse. The fact she saw both parents killed seems to have made her crazed. She goes by many names besides Morrigan. Should you meet her she might be Lilith, Moira, Morgian, or some other. She is extremely beautiful, though not as beautiful as was her sister, and she will use this beauty to lead you away from your duty.

She will attempt to win you over by offering you her favors. If you take her you will be in her power forever, and you will do her bidding in order to win her favors again. She uses her beauty for evil, she knows how to tempt the base side of a man, and the corruption in men will lead them to accept her offer. She calls herself the Queen of Air and Darkness, and believes she is. So be very careful for she uses; and then destroys what she uses."

As he talked of the woman Maeve grasped Kevin's arm in a death grip. He looked down at her hand wrapped around his arm, then at her. Her face was set as she whispered through clenched teeth. "Remember this, my love, you are mine, and I will kill her if she even looks at you." She paused, then, "And if you succumb to her I may have to kill you. If I did I would kill myself as well."

"Not to worry, acushla." Kevin whispered back. "My eyes are only for you. Believe me when I say that."

"You have all been warned." Myrdden continued. "The danger is great, so we must keep a constant lookout. Not only for her, but for those she might send to do what she feels she cannot accomplish by herself. Before the battle begins we must *sain* ourselves with prayers and runes, for it is only the protection of the High King of Heaven that will avail in this battle. Now, a good night's sleep is what we need. We should arrive at Swansea toward evening of the morrow."

As the sun disappeared over a line of hills they rolled up in their bratts, and slept. Unlike the king and other lords who traveled with an entire entourage of servants and tents, this group did not act as though they were special. Their attitude toward Arthur the next three years would determine much about the future. For Kevin and Tim, remembering the stories of Camelot, Launcelot, Guinevere, and the Knights of the Round Table, this news was disquieting. The rising sun found them again in their saddles and on their way toward Swansea.

The lane on which they traveled was obviously used by two wheeled carts, and was deeply rutted where the wheels had sunk into the soft loam. The forests pressed in on both sides as they rode from village to village where the clearings would suddenly appear with the strips of crops fanning out from both sides of the road. A few huts where the peasants lived would be empty for all would be in the fields caring for their crops, or helping a neighbor with theirs. When the sun was high in the sky they stopped by a brook with a small waterfall and ate cold hock, pieces of bread torn from the loaf, and drank the clear water. Then it was on the road again.

Evening found them in another clearing where there was fresh water. Once again they partook of the prepared foods that had been sent from the kitchen of Loch Dorca. Earlier they had turned away from the sea and headed inland where a fork in the road had indicated what might be a short cut.

Myrdden, who was familiar with this country, had pointed out the fact they could save a day by following this route.

Aieon set guards for the night, recognizing the hours of darkness gave a better chance for brigands to strike: a feat he had accomplished more than once. All of them slept with their swords near at hand, ready to do battle at the first sign of trouble. A quick breakfast and they were once again on their way in their usual formation. All eyes alert for anything that might be out of the ordinary.

It was late afternoon as the small group topped the hill overlooking Swansea. They sat their horses as they looked down at the small fishing village. The castle sat back from the waterfront. The total area encompassed by the walls was large, and appeared to hold about a hundred people, but to all appearances it was a rude affair. Unlike Dun Rowans this was an old style castle constructed of wood, sitting in the center of about three acres of cleared ground and surrounded by a wooden palisade.

A small group of guards were loafing on the catwalk of the front ramparts as they guarded the gate. Within the courtyard were stables, a cook house, seven mud houses for the servants, and a two story keep. All had thatched roofs. Outside the palisade were the houses of the locals who kept the king and court supplied with food and necessities. These huts were generally of wood or stone with thatched roofs.

"This was the castle of Uther Pendragon?" Kevin asked, his voice showing his amazement. "I thought all castles were of stone."

Tim shook his head as he looked at the grounds inside the palisade. "Whoever would build a castle there?" He asked. "And such a one as this. Why, it's the most vulnerable castle I've ever seen."

"What do you mean?" Fiona asked.

Tim waved his hand to take in the entire location. "Well, look at it. In the first place, it's of the old style, so it's made of wood. Even the ramparts forming the bailey are nothing but spiked poles. Yet, here we sit on the hilltop commanding a view of the entire courtyard and keep from this hill. If we desired we could shoot arrows into any part of it. If we shot fire down on them, the thatches would burn, the keep would burn, and with no loss to ourselves we would win the day. No, a better place for a castle would be where we now sit. Here on the high ground we could withstand an army, especially if our walls were built of stone. Whoever built that had no sense of modern warfare."

"Don't blame Uther for that. The castle is an old one and was taken by him when he conquered the city. Unfortunately he had little time here to build something stronger. The Saecsen came against him too soon to really fortify Swansea. Had he lived he was going to build a stone castle as a better protection and as you point out, in a better location." Myrdden explained.

"Unfortunately he met Vertigorm near the Avon River while we were in Tir na nOg and both armies were decimated. Uther and Vertigorm were killed, and their kingdoms fell apart. During the night, while you slept, I had conference with Oberon, the king of the fae of Britain. He informed me of the battle and its aftermath. The past year has seen a struggle between the small kings of Cymru, barons really, as they try to win the support of others, form a confederation, and have a High King over this land. None has succeeded in convincing the others he should be the one to lead the entire kingdom. One thing to say for them, they are talking instead of fighting.

"To the east Vertigorm's surviving captains are trying to place themselves in power. They are fighting among themselves and further weakening what's left of the Saecsen kingdom." Myrdden continued. He pointed to a small stone building closer to the waterfront. "There is the cathedral, still only half built. Ethelbert is financing its construction as penance for deserting Uther in his time of need. He was at the battle, but indecisive as to where to place his troops. As a result they merely sat on the hill and watched the battle until it was too late to be effective.

"Come, let us go down. There is a public house near the waterfront. We can get sustenance there before we present ourselves to King Ethelbert. Unlike Ireland, not all doors are open to travelers coming at mealtime."

The food at the pub was good. Since Swansea was a fishing village the meal consisted of a variety of fresh seafood served in a number of tasty dishes. Myrdden had warned against any discussion of their future so the tables were rather quiet as the group ate their food before presenting themselves at the castle.

* * *

Aione and his men waited outside what would have been the Great Hall in a castle built of stone. Myrdden and the others left their weapons with him before entering into the presence of Ethelbert. Once they were weaponless the captain of Ethelbert's guard opened the door for them. They stepped through into a room about thirty feet long and twenty feet wide. Ethelbert sat on a wooden chair at the opposite end of the hall. He beckoned them closer.

As they neared his rude throne they could see he was not a young man. His face had the appearance of a prune, and an expression as though he had just eaten sour fruit. He took in the appearance of the five approaching him, and finally nodded to Myrdden. "Ah, Myrdden. I was wondering what had happened to you. And who are these you have with you?"

"My companions are Kevin Mac Murrough and his sister Fiona, heirs to the throne of Leinster in Ireland. The Lady Maeve ni Grady and Lord Timothy Mac Egan, their companions."

Ethelbert nodded to each of them in turn. "Welcome to our humble castle. I wish we had more to offer you, but Uther's defeat has left all of Cymru in dire straits." After ordering chairs for them he shook his head as he turned his attention to Myrdden. "Since that battle nothing has seemed to go right. I hope you can fix things as you have in the past, Merlin. We certainly do need your help, and your magic."

"What has been happening here, your excellence?"

Ethelbert thought for a minute before answering. His face became even more sour than it had been before. "As you know, Uther had united Cymru and acted as High King over us. He was a good king, though he seemed ruled more by what was below his waist than by what was above his neck." He smiled wryly, "But you know when God told us to go forth and multiply we thought he was speaking directly to us. We've tried to do a good job of it, and Uther was at the forefront of that movement.

"Then Vertigorm came with his Saecsens and began trying to wrest the kingdom from him. Uther was able to resist for a while, but because he began courting the wives of some of the kings, he pushed a number of them outside the alliance. While they didn't join Vertigorm, they didn't help Uther either. Had they been at his side Cymru might still have a High King, as it is now there are ten small kingdoms such as Swansea.

"None of us is willing to join any of the others to make him High King. Oh, we have our alliances, but it is nothing like it was. Everyone wishes to be High King, but no one has succeeded. We only thank Heaven that Vertigorm is dead and his kingdom is in worse shape than this.

"Then, last month in the dark of the moon, this stone suddenly appeared in front of the cathedral. When we went to bed it wasn't there. When we woke it was. There is an anvil on top of the stone with a sword thrust through it and into the stone, almost to the hilt. I tried to pull it out, but couldn't budge it. Others have tried to pull it out as well. It is a lovely sword. A sword any warrior would love to have at his side, but no one is able to take it. Do you have any idea what it means?"

Myrdden smiled and nodded. “Aye, Sire, I do. The sword is enchanted.”

Ethelbert snorted, “I could have told you that. I know it is enchanted. My questions, and those of all my peers is, ‘Why is it enchanted, and what is its purpose?”

Myrdden leaned back in his chair. “The people of Faerie know of what is going on in Cymru and in Londinium. They do not like the Saecsens any more than you do, and decided to do something to assure the entire island a proper High King. The Lady of the Lake enchanted this sword and caused it to be placed before the cathedral. This is the seat of Uther, the High King, so she felt it only proper for the sword to appear here.”

“Yes, yes, man. I can understand that. But what is the purpose of the sword? It is stuck in that stone so tight no one can do a thing with it.”

Myrdden nodded. “I know. There is only one person who will be able to pull the sword from the stone, and he will do it as easily as though the anvil and stone were made of butter.”

“Merlin, you are testing my patience. I can quite understand what you are saying, but I want to know who this man will be?”

“Don’t expect that it might be a man, Sire. It could be a lad as well. Whoever it is, that person is the true High King of all of the island. No one but he will be able to move that sword.”

Ethelbert nodded and sighed a deep sigh. “So. I am not the High King.” He nodded with resignation, as he half smiled, “And I know at least a half dozen other kings who don’t qualify either.” He paused. “And when will it occur, this ability to pull the sword from its resting place?”

Myrdden shook his head. “I have no idea as to the timing. I do know it will not happen for a while, and then quite unexpectedly.” He shook his head. “I may be a seer and a seanachie, but there are some things that remain dark even for me. This is one of them.”

Ethelbert nodded his understanding. “Aye.” He shook his head as a half smile covered his face. “There are those things we are not to know until after they have occurred. But it would be nice to have some idea of what the future holds. My main desire is that it does not hold the Saecsen in rule over us.”

“True.” Myrdden agreed. “There are certain things and events that should not be. However, let us change the subject, my friend. I’ve been away for a while. Who are the new kings, and what type of man are they?”

Ethelbert sighed deeply as he thought. “Since the breakup of Uther’s realm there have risen a number of small kingships, much like this.” He chuckled ruefully, as he waved a hand at the world at large. “My kingdom.”

He said. "Extends more to the sea than to the land, for as you can see it is naught but a simple fishing village surrounded by small holdings.

"To the east lies Cardiff. There King Pelles still reigns, he who in his pride refused to give Uther his army. On him I lay the blame for Uther's defeat and the breaking up of what could have been a noble endeavor. Pelles is a man who takes an insult to heart and never forgives. To the west lies Pembroke and King Bagdemus. He you know not for King Garth was slain with Uther and Bagdemus, through trickery I believe, took the throne. I have found him to be one who tries to get others to do his knavery, and rises on their shoulders. I do envy him Pembroke Castle though, for it is nigh impenetrable. To the north is Aberysturth and King Accolon, a man who prefers to hunt the fox, the two legged kind mind you, rather than fight. I do not say he is a coward, but I have never seen him in arms of steel to this date, though he loves the soft arms of flesh. Further north at Anglesy there is King Damas. Of him I know little but that his kingdom is more akin to mine than to that of Pelles or Bagdemus. Across the bay to our south is Poole and King Garlon. I hold him in honor for he is a man of honor. His armies were allied with those of King Balin of Bath, and both fought well, leading their men into the heat of the battle. In Gore is King Urien. He quite enjoys the ladies and the banquet. He also enjoys the bard and the poet. A good sense of humor, and of humus: it is a pleasure to be with him. At Telford you will find King Rience. A brave warrior who, along with King Lot of Orkades, battled also by the side of Uther.

"None have yet heard of the sword or of its meaning, for it has only been before the cathedral for the space of one month. I have sent messengers to each with the news so they might attempt their strength in pulling it from the stone. Surely one of them will be the king who will unite us, and lead us against the Saecsen to drive him from our land."

Myrdden shook his head. "You may send for them to come and attempt to pull the sword from its steely rest, but I doubt not one will succeed. While I know not the future I have seen in a vision; the one that unsheathes the sword will be the one least expected to be able to do so." He chuckled, "In fact, I see much unbelief among these kings even as they see him do what none of them is able to accomplish. They must all remember the teaching of the church, the last shall be first and the first shall be last. It will serve them in good stead."

Ethelbert smiled sadly, "Aye. I wish them well, but if you say none of the kings of the west is the chosen one I will accept that. Still, the messengers are on their way. I have no doubt all will make the journey. I assume you and your colleagues will abide with me while we await the outcome of the various attempts to do the impossible, though it appears to be so easy."

"I thank you for your invitation, Sire, and accept for myself and my companions. I presume their men will abide with yours as well?"

Ethelbert nodded. "They may stay on, for I know they may not be too far from their wards. It is well. What then are your plans?"

"Once I've told all these kings the story of the sword I plan on traveling to see Sir Ector, his son Kay, and his charge Arthur. I have not seen them for many years and wish to find out how they are doing. I presume Kay is now a page and well on his way to warrior hood himself. I would go now, but it is very important all in this entire area know the story of the Lady of the Lake and her enchantment of the sword, that only he who is true High King may pull it from the stone and anvil. After that, well, we will see what fate holds for our future."

It was later in the evening when Fiona came to Kevin, who was walking in the outer bailey with Maeve. "Maeve, may I borrow my brother for a little while? I have something I wish to know." Without waiting for an answer, for the answer had to be yes due to the difference in station, she took Kevin's hand and led him toward the main gate. "Come brother; let us watch the tide come in." They walked in silence through the dusty street of Swansea, then turned to walk along the quay.

Finally, away from everyone, Fiona turned to him. "I do not know how to be devious, for father never taught us how to be devious. In this instance I fear I cannot be tactful either." She looked him in the eyes. "Who are you?"

Her question took Kevin aback. He looked at her in amazement. "What do you mean, who am I?"

"Just what I said." Fiona answered. "I ask because you are not the Kevin with whom I grew up." She paused, a slight frown on her face, then continued. "Nor is Tim the same Tim I have known for years. Oh, you both look the same as always, but there is a change in each of you I cannot fathom.

"Tim was your shadow. He emulated you in your cruel teasing, and you could tell him to do anything and he would. He was not his own man, he was your man. Now he is his own man. Yes, he is as polite and courteous as you are, but in a different way. He is no longer mimicking you. He is doing what he does because it is his nature; but it is a different nature than that of a few months ago. His nature has changed just as your nature has changed. I've wanted to ask, but trying to get you and Maeve apart has been impossible for the last month. Will you answer me?"

Kevin turned his gaze to the sea. The moon was the only light, the bay was dead calm, and its reflection was a silver pathway in the deep blue of the sea, leading one's eyes from shore to the horizon. He drew a deep breath and released it slowly.

He nodded toward the scene. "That is beautiful, is it not?" He turned to Fiona. "This is going to be a bit difficult to understand; or to believe. I am your brother, but at the same time I am not your brother. Remember the morning you found Tim and me unconscious in the hallway?" Fiona nodded. "I thought I was having a dream that morning, for only minutes before I had been with another Tim in that same hallway in the ruins of the same castle, and the year was two thousand years after the Christ."

Fiona opened her mouth to speak, but his upraised hand halted her. "You may choose not to believe what I am going to say. Yet what I say is truth. Tim and I, that is the Tim and I who now inhabit these bodies, come from a different age. Actually, it's our spirits or souls, I know not which, that come from that time, not our bodies. We were born in a period of time some fifteen hundred years in the future." He paused, and sighed his frustration.

"It is very difficult to explain what happened, but An Dubh, our half brother, actually killed Kevin and Tim that morning you found us on the floor of the passageway. Brian Connors and Myrdden told me the story. Because of the important events that will occur in our lifetime, and because I have the knowledge of what happened in this period of time, they transferred our spirits into that of the dying Kevin and Tim. Their spirits were sent to inhabit our future bodies, where they died." He sighed.

"Tim and I are now a part of this time, and cannot be sent back to our own time or bodies." He smiled sadly. "In a way I'm homesick for my own time, yet the nearness of Maeve makes me forget that time. I have fallen in love with her and now would not really want to go back, for I would no longer see her. Does that answer your question?"

Fiona stood amazed as she tried to assimilate what had just been said. She shook her head as if to clear it. "Then that is why Myrdden said you were brought from a different country, and are a seer into Arthur's problems."

Kevin nodded. "Yes. I know the history of what will occur unless certain things are changed. According to Myrdden I am supposed to help make sure they are changed. Now, after what he said last night, I see it will be a bit harder than I thought."

Fiona thought for a long time as she now gazed at the silver pathway that shone among the small wavelets of the bay. "It must have taken years to gain such knowledge." She mused. "And how many years had you lived in your future?"

"It took years, yes. Tim and I were in our fifty-fourth year of life when we were brought back. We both had a military background in that period of time. Both of us actually spent over thirty years in military service. That may be useful if there are battles to be fought, though battle here and battle in the future are two different breeds of cat. Now we are young again and will grow old and die here, unless we are killed in one of these battles yet to come."

"You told Maeve of this? Of your life in our future?"

"Yes. She was relieved. She was falling in love against her will, and she found out it was all right for I was not the same Kevin the Tease she knew."

"I thought as much. Her attitude changed toward you while we were in Tir na nOg, so I thought she knew something she wouldn't tell me; despite the fact she is my lady in waiting."

Kevin nodded. "Yes. Brian Connors did not want many people to know about us. He left it up to me to decide who to tell. Since you had discerned the change I felt you deserved knowing. I hope I was right."

"I believe it was right." Her face clouded as a question crossed her mind. "And what were your names in that future time?"

Kevin smiled. "You may not believe this either, but I am Kevin Mac Murrough then as now. Tim's name was Tim Keegan, because when his ancestors went to America from Ireland the name was written as Keegan rather than Mac Egan." They were silent for a while as Fiona thought things through.

"And were you both wed in your time?" Fiona asked in a small voice.

"No. Neither of us had wives. We were too often moved around and too often in battle to want to worry a wife with our safety."

Fiona smiled. "That is nice." She said. "Then I will be Tim's first and only wife." Somewhere on the hill behind them a fox barked, shortly followed by the sweet song of a nightingale. She continued gazing at the bright road the moon made on the face of the sea. Finally, "America?" She asked. "What is America? Is it like Tir na nOg, or Atlantis?"

Kevin pointed toward the moon. "If you go in that direction close to three thousand miles you will find another whole continent. It will not be known to Europe for hundreds of years, but it will be named America. Tim and I are direct descendants of those whose names we bear, which made it easier for Myrdden and others to bring our spirits back. They could not have done so had we not been in the direct lines." He chuckled wryly. "So you see, while you are my sister you are also an aunt many generations removed, and I may well be my own distant grandfather."

"I would that I were back home at Dun Rowans." Fiona's voice was sad. "I've never been this far away, and I don't know why we're here." She turned to face Kevin. "Why are we here? What is going to happen? Myrdden said you would know. Do you know of this witch of whom he talks? Tell me."

Kevin thought for a moment, and then nodded emphatically. "All right." He said, "But you must tell no one." She nodded assent. "There is a lad in the charge of Sir Ector. His name is Arthur. He is counted as a servant right now, and they call him 'Wart' because of his small stature." He smiled wryly. "Little they know. That lad is the future king for he will pull the sword from the stone in about three years. He will build a castle near here I think, no one has found it in my time, and call it Caer Maellot, though in my time it became known as Camelot.

"He will unite these people, win battles over the Saecsens, and all of the southern part of Britain will be under him as High King. He will make some good decisions and some bad decisions. It is Tim and my job to make sure certain of the bad decisions are not made. One of these bad decisions will be set up by Morrigan le Fae, as she will call herself. That one must be stopped at all costs. Unfortunately, I can't tell you what it is right now. I will when the time comes.

"Basically, that is what Myrdden has told me. My problem is that I have to guess at much of what will happen, for most of the history of this time has been lost to us. The only stories we have will be written a few hundred years in the future, and are where I obtain my limited knowledge of what I know about his reign. You and Maeve are here to give him feminine counsel, for he has never known his mother, and I'm not sure what counsel Sir Ector's wife has given."

Fiona absorbed the quickly told tale, nodded to herself more than to him, and finally said. "Well, now that I know this I feel much better in one way, and worried in another. I don't really understand everything you have told me, but it does explain much. Thank you, my brother, or whoever it is you really are. I am grateful. I'm not yet sure I believe everything you've said, but your actions tell me it is true. Leave us go back to the castle. I wish to discuss this with Maeve, I presume that is all right, and think on it more."

"Maeve knows, and now you know, so it is proper you discuss it with each other."

"I wish she had told me about this, but I can understand. She had a higher authority than me to answer to."

"Aye, and Brian Connors could do far more to her than you. Come. It's late and we should get our rest. It has been a rather busy day."

* * *

"Greetings, King Ethelbert, Prince Myrdden."

"Welcome, King Pelles. This is Prince Kevin Mac Murrough and his sister Fiona Ni Murrough of Leinster, and their companions Maeve ni Grady and Timothy Mac Egan. King Pelles of Cardiff."

Pelles bowed to Kevin and his retinue then turned to Ethelbert. "Let's cut to the quick of it. I'm a busy man and have only come to Swansea to claim my position as High King of Cymru. I understand there is a sword I must pull from some type of stone in order to prove myself worthy of the position. Where is it? I want to get this over with as soon as possible so I can return to Cardiff."

Myrdden chuckled at the pronouncement. "My lord king." He said. "I will lead you to where the sword is, but you must understand the situation. The sword is enchanted by the Lady of the Lake. I have been informed by her many will attempt to dislodge the sword, but only one will succeed. That one will be the true High King and deserve the respect and honor of the other kings of Cymru. It is possible you may not be the one able to dislodge the sword, and I beg you be aware of that."

Pelles frowned at Myrdden. "Sir. I consider you an upstart uninformed as to how to act in the presence of your betters. I am King of Cardiff and have held the throne for over twenty years. You are obviously little more than a stripling yourself, despite the title of prince; one which I am unsure of your right to claim. It seems apparent to me, as ruler of the largest of the realms of Cymru; I am the logical one to lead the others in their battles against the usurping Saecsens. Though I understand with the death of Vertigorm there is another attempting to rally them in Caer Londinium.

"I know not if he is Saecsen or not, but he calls himself the Black Dove. Now. Let us to the sword that I may take it in hand and claim my rightful position. I am ready to lead our armies against those of this Black Dove. Lead me to the place, Myrdden."

At the entrance of what would later be the cathedral Pelles strode to the sword. With what was almost a sneer on his face he took hold of the haft and gently lifted. Nothing happened. He then gripped the haft tightly and tugged. The sword was unmoving. His face darkening, he glanced at the onlookers, then took the haft in both hands and bent his weight into his attempt to pull it from its resting place. His face reddened as he struggled to move the sword even a millimeter, but it would not budge.

His face set in anger he strode to his retinue and beckoned one of his men. "Fergus! Use your stone cutting tools to bring me that sword!"

The man bowed, "Yes, Sire." He said. Collecting his tools from the saddlebags on his horse he approached the sword and the stone. Placing the wedge near the blade of the sword he struck it a blow with the hammer. Instead of even a chip flying off the stone, the wedge broke in half. He tried another with similar results. Turning to Pelles he said plaintively, "I am sorry, Sire. My tools break but there is no mark on the stone. I cannot do as you command."

Pelles turned to Myrdden. "What is the meaning of this?" He asked haughtily.

"I presume it means the Lady of the Lake does not deem you the proper person to become the High King. I told you in the keep she has placed a geis on the stone, the anvil and the sword. The one who is meant to assume the throne, and unite Britain, will easily pull the sword from its unusual sheath. There will be no need for the tools of a mason, or of a blacksmith, for it will seem to leap into the hand of its true owner. Many others will try, my lord King, and many will fail. It will be a surprise to all when the true High King makes his appearance. Yet even I am not truly sure who that shall be." Myrdden replied mildly.

Pelles appeared about to say something, thought better of it, turned on his heel and strode toward his horse. After mounting he turned to Myrdden. "I may not be the one destined to be High King, but I will refuse to honor the claim of one who does not come of royal stock."

Myrdden looked at him through eyes half closed, "The one who pulls the sword will be of royal stock, King Pelles, and it would behoove you to accept his leadership. If you do not your own leadership will end in a tragedy."

"You are threatening me, Prince Myrdden?"

Myrdden shook his head. "No. I am not threatening you. I am merely telling you the truth of what will occur. I can see the two roads that lie ahead of you. On the one you accept the king and prosper. On the other you reject him and die. I am a seer, as you well know, and I do not lie about what I see."

Pelles stated down at him for a moment, nodded (whether of acceptance or of goodbye no one could say) turned his horse and rode out of the town. Myrdden, Ethelbert, Kevin and his companions watched in silence as he and his entourage rode back to Cardiff. Finally Ethelbert, Tim, and the two women headed back to the castle. Kevin stood beside Myrdden as both looked at the rock, the anvil and the sword jutting out of both.

“Pelles said something about the Black Dove in Caer Londinium.” Kevin mused, almost to himself. “I don’t remember anything said about Black Dove in what I have read. I presume he is speaking of an Dubh.”

Myrdden was silent for a moment as he contemplated Kevin’s words. Then he nodded. “It is probably an Dubh.” He opined. “How well has the history of this time been recorded, Kevin? Is it possible an Dubh has been forgotten? And are you mentioned in the stories you read?”

Kevin shook his head. “Most of the stories of this time are the thing of myth.” He snorted softly, “Come to think of it even the events of five hundred years from now are really not well known. Oh, they’re being pieced together from the seanachie stories, but as you have said there may be some embellishment to these. No, the history of this period of time is scanty.”

“Then it is possible you were, will be, involved, and an Dubh has a part to play as well. It is also possible we are altering this history by having you appear and influence Arthur. An Dubh may not have been part of the old story, but may now be if only to make sure you don’t succeed. Morrigan may well have her spoon in this pot. I have noted that there is something that fights against the good conquering evil. It may well be we are already in such a battle now.”

Kevin sighed before replying. “You may be right.” He said, then turned to face Myrdden. “Pelles called in doubt that you are Prince Myrdden.” Kevin said. “May I ask where you come from and if you are a prince? You don’t have to tell me, of course, and I will still follow your directions.”

Myrdden smiled. “I suppose you have a right to know.” He said after thinking over the question. “I am a prince, among other things. My parents ruled the continent of Atlantis many years ago.”

Kevin’s eyebrows lifted in surprise. “Many years ago? Many thousands of years ago would be more like it. I always thought Atlantis was a myth, a fanciful legend.” He said.

“No, it was no legend. Atlantis existed, but was destroyed without a trace in a major disaster. A huge rock fell from the sky in a time many years after the land masses were one. The island Atlantis had drifted to the south and west of this land, though what is now these islands was once the mountain region of the north of Atlantis. Llyonesse, though slowly sinking, is also a part of the highlands of Atlantis. The rock caused an earthquake and the major part of Atlantis began to sink. I was a youth when my parents built a means for us to escape. They were killed before they could enter it. I was able to enter it, and after many days at sea, landed on the enchanted isle of Avalon, a part of Tir na nOg.

"Unfortunately, in the disaster that occurred and in protecting me, they had been killed by the tidal wave. They died before they could return to our home, and our boat. I was found near death and raised as part of that land and part of this, able to go between and take part in the destiny of Earth as well as dwell in Tir na nOg. Morrigan was also saved from Atlantis, and landed in a different part of Tir na nOg, where she became even more bitter because of the death of her parents. As you have found time in Tir na nOg is different than time here. A week there may be one year, or a hundred years, here. But, for that reason my age belies my appearance"

Kevin snorted his amusement. "I would say it does. That means you must be many hundreds of years old though you look only in your late twenties."

"Yes. I am almost of an age with King Brian, and he has been King of the Leprechauns for near three thousand years. In that time I have seen much history, most of it unsavory, and prefer to live in Tir na nOg over living here. Yet there is much to be done in this period if we are to alter the future of both this land, of Ireland, and of your country. It is important Arthur receive the right advice from you and your friends. Remember also, there will be much danger for you and them, as well as for me, before what we hope for is accomplished. And, of course, it could go either way depending on the decision young Arthur makes throughout his tenure as High King."

Kevin nodded his understanding. "Obviously Pelles is not High King, and obviously you believe this young Arthur is the one who will be High King. Are we going to wait here until he comes along?"

"No indeed, but first we must wait here until the kings have made their attempt to pull the sword from the stone. Many warriors will also try, none will succeed. This will take a bit of time, time I hope we have. Once all have tried we shall leave for Sir Ector's manor shortly thereafter. At Caer Garda we will get acquainted with him, his son Cai, and Arthur." He half smiled and gave a small shrug. "Then we shall see what happens next."

* * *

A very disheveled peasant appeared at the gate of Caer Londinium and called to the guard. "Would you tell my lord The Black Dove that Cardor of Swansea would desire audience?"

"And what gives you cause to think The Black Dove would have audience with the likes of you? Begone, knave!"

"Just tell him I have news of events in Swansea that will interest him greatly. Believe me when I say he wants to hear this news."

"Wait here. And if you are lying I'll have your lifeless body lying in the road for the dogs to eat." The guard snapped as he turned and headed toward the keep. Minutes later he returned to his post, made a feint with his pike, smiled nastily when Cardor ducked, and nodded his head toward the entrance of the keep. "Go in. He will hear your news."

Cardor approached the throne slowly, head lowered. Finally he heard a voice say, "Stop, and kneel before My Lord The Black Dove." He did as he was ordered. Another voice then said, "Tell me your news."

Cardor swallowed and raised his head to look at the black hair and beard of an Dubh. "My Lord." He began. "I bring news of events at Swansea I know will be of interest to you. I do need money to return to my home, however."

"Money, eh? If your information is important I will pay you handsomely. If it is not I will merely have you put to death. Speak!"

"Yes Sire. Two months ago a stone and anvil holding an enchanted sword appeared before Swanminster Cathedral, or what will be the Cathedral when it is finished. The story is that the sword can only be pulled from the stone by the one who is the rightful High King of all Britain. King Pelles has tried to pull it and failed. Others of the kings have since tried, and thus far all have failed."

"I know of the sword in the stone. It has been told me by others. Go on." An Dubh said in a disinterested voice.

Carnor licked his lips, his life depended on his news. He continued. "Visitors arrived from the west to visit King Ethelbert. They were eleven in number. One is called Merlin. The others are one called Prince Kevin, and his friend Sir Timothy. There are two women with them, a Princess Fiona, and Lady Maeve. These two, though women, dress and act like warriors. They had with them six ruffians as their entourage. They did not travel as nobility, but traveled as warriors all. I was surprised for I had never seen women dressed as warriors before."

An Dubh's face betrayed his interest as he leaned forward in the chair serving as his throne. "Are they still in Swansea?"

"I know not, My Lord King. I only know they were there when I left to come here to trade my wares. I did hear from one of the guards they were shortly to go to the north to visit Sir Ector in his demesne."

"Hmmmm!" an Dubh sighed deeply as he gazed at a far corner of the room. "So Kevin is not dead. I wasted my money on those men." He muttered as though to himself. Turning back to Carnor he asked. "Do you know the names of the men in the entourage?"

"Aye, Sire. The leader is one called Aione. He has two leftenants, Kyle and Finbar. The others are Eamon, Bran, and Duff, but they are merely men at arms."

"So Aione has joined Kevin." An Dubh mused. "Interesting! And Kevin is playing the warrior. Even more interesting!" He turned to his Chamberlain who was standing nearby. "Give this man a purse of gold. His news is of import to me." Turning back to Carnor he added, "Keep your eyes open and inform me of what is happening in Swansea if it is of import to me. I wish to know of the movements of this Kevin and his people, and especially of this Merlin. You may go now. Keep your eyes open and there will be more gold for you if your news will help me."

After Carnor had left he turned back to the Chamberlain. "Eventually we will have to kill him, of course, for if he will be traitor to his liege he would more rapidly be traitor to me. We will, however, wait until we have no more news from him: then dispatch him. It doesn't pay to have traitors in your midst for too long. They begin to get fancy ideas." He thought for a moment longer, than added, "Athol, fetch the Druid priest. Mayhap he will see what the future holds for us. After you send him to me tell my captains to assemble in the private hall. I believe I will have a job for them." The Chamberlain bowed and scurried away to do his bidding as an Dubh went to the room to await their appearance.

The death of Vertigorm had come as a blessing to an Dubh; a blessing he had not expected and one he would take full advantage of. Augustus, Vertigorm's son, was still too small to take over the throne. Colm an Dubh had been on the battlefield as Vertigorm had been killed by a stray arrow. At almost the same time he had seen Uther go down under a concerted rush of Vertigorm's pikemen who as yet had not known of the death of their leader. Once the two kings were dead the armies stopped fighting. They were confused, not knowing where to turn for leadership, and slowly left the field to tend to their wounds. They would leave the burial of the dead to the peasants who worked the land on which it had been fought.

An Dubh had watched from a safe position as Vertigorm's best leaders had gone down to arrow, sword, or spear. Once back in Londinium he had gone to the castle, Caer Londinium, to find a disheartened and dispirited group of men debating their future in this harsh land. Seeing no one was ready or willing to take over the leadership he had pushed himself forward as the Prince of Leinster and heir to the Irish throne. His expansion of his position had been accepted as truth by the men seeking someone to lead them, and he had quickly been elevated to the position vacated by Vertigorm. Now there was a small group of fiercely loyal officers willing to follow where he led, to take the orders he gave, and to prepare for the next battle against the Celts of Cymru.

The druid priest walked sedately into the Great Hall. When he reached the throne he bowed his head slightly in recognition of an Dubh's rank, then asked. "What is it you wish, Sire?"

"A group of men and women have come to Swansea from Ireland. I have a strange feeling they mean to do me and my kingdom ill. What is it you see in the future because of their arrival?"

The druid closed his eyes and bowed his head, his face set in stern lines as his breathing slowed and deepened. Slowly he raised his head, eyes still closed, and intoned in a voice unlike that he had used before. "I see a former druid high priest, now a priest of the new religion, as their leader. He has much power for he walks between two worlds. I see a new High King arise, a king who will have good counsel from those with this priest. There is war, battles will be fought. I see two possible roads from the final battle. If the one in the right wins there will be a long peace for more than a hundred years. If the one in the wrong wins there will be violence and bloodshed in the land for many years to come, and they will be conquered by a foe from another land. Uneasy will be the head under that crown." He shook himself as his breathing returned to normal and he opened his eyes.

"Tell me, old man, which kingdom is in the right and which in the wrong in this battle to come?"

The priest shook his head. "I know not of what you speak. When I use my powers to see the future I am in another realm, and am not allowed to remember what I saw. Only you, my liege, will be able to understand the portent when the time comes. At the moment only you know the message."

"Go then." An Dubh said bitterly. "I must needs think on what you have said." The old priest left the room as he had come, knowing his power and proud of that power over even the man who called himself king. "Old fool." An Dubh muttered softly, "A lot of good you did me. Athol, have my captains assembled?"

"Aye, Sire. They are in the private room."

"Good. Now we'll see who is in the right and who in the wrong." He said as he departed the throne for the meeting.

"If our plan is to succeed we must act now." He said as he stood before the small group "There is a usurper to my throne in Ireland. Kevin

MacMurrough, his sister, and their companions. There is a small retinue with them, all warriors, and all working against our interests. As I see it there are three things we must do. First: Ando, I want you to delegate two or three of your best men to go to Swansea, find one who calls himself Kevin Mac Murrough, and make sure he doesn't return to Ireland. Second: Galdor and Kormon, each of you take a platoon of men and scour the countryside for the remnants of the old army. Bring them back to Londinium so they can be restored to their former glory to prepare for the battle to come. Third: Lindemor, I place you in charge of getting the armory back into shape. We will need to find good smiths to make the necessary swords, spears, and armor. We will need good bowyers, arrowsmiths, and fletchers if we are go have enough archers to thin the ranks of the foe before the hand to hand fighting. Also, we will need barracks for the men Galdor and Kormon bring back. That done we will also need the necessary cooks and food to feed them. Yours will be the hardest job, for you will have to coordinate all of this in time to meet the needs of the army as it gathers. Any questions?"

The officers thought over their assignments as an Dubh waited, his eyes moving from face to face as they did so. Finally Lindemor looked up. "Sire. Since Ando merely has to choose two or three men to carry out the assassination, wouldn't it be wise if he and I worked together on the armory, and other details? Each of us could take on certain of the duties, coordinate our jobs, and get the whole thing done faster than one man could if he did it by himself."

An Dubh considered the suggestion, then nodded his head. "Good thinking, Lindemor. Ando, you will work with Lindemor on this project. Understood?"

Ando bowed his head in acknowledgement of his orders. "Aye Sire. Understood. We can meet after leaving here and divide the duty so each of us is doing that job he is best at."

"Good. Any other questions? Ando, stay a moment after the others leave." The meeting disbanded. An Dubh watched the men leave, a faint smile on his face. Kevin had turned out to be harder to kill than he had thought. The man he had considered a weakling and joker had turned out to be more of a warrior than appeared on the surface. He turned to Ando. "I gave you the name of one I wish killed. There are others. In fact there are possibly eleven all told, so you will have to select more than one to do this job." Ando waited silently for an Dubh to continue.

"Another who must be killed, and I mean must, is Fiona ni Murrough. She is as much a danger to our plans as is Kevin. The third is a man called

Myrdden, or Merlin, or Emrys, or perhaps some other name. He will be with them, however, and on an equal footing with Kevin. He also must die, for I believe he is at least as dangerous as the others put together. I've heard tales of his prowess with blade, but he is also a seer. Your men must be careful. Understood?"

"Understood Sire. I will do my best to find our best men for this job. I believe I know the one's who will be best. They will do the job, or die in the attempt."

An Dubh nodded. "All right. If they die in the attempt so much the better for them, for if they fail in the attempt and return here I assure you they will die. I will not stand for failure. I have seen too much of it already. Go!" Ando hurried from the room, a little concerned for his own future welfare if things went wrong with these assassinations.

An Dubh walked back to the empty throne room, his mind working over his plans to conquer Cymru and kill Kevin. As he moved to sit on his throne he heard a soft voice behind him. "Greetings, an Dragan." Startled, he turned swiftly to behold the most beautiful woman he had ever seen. Her dark black hair outlined a perfect face, her almond eyes were deep blue, and her ruby lips were smiling sardonically at him. She was wearing a long green cloak, the hood thrown back to outline her hair against the sheen of the satin lining. His breath exploded in a gasp as he beheld her. Finally, catching himself up, he asked, "Who are you, and how came you into this room?"

She moved seductively closer, the sardonic smile never leaving her face. It seemed she was very amused at his reaction to her presence. "Why, an Dragan, you may call me Morrigan. I am here to help you achieve that which you most desire." As she spoke softly she moved closer and the robe she wore seemed to open of its own volition to reveal a long, tapering leg up to her thigh, and as the top slid off her shoulder it revealed the perfect roundness of a pink tipped breast. "With my help there is no doubt as to the winning of all Britain for you. You know of the power of Myrdden? My power is greater, and my desire is to see his power vanquished. Together we can do much, and each of us will gain our end. Would you like to try me out?" She asked, as her left eyebrow arched to ask a deeper question.

An Dubh licked his lips as his eyes devoured what she had revealed. "Yes." He croaked.

Morrigan let the robe drop to the floor. She wore nothing beneath. "Here?" She asked, "Or in your rooms?"

"Let us go to my rooms where we can discuss this in private." He stammered his mouth strangely dry.

"Yes. Leave us go." Leaving the cloak lying on the floor she turned to lead the way, an Dubh following docilely in her wake.

Later, as he lay at her side on his bed, he asked. "Why did you call me an Dragan?"

"Because, my love, a dove is a symbol of weakness. With my help you will be strong as the dragon, and will be called that by all. Together we will bring the kings of Britain, Cymru, Eire, and Alba under the rule of a High King called an Dragan. You and you alone will rule both islands as one kingdom." She smiled, but while her lips were warm her eyes were cold. "Believe me, an Dragan, with my help you will win this battle over Myrdden and those he is with." She caught his neck in her arm and drew him down to her. "Now, let us love again. It has been too long, much too long."

chapter 2
Caer Garda

Kevin and Maeve entered the public house, now renamed The Sword and Stone, and looked around. The room was about 30 feet by 20, rustic tables and chairs scattered throughout. In the sconces, set about four feet apart, candles guttered, the walls above them sooty from the ill burning wicks. Kevin looked over the crowd. Fishermen, shepherds, and some townspeople were in small groups either at the wide plank set on sawhorses that was the bar, or at several of the tables. Two fishermen, seeing them enter and noting their rank, rose from a table and moved to the long plank of the bar. Kevin nodded his thanks and led Maeve to the table. As the landlord bustled over to take their order Maeve noted Aione and Kyle enter, shoo two others from a nearby table, and sit down. After the landlord left she said, "I see Aione and Kyle are here as well; our ever present watchdogs."

Kevin nodded. "Yes. I asked Aione about their being near us all the time. It seems Myrdden has talked to them. Aione has designated himself as my guard, Kyle is yours."

"What of the others, do they also have their guardians?"

"Oh yes. Finbar is to watch over Tim, Bran over Fiona, while Eamon and Duff have been told to guard Myrdden himself. I doubt it was Myrdden's idea, but in Aione's mind Myrdden is the most valuable of all because of his powers. He doesn't call what he does 'magic', but only the natural things that can be done because of his association with Tir na nOg."

As Kevin turned his attention back to Maeve Aione's eyes were examining everyone in the bar. He nudged Kyle and nodded slightly to two men who had just entered, then called Kyle's attention to another couple at the bar. He gave Kyle a meaningful look and whispered, "Their boots." He muttered. "Be ready."

Kevin hadn't noticed Aione and Kyle's observances. His attention was on Maeve, and he continued his conversation. "At the same time he is fearful because of Morrigan. I suspect you know he's in touch with the fae of this land. They informed him that Morrigan is about. The fae have little love for her. They apparently have had traffic with her before, and have found she can't bc trusted."

"What do they say about her?" Maeve asked as she lifted the tankard the landlord had just placed before her.

"According to Myrdden they found she has no sense of honor. She is completely involved with her own schemes, will say anything to get others to do as she wants, but when the time comes when their plans are failing, and they need her to bring them to fruition, she will abandon them to assure her own desires. They say she uses people, and when she is done with them she discards them for someone she feels will benefit her more."

"Have you heard more of her looks than what Myrdden told us the first night?"

Kevin shook his head. "No, though it wouldn't do much good. He says she can change her looks to suit her fancy, though she always makes sure she is beautiful and alluring in the sight of men."

"Just make sure you don't..."Maeve was interrupted as a fight broke out at the end of the bar. Both she and Kevin turned to see what the uproar was about. The fight ended as quickly as it had begun and when they turned back they saw Aione cleaning the blood from his short sword with the robe of a body on the floor. At his feet lay the body of a man with a dagger in his outstretched hand. Maeve looked at the body, then at Aione, "What happened?" She asked.

"The fight was meant to get your attention. I noticed one of the men wore boots of Saecsen make, so I suspected the ruse. I wasted no time on the fight, but quickly turned to see why the Saecsen started it. I saw this other Saecsen as he attempted to kill Sir Kevin. I stopped him."

Kevin got to his feet and clapped Aione on the shoulder. "Thank you, my friend, for once again saving my life. Come. Let us depart this place for somewhere quieter."

A quick smile touched Aione's face as he nodded and sheathed his knife. Kevin had called him friend, giving him a sense of pride he hadn't had before. "Aye, Sire. I quite agree." He said as the publican, a disgusted look on his face, grabbed the body and dragged it outside. Fights, and death, were not an unknown event in the pubs. Since the death of Uther, and Ethelbert's weak rule, there seemed to be no law in Swansea but that one made for oneself.

Little attention had been paid to the quick death of the would-be assassin. As the publican returned to his place behind the bar he muttered, 'Should have taken care of your own trash.' as he passed Aione.

They left the public house and walked toward the quiet of the quay. Aione and Kyle stayed behind to make sure no one disturbed them. As they stood at the end of the pier Maeve leaned against Kevin. "You are a target, m'acushla, and I don't like it."

"I can't say I think much of the idea myself." Kevin agreed. "I guess we will have to be a little more careful than we have been. Thank God Aione has his wits about him."

Maeve turned to him and put her arms around his neck, pressing herself against him as she did so. "M'acushla." She whispered. "I burn for you, and I feel you burn for me as well. I do not wish to die before I become Maeve Bean Mhic Murrough. I wish to know you and have you know me as wife before that time comes. Will you grant my desire?"

Kevin pulled her closer and kissed her soundly. "Gladly." He said. "Though that's the first time I've been proposed to."

"I gave up waiting for you to make the time." She laid her head on his shoulder and whispered, "Though I wonder if it is because of the hundred pieces of gold my dowry holds."

Kevin held her close as he whispered back, "Beautiful Maeve, I would love you just as much if your dowry was only ninety-nine pieces of gold."

Maeve backed away and stared at his face as he tried to hold himself back from grinning. "Sure and what kind of an answer is that. Why I have half a mind to mmmfff." as he stopped her with a hearty kiss.

"Dear heart." He said as he pulled her head back to his shoulder. "After tonight you will be Princess Maeve Bean Mihc Murrough, and the hundred pieces of gold will hardly add a great deal to the treasure already there. I marry you because I love you."

"I'm sorry. I was just remembering what the old Kevin was like. This is a good time for our wedding."

"Aye. It is." He turned toward shore. "Kyle!" He called. "Would you find Sir Tim and Lady Fiona, and Myrdden. Oh. Make sure their guards come to meet us at the cathedral."

"Aye, Sire." Came the answer, and Kyle headed toward the castle.

"Now?" Maeve asked.

Kevin smiled. "Now, my beauty. Myrdden is a priest, as you know, and since we really know none here but our guards and Ethelbert, who is probably asleep and wouldn't be too excited about our wedding, we will have a private one with just our friends attending. Does that meet with your approval, Maeve Ni Grady."

Maeve smiled and nodded. "Aye, m'acushla, it very much meets my approval. Though I do wish our folk were here to celebrate with us." She lifted her head for a kiss, which was quickly bestowed, then murmured, "Let us to the cathedral. I wish to be on time for my wedding."

After the ceremony Myrdden looked at the couple and said, "You realize this is going to upset the current sleeping arrangement. Either Fiona or Tim will have to move from their quarters, or we have to find another room for you at this late hour."

Tim smiled sheepishly and muttered, "Well, if Fiona would marry me the arrangements would be put back together, wouldn't they? We'd just have different sleeping partners." He looked at Fiona, "What do you say, will you marry me?"

"Well, it's certainly about time you asked." Fiona said in mock seriousness. "I was beginning to think I would die a spinster. Of course I'll marry you." She looked at Myrdden, "Sometimes I think these Irish men have skulls as thick as an oak."

* * *

Caer Garda was not an imposing castle. The hill on which it stood overlooked a main road leading from Pembroke to the Thames River, and thence to Londinium. Though it only covered the top of the hill, so the inner court was small, and the keep had only two separate stories, Sir Ector had made certain the pass was well guarded. There was an ever alert group of men walking the parapet behind the drystone ramparts at the top of the bailey, for the threat of Saecsen attack was always present. While the news indicated the Saecsens were in a state of confusion, it also indicated someone was holding them together and reforming their army; and that someone was not a Saecsen. Somehow that someone had usurped the place of Vertigorm's son: and that son was forming an army of his own to take back the role of Chieftain of his own people. If that be true, everyone said, it would be some of the best news they had heard for years. Still, vigilance was the watchword. Too many friends had been lost to Saecsen blades.

So when the small group of travelers, obviously warriors from their dress, approached the closed gates they were stopped with an inquiry as to who they were and what business they had there. Myrdden looked up at the sentinel and said, "Inform Sir Ector Prince Myrdden is here with his warriors."

"Hold where you are, Sire, and I will inform Sir Ector of your presence." A few moments passed and the portcullis began to rise. The creaking of the windlass could be heard as the well oiled chain was slowly wrapped around it. As it opened far enough for a man to go through the figure of an older warrior came out.

"Myrdden, my friend. *Caed mille failte*, a hundred thousand welcomes. It is good to see you again." He said with enthusiasm. Then he called, "Arthur, come! Take these horses to the stables, rub them down well, and feed them. They have come far and deserve as good a treatment as their masters will receive." Then, "Dismount, my friends, and enjoy the hospitality of Caer Garda. You will stay for awhile, will you not?"

"With your blessing, my friend, we will stay until the new High King is crowned, and maybe longer."

Sir Ector laughed, "And you will be welcome that entire time. Now, who are your friends that I might receive them properly?" After the introductions Sir Ector bowed his welcome. "I am honored with your presence, my lords. I will attempt to make your visit as pleasant as possible. Come, let us to the Great Hall were we can eat and gossip. There is much news I wish to hear, and I know I have much news for your ears as well." He led the way to the keep, calling as he did so, "Food and drink for our honored guests."

"You are using Arthur as one of your servants?" Myrdden asked Ector as they dined in the Great Hall.

"Oh, no." Ector replied. "Arthur is page to my son Cai. Cai was warriored last year. Since Arthur was then fourteen years of age, and eligible for the position, I made him page. He has a way with horses, however. Wanting the best care for your steeds I felt he would be better with them than one of serfs who does not care that much."

Myrdden nodded understanding. "So Arthur is now fifteen years of age. I had thought him only twelve. Cai must be eighteen at least, then. When did he do his vigil?"

"In the spring of the last year. He is looking forward to the tourney to be held in Swansea two years hence. He has been practicing the use of the sword and the lance on the courses in the valley below. He is becoming quite adept at their use. Arthur has also been practicing with the sword, for one day he will be warriored. Once he has served his term as page, of course."

"Of course." Myrdden speared a small game hen on his scian. "And what word have you heard from the east?"

"It is bruited that he who calls himself the Black Dove is now being called The Dragon. He has usurped the place of Augustus, Vertigorm's son, and is assembling an army under the captains of Vertigorm's host. It is said there came a very beautiful woman who has captivated The Dragon, and also said he does her bidding as though she were the one in charge of the forces. She seems to have him under her thumb."

Myrdden's head turned sharply to look closely at Ector. "And what do they say her name is?"

Ector's face knotted in thought. "I believe she is called Morrigan." He answered.

Myrdden turned his face toward his companion. "Morrigan." He said somberly. 'This is the one I warned you of. We must be constantly on watch now." Turning back to Ector he asked, "And what do they tell of her appearance?"

"She is lovely, of raven hair, and the blue gowns she favors do make her very appealing, according to those who have seen her. She sits the throne at the side of The Dragon, and he consults her about everything that goes on."

"So." Myrdden mused. "This time she is of raven tresses." He smiled sadly, "Always beautiful, always evil. I would give much to know her plans. Whatever they are they will do us nothing but ill."

* * *

"Adrik, I needs must get away from this camp for a little while that I might collect my wits and make plans. I will ride alone along the river. There is a clearing near a falls where I might commune with our gods. See I am not disturbed."

"Your desire will be obeyed, Sire. I wish you good meditation that we might win over the upstart who usurped your place after the death of your father."

Augustus mounted his charger and rode out along the river path, his head bowed in thought as the soft thud of the hoofs slowly covered all but his thoughts of how he might come against the man who now called himself An Dragan. The day was soft for an early spring afternoon, and the warmth of the sun soon caused him to divest himself of the maroon cloak he wore. The bronze helm plumed with maroon dyed horsehair was hot, but he kept it on. One never knew in these woods when a lone rider might be attacked. Yet, he must go to the falls so the soothing sound of the falling water would help him think.

He had hardly dismounted to sit near the bank of the river when a low voice, barely louder than the roar of the falls, sounded behind him. "My lord. You seem to be troubled."

He turned his head to see a very beautiful damsel of flaxen hair standing near the line of trees at the back of the clearing. He sighed, caught between the desire for her that suddenly came upon him, and his desire to clear his mind for the upcoming battle plans that must be made. The latter won as he spoke sharply, "Begone lass. I need to be alone with my thoughts."

Her smile was radiant as she walked to him. "I know, my lord, but if your thoughts are of winning over An Dragan perhaps I might help."

"And who might such a slip of a girl be who would help me, a leader of the Saecsen army?"

Her smile was bright as she said, "You might call me Lilith, my lord, and I am skilled in much more than that which is so apparent on you mind." She sat next to him then lay back on the soft moss of the bank. "Would you like to make plans now, or after?" She asked through half closed eyes. "I do believe I have the perfect sheath for your sword, if you wish to try it."

Augustus turned to lay beside her, his kisses covering her face. Moments later she exclaimed, "Ah, my lord, you are like a young stallion with his first mare."

Afterward, as they lay on the bank she whispered, "Shall we now discuss plans on winning over all of this land? Not just the part now held by An Dragan, but the land of Cymru, and of Alba as well. You, my lord will be mighty in all of this land. Then we might think of winning Eirrean as well."

"You sound as though you have a plan to accomplish this."

"Oh, I do, my lord, I do."

"And what, may I ask, will your reward be if you are able to help me?"

"Why, to rule at your side so I might satisfy your every whim."

"You say your name is Lilith? Of what kingdom do you come?"

"One you have yet to hear of, the kingdom of Llyonesse." Her face grew sad as she thought of her home. "A kingdom that no longer lives, but shall again in some future time."

"It has been conquered then?"

She sighed. "Aye, my lord, conquered by King Lir, for the sea swallowed it and it now lies leagues deep beneath the waters of Muir Nicht to the south of this land."

"You were of some authority in that land, I take it."

Lilith's face grew stern, her eyes like flint, as she said, "I was a princess and the leader of the armies of Llyonesse. In our land women fought beside their men so the men would know how strong the love for them could be. This was many years ago."

"Yet, you seem so young."

Her radiant smile again broke through. "I have lived many years in Avalon, where one does not age rapidly. Once we have won this land I may take you there so you can see the beauty of such a place. Now, however, let us make plans for the winning of this land."

* * *

"I would ask a boon, Sir Ector." Kevin entered the great hall where Ector was sitting behind the long table reviewing reports from his chamberlain. He looked up as Kevin approached.

"A boon? And what sort of boon would you ask, Lord Kevin?"

"I have noticed young Arthur. He seems to be very quick, and very sharp. I would ask for him as a squire while I am here."

Ector's left eyebrow lifted as he surveyed Kevin, a puzzled look on his face. "But my Lord, at the moment Arthur is page to my son, Cai. Why do you not select the son of the chamberlain, who is well born?"

Kevin smiled. "Aye, Sir Ector, I realize Arthur is page to Cai, yet I believe I can help him more, for I have been a warrior for more years than has Cai."

Ector shook his head. "Sire, it is unheard of that one of lowly birth become more than a page."

Kevin nodded understanding. "Aye, you may well be right. But think for a moment, Sir Ector, of our own ancestors. Were all of them selected by God to be rulers, or were some at one time of no more import than Arthur. Yet, through their mind or through their strength they became strong and took command of a group of men who looked on them as leaders. Then, as leaders, they conquered other men and in time took rulership of a land. Or, on the other hand, they may have sworn fealty to some strong man who gave them a title of baron or earl, and land to go with it."

He shook his head. "No, Sir Ector, I believe all of us have risen from lowly positions to positions of power through no other means than that our forebears took from those weaker than themselves and became rulers. Mine became kings, yours became nobility, but they came from the same stock."

Ector sighed, rose from his chair, and walked to the window overlooking the bailey. He gazed out at the ramparts for a long moment then slowly turned. He looked at Kevin with a lopsided grin on his face and shrugged. "Aye, you may well be right, Sire. Not too long ago I was a swordsman in the army of

King Uther. In battle I saved King Uther's life and was sore wounded when I did so. He rewarded me by giving me this land and making me a baron. Now I will pass the barony on to my son who is able to become a warrior because I am a warrior."

He turned back to the window and was silent again. Kevin waited. "You may have Arthur. I have noticed he is quick of mind, and shows ability beyond that shown by others his own age. I hope he proves out." He smiled again, "Besides, how could I, a mere baron, say no to the Prince of Leinster?"

"Oh, you could, Sir Ector, for I would have accepted it if you had, though I would have attempted to argue you into seeing my side. I thank you for your willingness to accede to my wishes. I do not believe you will be sorry."

"I hope you're right, and I wish both of you my best. I presume you will place him in the tutelage of Aeion for training in swordsmanship."

"Aye. Aeion and Maeve, though I may take a bit of a hand in it myself. After all, if he's to be my squire I should have some small say in how he learns, don't you think? I believe I'll go for a short ride with him and see how he reacts."

"Good idea. I'll have your horses saddled."

* * *

The sun was slowly sinking toward the hills to the west, painting the clouds with the soft hues of orange, pink, blue, and lavender, when Kevin, Arthur, and the ever present Aione rode through the wooden gates of Caer Garda. They looked in astonishment at the change to the keep. During their absence it had been decked in multi hued flags and buntings, giving it the appearance of a gala festival. As they dismounted Kevin asked the ostler, "What has happened?"

"Oh, Sire, a troupe of bards and entertainers has graced our halls this afternoon. Sir Ector has made them welcome, and has bedecked the keep in honor of their coming. They bring news of the events in the east, songs, poems, stories, jesters, and acrobats. There will be a gala feast for all, and all are invited into the Great Hall to be entertained. Sir Ector is indeed a wonderful master."

Kevin clapped his newly appointed squire on the shoulder. "Well, Arthur, tonight should be very interesting."

Arthur nodded assent, then said, "I thank you, Prince Kevin, for giving me opportunity to be your squire. I will serve you well."

"Aye, that you will. And before long you will be a warrior yourself."

Arthur smiled a weak smile. "Oh that that could happen, Sire." He shook his head sadly. "Such things never happen to those who are of lowly birth."

"Ah, but they do. Take Sir Ector as an example. He was of lowly birth, yet became a warrior and obtained this land to pass on to his heirs. Trust me when I tell you this. You will become a warrior, and many people in the future will hear of the legend of Arthur and his fellow warriors."

Arthur grinned broadly, "Ah Sire. You jest. But your jest does make me feel good. Would that it could be true."

"We will wait and see, eh Arthur?" He turned to the keep. "Now let us find some refreshment. The ride was long and I am dry. Do you think they have some ale for the weary traveler?"

"Sir Ector always has food and drink for the weary traveler, Sire. I am sure you will find some. While you do that I will take care of your arms and trappings."

Kevin shook his head. "No. Come with me, for you too are thirsty. Aione, will you take care of our kit?"

"Of course, Sire."

"Thank you. Once done find me in the hall and I shall have a flagon of good ale for you, and possibly a loin of beef to fill that emptiness in your midsection." He looked at that area as he spoke, "Though methinks it is a bit larger than it was when I first saw you."

Aione laughed. "Unfortunately true, Sire. You feed me too well. We need a good fight to help us lose a bit of our roundness. Mayhap you can supply us with one."

"Perhaps we will have a bit of swordplay tomorrow, my friend. I believe all of us could use practice. We've been busy traveling and enjoying ourselves." He glanced at Arthur. "And our young squire should be given some lessons by a master swordsman. You are, I presume, ready to teach him."

Aione bowed. "Aye. I will teach him all I know. When I am done I will turn him over to you to finish the job, for you are my superior with sword as well as with place. Now I will go to take care of your kit."

"Don't forget to come to the Great Hall for food and drink." He called as Aione walked away. "Now, let us find ourselves some of the viands Sir Ector has provided."

The Great Hall was lit by torches burning in sconces along the walls, and at the far end was a long table filled with various meats, vegetables, fruits, and liquids. As Kevin and Arthur took pewter plates and began filling them with a variety of foods Myrdden came into the Hall from a door at the back. His face was grim as his eyes scanned the room for one of his party. When he spotted Kevin he motioned for him to come to where he was, found a seat, and waited.

Kevin left Arthur and walked across the relatively open room. As yet few people had appeared, waiting until they received word it was all right to assemble. Servants were still coming in with steaming bowls and platters as Kevin sat next to Myrdden. "You seem rather unhappy." He said as he lifted a drumstick to his mouth. His flagon of ale sat on the chair next to him.

"Yes." Myrdden answered. "I have been talking to Oberon and Titania. They came to me with news of what is happening in Londinium. You will remember I warned you of Morrigan a few months ago."

Kevin nodded. "You said she was lovely, evil, and used men to her own ends, and we should avoid her at all costs." He threw the chicken bone on the floor as he picked up a second drumstick.

"From what I can gather she has appeared in Londinium, and in another of her guises, to the north in the camp of Augustus near the fens."

"What makes you think this?"

"There is a woman of great beauty, dark of hair, blue of eye, and well formed who is now mistress of the castle in which An Dubh has taken residence. He is in her thrall, for she shares his bed, though not every night. She has given him a new name, An Dubh Dragan, The Black Dragon, and has him gathering his armies to fight those of Augustus for full leadership of the Saecsen horde."

"This sounds bad."

"Not the worst. There is another of great beauty of yellow hair, blue of eye, and well formed who now shares Augustus bed, though not every night. She is leading him to call other fighting men to his army to fight your half brother for control of that same leadership."

"She seems to be playing both of them against each other so she will win no matter which of them loses."

"Exactly. Once the armies have fought they will rejoin forces under the leadership of one of these two, and the remnant will be greater than either of the armies when it began. Then she will recruit new men into this army to come against the west. Her hope is to be the queen of all this land."

"That will take years."

"Aye. Years. But she has time on her side for she is of my country, and has lived in Lyonnesse, which is a part of Tir na nOg. Like me she has a long life.

Thank the High King of Heaven we have a few years of our own. It will be a bit more than a year now before the tournament at Swansea. There Arthur will prove himself. Morrigan does not know of Arthur, nor his forebears, though she will find out, I believe. She knows we are here, and her plans are shaping against us for she and I are deadly enemies."

"She knows you are here? How?"

Myrdden shrugged. "There are always traitors and informers who will do anything for a bag of gold. A trader from Swansea informed An Dubh of our presence. An Dubh told her, and my name was mentioned. She cares little about you personally, for it is me she hates, but since an Dubh hates you she will try to kill you as well. To her you are little more than a pesky fly she can swat at will. She knows my power and believes hers to be as great or greater. It is there the test will come. Not yet: later. We must be on constant guard as the years progress, for as they do so too will her desire to crush us. Be warned, and inform the others, as shall I. Now I must make some other preparations."

* * *

Myrdden rode alone in late afternoon the following day. Leaving Caer Garda he followed the trail to the east and north. At a small rill he dismounted and waded into the water. Reaching into the stream he searched until he had found twenty-eight small white rocks and four larger ones. Placing these in a leather pouch at his belt he mounted and rode further. Coming to the hill called Myddfai he left the horse at the base and walked along a faint path to the top. At the very top there was a large rock, carefully hollowed to form a cup. He poured oil into the stone cup, placed a piece of braided hemp in the oil, and left a portion lying over the rock lip. Then, in the approaching dusk, he carefully placed one of the larger white stones to the north, and the others at the east, south, and west of the center rock. The smaller stones he placed at the compass points between the larger ones, some toward the inside, some toward the outside.

As the rim of the sun disappeared over the ridge to the west, and darkness began to cover the hill top, he lit the wick of the lamp that was the center stone, planted his staff firmly in the soil, stood in the center of the circle, and prayed, "Oh, High King of Heaven, I ask your protection and help in what I am about to do. I ask your protection and help in furthering this project with young Arthur. I also ask that you sain me as I make this call. I am yours and under your protection in this entire undertaking, for I do what you have asked me to do. Thank you for your blessing." Turning to the east he called loudly:

"The stones of calling have now been placed.
The sun has orbited to its resting place
As the moon now rises to her lonely space,
And this place of meeting is lighted by moon and wick
I call you Morrigan to this lonely hill
To meet and only the truth to tell."

Lifting his head he shouted "Morrigan, come to me. This I command in the name of the High King of Heaven!" Having said this he waited as a crescent moon began to appear over the peak to the east. He waited. He thought of calling again, but knew the one call was enough.

"You wanted me?" A voice came from the darkness outside the circle of stones.

"You are here." He said flatly as the figure of Morrigan approached the circle. She stopped just outside and examined the white stones with a wry look on her face.

"So." She said softly. "You have sained yourself and stand protected. Why, my dear brother, do you do such a thing? Do you fear my power that much?"

"Fear you? No, I do not fear your power. I am leery of your wiles that lead to killing those who stand in your way. I remember Sheila well."

Morrigan's lips curled in what was more a grimace than a smile. "Our dear sister, Sheila." She said dryly. "Poor beautiful Sheila. She did not have our power, Myrdden. She was weak, and felt pity for these creatures who occupy this land. She stood in my way as Queen of the Air and Darkness. She had to die."

Myrdden sighed. "You have no knowledge of compassion." He said. "You live only for yourself. What are your plans regarding the Saecsens and Anglos? What are your plans for the one you have dubbed An Dragan? I also hear you have seduced both he and Augustus. Now they eat from your hand. Am I right?"

"So many questions, brother dear. My, my. You are the curious one, aren't you? Why don't you let me inside the circle? We could sit by the lamp and discuss these things as brother and sister, as in the old days."

Myrdden shook his head. "Those old days are only in your mind. No, I believe this is a fine arrangement. Now, please answer my questions."

Morrigan sighed and mocked, "Ever the polite one, aren't we? Well, my plan with these two is to bring them together to form one army. It will take a little while, but you know I can do it. They are in my thrall now. Then, with that army we shall march against you and those with you, defeat you, and continue until we rule this entire island. From there we cross to Ireland and conquer it. Then, when everything is in our hands, I will take control from my two mighty warriors and rule as their queen." She laughed, "You see, Myrdden, they will fight over me and both will, unfortunately, perish leaving me the sole ruler."

"I had heard you planned on their fighting each other."

Morrigan smiled slyly. "At first I thought that would be a goal. Then I considered the size of the armies, and felt it best to have both armies as one rather than two enemy armies still angry with each other. I believe this way I will be better able to defeat you and your armies here. It may take a little time, but time I have plenty of."

"You will not accomplish this if I have anything to say about it."

Morrigan laughed, a mocking tone in her voice. "You have nothing to say about it, my loving brother, nothing at all. My power as Queen of the Air and Darkness is greater than yours, despite your calling on the High King of Heaven. He who I serve is greater. Now, if you don't mind, I will go back to where you summoned me from and carry out my plans. Don't try to stop me. If you do I will grind you into the soil. My will shall be accomplished. Goodbye, and bad cess to you." Myrdden sensed her presence leave the hill. He waited, sitting by the center stone, until he was sure she was gone. Then he picked up the stones and placed them in his pouch, took his staff, and returned to his horse. It was dawn when he rode into Caer Garda, a thoughtful look still on his face.

chapter 3
In Enemy Territory

Spring had come; a wet spring with a bone chilling cold the wind from the north did nothing to alleviate. The low road was a sea of mud as it wound through the valley. The south side of the hills still sported large patches of snow that remained as if defying the oncoming warm weather. A falcon, roosting comfortably in the shelter of early leaves, regarded a group of travelers riding east. Their garb was the tightly woven wool cloaks of the Irish, so little color was seen to indicate the rank of those hidden by the dark gray of the cloak. They rode, head down beneath the hoods, as they tried to keep the cold drizzle from running down the inside of their clothing.

"Springtime in Britain," Aione observed, "isn't much different from springtime in Ireland."

"True." Myrdden answered, "Though I do believe the breezes are a bit warmer in Ireland. At least we have our bratts to keep us warm." As he said this he drew the cloak a bit closer around his neck.

"And just how much further do we have to travel?" Maeve asked.

"Far enough to make me long for the warm waters of Bath." Kevin observed. "Right now I crave nothing more than to bask these frozen bones in the heat of one of the tubs in the public bathhouse."

"What are you talking about?" Maeve asked.

Kevin laughed. "When the Romans conquered this land they found warm springs beneath the town we go to. These are mineral springs that are presumed to aid one's health. The Romans then built a large house to cover these springs, and they used the springs to both refresh and to bathe themselves, especially on cold and wet days. I see nothing wrong in doing the same. After all, when in Bath do as the Romans did."

Myrdden broke in, "To answer your question, Maeve, we should be there shortly after the sun is directly overhead. Since we started this portion of our journey at dawning, and the trip along this road is one of about half a day, we might expect to be in King Balin's presence shortly after the noon meal."

"I hope he saves something for us." Maeve murmured. "I find my stomach wondering if my mouth has been sewn shut."

"There will be plenty at the castle in Bath, for King Balin is noted for his hospitality. There should also be much more information about events in the east. The closer we get to Londinium the more we should learn. Bath is the furthest bastion of those aligned to Uther, and Balin was one of his friends. Morrigan told me she is using both Colm and Augustus. She plans on trying to unite their armies to march against the west. She told me she is trying to unite them, though her plans are as changeable as a day in May." As if on cue the clouds scudding across the sky broke, the rain stopped, and the sun suddenly shone about them. "And you see what I mean about changeable weather." Myrdden chuckled.

"Can you tell us more of this Morrigan?" Maeve asked. "What you told us after we arrived on these shores didn't give us much real information regarding her."

Myrdden thought for a moment. "Well, as I've said before, Morrigan and I both come from Atlantis. Atlantis was a large island continent that was in what is now the Maer Nicht. A narrow neck of land connected the main island to this island. My home was on the southern part of the continent. Morrigan's was in the north.

"When I was a youth a great rock fell from the sky and caused the major part of Atlantis to sink. Both Morrigan and I as youths were placed in a small boat in order to escape the destruction. Unfortunately, my parents were killed before they could reach me and the boat. Her parents were in the boat with her, but were unable to tie themselves in for safety. In the battering they got from the sea both were killed. I believe it has affected her mind.

"Both of us possess certain powers natural to those born in Atlantis, but looked on as magic in this land. Llyonesse is still connected to Cornwall, but now lies under the sea. "

Unlike you, Maeve, Morrigan takes an unusually great pride in her beauty and powers. She has turned her obsession with herself into an unnatural desire for more power and to be a queen worshipped for her beauty. She plans eventually on ruling all of this land and of Ireland. What stands in her way are the armies of the west. To accomplish her plans she must conquer our armies, those of Alba, and then of Ireland. In order to do that she must have a large army herself. The stories we have heard of the blonde woman who is privy to Augustus ear, and the dark haired woman in league with Colm an Dubh, I would say are the same person." He paused. "And that person is Morrigan. She will call herself by many names, but it is the same person no matter what the name."

Kevin nodded and said, almost to himself, "A rose is a rose is a rose."

"Exactly." Myrdden agreed. "If you called it a lily of the field a rose would still be a rose. It cannot hide its true nature any more than Morrigan can hide hers whether she is called Lilith, Moira, or Morrigan."

Maeve threw her hood back and shook her head to loosen her auburn hair. Kevin looked at her and said, "When you do that you excite me."

Maeve gave him a sidelong glance, and smiled, "And why do you think I do it, acushla? I love to excite you. When I stop exciting you I will be very worried."

"You do that on purpose, don't you?"

"Of course. I know your weakness."

"You do, eh? And what is my weakness?"

Maeve laughed and turned her head to him as she smiled, "Me." She said.

Kevin sighed and answered her smile. "You're right." He said. "And it has been since I first saw you bending over me in the passageway at Dun Rowans. I'll never be the same as I was before I saw you."

"Good." Maeve nodded. "I want you the way you are now. That other Kevin was not a nice person, though I found myself drawn to him in a different way. Now you are the pulse of my heart, for I bear a part of both of us within."

"You are with child?"

"Aye. The next heir to Leinster will be ours."

Kevin smiled as he rode on with a new thought on his mind.

* * *

The hills turned into a plain and they rode by the blossoming rhododendrons that lined the hedgerows of the valley. To their right was a meandering river, and ahead on the hillside stood the village of Bath. Atop the hill stood the palisade and a wooden structure they recognized as the castle of Balin. A rift in the clouds allowed a shaft of sunlight to highlight the wooden walls and keep. In the fields on each side the peasants stopped their digging and watched the troop of horsemen with curiosity. As they rode the clouds again broke, the sun came out, and the day began to warm up. They discarded their cloaks and rode in the trappings that set off their ranks.

A stone bridge allowed them to cross the river and enter the town of Bath. On their left was the building built by the Romans to house the mineral springs, and as they rode up the narrow muddy streets of the village the thatch of the roofs still dripped the last of the rain onto the streets. The old women looked up from their preparation of supper at the sight of the troop of travelers passing their doors. One look and they knew these were not bards on the way to entertain. Since what happened at the castle was none of their business they went back to stirring and cutting as they prepared the stew for the evening meal. Gossip for the evening, wonder at what the visitors were about, but no matter what it was their lot would not change a whit.

As they approached the palisade the gate opened to allow entrance, and closed once they were inside. As their horses were taken to the stables a page led them into the castle and the Great Hall. Balin sat in a large chair a little removed from the long table that would later serve as their dining table. He smiled. "Greetings, Merlin. I heard you were in Cymru and wondered if you would honor me with a visit. I understand your companions are foreigners."

Merlin chuckled. "Ah, Balin, you ever have the dry wit. I suspect your spies have already told you these two are the heirs to the throne of Leinster, and these are their men at arms and guards. We have already found them to be necessary. Prince Kevin MacMurrough and Maeve Bean MichMurrough, this is King Balin of Bath."

"I am honored to meet you, Sire, and bring greetings from my father, Dermot Murrough, King of Leinster."

Balin nodded his acceptance. "Welcome Prince Kevin. When you return to your own land give your father my greetings and best wishes." He nodded to Maeve. "Welcome Princess Maeve. May your stay be pleasant." The amenities finished he turned his attention to Merlin. "I presume you come to find out what is happening to our east?"

"Indeed. I can give news of the west, but it is important for the west to understand what is happening in Londinium and in the fen country to the north. I understand Augustus is camped there and preparing an army to war on those of us in the west."

Balin frowned and nodded. "Aye. That is true. It is not the worst of it, however. There is a woman in Londinium who is fomenting trouble with the one who now calls himself the Black Dragon. He has sent scouting parties as far as Bath to ascertain the lay of the land, and how many troops may be available to us." He paused.

"But you are tired from your journey. Allow me to open the baths to you that you may refresh yourselves. Once you have enjoyed the bath, and we have supped, we can better discuss what is happening to our east, and make plans for the future."

* * *

A traveling troupe of entertainers had arrived while Kevin and his friends were in the bath. The meal provided by Balin was sumptuous, and the tables filled the Great Hall so those associated with the castle could enjoy both it and the entertainment. Joints of beef, mutton, lamb, chickens, and guinea hens, interspersed with platters of the local vegetables, were placed at easy reach of the diners. As usual, the bards sang the old songs and brought the news of events in the east through newly minted songs and poems.

It was very apparent little escaped Balin's notice. Even as his attention seemed riveted on the entertainment, he caught Kevin's use of the fork he had brought with him. "Interesting device." Balin said. "Perhaps you can tell my blacksmith how to make me one of those. It would save me cutting my mouth every now and then." The comment was made without taking his eyes off the acrobats in the center of the room.

Later, when the company had been dismissed and the tables replaced only he and his guests remained in the Great Hall. "From what the bard said tonight there are interesting things are happening in the east." Balin said as he turned in his chair and put one leg on the table. "I like not the story of the raven tressed mistress of the usurper in Londinium. I like less the story of the flaxen haired trollop in the Fen Country. Neither of them bode us good, I ween." He took a flagon of mead and sipped it thoughtfully. Turning to Merlin he asked, "What do you think, sir? Are we in trouble yet?"

Merlin didn't answer immediately, but thought of the implications of the news brought by the entertainers. "I don't believe so." He answered, his words emerging slowly as he continued to think. "Much depends on Morrigan's strategy, for it is her, you know." He smiled crookedly. "Her in both places. She has abilities others do not possess because of her lineage. I believe she is going to try to unite the two factions into one big army. This will be a problem, though, for Augustus considers himself the rightful leader after his father. "

Colm an Dubh," he smiled without humor, "now dubbed an Dragan, is a usurper. It will be a while before she can bring them together, if ever. If alliance fails, as well it may, she will pit them against each other in warfare." He shook his head. "This I doubt she wants, for it would decimate both armies and render ineffective her desires to take over this land. She recognizes this, for she is very astute in these matters." He paused as he shook his head, "No. I do not believe we are in trouble at this time. I believe we have time to consolidate the forces of the west once we find the rightful king."

Balin smiled as he placed the flagon on the table. "Well. I know I'm not the one. I went to Swansea and tried to pull the sword from the anvil." He shook his head at the memory. "I strained so much I almost busted a gut. I couldn't budge it at all." He chuckled mirthlessly. "I doubt you will find anyone who could move it a fingerwidth, let alone pull it out completely."

"We shall see, Balin, we shall see. I believe I have someone who will be able to accomplish the feat."

"Aye, Merlin, but will the other kings follow him?"

"I believe they will, once they know who he really is."

"For all our sakes, I hope so." He picked up the flagon, refilled by an almost invisible servant, and raised it to his lips. "Now, what should our strategy be?"

"Lord Kevin is part of our strategy. He has some knowledge of the future king, and of his reign. What is your reading of this period in his life, Kevin?"

Kevin shrugged his shoulders and shook his head. "I know little of his life prior to his pulling the sword from the stone and anvil. Once he has appeared on the scene by doing that I have a reasonable idea regarding certain events in his life and reign. I know many things he should not do, and many things he should. If we can prevent him from doing those things that will lead to future trouble, his kingdom should live long and be prosperous. If he insists on not following our advice..." Kevin shook his head sadly, "things will go badly for his kingdom, for it will disappear within no more than twenty years, and he will have only one son, who will kill him in battle. It is not a pretty picture, and I can see it going in two different directions depending on his actions."

Balin listened intently, nodding as Kevin spoke. "But what of the kingdom and army to the east?"

"I see the future king dominating the entire island, if he does not take certain actions. Unfortunately, there is a beautiful woman involved, and this is his half-sister, though he doesn't know it at the moment."

"Then he must be warned of her."

Kevin nodded agreement. "Aye, King Balin, he must be, and he will be."

* * *

"Enough of practice, young Arthur, leave us move on to another sport." Kevin lowered his sword, a movement echoed by Arthur. "I believe it would be a good afternoon's endeavor to see if we are smarter than the fish."

Arthur smiled broadly as he removed the protective covering from his head. "I thank you, Sir Kevin, for the lesson. I further thank you for including me in this other sport. I shall gather my pole and gladly join you."

"And I shall see the cook about a bit of food to tide us over as we search for the wily trout that inhabits yonder river."

They ground tied their horses as they went to the riverbank. "Careful, Sir Kevin, for you know it is dangerous to immerse yourself in water."

"Why do you say that?" Kevin asked as he baited a hook.

"Why, all the old wives tell the stories of those who were immersed and then died. Water is deadly to the human body. I thought everyone knew that."

"'Tis but an old wives tale, Arthur. Water will not harm us. We drink water, we use it for cooking; we use it in many ways. Why, if we do not die when we take it inside is it bad when we use it on the outside?"

Arthur pondered the question as he baited his hook. "I shall have to think of this." He said as he cast the hook into a deep pond. "I trust the old women for they have become wise over the years. I also trust you. I know not which of you has the proper answer to the question. AHA! I think I have something." Arthur's pole was bending as the line tightened. He played the fish and slowly brought it toward the bank, pulling the line with his free hand as his other held the pole. Finally the fish was near the shore.

Arthur bent over to retrieve his catch, sliding his hand down the line toward the hook. As he did so a ram, in the field to service the ewes, spotted the appealing target. Without warning the ram ran toward Arthur's unprotected rear and, just as he was reaching the trout, butted him into the pool. Pole and line were forgotten as Arthur began flailing the water, dipping beneath the surface to come up spluttering and gasping for breath. Kevin's weapons were dropped to the ground as he dove into the pool after his squire. Staying beneath the water he grasped Arthur's legs and turned him around so he could come up behind him. Catching Arthur across the chest to keep his head above water Kevin used his free arm to swim to shore. Arthur lay on the greensward coughing up the water he had swallowed.

He finally lay supine and looked at Kevin's worried face bending over him. "Thank you, Sir Kevin, but I fear now we will both die. We have both been immersed in the stream."

Kevin smiled. "I think not, Arthur. You will see. We will survive, and be the wiser for our ordeal. Now, let up cover with our cloaks so we don't chill. That might lead to some severe disease, but it would not be caused by our being in the water. Why don't you gather some dry wood for a fire? I believe I have the makings in my bratt."

While Arthur gathered the small wood Kevin got out the flint and his scian, found some dry grass, and began to lay the tinder for the smaller twigs Arthur had brought. In moments there was a good enough blaze to add larger pieces of dry wood.

Looking at the pond Kevin saw Arthur's pole near the shore. The trout was still hooked. He smiled, "It looks as though we have some meat to go with the rest of our lunch. A good meal will set things right and warm up our insides, eh Arthur?"

Arthur was still apprehensive, "If you say so, Sir Kevin."

Kevin placed a hand on his shoulder. "Trust me, my friend, trust me." He turned at the sound of a horse approaching.

"Sire." Aione tried not to sound as though he was scolding Kevin, but his voice betrayed him. "I was worried. You didn't tell me you were going off alone. You should have let me know so I would be there to help you in case of need."

"I'm sorry, my friend, I had other things on my mind. I'll try not to neglect you of your duty in the future. Meanwhile, come join us in our meal. Arthur has caught a trout that we will cook to go along with the provender the cook gave us."

Aione dismounted. "Sire, your clothing is wet, as is Arthur's. What, pray tell, has caused this?"

Kevin smiled. "Arthur was pushed into the stream by that ram." He pointed to the ram that was now eyeing one of the ewes. "Arthur couldn't swim, so I went in the water to save him."

"Swim?" Aione shook his head, "I know not the word, but I do know you have put your life at risk by immersing yourself in the river. I have heard of a woman who befriends the people of Faerie, and has a gift of healing. I shall ride for her immediately. You may still be saved."

Kevin shook his head. "No, Aione, stay with us. No harm will come to us because of this unexpected wetting. I give you my word. Sit. Open the package of food, and we will all eat. We may even catch some more fish to take back to Caer Garda with us." With some trepidation Aione sat and began eating, eyeing both Arthur and Kevin as though waiting for them to fall dead before his very eyes.

Nothing happened. Both Kevin and Arthur appeared in the best of health, nothing seemed amiss after their unexpected swim, so Aione calmed down and joined in the conversation regarding the coming tournament in Swansea. The town below the Caer was anxiously waiting for news as to who of the warriors would attempt to win the prize for the best jouster. Instead of the normal sharpened iron points the lances would be blunted with a padded pillow of leather fronting a specially made blunted lance.

Aione, who had been in town only that morning, reported that the people were expecting Cai, young as he was, to win one of the prizes. They recognized him as a warrior who was already proficient with sword or lance. They also recognized, with the ever present threat of the Saecsen host encamped both north and south of Londinium, to use the real tools of war would cause the death of some of those taking place in this tourney. Best to use blunt edged swords and pillow covered lances. Bruises gained from being knocked from a horse, or from the edge of a blunt sword, would heal. Once buried, always buried. The loss of a good fighting man was something no one wanted. Aione was full of the information he had gained as he had had a flagon of ale at the town's public house; a meeting place for most of the men at one time or another throughout the morning.

"Oh, yes," he said around a mouthful of cold venison, "I almost forgot. When I left Caer Garda the Lady Maeve was in pain. Some of the ladies said she was going to give birth. They told me to let you know." He made a wry face, "Sorry, m'lord, but the news flying about in Llianfir was so interesting it slipped my mind."

Kevin half smiled as he stood to his feet. "I understand." He said. "To a fighting man the events going on in the life of a woman are of less consequence than the news of a tourney or a battle. Pack these things up and come back with Arthur. I'll ride on ahead and see how things are at the Caer."

Aione had a rueful smile on his face as he stood up. "Aye, Sir, I'll follow in a few minutes." Arthur stood near his horse, his body shaking with subdued laughter at Aione's discomfort. As Kevin rode off Aione looked at him. "My suggestion, young squire, is that you keep your mirth to yourself. If I hear so much as one chuckle you will feel the flat of my sword on the same area you felt the horns of the ram. Be ye warned. Now, let us be on our way. Mayhap our lord will have news of a new heir to Leinster."

* * *

"Ah, my Dragan, have you seen this?" Morrigan held out a sheet of parchment on which the announcement of the tourney at Swansea was printed. "One of our men brought this back from Bath. Not being able to find you, and realizing the importance of this announcement, he brought it to me."

An Dubh took the parchment as he gave her a sour look. "Many things seem to find their way to your hands before they find mine." He commented petulantly. "Let me see what this means." He read the announcement slowly. He tossed the parchment on the table as he shrugged. "And what bruits this to me? It is a tourney in Swansea open to all warriors in Cymru and the barony of Lord Balin, those with whom we are at war though we do not fight at the moment."

Morrigan arched an eyebrow, a half smile on her face. "Ah, my Dragan, it could mean much to you." She said as she shook her head slowly from side to side.

"Why, pray tell, does a tourney for the Cymru warriors have anything to do with our Saecsen warriors?"

Morrigan sat down on the opposite side of the table. "It could mean much, love. It says the weapons will be blunted so they do not lose manpower through their warriors being killed in the tourney. Their lances will have blunt tips covered with flax stuffed stockings of sheep skin. Their swords will have blunt edges. They will be wearing protective coverings to ward against bruises or broken limbs.

"Now if some of our warriors disguised as Cymruan warriors were to enter the lists with metal pointed tips covered with thin skin. The tip will cut through when it hits and they will lose a warrior. Our swords could be made with a false blunt edge that can be discarded just before they engage the Cymruan foe. In such a contest our men would easily defeat and kill their warriors so when the final battle come their armies will be decimated. We could march through Cymru without losing many men. Once Cymru is conquered what is to keep us from Alba; and then your beloved Leinster?"

She sat back in the chair and gazed at him with hooded eyes as he digested her plan. Finally he nodded, a thoughtful look on his face. "Yes." He said slowly. "It might work, though I doubt the warriors who go to the tourney would return to us at its finish."

"True," Morrigan offered, "but before they died they would take four or five of the enemy with them. Those are good odds. We could start our smith making those swords now so they will be ready for the tourney next spring."

An Dubh head bobbed slowly up and down as he thought of the inroads such a plan would cause. A slow smile spread across his face, and Morrigan knew she had won; he would once again do as she wished.

* * *

Kevin burst into the room where Maeve lay. Cradled between her arm and side was the small head of the latest Murrough. She smiled at him as he looked at the sleeping infant, "Aye, love, there is a new heir to the throne at Dun Rowans, and what are you going to name your son?"

Kevin smiled broadly at the news. "We'll name him after his grandfather, Dermot. He will be known as Dermot Patrick Murrough. And how do you feel now, lovely Maeve?"

"Tired, sore, and altogether happy. How did you find out about the birth?"

Kevin chuckled, and told her the story of Aione's visit to streamside. "He was more interested in telling me the gossip concerning the tourney than in giving me news about my wife."

Maeve nodded knowingly. "Aye. 'Tis what is on men's minds right now even though the tourney is months away. But now, love, leave me. I have labored hard this morning and needs must rest. Best you be off to practice swordplay for the tourney. Leave, and let me sleep. Bridget will stay with me while I sleep, and if anything untoward happens she will let you know." Kevin bent, kissed her gently, kissed his son, and paused to look back as he stood in the doorway. "Go, love. I am in good hands."

chapter 4
The Tourney at Swansea

May bloomed. The hillsides were covered with the bursting blossoms of rhododendron, gorse, and field flowers galore. The time of the tourney had arrived. To the west of Swansea Ethelbert had prepared the lists. The field lay in an open area large enough to have the preparation tents for the participants, the galleries and pavilions where nobles could sit, a viewing area for the common folk, and the fields on which the games would be played. With all that there was plenty of room for the vendors to set up their tents and tables where the crowds could buy of their wares during the lull between contests.

To the east of town the camping area where the tents of the kings, warriors, and their retinues were to stay was laid out on a large field. This field was large enough to allow all plenty of room for themselves and their retinue. As each group of nobles and warriors arrived they rode through the town. Some distance ahead of the royal party were pages and squires with the colorful flags associated with each of the kings and their followers.

All knew in advance the section of the plain they would occupy. Once there the flags were placed before the tents of their owners so all would know where each warrior or noble was bedded. The same flag would accompany its owner when he was embattled on the field of the tourney or when he sat in the gallery and watched.

The majority of participants had arrived by the end of the second day before the tourney. Banquet tables were set up in several of the larger tents, as the kings vied with each other to see who could present the best feast. Each had arrived with the fruit of his own land as an offering for the feast he would present. The most anticipated of all the offerings were the barrels of heady ales and beers produced by the various small kingdoms. Sampling these was the most popular of the pastimes during the hiatus before the first of the games would begin.

Arthur rode ahead of Kevin and Maeve with the flag with Kevin's coat of arms proudly floating above him. Both Kevin and Maeve were dressed in their personal armor. Not far behind rode Aione and Kyle, their eyes alert to anything that might seem untoward as the group approached their allotted area. Since Caer Garda was in the kingdom of Anglesy their tents were near those occupied by King Damas. Not far behind were Sir Ector and Sir Cai, Cai following the flag of St. George since he as yet had no coat of arms. Instead, he would wear those of Ector until his own were granted.

Each of the fighting men, warriors included, wore the protective covering made popular by the Romans: a thick leather cuirass studded with overlapping iron rings; rings that would turn the edge of a blade, though not stop the puncture of a metal tipped lance. The cuirass worn by the kings was of beaten bronze, but few of the warriors were wealthy enough to afford such an expensive device.

It was early morning when Kevin stepped from the tent, a morning that was dawning fair and calm. Behind him Maeve was suckling young Dermot, now all of six months old and fast showing the attributes of his forebears. As he stood looking at the crowd of tents surrounding him Aione stepped to his side. "Don't you ever sleep?" Kevin asked with a smile, "It seems whenever I go anywhere you are my shadow."

"Aye, Sire, and always shall be." He answered then nodded toward the center of their circle of tents. "Kyle has breakfast ready, Sire. If you and Lady Maeve are ready to break the night's fast." Even as he spoke Aione's head was turning to watch all going on around him.

Myrdden appeared at his tent opening, stretched, and sniffed the morning air. "Aha. Besides the freshness of this morning I believe I smell the enticing aroma of ham being broiled over a fire. Am I right Aione?"

Aione nodded. "Aye, Lord Myrdden. You are right. We only wait the ladies Maeve and Fiona, and Sir Timothy."

Kevin laughed. "Lady Maeve is almost ready, I believe, but if Sir Timothy and Lady Fiona wish to sleep, and miss breakfast, it means all the more for us. Ah, here is the Lady Maeve and young Dermot. Now, my friend, we can break our fast. Afterward we will ride to look over the tourney field."

* * *

The group drew their horses to a halt just inside the entrance to the tourney grounds. Kevin and Tim were seeing the lists for the first time, having only read about the jousts in the literature of their time. Their heads moved as they slowly scanned the entire area. Tents where the participants could prepare themselves were set up at each end of an area the size of a football field. Down the center, separating two paths, was a wooden fence that stood about a yard high. Off to one side was an open grandstand already decorated with the flags of the nobility who would sit in the gallery. The whole area had assumed an air of the festivity that would take place the following day.

Besides the flags of the nobility there were buntings of various colors flying from poles set in a circle around the lists. Ropes were tied to these poles so spectators could watch from an area opposite the grandstand. Nearby were areas set aside for the sword fights, and a special arena backed by a hillside was set up for the archers. Only the nobles would joust with the blunted wooden lances. Others, like Aione, would contend in the sword fights. The archers would have their own contest to see who might be the best with bow and arrow since each king had brought only his best archers. Besides the contests a joust was a good place to get to know others of your skills with whom you might be allied in the not too far distant future.

Tim sighed and shook his head in wonder at the sight. "Amazing, isn't it?" He asked of Kevin. "I never imagined it would look this way when I was reading about these things. I always thought it was a somewhat drab occurrence. Instead…" He looked around him at the flags and bunting, "look at all that color, and there's an excitement in the air I can almost feel."

Kevin nodded his agreement. "Aye. It's far different in person than in the books. Of course, the black and white woodcuts didn't show all the flags, pennants, and bunting. I think this is going to be a fun week, and an interesting one." He nudged his heels into the flanks of his horse and moved forward into the tourney area itself. The others followed.

Behind the spectator viewing area merchants were already setting up their tents, tables, cooking areas, and places they could sell the merchandise they had brought from their own kingdoms. Kevin smiled as he noted the animated conversations between merchants who sometimes only saw each other on occasions such as this, or at the fairs held in several locations throughout the many kingdoms. Not all were friendly conversations, as when someone felt another person was intruding on their space, but there were guards policing the area so no dispute went unsettled for long.

"It's a good thing we're using blunted lances." Kevin said as he rode the length of the list, turned, and looked back along the fence. "A horse can get pretty fast before it gets to the center, and a metal point on a lance could skewer another rider if it hit right. We don't want to lose any fighters in this tourney. What we want to do is to be able to recognize the best we have. There's going to be a battle coming up, probably with the Saecsen, and we don't want to lose it."

He turned his head toward the vendor's area and sniffed. "It must be close to noon. At least my stomach says it is. Let's go over and see if there is anything ready to eat. After all, someone has to feed all those people putting up their tents."

He was right, for two of the tents where one could buy meals were already doing a lively business with other shopkeepers. All moved aside as the riders dismounted. The proprietor scurried to where they stood at the rough plank he had put up for a bar. "Aye, my lords. Might I be of service?"

"And what might be your offering today?" Aione inquired.

"We have both roast pork and beef. Or if you would rather I could broil a loin especially for you over the coals. It wouldn't take too long if you'd like to wait."

Kevin nodded. "I could go for a steak right now." He said. "Let's do that."

"Begging your pardon, Sir." The proprietor said after calling to his wife to putt the steaks on the homemade grill. "I thought the tourney was for the kingdoms of Cymru."

"It is." Kevin said. "It is to find out who our best fighters are from the several kingdoms."

"I thought as much." The man answered. "But this morning, early, several men dressed as warriors of Orkades were here." He shook his head. "But they weren't men of Orkades no matter they tried to appear as such."

"And what makes you think that?" Kevin asked as Myrdden joined him.

"Well, Sire, I judge men by the way they're shod. Men of Cymru, though they come from other kingdoms, have a certain style shoe they wear. I can tell which of the kingdoms a man is from by looking at his shoes. You, for example, are coming from Anglesy, for you wear shoes made in that area. These men wore shoes of a Saecsen make. I fought with Uther against them. In the battles I was able to take note of the type shoe they wear. These men, there were four of them, were trying to make me believe they were from Orkades, but their shoes betrayed them."

"What you say is very interesting." Myrdden spoke up. "But how is it you know so much about shoes?"

The man smiled broadly. “I am a shoemaker, Sire. But right now,” he looked at the crowds milling around the tourney areas, “there is little call for shoes at my shop. So I help my wife with the serving here. Besides, this is more fun than sitting in an empty cobbler’s shop.”

Myrdden laughed heartily. “You speak truth. This is much more exciting than an empty room. We thank you for your information; it may prove very valuable to us. Here, take this for your trouble, and if you see them again while we are here I would appreciate your pointing them out.”

The proprietor bowed deeply as he took the coins Myrdden offered him. “Thank you, my lord, I will keep a sharp eye for them, and let you know immediately I see them. Ah, here comes your food. Enjoy, Sire. I know you will, for my wife is the best cook in Swansea.” With that he went off to take care of his other customers. The nobility had been served, now the common folk could eat.

As they began to eat Myrdden warned. “It would seem one of their two kings has sent men to spy on us. We must be on our guard. We know an Dubh has been trying to kill Kevin, and probably Fiona as well. He doesn’t know of Dermot yet, so I don’t believe he is sending spies or assassins against Kevin at this time. I feel the fine hand of Morrigan in this. I doubt an Dubh would come up with the idea of disguising his men as ours and sending them to take part in this tourney. I just wonder what devious plan she has come up with.” He paused, then shrugged. “Well, nothing we can do about it right now. We’ve been warned, that will have to suffice for the moment. Meanwhile, Aione and Kyle, be on double alert while the tourney is on. They will give themselves away, have no fear.”

* * *

It had rained during the night, but morning dawned bright and fair. Once having broken their fast the camp emptied rapidly as everyone headed through the village to the lists. Seats had been set up in the front row for the kings and their higher nobles. Smaller seats had been set up behind to accommodate the lesser nobles. Across the way and behind the ropes the standing crowd of commoners noisily awaited the first of the jousts. According to the roster that had been announced by pages, for many of the nobles and the majority of the common people could not read, there were to be three jousts with lances. These were to be followed by three demonstrations of swordsmanship by warriors from various kingdoms, followed by the first of the archery contests. After breaking for dinner a similar agenda was to be followed in the afternoon. The contests would last for the week, at the end of which the major winners would be announced.

Aione and his men lounged against the sides of the pavilion. Three were on one side, three on the other. Though they appeared to be mere spectators they were watching every new entrant with interest. As the trumpet sounded to announce the first joust of the day the two warriors took their places at either end of the long strip, one on each side of the fence running down the middle. While they wore helmets of metal their only armor was the thick rawhide cuirass covered with metal rings, and the thick rawhide shield emblazoned with the arms of their barony. The trumpet sounded a different note and both men spurred their horses, thundering down the line toward each other, padded lance tips aimed at the other rider. They met with a crash as lances splintered against the shield each held up to fend off the other's lance, but the warrior from Pembroke lost his stirrups and was pushed over the tail of his horse to land ignominiously on the ground as his steed thundered on. Loud applause and cheers broke out for the warrior from Swansea who had won the right to go on to the next level of the contest.

The next two warriors were more experienced, for neither was unhorsed on the first run. New lances replaced the broken ones and they rode down the line once again, only to have both again sitting on their horses as they reached the ends of the fence. A new set of lances, a new ride, and the warrior from Anglesy unseated the one from Gore. The winner of the third match, after two tries was from Bath.

With that the area was cleared for the sword fights that would follow. There would be a number of bouts with short swords of about two and a half feet in length. Later there would be bouts with the longer two-handed swords. All bouts would be with blunted swords, and last until one of the two had demonstrated more prowess by being able to touch his opponent more times in fifteen minutes. An hourglass was set up with enough sand in it to last the fifteen minutes allotted for the contests. Off to one side, dressed as men from Orkades, four warriors huddled together, eyes narrowed, as they watched the first bout.

"Are you sure these swords will work?" Mordant whispered. "They seem to be pretty blunt to me."

"You know as well as I the covering over the real blade isn't really metal. When you strike a blow, even to the shield, it will crumble to powder and you will have a real sword in your hand. The men of Cymru are not as strong as we Saecsens, so you should be able to disable your opponent easily. Besides, we went to the witch woman and she put a spell on our swords that no one would see the powder or the wounds the sword makes. She is very powerful, more powerful than any here, so we are safe."

"That may be true, but I'll be glad when we have finished our matches and can go back. I feel very vulnerable in the midst of so many we will be fighting. I have a bad feeling about what we are doing."

"You do not believe we are in the right?"

"I believe we are in the right. Yet I fear we will be caught and never make it back to our own land."

"Worry not. The witch woman has given us her promises we will return with honor. There are many of their fighters here. We only have to disable a few, and those should be their best. Watch closely for we wish to make sure we keep their best from being able to fight."

"I'll watch, but I still fear for our future."

Argonan smiled cruelly. "Good. Fear is the best ally of a fighter. You will do well, Mordant, never fear." They watched as the first bout came to an end with the warrior from Pembroke being declared winner for having the most body hits.

After the first of the archery contests the crowd dispersed to the dining area where more tents had been set up to handle them. Aione and his men followed Myrdden and their watch to the tent of the man they had seen the day before. He bustled over to them and led them to a rude table to one side where he signaled a lackey to bring bowls of the thick stew to the party. This done he turned to Myrdden. "They are here, my lord. I saw them only moments ago. They dress as men of Orkades, but they still wear the shoes they wore yesterday."

Myrdden nodded. "Given your experience in battle, what contests do you think they plan on entering?"

"Three are dressed for the sword fighting, the other for jousting. I saw this for he is dressed as a warrior might dress, but he is very close to the others. It was singular for they did not visit with others dressed as men of Orkades, but held to themselves completely. This was suspicious to me, so I examined them more closely. They are the same four I saw yesterday."

Myrdden smiled and handed some coins to the man. "Thank you, your information is valuable to me. Keep being our eyes and try to point them out to Finbar. Finbar, you will remain with, what is your name, sirrah?"

"Armand, my lord."

Myrdden nodded. “Remain with Armand and he will point these men out to you. Once you recognize them and their garb you may return to show us who to watch for.”

“Aye, my lord. It will be done.”

* * *

The man who called himself Orkin of Orkades was second in the lists for jousting. As he thundered down his side of the fence, buffered lance held steady ahead of him, he smiled. A direct hit on the mailed cuirass would put his opponent out of the tourney, and perhaps out of the coming war, permanently. His opponent, Paidraig of Poole was, however, a man of some experience. The stout leather shield deflected the blow, but drove the padding far down the body of the lance, exposing the sharp iron point the pad had hidden. Myrdden saw it immediately, called it to Ethelbert’s attention, and the man was immediately brought down from his horse by the stewards at that end of the fence. Both man and lance were brought to the royal box where Ethelbert examined the tip.

“So!” Ethelbert turned to the warrior. “What is your excuse for this attempt at killing your opponent?”

“Myrdden interrupted. “Look at his shoes, my lord king. Those are not Orkadian shoes. Those are shoes worn by the Saecsen. This man is not of Orkades.”

Ethelbert nodded his acceptance. “I know not why you are here but to deliver death or injury to the warriors of Cymru. For your crime against our tourney I sentence you to death. Guard, you may take him away and carry out the sentence.”

Myrdden watched as the guard led the man from the grounds. “There are still three more, Ethelbert. I believe, from what I have been told, they will take part in the sword fighting. We can expect more attempts on the lives or health of our champions.”

“And we will deal with them in the same manner.” Ethelbert’s voice was stern.

The warriors who were participating in the sword fighting contests had two swords they could use. One was the short sword; the second was the heavy two-handed sword with a blade that could be up to four feet long. The afternoon contests were with the shorter of the two, a weapon more often carried on one’s person. The longer weapon was used more in actual battle than in these contests.

Mordant of Orkades took his short sword and entered the tourney area. Myrdden's eyes narrowed as he took in the man's garb. He was dressed as an Orkadian, of that there was no doubt. His shoes, however, resembled those of the man who had been killed earlier. The two warriors circled each other warily, swords held ready for the first blow, shields held before them to parry the blow of the opponent. Mordant swung his sword in a short arc, hitting the shield of his opponent. As promised the frangible covering the actual blade turned to a powder to expose the sharp edges.

No one seemed to notice, a fact that intrigued Myrdden, who had seen the outer cover disintegrate. His lips thinned as he whispered words in an arcane language. Now the blade shone brightly as Mordant swung again. The other's shield came up to ward off the blow as his sword was swung sideways, aimed at Mordant's left side. The edge of Mordant's sword sliced into the heavy leather of the shield, stuck, and as he tried to free it he received three quick blows to his own ribs. By this time Myrdden's counterspell had allowed all to see Mordant had a real sword rather than the blunted one allowed in the tourney. He quickly met the same fate as his companion.

"Sir Cai." The captain of the tourney called as he walked to where Cai was sitting. "Sir Cai, there has been some trouble in the sword fighting. Would you be so kind as to prepare to be one of the contestants in the third bout?"

Cai hadn't expected to have to fight until the following day. "How long do I have?" He asked.

"There is a delay right now due to irregularities in the first bout. I would estimate you would have two glasses." He was referring to the manner of keeping time for the tourney by use of an hourglass.

"I am honored you have asked me. I will be ready." It was only after the captain had left he notice his own sword was not handy. Not expecting to be called for this day's fight he had left the blunted sword back in his tent. "Arthur." He called. "Would you go back to camp and bring the tourney sword? I will need it for the third bout. I believe it is under the cot."

Arthur nodded. "Yes, sire. I'll fetch it."

Since the lists were outside town on the west and the camp was at least a mile to the east of Swansea the round trip would take close to an hour. Arthur had heard the captain say there would be at least two glasses turned, but that would be a half hour. He thought of this as he hurried through the town. He didn't believe he had enough time. It was then he spied the sword resting in the anvil. He hurried over to it. It was a blunted sword, for the edges were rounded instead of sharp. He smiled as he took the hilt in his hand and lifted upward. The sword slid from the stone and anvil as though it were only butter. He sighed as he looked at it, then turned and hurried back to the lists.

"Here you are, Sir Cai. Here is a blunted sword that you might use. I didn't have time to go all the way back to camp, so I brought this instead."

Cai looked at the sword Arthur handed him. His eyes widened and his face lighted up. He held the sword above his head as he ran toward the pavilion where the kings sat. "I have the sword in the anvil." He shouted. "I am the rightful king of Cymru."

"May we see the sword." Ethelbert asked as Cai stopped before the royal pavilion. Cai handed it to him. "This is the sword, my lords." He said as he handed it to them to examine. Turning back to Cai he asked, "And when did you acquire this sword?"

"A few moments ago, my liege. I had left my own at camp, not expecting to fight until the morrow. When asked I knew I didn't have enough time to go back, so I was able to get this one instead. Having it makes me the rightful king."

"Not so fast, young warrior." Bagdemus of Pembroke broke in. "Who, pray tell, saw you take this sword from the stone?"

"Why, no one, my lord. All are here at the tourney. Yet, as you can see, I have the sword."

Bagdemus nodded, a wry smile on his face. "Aye, you have the sword, of that there is no doubt. Yet no one saw you remove the sword from its resting place. I, for one, having tried to no avail to wrest it from the anvil, would enjoy seeing someone pull it out." He turned to the other kings. "Gentle sirs, I believe we should take this young warrior to the stone, insert the sword, and watch as he draws it again. Do you not agree?"

Damas nodded soberly. "Aye. That seems something that should be done. I, for one, will follow he who can pull it from its prison, but I must see it happen before I will believe it. I found I could not make it quiver when I tried. I see the sword, now I would like to see it removed before my very eyes."

Ethelbert spoke up. "You speak for all I believe. Come, let us go to the sword and do as Bagdemus and Damas suggest. I wish to see Sir Cai remove the sword as well."

The group mounted their horses and rode back to Swansea and the cathedral. "Now, Sir Cai, please insert the sword in the anvil." Cai bit his lips, took the sword, and placed the tip in the hole in the anvil. It was as though the anvil desired the sword, for the sword leaped from his hands and was drawn back to its original position.

"Interesting." Damas mused. "Now, Sir Cai, please draw the sword from the anvil." Cai grasped the hilt and pulled. There was no response from the sword. It didn't move. Cai mounted the anvil, one foot on each side of the sword, and pulled with all his might. Nothing happened.

Pelles looked at him. "It seems obvious it was not you who pulled the sword from its resting place. Please inform us of where you got it."

Cai dismounted from the stone. He hung his head before the kings. "I had forgotten my own sword," he said, "so I sent Arthur to get it. He is the one who brought this sword to me."

"Arthur?" Damas blurted, "He is but a commoner. How could he pull the sword?" He turned to look at the crowd and spotted Arthur, who was trying to hide behind Kevin. "Come here, young squire." He ordered. Arthur advanced. "Did you pull this sword from its resting place?"

"Aye, Sire. I'm sorry. I meant no harm." Arthur's voice quavered as he stood before Damas.

"You say you drew it from the anvil and stone." Ethelbert stepped to one side. He had a twisted smile on his face. "Pray demonstrate how you did this deed."

Arthur looked at Kevin, who nodded slightly. Taking a deep breath Arthur walked to the stone, placed his hand on the hilt of the sword, and lifted. The sword again came out of the stone as if it had been thrust into a pod of butter. He handed the sword to Ethelbert.

It was then Myrdden stepped forward. "My lords." He said. "You have seen King Arthur draw the sword from the anvil and stone. King Damas was wrong in his statement regarding Arthur. His true name is Arthur of Pendragon, for he is the lawful son of Uther of Pendragon, and as his heir is the true king of Cymru. I would ask all of you to swear fealty to him."

"Swear to a lowly squire?" Pelles was angry. "Why should I believe you that this stripling is who you say he is?"

Myrdden stared at Pelles, who lowered his gaze after a few long moments. "You should believe me because you have seen him do what you were unable to do, though you tried very hard to pull it yourself. You should believe me because you know who I am, and I am not one to tell an untruth. You should believe me because you know what the Lady who placed the stone there has told all of us regarding the one who pulls the sword from the stone. Now swear fealty and prepare to follow King Arthur. He will be trained in leadership, and he will lead us against the Saecsen, for it is his right so to do."

* * *

"So!" Morrigan said after the two remaining warriors had made their report. She took a deep breath, her face set, her eyes two slits of black, showing no white for the first time since an Dubh had fallen under her spell. He sat back on his throne and eyed her warily. "So!" she repeated. "At least he is a stripling, and should be easily led astray. Had he been one of the older warriors it would have been more difficult to bring him to me, but with a stripling it is no problem.

"Yet," She paused, her set face giving evidence of her thought processes. "Myrdden is mixed up in this. Of that I have no doubt. He and that insufferable foursome he has with him will attempt to undermine my attempts to bring him to my side." She shot a quick glance at an Dubh, "Our side, I mean."

"Just who is this Myrdden?" An Dubh asked. A note of caution was in his voice.

"Myrdden? A mage from the same country I come from. He has some powers, has many friends among the *Sidhe* and at Tir na nOg. I am not sure of this Kevin or Timothy the reports indicate are with him. I know not who they really are."

"Kevin is my half brother and heir to the throne of Leinster. Timothy is his man and friend. It is these two I must kill, and my half sister Fiona, to gain the throne for myself." An Dubh told her.

Morrigan stood tall and straight, as a look of triumph slowly spreading over her face. "Ah." She said. "That helps matters tremendously. You should have given me that information earlier. If we can eliminate Kevin and Timothy we may also get to Myrdden, and then we can have the boy to ourselves." She turned abruptly. "We must make peace with Augustus. Only then can we unite the two armies and expect to win a battle over the armies of Cymru."

"But Augustus hates me. I doubt he will offer to come under my command. After all, his father was the chief of both armies before either of us took control of what we have." An Dubh spread his hands wide as he explained his feelings.

"Then, my dear an Dragan," Morrigan's voice dripped with venom. "you will fall under his command. I care not who hates who. I want to win over Cymru, and if it means Augustus controls the armies, or you who control the armies, it makes little difference to me. It is my will that will survive over both of you. Do you understand me?"

An Dubh cowered back in his seat. He recognized a power greater than that of any mere mortal was facing him. He nodded as he licked suddenly dry lips. "I understand."

"Good! Now let us begin our preparations."

part two
The Caer Maellot

chapter 1
Arthur's Challenge

Morrigan was angry. Of that fact there could be no doubt. She paced the throne room as Colm an Dragan watched from the high seat. Her face was rigid, her eyes narrow slits matching her strained frown and thin lips. An Dubh sat back, eyeing her warily, wondering just when she would erupt. He knew she wouldn't disappoint him, and silently rued the day she appeared in court, and the events leading up to his becoming her thrall rather than she his.

She suddenly stopped and turned her fierce gaze on him. "It's been four years since that bastard son of Uther pulled the sword from that cursed stone. Four years that he's been playing up to the kings of Cymru. Now he's even gotten them to contribute workers and artisans to build a castle for him. High King indeed! Just because he's the only one who could pull the sword doesn't make him High King in my sight. But work has started on the castle, and it will be made of stone, not wood. That will make it harder to attack. And it is being built on top of a hill to make it even more difficult.

"I see your brother's fine hand in this. He has ideas that don't seem to come easily to you. Too, he seems to be advising that upstart in almost all his decisions. On top of that his brattling is four years old, and if anything happens to him the brat will take the throne, not you."

Colm cowered back in his throne. "What do you want me to do about it?" He asked, a quaver in his voice. "Kevin knows I've tried to have him killed. He knows how much I hate him. He certainly won't listen to me. If I went there he'd probably have me seized and beheaded."

"You and Augustus must come to terms. I've told you that time and time again, yet you dally and refuse to take my counsel."

"Augustus doesn't like me, in fact, he hates me. I took half his men away from him when Vertigorm was killed. Our armies are almost equal so if we fight both will come to naught."

"I didn't mention a fight. I said you must become allies. You and he must join forces so both armies will become united. Only then will we possibly defeat Arthur and the armies of Cymru that even now train to become united into one whole."

"But Augustus would never agree to become my captain. He's too proud."

Morrigan's eyes narrowed even further as her face showed her disgust with Colm. "Then, dear heart," her voice dripped with sarcasm, "as I have oft told you, if he will not become your captain you will become his. The armies must become as one, and I care not who leads that army. I care about defeating the armies of Cymru. Think it over, my sweet, and come to your own terms with my decision."

Morrigan returned to her pacing, face again set in thought as an Dubh, frustrated, clenched his fists in anger, but was fearful of saying anything further. Morrigan's rages frightened him for he had seen them often in the past four years, and some of his men lay dead now because of her. Over the course of the four years she had been with him he had found once he had lain with her there was little love in her heart for anyone but herself. Her desires were what mattered, and no other person ever entered her mind when she had set her heart on having something. Now her heart was set on Cymru, and his desires or fears had no bearing on her will.

"I must go to Tintagel." She said suddenly as she stopped her pacing.

"Tintagel? What and where is Tintagel?"

Morrigan sneered as she turned to face him. "Tintagel is where Queen Igraine lives. She is the mother of Arthur Pendragon, though he knows it not. She has a daughter, Arthur's half sister. She is a year or so older than Arthur, and quite lovely. If I can get Arthur to lay with her we might still accomplish our ends."

"She is his half sister? How, pray tell, could that be?"

"Because, dolt, she was wife to Gorlois whom Uther slew, and disguised as Gorlois he lay with Igraine and she conceived Arthur. Merlin, that bumbling idiot, took the babe immediately it was born and gave it to the keeping of a warrior to bring up. He didn't tell the warrior who the father was, or even that he had noble blood. He was raised as a commoner should be: not as a royal child. He now knows his father was Uther, as does every king in Cymru. He doesn't know his mother, or that he has a sister.

"Next month he is to have a meeting of those under his reign. Igraine will go for she never wed after the death of Gorlois so is the ruler of the lands over which Gorlois held fief. Neither does she know Arthur is her son. I will have her take the daughter, Maerie, with her. When Arthur sees her, if he is anything like his father, he will lust after her and have her at any cost. It will be a liaison made in Hell," she grimaced in what became an evil smile, "though he will not realize it until it is too late." She nodded as she made up her mind. "Yes. I will leave for Tintagel. Have the servants get my things ready. I will ride as soon as they are prepared." She turned on her heel and left the room to prepare herself for the long ride to Penzance.

* * *

Shortly after Morrigan departed Londinium Lilith walked into the castle Augustus occupied in the fens. She nodded to him, "My lord, we must do something about the rift between you and the man who calls himself an Dragan. He has a large army, half of the army your father commanded, but it is still too small to defeat the armies now banded together in Cymru. The two of you must become allies. It is only thus you will be able to realize your rightful claim to the rule of this island. With the united army you should be able to conquer not only Cymru, but then move on to capture Alba as well. With all of these armies under your command the taking of the Island of Eirrean will be easily accomplished."

"This may be true," Augustus countered, "but the usurper and I will not make good bedfellows. He stole my men from me while I was otherwise occupied. For this I can never forgive him. We are deadly enemies, and if I see him I will surely kill him."

Lilith was silent for a moment as she looked at Augustus. His demeanor made it obvious he was a strong ruler, and one who did not easily bend with the wind. For some reason she could not get him to fear her as an Dubh did when she was Morrigan. Augustus' ice blue eyes were steady as he watched her. "For some reason he has obtained the loyalty of the officers in command of that contingent of men. I fear if you tried to lure them away they might turn on you. It would be best if you and an Dragan became friends. It matters not who is in command of…"

"What do you mean it matters not?" Augustus interrupted. His tone was icy. "These were men commanded by my father. They should be loyal to me, not to that bastard son of an Irish king. If, and I say IF, the two armies are united it will be totally under my command. This usurper will be far down the list of command, or he will die. I will not tolerate any of those officers who have gone over to him. They are turncoats. They will also die. I will appoint other officers to take their place, but never will I have anyone in my army who is not loyal to me. Do you understand me?" Lilith nodded and remained silent.

"Then," Augustus continued, "let us not have any more of this prattle of joining hands together to defeat the enemy to the west. This will not occur unless he comes to me on his knees, begging my pardon for his acts of disloyalty, and returning my army to my command. Once he has done that I may, and I mean may, allow him to have a small regiment to command. My men, men loyal to me, will command the important units."

As he thundered forth his tirade Augustus had risen to his feet, his fist pounding the table as he spoke. He paused, staring coldly at her for a moment, then settled back in his chair and regarded her with an upraised eyebrow. "Now, what other news of import do you have to offer?"

"Arthur has a sister residing in the castle Tintagel in Cornwall. I would visit her with your approval. Arthur is having a conference with all rulers of the lands he rules as High King. Igraine, queen of Tintagel, never remarried after her husband was killed by Uther. I will talk to the sister, who I understand is quite lovely; have her seduce her brother so she will bear his child. It will be a boy. While it is a long-range plan, at some time in the future this son will learn to hate his father. I expect him to rally armies against Arthur to defeat him." She spread her hands, "As I said, my lord, it is a long range plan, but one that can be quickly put in motion."

Augustus pursed his lips in thought. He smiled cruelly as he nodded. "It is long-range, but it is one that has merit. Go. You have my permission. I will write letters of pass for my officers so they will allow you freedom of travel. Report back to me when you have finished your work. Then we will make other plans to retrieve my army."

Lilith bowed her head as she backed from his presence, "Yes, my lord. It shall be done." As she left her fingernails dug into the hands of her palms in frustration as she wondered why Augustus would not bend to her will as easily as an Dubh.

* * *

Arthur and Kevin walked around the site of the future castle. Some stonemasons were busily laying stone on the walls of the keep. From what would be the keep there was a wide clear area, the inner bailey, before one reached the stone wall that was also being raised. Beyond that wall was a wider expanse of an outer bailey that would be enclosed with another wall. That wall, like the inner, would be wide enough for four horses to ride on it side by side. In Kevin's mind these walls would be barracks and armories for those who would be Arthur's army.

Their way took them outside the outer wall to a wooded area that came almost to the wall. Arthur looked over the walls to the future keep, a satisfied smile on his face. The keep sat back toward the edge of a cliff, yet a battlement was being built behind it, adding to the height. The walls would be sheer from the top of the battlements to the edge of the beach hundreds of feet below. He nodded his approval. "This will be a strong castle. If the Saecsens attempt to take it they will have a very difficult time."

Kevin nodded. "This may be true, Arthur, but there is more to be done out here as well."

Arthur's face lost its satisfied smile. Turning to Kevin he asked. "And what do you think should be done out here?"

Kevin gestured to the forest just behind them. "An army could approach the outer battlements before any of the sentries could see them. They could be right at this wall, and possibly scale it, before your men would know of their approach or their presence."

Arthur pursed his lips in thought and finally nodded. "I see that." He said. "What is to be done?"

"I would suggest we clear an area from the edge of the outer battlements to the edge of the woods. I believe it should be as far as an arrow can travel if shot from the top of the battlement to the woods. That way the enemy, and we know there will eventually be a Saecsen army coming to defeat you, will have to cross a wide, clear, area before reaching the wall. That will give your archers time to man the battlements and send volley after volley of arrows on their approaching lines. Far fewer would reach the wall, and fewer still would be able to scale it. Also, I would make the wall wide enough to house barracks for your men at arms. That way they would have shorter distances to go to defend their portion of the walls."

"I see that also." Arthur said. "Let us go see the chief architect and tell him of your ideas. It will take a bit longer to build, but it will be far stronger."

"While we're making our plans let's put the main door to the keep about twelve feet from the ground with an archway before it. Above the area before the door we could place an iron grating through which boiling oil could be poured on those who attempt to storm the keep itself. That is, if any could breach the two walls leading to the keep."

Arthur turned to Kevin, a serious look on his face. "When do you expect the battle to occur?"

"The Saecsen are still divided at the moment. My half brother Colm has control of half of Vertigorm's old army. His son, Augustus, has control of the other half. If these two join hands to attack us they have an army a bit larger than ours. Remember what Myrdden told us about the evil woman that has influenced both of them; though neither still know she is advising the other. Morrigan is from his country and has powers similar to his. Because of this he fears she will be able to bring these two together. He doesn't know when this will occur, but when it does they will come against us in war once again. I feel we should be well prepared for such an event."

Arthur nodded understanding as he turned to look on the work on the castle. He pursed his lips in thought as he surveyed the work going on. "It will take even longer than I thought, and I hope we have the time, but we will incorporate your ideas into my castle," he smiled thoughtfully. "in hopes that it will exist in a peaceful land. This was once called Caerleon, but I believe I will name it Caer Maellot."

"Caer Maellot, eh?" Kevin smiled. "That has a familiar ring to it. I like it."

"Good! Caer Maellot it is. Now, let us see to the architect."

* * *

Kevin stood with arms folded across his chest as he watched the serfs working at the clearing of the forest. Already the walls along the cliff above the river were rising higher. No foe would be able to scale those battlements. The walls along the sides were now reaching close to thirty feet in height and twenty feet wide. Rooms to lodge men at arms, the armory, and food supplies had also been added. Toward the rear was a small, disguised, gate in case an enemy did make it inside the walls, but the large gate in front would be the main entrance. The clearing of the land would give another means of defense. Caer Maellot would be well protected from any external enemy. He turned as he heard footsteps approaching.

"What next?" Tim asked as he stood by Kevin's side.

"With Myrdden gone for the time being we're on our own. I wish he was here for the meeting Arthur has called." He turned to look at the construction behind them. "The keep is almost finished. We should be able to have the meeting here." He turned back to Tim. "According to what I remember in the books I read about Arthur's life, he has to worry most about what comes internally rather than externally."

"What do you mean, internally?"

"Well, the Saecsen armies are still divided. We don't have much to fear from any armed conflict at the moment. That will come later if I remember correctly. But Igraine has always harbored hatred for Uther for what he did. He disguised himself as her husband, came to her while her husband was in battle with Uther's troops, and he bedded her at almost the same time her husband was killed. She already had a daughter who is a year or so older than Arthur. When Arthur was born Myrdden took him and placed him with Ector. Igraine lost her son at that moment and had no idea where he was…until now. She hated Uther for what he did, and that hatred has been transferred to Arthur.

"According to the legends Uther had a strong sexual drive. He loved to exert the rights of the lord over the young girls who caught his fancy." He smiled crookedly. "I've heard from some of the warriors who fought under him that half the children in his barony had him as father. When he saw Igraine he wanted her, and conspired to get her. I fear Arthur has inherited his father's weakness. I also understand his sister, whom he doesn't know is his sister, is a very lovely young woman. She has inherited her mother's beauty. Arthur is going to want her, and we have to keep him from taking her to bed."

Tim thought for a moment. "I can understand the bans against incest. If the old legends tell of his taking her, why should we change them?"

"Because, my friend, when he takes her and gets her pregnant she will have a son…a son named Mordred. Some of the books talk of Mordred being his nephew, others say he is Arthur's son. The thing is, in a future battle Mordred will kill Arthur and the era of peace and plenty in this land will be over for more than a thousand years. We must make sure Arthur and his sister don't have sex."

"Yeah, but do you think Igraine would allow her daughter to sleep with Arthur? After all, the law is pretty rigid regarding incest."

"True. But who knows the woman is Arthur's sister besides Igraine, the girl, and us? If no one knows they are related no one will care if Arthur satisfies his lusts with her. The thing is, after the birth of Mordred his sister and his mother will train him to hate Arthur. They will use him as a weapon to satisfy their own hatred. Igraine has been patient up to this point; she will be patient in her training as well."

They stood silently watching as the serfs felled more trees, stripped them of their branches, and had the logs dragged to one side. They would later be used to make pillars and beams for use in the keep and the barracks. Finally

Tim broke the silence. "But I always thought Guinnevere was the main trouble spot in Arthur's life. I remember the movies about her and Lancelot."

Kevin nodded. "Aye. That's another trouble spot, and the movies probably got it all wrong. Still, it won't happen for quite a while. I think Arthur will be in his forties when he meets Gwyndevehr." He chuckled mirthlessly. "She's probably just being born. There was quite a span of years between them. That's why Lancelot was so successful in seducing her.

"According to the stories by that time Arthur was more interested in the Round Table and the search for the Holy Grail than in women. He went on long crusades against the Albanese as he tried to unite the country. Gwyndevehr was young, and the Celtic people are hot blooded. When God told man to go out and populate the Earth they acted as though he were speaking only to them. Lancelot was young and handsome. Gwyndevehr was being neglected, so things took their natural course."

He chuckled again. "Look at me. I'm talking about the future as though it were the past. Of course, for us it is the past, but it is still the future in this period of time. We have to be careful about Arthur's future and use our knowledge of his life to keep him from making those mistakes."

"And how are you going to keep him from taking his sister to bed when you don't even know her name? Anyway, Igraine's husband may come in her place." Tim asked.

Kevin nodded. "Aye, and there's another problem. She never remarried. Her hatred kept her from marriage. From what I've heard she has kept to herself, kept her daughter to herself, and has given her the same hatred. Since she is the ruler of that barony, or kingdom, she will come to this meeting. Arthur, in his innocence will see the girl and want her immediately. How am I going to let him know the lady is his sister?" Of course, once I find out the girl's name it might help. Keep your ears open. Better yet, let's make some inquiries of some of the warriors who might have been in Cornwall. Perhaps they have heard of the young lady."

"True. I don't believe we're needed here. The foremen seem to be doing a good job of keeping the workers in line. Let's go back to the old castle and see what some of the visitors might know. I understand a group of bards and acrobats have been seen heading in this direction. They might know something as well." He looked back at the construction of the new caer called Caer Maellot. "That place is going to be massive."

Kevin nodded. "And the keep is almost finished: fast work for this period of time. I wonder how much longer it will be to finish the battlements." They mounted their horses and headed back toward Harlech and Arthur.

* * *

Arthur looked up as Kevin and Tim entered the family room where he was reading. "Merlin was called away. Apparently there is some need for him to be in Tir na nOg, so he told me I should talk over the assembly of the kings with you two. I'm new at this being the High King, and some of the older men still don't accept me as someone they should obey. They say I'm too young to be High King." He motioned them to seats near the table at which he was sitting. "What do you think?"

"Well." Kevin began. "First off, they have to accept you because you are the only one who could draw the sword from the anvil and stone. The Lady of the Lake had that test especially prepared to show everyone who the true king would be. It's good you had training, and grew up as someone who was born of lowly parentage. You see how the common man lives and is treated. That gives you some insight into rule the other kings lack. It may also give you an advantage they don't have in obtaining the loyalty of the common people. Of course, getting their loyalty will depend on how you treat them.

"Secondly, you are High King, but basically you are first among equals. You are a warrior and a king, they are warriors and kings. What you have to do, in my estimation, is to show them you are not going to force them to accept your authority. Loyalty and trust cannot be commanded, they must be earned. So your job, while we still have time before the Saecsen troops join together, is to earn that loyalty and trust.

"Third, you should always remember that kings are merely men with a duty to lead, but that leadership also means serving the needs of others."

Arthur's forehead wrinkled in a frown. He raised his left eyebrow as a sign of inquiry as he shook his head and said. "I don't understand."

Kevin smiled. "I know. We're on foreign soil when we talk of this since none of the kings you know have ever thought of their being called to serve their subjects. All you, and they, have seen so far is that the subjects live to serve them. The trouble with that is much of the service is given with resentment. Let me give you an example. You expect the farmers to give you one tenth of their produce to feed those who live and work at the castle." Arthur nodded, and Kevin went on.

"But you have fox hunts and ride through their fields, trampling the corn so it never ripens, and never think that you are ruining their ability to feed themselves if they give their produce to you. It does no good having subjects if you starve them to death."

Arthur sat back as he began to think about this new idea Kevin had given him. "I never thought of it that way." He finally said. "I doubt any of the other kings have given that any thought either. They just demand that they get enough food to feed the castle without thinking of how much food the peasant has."

"You see what I mean." Kevin continued. "The peasant sends the food to the castle and gets nothing for it. On top of that he must sell some of his output in order to get the money you demand in taxes. This further lowers his ability to buy things he might need for himself and his family. You want to gain their loyalty out of their regard for you, not out of their fear of you. In order to do that you must gain their trust. To get that trust means you must do things that they recognize benefit them. In other words, you must serve them if you expect them to serve you."

"So what do we do?"

"We might start with the kings. You will be first among equals." He smiled slyly. "I suggest when they arrive you greet them warmly and give each a gift that is aimed directly at him and his interests. They will be coming with gifts for you, as has always been expected. Kings have always been the recipients of the gifts, looking on it as their right as ruler of over their domain. You will be different. You will give as well as receive. Don't expect everyone to appreciate what you do, because the smarter ones will recognize this as a change in tradition and a threat to their sovereignty."

"If that's the case I'll wind up with enemies rather than those loyal to me because they love me."

"Ah yes, but there's a way out of that dilemma. Make a new order of warriorhood and induct them into it. Perhaps The Warriors of the Golden Chain, or... that's not a good name. Let me think." Silence filled the room as Kevin sat back, a thoughtful look on his face. Finally he smiled. "I think I've got it." He said. "Let's call it the Warriors of the Round Table."

"Warriors of the Round Table." Arthur repeated. "That sounds good." His left eyebrow went up. "What does it mean and how would it work?"

"We'll have the carpenter build a huge table to be placed in a special room in the castle. If everyone sits at a round table there is no difference one to another. It's not like the seating at meal at the castle where certain nobles sit above the salt in special seats denoting their rank, and lesser ones sit below the salt to show they are not of as noble a birth. At the round table all are equal. There is no above or below the salt. Each would have an equal voice, and you as High King would have no more voice than anyone else at that table. In this way they will see you as a person who accepts them as equal, and more will come to have trust and loyalty to your crown. Still, be warned, there are those who look on everything and everyone with distrust, and will question your motives. No matter what you do you will always have enemies, some even in your own ranks."

Arthur drew a deep breath and released it slowly. He nodded. "I suppose you're right. Let me think this new idea over. I'm just not sure it would work."

"Certainly. Though I can assure you, it will work."

"I'll have to trust you, I guess." Arthur put the book down. "You were at Caer Maellot today? How are things coming?"

"We should be able to hold the ceremonies in the Great Hall. The keep should be finished in a few days. Then all that has to be done is to move the furnishings in. We can accomplish that during the next fortnight. Since the convocation won't be for another month everything should be finished in plenty of time. Of course, the battlements will take a bit longer, and both baileys will still be a bit rough, but everyone can see what the place will be like when it is complete."

"That's good. I like it that it's convenient to Harlech. It's good to have a town nearby, especially on the sea, where the men at arms and the servants can live and enjoy themselves. I want to be known as a King of Peace."

"Unfortunately you're going to have to be a King of War until the Saecsen is defeated."

Arthur nodded sadly. "I know." He said softly. "I know. Yet, perhaps someday this land will live in peace and plenty. Let's hope so anyway."

* * *

Arthur and Kevin stood in the balcony overlooking the Great Hall. Below them those rulers who were the first to arrive were milling around. Maeve and Fiona, both dressed in green gowns were talking with two other ladies who were among the assembly. Arthur's eyes were resting on the younger of the two, a statuesque blonde of undeniable beauty who bore strong resemblance to the older woman she accompanied. Kevin noticed how his attention seemed only on her, neglecting the rest of the assemblage. He studied the two women more closely, watching their mannerisms as they chatted with Maeve and Fiona.

Arthur poked an elbow into Kevin's arm without taking his eyes from the blonde beauty below. "She is so beautiful. I must have her."

"I would be a bit careful, Arthur." Kevin admonished. "She is beautiful, but there may be drawbacks."

"I am High King." Arthur stated. "I can have whoever I want; and I want her."

"I understand," Kevin answered, "but let's look at a couple things first. One should never attack until one is sure of his objective."

"Oh, I'm sure, believe me."

"That's not what I meant. One must make sure he has all the information about the object one is advancing toward. That rule holds true in love as it does in war. Let's observe the two more closely. All right?" A reluctant Arthur agreed. Kevin tilted his head to one side, a serious look on his face. "Notice how the older lady raises her left eyebrow when inquiring about a statement?" Arthur watched closely and nodded as Kevin went on. "Notice how the young lady has the same mannerism? There. She raised her left eyebrow at Maeve just then."

"I saw it." Arthur said.

"It seems to be a family trait, wouldn't you agree?"

Arthur shrugged nonchalantly. "I suppose so."

"Like mother, like daughter." Kevin paused. "Like son." He added.

Arthur's left eyebrow raised as he turned toward Kevin. "What do you mean? Like son?"

Kevin sighed. "Your left eyebrow just raised up. You have the same mannerism as your mother."

Both of Arthur's eyebrows went up, then his face settled in a frown. He shook his head, perplexed. "I don't understand." He said.

"Simple. The older lady is Queen Igraine. She happens to be your mother. The young lady is Maire, your sister. There's a strong family resemblance between the three of you. Didn't anyone tell you who your parents are?"

Arthur shook his head, still frowning. "No. Not yet. But I think someone should, and right now."

"Let's go into the library for a few minutes. I'll fill you in."

Arthur paced the room as Kevin told him the story. "Some twenty years ago Gorlois and Igraine came to a meeting similar to this when Uther, your father, became High King. Igraine, as you saw, is a very lovely lady even yet. He wanted her. He got Myrdden to aid him. At the time Gorlois and Uther were fighting due to Uther's designs on Igraine. By aid of deception and, I believe, Myrdden's ability to cloud one's mind, Igraine thought Uther was Gorlois. You were conceived at the same time Gorlois was killed by Uther's men. Igraine's hatred of Uther began when she found the truth. She didn't want Uther's son. Since Myrdden had made Uther promise you to him he placed you under the rule of Ector. You grew up knowing neither your true father nor mother. Ector wasn't told of your parentage, so wasn't able to give you that information either.

"Igraine had a daughter by Gorlois two years before you were born. That daughter is Maire, your half sister." Kevin waited for Arthur to speak before continuing. Arthur continued his silent pacing of the floor. "I believe Maire doesn't know you are her brother and has come here with a plan to seduce you. If that occurs she will have a son, and that son will grow up to hate you because of both Igraine and Maire. When that son is in his twenties he will contest you for the throne…and he will kill you."

Arthur turned to face Kevin, his left eyebrow raised in inquiry. "And how do you know this, Sir?"

"As Myrdden told you, I am a seer and a seanachie. I have a clear picture of certain parts of your reign, and a cloudy picture of other parts. I know who you should choose to be on the Round Table later, even though these kings will be on it now. I know not all about your reign and of all events of the Round Table, but I do know things that will cause your desire for a peaceful kingdom to stop with your death. I also believe if you follow my advice in the things that matter, such as this one, your desire for a peaceful kingdom will continue long after your death."

He drew a deep breath and let it out slowly. He smiled wryly, "The choices, however, are always up to you. You can take your sister to bed, or thwart Igraine's plan by not doing so. I have no ability to do other than tell you the truth of events and warn you of your actions."

Arthur walked to the window and gazed at the sun as it touched the Mountains of Mourne across the Irish Sea. He turned, a wry smile on his face. "Shall we go down and greet my mother?" He asked.

They entered the hall and walked to the huge fireplace where Igraine and Maire were still in conversation with Maeve and Fiona. The latter stepped aside as Arthur strode into their midst. Igraine and Maire both curtsied and bent their heads. "My Lord." Igraine said as she smiled with her mouth but not with her eyes.

"Greetings Lady Igraine and Lady Maire." Arthur said as he bowed. "I do hope you find your stay in Caer Maellot pleasant." He turned to Igraine, smiling broadly, "Or should I say, Greetings Mother, my home is your home and I hope you treat it as such." Turning to Maire he added. "And for you also, my sister, I wish you all the warmth of the castle as though it were your own. I am exceedingly happy you were able to come. Now you must excuse me as I greet my other guests."

When he was well away Maire turned to her mother. "You knew we were brother and sister and you never told me. How can I do what you and Lilith want when it would be a crime against God for me to do so? How can you have plotted to send me to Hell so you could have revenge against Uther? Uther is dead and his son is now High King, and the High King is your son as well. Oh, Mother, what am I to think? My head is in a whirl."

Igraine's eyes were on Arthur as he talked to King Bagdemus. Her face was set in a scowl. "How did he find out?" She asked aloud. "No one but myself and Myrdden knew of this; and Myrdden's honor would never allow him to tell Arthur. How did he find out?"

chapter 2
The First Round Table

"King Bagdemus, I welcome you to Caer Maellot and do hope you enjoy your stay with us."

"Thank you, Sire. I appreciate your hospitality and hope you bear me no ill will for my actions when I thought you a usurper rather than a pretender for the throne."

Arthur laughed and shook his head. "I feel no ill will, Sir. I am appreciative of the fact you were willing to come to this gathering of the kings of Cymru. I am desirous of having a discussion with you, however. Since you are the first of the kings to arrive, as well as the most powerful, I wish to gain your wisdom on a project I have in mind. If you wouldn't mind Prince Kevin, Sir Timothy, you, and I could retire to the library upstairs and have a private conversation."

Bagdemus bowed his head as he said, "You wish is my command, Sire. I hope I will be able to atone for my serious blunders during the past four years."

Again Arthur shook his head. "Do not trouble yourself. I have found out already that to harbor a grudge is to let the other person hold control over your thoughts. Better to forgive, forget, and move on in hopes of winning the other person to your side. Come, let us upstairs."

Bagdemus' smile was a bit lopsided. "You say you wish my wisdom, but I believe yours is already greater than mine, for I have found it difficult to forgive, let alone forget, the evil others have done. My desire is always to seek revenge."

"There are times when one must return a blow, if only in self defense. When I say forgive and forget I am not talking of war, but of the everyday slights one receives from both friends and allies. I am not in favor of allowing the Saecsen hosts to invade our lands, to desecrate our soil and faith, or kill our people without taking them to task for their misdeeds."

Bagdemus smiled. "It is good to hear you say that, Sire. I was afraid you might attempt to appease the enemy and bring destruction down on us."

They reached the library and the four entered to find seats around the table. Arthur looked at Kevin and Tim, "Feel free to discuss these plans with us, for I believe we are all equals here and with input from all we will better be able to bring a good plan to the attention of the other kings when they arrive." He leaned back in his chair and gazed at Bagdemus. "It is my desire to start a new order, and the kings of Cymru will be the first in that order. Later we will induct other champions in as they appear, but they will have equal status with those of us who are the forerunners of the order."

Bagdemus nodded thoughtfully. "A new order…" He mused. "I recognize the need for recognition of those warriors who are our champions. In each of our armies there are those who stand out from the rest. We give them more recognition and responsibility, but they stay within their station. What do you suggest we do?"

"Many of the champions, as you know, call themselves warriors. As yet such a title is pretty much self-bestowed. They serve time as a page, then as a squire, and move on to become a warrior. Some develop much better skills than other warriors, and their peers recognize these skills. They then become leaders and teachers. Still, they feel something is lacking. I would create a new order for these men who are our champions. Warrior seems to be a distinction many of lesser prowess already own. We need a new title to bestow on these to recognize they are a cut above the rest" His face buckled in thought. "We might call this new order that of the 'knight'. Sir Kevin has suggested that this order of knighthood give them rank and privilege in all the kingdoms. I would call this new order the Knights of the Round Table, and make knighthood a badge of honor as well as a title to be given to the best of our warriors."

"Knights of the Round Table, eh? Just exactly how do you think this new order should be organized?"

"I've only begun to think about the organization, and it is not yet clear to me. I believe we should start with the kings of Cymru. We would form an organization where all would have equal authority within the order. The round table is just that. A round table has no head where the ruler sits and orders things done. Here everyone would be on an equal basis, everyone would have a voice in what was to be done, and when the majority has decided on an action, all would join in that action."

Bagdemus leaned back in his chair and stared at the ceiling as he thought. "Equality, eh?" he muttered to himself. "What an unusual thought. Rule by the majority. Interesting." He finally returned his gaze to Arthur. "If you don't mind I would like to mull these ideas over. Perhaps when the others arrive we can meet and try out this idea with them in attendance. I appreciate your letting me know of this first, but there are some problems I think I can see."

Arthur nodded. "I understand. These are new ideas. Good! We will wait and talk to the others. Everyone should be here by tomorrow." He smiled broadly. "Now, let us repair to the Great Hall and enjoy ourselves. A group of entertainers arrived just in time for the festivities. I am sure we will be well looked after."

* * *

"What you say sounds good," Balin offered from his seat at the round table "but I can see problems if we kings are to be the warriors you talk about."

Arthur nodded. "Go on."

Balin sighed, a rueful smile on his face. "Take a good look at the men around this table. You are a young man of twenty years or so. Any of us is old enough to be your father." He gestured down the table. "Why Garlon is probably the youngest of us, and even he's too old to be a champion. No. The rest of us are on the downward side of our fighting days."

He paused and thought for a moment. "Another thing. It's a long trip from Bath to Caer Maellot, or from Swansea or Cardiff. Poole is even further. We are kings of small kingdoms, and those kingdoms need our presence to maintain order and justice. I'm not sure, but I believe the others around this table would agree with me."

There was a general nodding of heads. "My lord Balin is right." Garlon spoke up. "Why even Accolon takes a day to get here, and he's the closest of all of us to your throne. While Balin was talking a thought struck me. I was talking to Bagdemus when I arrived, and he mentioned the fact of a number of our best warriors being called knights to distinguish their prowess at arms as well as their leadership. These are generally young men looking for adventure. They are the warriors who go to the jousts and tourneys to prove themselves against warriors from other kingdoms. Would it not be proper for us to send the very best of our warriors to Caer Maellot to be granted the accolades of the Round Table. Because of their recognition as a knight they could be leaders of the various armies, as well as making sure there is good communication between the various kingdoms; something lacking at the moment." He rose from his seat and paced back and forth as the others waited for his further thought.

"We all know the Saecsen is going to invade at some time in the near future. Having these warriors in place and ready to serve would aid in our fight against our common enemy." He looked around the table at his peers. "What do you other gentlemen think?"

Arthur sat back and listened as the others agreed among themselves they were too busy, too old, and too out of practice to be the actual warriors who would fight from the Round Table. After a time of discussion all finally agreed to send their best warriors to Arthur for training. These would be trained to be the leaders of the various armies of Cymru when the Saecsen invasion came. Finally quiet settled on the room and their attention turned to Arthur.

"What you have said makes a great deal of sense. Still, I would have honor bestowed on each of you as well. Therefore, if you accept, I will make you Knights of the Round Table, though of an emeritus status. The men you send me will be those who will be the knights who lead the armies, and maintain justice once peace has settled on our land. Now let us discuss ways in which we can assure the common people a new place in our kingdoms."

To grant the commoner a status was unheard of, and everyone in the room tried to talk at once. Arthur waited a few moments then rapped on the table to get their attention. "Sirrahs." He said. "There are good reasons to give the common people our attention. I am going to ask Prince MacMurrough of Leinster to outline my plan. He has been a faithful adviser for a number of years, and I ask you to hear him out."

"We have a tendency to look on the common person as a slave." Kevin began. "To most of us he might be, yet they do have some property of their own though they tend our fields as well. In Kilbourne the king and his court," he smiled a half smile, "much as we do in our kingdoms, would hunt the fox or the deer. In doing so the troop of horsemen would ravage the crops of the people. These crops were meant to feed the peers as well as the commoners. Even though the crops were destroyed the levy of food placed on the farmers remained the same. This meant those who were farming had to starve themselves to feed those in the castle who did none of the work in raising those crops.

"The king dismissed the complaints of the people and continued his hunts. Finally, in desperation, the people rose against the king and his court. They came against the castle with pitchfork and mattock. Since the army was made up of sons of the peasants drafted into service by the king, the army did nothing to stop them. The king and court had to flee for their lives, and the people appointed one of the peerage who was recognized as a friend to be king.

"It is important for all of us that the commoner be loyal. Yet, loyalty is something earned, and cannot be achieved by merely ordering someone to be loyal. We expect much from the people but give little in return. It would seem loyalty should be a two-way road. If we expect their loyalty we should show them a loyalty in return. A healthy people make a stalwart army. It is the food they grow that feeds us, and to deprive them of their needs to satisfy our own can very well lead to our downfall. I suggest we discuss some ways in which we can gain the loyalty and respect of those people over whom we rule.

"While we do expect ten percent of their output as a right, many times we take more and do not give anything in return. They must come up with payment for things they need. I suggest as a start we give market price for anything over the levy so they are able to purchase things they need. Many of the tools they need are used to help feed us. Since we are around the Round Table all are equal. Let us hear what you have to say."

"I, for one, am against it. It flies in the face of tradition. How can these people respect us unless we show them we have the God given right to rule?" Damas eyes seemed to flash in anger as he spoke.

"What makes you think they respect you now?" Kevin asked mildly. "They bow to you because if they didn't they would be struck down by your guards. Is that respect; or is it fear?" Kevin paused for a moment. "Let me give you an example. There was a king named Wenceslaus who, on the eve of a feast day in the midst of winter, saw a poor peasant gathering fuel for his hut. His page knew the man and that he had neither food nor heat because the baron of that land had ridden over the cropland and destroyed all. Wenceslaus had his people gather food, warm clothes, and wood to take to the man's hut. He himself broke the path through the snow, following the page's instructions, and made sure the provisions were duly delivered. Besides gratitude, what do you think the poor man now thought of his king? Do you think he felt him a fool for what he did; or did he gain respect for him, so much so that he would now do anything for that ruler?"

"But tradition, Sir, tradition."

"Our people can't eat tradition. It isn't tradition that makes them follow us. Right now it may be fear. If, however, the ruler is too traditional, and tradition is harsh, the people might desert to an invading army in hopes of having a better life. We are faced with an enemy we know is cruel and gives no quarter. So I have little fear of defection against them; but what of another enemy with a more savory reputation? I know there are those who will rebel even under the kindest of leaders, but they are few. More rebel against oppression. Let us undermine that before it gets a foothold." The discussion continued throughout the afternoon, and the participants left with many ideas to think over.

* * *

"We must get together with Augustus before it is too late." Morrigan was pacing the Great Hall of the castle in Londinium. "Arthur has had a meeting with all of the kings of Cymru in his new castle at Caer Maellot. The castle itself is as close to impregnable as it can be. The cliffs on the Irish Sea rise tall outside of Harlech and he has builded Caer Maellot so all of one wall and a portion of another extend above the sheer cliff. The outer wall is thick enough to house rooms for his men inside. You and Augustus must find some way to draw him out so we don't have to attack the castle itself. It's all your half brother's fault. He was the one who designed the structure else that strong a fort would never have been built by Arthur."

She stopped her pacing for a moment and turned a fierce countenance on the cowering an Dubh. "To go even further he has established a new order: something he calls knights. The champions of the various kingdoms will assemble at Caerleon to become Knights of the Round Table. All, including Arthur, will be equal when seated at the round table, for there is no head at such a table. These champions will become the generals of the various armies when the war comes. Again, I understand your brother is teaching them things about battle and fighting never heard before. They go against all tradition. We must do something, and it must be done before it becomes too late."

An Dubh spread his empty hands in what appeared to be an apology. "But what am I able to do? Augustus hates me and would kill me the moment I appeared before him. The army I command is not enough to do battle with the armies of Cymru. Besides, who are these champions that are assembling at Caer Maellot? Have we heard of any of them before?"

Morrigan nodded, her face stern. "Ah yes, we've heard of them. From what I understand each of them is better than our best. There's Gawain from Poole, Galahad from Anglesy, Percival from Gore, Cai from Swansea, and others from each of the kingdoms. Somehow Arthur found out Igraine was his mother and Maire his sister, so that plan went awry. Now we must rely on the armies of you and Augustus to carry out or plans."

"How can we meet with Augustus? I could never go there and he would never come here."

Morrigan smiled with her lips, but the unsmiling eyes turned the gesture into more of a grimace. "I will go to him on your behalf and I will plan with him the way we will approach this battle. When I return I will give you instructions on what you are to do when the battle starts. Do you understand?"

An Dubh nodded, his body showing his resignation to what she said. "Yes. I will await the plans for myself and my army."

"You are a weak fool," She said sarcastically, "but you may still be useful to my plans." Then she turned and marched out of the throne room. An Dubh watched her go with hatred in his eyes, but breathed a sigh of relief at her departure.

* * *

Kevin walked the battlements with Tim, Maeve, and Fiona. He stood and looked out over the expanse of greensward between them and the forest. He sighed as he rested his chin on arms resting on the top the parapet. "I don't understand." He muttered. "We now have Gawain, Galahad, Percival, Cai, Tristam, and even Lancelot." He shook his head in bewilderment. "According to the stories Galahad is the son of Lancelot du Lake, and none of the others really appear until Arthur is at least in his thirties."

"What do you mean?" Maeve asked. "What stories are told of Arthur and these Knights of the Table Round? It has just been made."

Kevin took Maeve's hand and smiled gently. "Remember, my heart, what I told you years ago at Swansea. You found it difficult to believe, if you ever did, but both Tim and I are not of this age. Merlin and Brian were able to bring our essences back to inhabit these bodies, but we know Arthur's future."

Maeve nodded slowly, her face a study in perplexity. "I remember. But I have trouble believing yet."

Tim interrupted. "When were these stories written?" He asked. "What I mean is, how long after Arthur's reign did they appear?"

"Well, the most famous is Mallory's, and that is about five hundred years from now. There were some written in the next hundred years, but they were ramblings and didn't have the texture of Mallory's Morte de Arthur."

"Okay. Look at our own history. We had about four hundred years from the first colonies, and how many variations on the same story have you heard regarding events in the sixteen hundreds. Or even a later period: how about Washington and the cherry tree? If you want to make a good story you have to embellish it a bit, alter certain events as far as time is concerned, and maybe invent a few things that you aren't sure happened in order to make a better story. Perhaps these warriors did come at this time, or perhaps these aren't uncommon names and there are some similarly named warriors at a later time."

"You may be right." Kevin put his arm around Maeve's shoulder and drew her closer. "You may be right, and so we will work with the men we have. I have a gut feeling we will see war before too long. Merlin returned yesterday, as you know, and he says Morrigan is getting anxious." He chuckled mirthlessly. "On top of that he tells me a warrior princess named Gwyndevere is on her way here. She's a champion from Cardiff, and she's coming with another champion named Bors. So it gets a bit sticky as far as history is concerned."

Tim shook his head, grinning broadly, "Not history, Kev. Don't forget, in our time they don't yet know whether Arthur lived or is just a myth. Some have him the humanizing of one of the Celtic gods, and these stories are of how Cymru, or Beigh, or Wales, whatever you want to call it, became part of the British Empire."

Kevin nodded, took a deep breath and expelled it slowly. "You're right, my friend. I guess we play this whole thing by ear, but if we're going to beat the Saecsen army we'd best start teaching these fellows a few nontraditional tricks."

Maeve looked up at Kevin and said, "When the battle comes, my heart's blood, I will be at your side."

Kevin shook his head. "No, love, I would have you stay with Dermot where you will be safe."

"You are my life. I am yours. I will go with you into battle. It is settled. Both Fiona and I will fight with our men. We are just as good with sword and snee as are you. I will hear no argument from either of you."

"Your mind is made up?"

"It is!"

"Then we fight together as one."

"Yes. Now let us go together and become one."

* * *

"Sire. An emissary of Augustus comes under a flag of truce. He desires to have audience." A guard from the main gate brought the information to an Dubh.

"Show him in."

"Aye, Sire."

The man, obviously an officer of Augustus army, entered and bowed his head. "I am Captain Adric of the army of King Augustus. My lord sent me to negotiate a way in which our armies might unite. He recognizes that neither of you is willing to give up full leadership of the men you command, and neither wishes to be under the authority of the other. He also recognizes neither of you wishes to be on the same field of battle as the other." He smiled sardonically. "The hate he has for you, and the fear you have of him, would soon cause one of you to meet death early."

Colm drew a measured breath and let it out slowly. "There is no need to be insulting." He said to the man. "I could have you cut down for those remarks."

Adric kept the sardonic smile on his face as he answered. "Aye, you could, but you won't because you fear Augustus and the revenge he would take on my death. That knowledge will keep you from committing such a cowardly act. I must agree with King Augustus. You are a crusty botch of nature, the spawn of a woman of easy ways. Therefore I will make my business short and then take leave of your putrid presence. King Augustus is planning a siege on Caer Maellot, or Caerleon, in the spring. He will attack from the northeast. He would have you attack from the southeast at the same time. Because of the defenses of the castle his desire is to induce Arthur and his men outside to do battle. The attack will occur a fortnight after St. Patrick's Feast. He, ah, requests your presence at the battle."

"You may inform your, ah, king I am not afraid of him, and I will be there with the armies at my command at the appointed hour." Without waiting for dismissal Adric nodded, turned on his heel, and walked out as an Dubh seethed at the insult. He thought of having Adric slain, but realized Augustus would then send his armies after him. Too, it would then be a fight between the men he commanded and those under Augustus command. Since an

Dubh's men at arms were actually part of the army of Vertigorm, and nominally under Augustus, he wondered if they would protect him if their former leader attacked. He decided not to take the chance.

* * *

The outriders brought news of the armies of Augustus and an Dubh shortly after they left Londinium. Balin of Bath was informed as they rode west, formed his men at arms and marched toward Caer Maellot. As the riders warned other kings on their way to Arthur the armies formed and marched west. Immediately on the arrival of the warning each king sent messengers posthaste to those not on the route of the outriders. In that way the warning was quickly passed, armies formed, and the battleground selected. Each of the armies camped so as to surround the castle. Attack had to be from the east since the western approach was impassable.

"Let's see." Tim said as he and Kevin walked the battlements. They paused on the parapet and looked over the expanse of tents and men ringing the castle. Behind them, in the area between the wall and the keep, was another group of tents and men. "The armies of Cymru seem to be quite strong. Stronger than I had imagined, I believe. I wonder how large the armies of Augustus and Colm are. Did any of the outriders have an estimate?"

Kevin leaned on a battlement. "It seems the armies were somewhat evenly divided when Colm induced those men away. I guess there are somewhere around ten thousand men in each of their divisions. I think we have somewhere a total of fifteen thousand men to fight them. Of course, we have this fortified position, and they will be in the open. We can only hope our men will be stronger than the Saecsen. One good thing is we have our champions scattered throughout the armies to give advice and strategy to those leaders unfamiliar with the terrain around Caer Maellot." He smiled. "If we get through this battle, and Arthur wins, the southern part of this island will be secure. If not, things will take a turn for the worse in the future."

"Even worse than what it was in our time?"

Kevin shrugged. "Hard to say. But the way things are happening here aren't the same as the way they were written in the books. Timothy, me boy, we are playing it by ear from now on. When Myrddin brought us back in time he was under the misapprehension we knew this history." He chuckled mirthlessly as he looked out over the field of men at arms. "Boy, was he mistaken."

* * *

Five miles away Colm walked into his tent after reviewing his troops and making sure the food supply was adequate. By doing so he hoped to inspire his men with the fact their leader was with them, let them know what he looked like in his armor, and in general attempt to raise their morale. Now, inside the walls of the tent, he removed his armor and sat on the chair he had ordered brought with them. Leaning his head on its back he closed his eyes and relaxed.

"Colm an Dubh." The soft voice of a woman jarred him from his reverie. He opened his eyes to see the form of a young woman, long auburn hair hanging to her waist, her green eyes staring mockingly at him. He started to his feet and glared at her. At the door the two guards stared outward, seemingly unconscious of the presence of the woman in his tent.

He shook his head in amazement. "Who are you and how did you get in here without my guards alerting me?"

Her mocking smile now had a touch of sadness. "No one may see or hear me but you."

Colm frowned and shook his head. "I don't understand."

"I am assigned to Clann Murrough, so only those of Clann Murrough may see or hear me when I have news to bring them."

Colm's heart fell, and his face sagged in fear. "You are a bean *Sidhe* " He whispered, the fear in his voice a palpable thing.

The woman nodded. "Aye. I am the bean *Sidhe* of the Murroughs."

He drew a halting breath. "You are only sent to inform one of their impending death."

She nodded slowly. "That is true."

He drew another deeper breath and raised his chin. "Then Kevin will die on the morrow, and you are informing me of his impending death."

"No. Kevin will have a long life, as will his son. Tomorrow you will die in battle. Be forewarned. Nothing you do will avert your fate."

"Who is it will kill me?"

She shook her head. "That I cannot say for it depends on where you are at the appointed time. Farewell, Colm an dubh, son of Dermot Murrough." With a fearful screech no one but he heard she faded from his sight. With her disappearance the life seemed to desert his legs and he sat in the chair with a thump, still staring at the spot where she had been standing. He closed his eyes and leaned his head on the back of the chair. "Nothing." He whispered. "She said nothing I do will help me."

chapter 3
Battle and Beyond

Augustus led his armies into battle against the combined men at arms of six of the twelve kingdoms. In the south Colm ordered his men against the men at arms of the other six kingdoms. Augustus rode a large white horse at the head of his armies, a man holding his flag flanking the horse on either side. His men knew where he was at all times, and where to rally when the battle became too much.

Colm sat on a small hill to the rear, his flags also on each side of his position, and directed the battle from that vantage point. Flanking him on all sides was a company of men set there to make sure he came to no harm. Had they been able to see the fighting to their north they would have seen their former commander leading his men in battle. Colm stood up in his stirrups to see how the fight in the valley below was going. It was obvious the army facing them, led by three of the Knights of the Round Table, was being commanded much better. The Knights each wore a cuirass of overlapping strips of iron, with another strip draped over each shoulder. Their helm was fashioned after the Roman helm with a strip hanging down the front to protect their nose. These, too, were in the forefront of the fight giving the men behind them of their courage.

Augustus noted the men he was fighting were also led by men dressed in a similar fashion. The peculiar armor they wore set them aside from the rest, giving the men they led a good view of where they were at all times. Here, too, the battle was going against the Saecsen army. Augustus decided he must face at least one of these leaders to rally his men, falling slowly back before the fierceness of the Cymru army, so he rode boldly toward the one known as Bors. Bors watched as he rode closer, sliced through the neck of a foot soldier in front of him then fell into a sword fight on horseback as Augustus came upon him. Their swords were almost identical. With one hand they maneuvered their horse, with the other they sliced and parried at each other as opportunity presented. On either side the foot soldiers fell back and formed a circle around the fighters.

With the ground clear on all sides the two continued to slash and parry. Finally Bors, his sword sliding off that of Augustus, sliced through the throat of his rival's horse. The horse fell to its knees throwing Augustus over its head. As he lifted his arms to break his fall he lost his sword. Bors immediately swung off his horse and approached Augustus. On his way he picked up the other's sword, and as Augustus lay on the ground, handed it back to him. He then backed off to allow his enemy time to rise from the ground to resume the battle. On his feet once more Augustus bowed his head to acknowledge the honor then raised his sword to do battle once again.

Now the two men circled each other warily as each looked for an advantage in what they knew was a duel to the death. Augustus feinted a blow. Bors made as to parry it but Augustus sword snuck to one side and sliced open Bors' arm. Bors arm went numb as he tossed his sword to his other hand to continue the fight. Now they again slashed at each other, Bors using his left hand to fight as his right arm dripped blood onto the ground. Now he made as if to slash a body blow, Augustus attempted to parry the blow to his abdomen. As he did so Bors' sword swung up and across Augustus neck. Augustus' eyes widened as a gush of blood spurt from his mouth while that from his neck painted his leather armor crimson. He dropped to the ground as gurgling breaths came from his throat. He attempted to rise, fell back, and no sound came from him. Bors gave him a warrior's salute, raising the hilt of his own sword to his lips then turned to face the other army.

The cry went up. "Augustus is dead. We have no leader." Weapons began to drop as the Saecsen troops surrendered. With no leader there was no desire to fight, and no need to continue a battle with no purpose left. The army led by Bors, Galahad, and Percival surrounded the Saecsen and began herding them toward the north side of the castle.

Meanwhile, in the south, the battle was also going badly. Here, with no leader on which to rally, the men began slowly moving back as the southern part of the Cymru army fought behind the leadership of Gawain, Lancelot, and Gwyndevere. Nearby Kevin, Tim, Maeve and Fiona were also involved in their own battle.

As the army of Colm continued to fall back one of the men near him said, in a scornful tone, "Are you not going to rally your men, my lord? They need your presence." Colm sat still on his horse, watching the men fall before the swords and pikes of the other army. Then those who had been his guards suddenly ran toward the fight, leaving him alone on the hill. He glanced quickly around him to see he was quite alone. He tugged the reins to turn the horse around, prepared to run from the battle. Facing him as he did so was one of the leaders of the other army who had flanked the fighting and come around behind. Colm drew his sword to fight, but hardly had it out of its sheath before the other's sword was thrust through his chest. He looked down at the half blade he could see.

His eyes followed the blade to the hilt, the man's hand and arm, then to the fierce eyes glaring at him from the helm. The other jerked his arm back to pull the sword from his body, and Colm saw the spurt of blood as it seemed to leap from his body. His arms and legs were weak, so he decided to dismount, and fell into the grass of the hillside as he breathed a last breath.

Meanwhile, not realizing their leader had died a group of men were fighting Kevin and Tim. It was four against the two of them as both men, standing back to back, parried and thrust at the men surrounding them. Maeve and Fiona, standing just outside the circle, were trying to get their swords into play as well. One of the men, seeing Kevin engaged with one of his mates, lifted his sword to swing at Kevin's head. Maeve's sword was swifter as she swung it downward and through the other's arm. His arm flopped on the ground, sword still clutched in its fist as he caught the stump of his arm with his good hand in an attempt to staunch the flow of blood.

A shout echoed over the battlefield. "Colm an Dragan is dead. We have no leader. Lay down your arms." On all sides the fighting stopped as the Saecsen army looked to see there was no one in command. Then the word came from the north that Augustus was also dead. Surrounded by the army of Cymru they began a walk toward Caer Maellot and the judgement of Arthur.

* * *

"Ah. Sir Gawain the Dragan slayer, and Sir Bors. Please come forward." Arthur said as he called Gawain before him in the Great Hall of Caer Maellot. He rose to his feet as Gawain knelt before him. "I wish to honor this brave warrior, and all the Knights of the Round Table." Arthur announced. "Because of their deeds on the field of battle this war was short lived. I hereby announce a new honor for those who do great deeds of valor in times of stress. I hereby make each of these warriors, Knights of the Golden Helm. Rise Sir

Gawain and Sir Bors. You have the hearty thanks of the people of all Cymru." He sat down as the two warriors moved to one side.

"Now. Who is the new leader of the armies of the Saecsen?" He asked.

"I am, my lord. I hight Adric the Bold. With the death of Augustus and Colm an Dragan I have assumed command of these armies."

"Good. Come forward and receive your punishment."

Adric walked slowly to a spot below the throne. At the foot of the stairs he knelt before Arthur. "I beg you if you take my life to spare the lives of my men." He said.

"No. I will not take your life, Adric the Bold, but I do have punishment for you. You and your men will be placed on ships and will be exiled from this land forever more. You may return to your own land, but if you ever sully the soil of this island again you will be summarily executed. Rise, Adric the Bold, and prepare your men for the journey before you."

"Thank you, Sire, for your mercy. We will go home and not return. You have my word."

Arthur waited until the Saecsen had departed the hall under the guard of his own men at arms. He smiled at the assembled company. "In honor of our victory, and of Sir Gawain and Sir Bors, we will have a ball to which all are invited. This is a day for celebration."

* * *

Myrdden sat in the library with Kevin, Tim, Maeve and Fiona. "I have what I believe to be good news." He said. "I have been in conference with Queen Titania, King Lir, and King Brian Connor. It would seem we have the ability to send you back to your own time and land just before the rock fell on your heads in the ruined castle. We will, of course, have to go back to Dun Rowans to accomplish this, but it can be done."

With the news Maeve gasped, but quickly caught herself and looked solemnly at Kevin. Kevin looked at Tim with an astonished look on his face then turned to Myrdden. "I thought you said such a thing would be impossible."

Myrdden nodded. "I did. But that was almost six years ago and much has happened in that time. King Lir and Queen Titania have been examining the various ways in which this might be done and they say they will be able to do it. So if you wish to return to your own time and bodies, we can make it happen."

Kevin turned his attention on Maeve, and could see the glistening at her eyes even though her face was stoic. He looked at her for a moment, half smiled, then turned back to Myrdden. "When I woke up in Dun Rowan for the first time my eyes beheld the most beautiful woman I had ever seen. She had rich auburn hair, green eyes, and was dressed in a lovely green gown. She didn't like me then, but since then has changed her mind. I don't know about Tim, but I could never leave Maeve. It would be like cutting the heart from my body. No, Myrdden. Thank you, but no thanks. I couldn't leave the only one who makes me into a whole person."

Myrdden nodded and turned his attention to Tim. As he did so Maeve quickly moved to Kevin, wrapped her arms around him and kissed him soundly. "There are more where that came from," She whispered in his ear, "and other things, too. *Oh, gra mo cre me, acushla*."

Tim watched the two as they hugged, turned to Myrdden and said with a grin. "I'm with him. I mean, how could he ever get along without me? I've had to watch over him while we were SEALs, now I guess I'll have to watch over him while we're here. Besides, without Fiona I'm a hopeless wreck. No, I'll stick it out here. Life up there wasn't as exciting as life here."

Myrdden nodded. "Then I have other news. First, Morrigan has gone back to that part of Avalon from whence she came. When she will return I know not. Then, Kevin, your father is ill and needs you home. He feels he is no longer able to rule as he should and wishes you to take the throne. You should leave as soon as possible."

"All right. Tim. Are you coming with me or staying here with Arthur?"

"Good question. What's your opinion on this?"

Kevin thought for a minute. "Well, I'm just on the other side of the Irish Sea, and that's not such a bad trip. Arthur is going to need advice from someone who has some idea of what will happen, even though it seems every story was pretty much fiction. Make sure he doesn't go after the Holy Grail. That was the cause of his downfall before. I don't know what to tell you about Gwyndevere. I think he is going to marry her, and the stories don't have that happening for another ten to fifteen years. I guess we play it by ear. Just make sure he doesn't try to invade Ireland. The stories have him doing that after winning in Alba."

* * *

“I am sorry to see you go.” Arthur said as he and Kevin watched the sun set over the Irish coastline. “I understand how it is, though. A king must give many things up if he is to rule with justice. I have found your advice to be good. I only wish I could continue to receive it.”

“Well, Arthur, you will have Timothy here, and he is very knowledgeable about future events as well. Besides, I will be just over there,” he gestured toward the opposite shore, “and I will be happy to have you as a guest, or be a guest of yours if trouble does come. Don’t be afraid to call me if you need me.”

“You have earned my respect and my trust. Tomorrow I will honor you before you leave by making you a Knight of the Golden Helm along with Sir Timothy. I am right happy you will leave him behind to help me. Now the Saecsen has been taken from our land there is much work to do.”

Kevin nodded. “Yes. Don’t forget, however, you will always have enemies jealous of your rule and the trust people have in you. Don’t let them throw you off the course you have set for yourself and your people.”

Arthur chuckled. “We have set. Without you I would never have tried these things. For that I owe you another debt.” The sun set below the horizon as the two men left the battlements overlooking the Irish Sea and went to the keep: one to continue his reign in what would later become Great Caer Maellot, and the other in his kingdom of Leinster.

book three
Caer Maellot

chapter 1
Arthur

Kevin MacMurrough stopped by the window on the fourth floor of Dun Rowans, leaned his elbows on the sill, and gazed at the view. Beyond the walls of the battlement lay green fields surrounded by dry stone walls. In their enclosed space sheep grazed contentedly. Woods of oak, maple, and beech grew down the hill above the outcrop of a cliff that had supplied the rock for the keep and battlement walls. Half a league into the ocean was a long green island with a round stone tower at the lower end. Kevin drank the view in with a half smile on his face.

"And what are you thinking, *acushla*?" The soft, throaty, voice of Maeve asked as she laid a gentle hand on his shoulder.

Kevin turned to look into the elfin face surrounded by a wealth of auburn hair. He smiled as he enclosed her in his arms and pulled her to him. "I was thinking of a time, so long ago, when I was retired from the SEALs and found I had inherited a broken down old castle in Ireland. Tim and I flew here to look at it. While we stood looking out this window of the ruined building that stone," he pointed to a stone above the opening, "fell and hit both of us on the head. Next thing I knew I was laying on this carpet in this castle looking into the face of the most beautiful girl in the world. Unfortunately, this beautiful girl hated me."

Maeve looked up into his eyes and smiled tenderly. "Aye, that she did. But, *acushla*, she no longer hates you. She loves you very dearly. Besides, you aren't the same person I hated back then. You may look like him, but you are you, and I am ever so thankful Myrdden, Brian, and the others were able to bring you back so I could have you." She looked out the window. "Was the view so different then?"

Kevin sighed. "Aye. That it was. The Saecsens had defeated Arthur and eventually took over this land as well. They tried to kill all the Celts because our religion was not the same as theirs, though we worship the same God. That is why it is so important that Arthur win and establish a peaceful land where there can be peace and plenty for all."

Maeve nodded. "And is that why you made our family motto *Siochin agus fiurse*?"

"Well, that and the fact I wanted it for all our people, not just for us."

"You are a good ruler, love, and there is peace and plenty in the land right now." She fell silent as she gazed at the scene outside. Finally she said. "I wonder how Arthur is, and Tim and Fiona. I miss them. After all, it has been four years since we saw them last." She looked up at him. "Perhaps we could visit them."

Kevin thought, then said. "Why not? I'll send a messenger over to let them know of our desire, and when we get word from Arthur, we shall go." He smiled as he took a last look from the window. "For now, let us go into town. I have a thirst, and would like to take a walk."

"A thirst can be slaked in the keep. We have plenty of ale on hand."

"Aye, but not the walk. Remember the publican when Aione and Kyle first saved us," he chuckled, "so many years ago? I believe I would like to go to his pub once again. After all, it was where you first said you had begun to have tender thoughts of me."

Maeve shook her head in mock dismay. "Acushla, I would think it more of Tir na nOg when King Brian told me the story. Sure that was the time my mind was set at ease, for then I knew though you looked like the Nasty Tease, you were not. That meant I could give you my heart and know it would be safe. But if you wish to wallow in remembrance, I will wallow with you."

At the entrance servants brought cloaks to cover the ankle length tunics they wore in the caer. Maeve's cloak, as usual, was a green that set off her auburn hair. Kevin's cloak was of an autumn red. Both reached from neck to ankle so the only thing to set them off from the rest of the people would be the thin golden circlet each wore around their throat. As they prepared to leave Aione and Kyle rose from positions inside the guard's room, took their own cloaks, and followed them out. Between them and Kevin a large Irish wolfhound followed at Kevin's heels.

The town was bustling this day as they walked down the dusty road toward the pub. Carts laden with dried turf for the fire were pulled through the street by cattle. The turf was supplied free to those who needed it with the only payment being for the labor of delivery. The various shops were set up to supply the necessities that couldn't be grown or made on the farms surrounding the town. As they passed the people would touch their forehead, and nod, as a note of respect. Kevin's walks through the town were well known. At first the people had been in awe of his presence, but over the past few years had become accustomed to seeing him. When he first arrived back from Cymru there had been doubts as people remembered the man who had left years before. Over the years he had become a beloved leader.

Michael, the publican, greeted him when he entered. "Ah, my lord, it is an honor to have you in my pub. Here, let me give you this table in the corner. From it you can see all that is going on. Aione, Kyle, greetings. Here. You sit at the next table." He turned back to Kevin. "My lord. It is almost the noon hour. My wife, Aine, has made a most wonderful stew. Allow me to serve you and our beautiful queen so you might have it along with your ale."

Maeve nodded her appreciation. "And would you also make sure Aione and Kyle are well served as well? You know to send your fees to Brand."

Michael smiled. "Aye, my lady, but I would gladly give you this free for all you have done for us."

"Nay. A workman is worthy of his compensation. Though, if the meal is as wonderful as you say, perhaps we might have Aine come to the caer to prepare it for us a few days during the month."

"It would be our honor, my lady. And believe me when I say you will find I do not lie about this meal." He bustled away to fill the orders.

Maeve smiled warmly as she watched him depart. "He is so proud of his lovely wife." She said as she laid her hand on Kevin's. "Almost as proud as I am of my braw husband."

A hearty baritone voice broke her reverie. "Aha! They were right. They said I'd find you here." The owner of the voice pulled two chairs from another table. His blonde haired and blue-eyed companion sat as he handed her to one chair, then he sat down. He opened his own cloak of midnight blue and rested his elbows on the table. "And how does it go with you two?" He said as Eamon and Duff joined Aione and Kyle at their table amid much pounding of backs and shoulders as old friends met after four years absence.

"Ah, Myrdden," Maeve said as she kissed his cheek, "it is good to see you again. You look just as young and handsome as ever; and who is this lovely lady?"

Myrdden looked fondly on his companion. "Oh, I've told you of her before. This is Nimue, and these are King Kevin MacMurrough and Queen

Maeve." He turned back to Kevin. "I felt it wise to bring Nimue with me this time. While we are here we age much faster than in Tir na nOg, and I don't wish to be an old man with a young wife."

Kevin, meanwhile, caught Michael's eye and pointed to the new arrivals to indicate he should also bring food and drink for them. Then he and Myrdden caught each other's hands in a warm handshake. "And what have you been doing since last we saw you?"

Myrdden leaned back as Michael brought a tray laden with four bowls of a steaming stew, two loaves of freshly baked bread, a large tub of butter, and four tankards of ale. "As you can see, I've been to Tir na nOg, "he said as he broke off a piece of the loaf and buttered it, "then back to Beigh, or Cymru, whichever you prefer." He took a spoonful of stew and his face showed his appreciation of its flavor.

"Arthur has consolidated his power there, and has the backing of the lesser kings. The Round Table is proving to be a good place for the leaders of his army to meet. Since he sits at it as well it is as though all are equal to each other. That alone makes for good relations among the leaders."

He smiled wryly. "Morrigan, on the other hand, was not defeated along with Augustus and an Dubh. It was said she went to Avalon, but the rumor was false. She had remained in Londinium, though they have shortened its name to London. Once she heard of the defeat she sent one of the lesser captains to the continent. While Arthur was consolidating Cymru into a united land she was working to undermine everything." He leaned back and shook his head, a wry expression on his face.

"Under her direction more Saecsens have entered the country and again have a sizeable force in and near London. Morrigan doesn't wish to display too much of her power, so is again running things from the shadow of a Saecsen named Marduch. There have been minor skirmishes along the border river, but there will be larger scale battles in the near future, I believe. "

Because of this I deemed it necessary to come here to inform you of events, and to ask you to return to Caer Maellot. Timothy has been quite helpful in organizing the kings, and preparing the men for the battles that may come. His command of tactics is well recognized by all. Still, you are the one who has more knowledge of the future of Arthur's reign, especially of the pitfalls he may face. I can see certain things from the Stone of Seeing at Lough Dorca, but you have read more of this coming time from that world of the future."

Kevin nodded thoughtfully. "Aye. What you say is true, but already things are not as I have read of them at that time. Besides, most people of my time think of Arthur as a fictional character made up by a number of authors who won't be born for a long time in the future. Historical knowledge of him has disappeared."

"In what way is it different?"

"Well, for one thing, Gwyndenvere here is a warrior princess, much like Maeve. In the books she is a young maiden who is married to Arthur when he is in his forties. Lancelot is a young man who doesn't show up until Arthur is in his forties, and he and Gwyndenvere fall in love while Arthur is away on one of his forages into Alba. Here Lancelot is one who is of Arthur's age and will probably go with him on those forages."

Merlin absorbed Kevin's words. "It may well be true regarding Arthur's personal life, but you also know of his battles and conquests. From what you have told me before Arthur's realm crumbles when he is defeated in battle against Lancelot. What needs be done is to retain the realm so it, and the dream, can be passed on to the future. A kingdom of learned men who will be ambassadors of peace would make a good legacy.

"Rome has become decadent and will not last much longer. The citizens of Rome no longer fight for her but hire their fighting done by foreigners willing to do battle for money rather than love of country. A country that depends on mercenaries cannot long last.

"Rome, though they were a very cruel people, held the world together through its military might. That might is no longer there. I fear when Rome falls there will be a long period of barbarism unless there is a land and a people to take on the burden of assuring peace and prosperity through their own might of arms."

"Aye, Myrdden that is exactly what happened." Kevin said as he leaned forward and rested his elbows on the table. "If I'm not mistaken, Constantine moved the actual Roman Empire to Byzantium a couple hundred years ago. What we call Rome today is a shadow empire, and when Rome finally disintegrated the continent became populated with small principalities while the church that operated out of Rome held it together. Then the church became a political power ruling through fear. Even the princes feared the power of the head of the church to keep them from gaining heaven when they died. It took almost a thousand years before that yoke could be broken. We call that period of time the 'dark ages'. It was only through the monks at the monasteries in Ireland that the learning of the ages wasn't lost. Many of the monasteries in Europe were actually begun by Irish monks."

Myrdden nodded thoughtfully. "Yes, and even now the beginnings of that are being felt. Rome has burned libraries in many of the cities they occupied.

I know the monks and followers of Padraig here in Eire are collecting the books and learning of other lands, copying them, and making sure they are preserved. I heard monks are leaving here to found monasteries on the continent to alleviate the events of the breakup or Rome. What you must do is help Arthur through the campaigns and, hopefully, assure the continuation of what he has started. If you can do this it will mean those 'dark ages' you talk about may not happen, at least on these islands."

Kevin looked at Maeve and smiled. "Well, we were already discussing going to Cymru to see Arthur. From the looks of things you have made up our minds for us."

"Good!" Myrdden lifted his mug of ale. "To a successful life! Now, if I can get some more of that stew…and find out who your friend is."

Kevin looked down at the dog lying at his feet. "This is Beog."

Myrdden snorted. "Beog, eh? He should be called Mor. He certainly doesn't look Tiny to me."

"When we found him he was pretty small, so the name was appropriate. Now," he glanced down again, "he has outgrown the name, but he's used to it so it stuck."

Myrdden reached down to let Beog sniff his hand. "Hello, Beog. I hope we will become good friends too." He glanced around and caught the innkeeper's eye. "Another bowl, if you please, landlord. I'm famished from a long journey."

* * *

Dun Rowans was bustling with the preparations for the trip across the Irish Sea. Kevin was in the library going over records of the men at arms. He looked up from the books, a thoughtful expression on his face, nodded, and said, "Thomas."

A servant standing outside the door entered and stood before the table. "Yes Sire."

"Would you be so kind as to find Aione and have him come to the library?"

"Yes Sire. Immediately." Thomas left on his errand as Kevin went back to the records. Minutes later Aione entered the library. "You called for me sir?"

Kevin looked up and smiled. "Yes I did. Sit down, my friend, I wish to talk with you."

Aione sat nervously, a worried look on his face. "Have I done something to displease you, sir?"

"No, nothing of the sort. I am quite happy with your service, so relax. Pour us a glass of wine. I have something I want to discuss with you." Aione rose, poured a glass and brought it to Kevin who added, a smile on his face, "I said pour 'us' a glass, so pour one for yourself now, sit, and relax." Aione did so cautiously. This familiarity was something quite new, though he had often experienced the largesse when sitting with his men at a table nearby when guarding his king. They never had to pay for food or drink when with him, and Aione made sure none imbibed so much they lost track of their duty. Something was afoot, he knew not what, and wondered what it would mean for him. He sat, still somewhat stiffly, and placed his glass on the edge of the table.

"I was just going over the records of the men at arms." Kevin paused to sip his wine. "I am thinking of retiring Hogan as Captain of the Guard. What do you think of my decision?"

"Hogan is a good man, sir, and has done an excellent job for you. The men all respect him." Aione was thoughtful in his reply. "Has he done something to offend you that you would let him go?"

"On the contrary. I believe he has done a remarkable job. He is getting a bit older and slower, however. When I say retire him I mean just that. He will keep his regular pay, he will have all the rights and privileges he now enjoys, and keep his house and garden area as well. He will no longer have the responsibility of command, will have the time to enjoy his family, and be able to enjoy the companionship of the men without having to order them around, and be able to enjoy the salmon fishing in the river."

Aione nodded. "That is good, sir. I'm sure Hogan will appreciate the fact he retains all he has earned through the years, and would still be part of the household. He has told me more than once how he loves being a part of this house."

"Thank you for your approval. Now, as for his replacement…"

Aione interrupted, "Roark would be a good man, sir. I've watched him the past eight years I've been with you. He has the respect of the men, is a good swordsman, and would do well as Captain of the Guard," he caught himself, "sorry sir, I spoke out of turn."

"Be at ease, Aione that is just why I brought you here. I want to hear your opinion regarding the men. I trust you, but I was thinking also. We have been together for eight years and you have been content to be a guard over me for that time. I see by the records you and Kyle have remained mere men at arms over that period. You have the respect of the men as well. I was thinking of making you Captain of the Guard."

Aione's face fell. He swallowed the sip of wine he had taken. "Have I not met with your approval in doing my job?"

"Of course you've met with my approval."

"Then why would you wish to transfer me to a different position?"

Kevin was surprised. "Why man, I was thinking of rewarding you for a job done so well. Captain of the Guard is a promotion. It will give you more pay and more responsibility. I know you get along with all of the men. You deserve more than you have. I was going to promote Kyle to your lieutenant as well."

"With all due respect, sir, I would prefer to remain with you. I know Kyle feels the same way. Our job is to make sure you and Queen Maeve are safe. We know how to do our job. I wouldn't really trust any of the other men to do my work. Over the years we have gotten to know both of you, how you travel, and how you are not always conscious of what is going on around you. No sir. I would worry about your safety far more as Captain of the Guard than I do when I am nearby. Promote Roark as Captain, and if you need a lieutenant young Ewan would be a good man. I prefer to remain at your side."

Kevin was obviously taken aback at this turn of affairs. He leaned back in his chair and stared at Aione, who stared back. His face showed his determination. Finally Kevin gave a deep sigh, and nodded his decision. "All right then, you obstinate Irishman, I am still determined to reward you. You are hereby sentenced to remain as my personal guard. This is a job, if I remember correctly, to which you appointed yourself when we were in Swansea. I now make it official. The same order will apply to Kyle. He will be officially the guard to Queen Maeve." He paused as a broad smile lit up Aione's face.

"Since such a position requires an officer rather than a mere man-at-arms you are hereby promoted to the position of Lieutenant of the Guard. The same promotion is awarded Kyle. Roark will be made Captain of the Guard." He smiled and shook his head as he chuckled. "Now finish your drink and get out of here, you ungrateful wretch. And thank you for your loyalty. You may tell Kyle of his promotion as well, and I will personally place it in these records to make it official. Now don't spend all your new found wealth in one place."

Aione rose to his feet, the smile still on his face. "Thank you, sir. You shall never regret it."

"I haven't yet, my friend, I haven't yet."

* * *

The Great Hall of Caer Maellot was ablaze with light from the large candelabra hanging from its chain and from the candles in sconces that lined the walls. Colorful banners festooned the walls, draped from staffs in wall holders, and hung from ropes stretched across the ceiling. On the balcony above the entrance the court musicians were playing a popular tune for those seated at long tables arranged in a large 'U' that left the center available for dancing or entertainment. Arthur and Gwendenvere sat in the two center chairs of the head table. Myrdden sat to Arthur's right with Kevin to his right, and Tim to the right of Kevin. Maeve sat to the left of Gwyndenvere with Fiona to her left and Nimue at her side. The kings and queens, and Myrdden, wore gold torcs while the others wore torcs of silver. On each side of the royal pair and their guests the others descended in order of their rank, with those below the salt being guests not of the aristocracy.

Arthur leaned forward. "It is good to have you back in court, Myrdden and Kevin." He said to the two. A grin broke his face as he added, "And good to see Myrdden has finally been able to bring his lady with him. She is as lovely as you said, my friend, and I see the ladies are finding her as companionable as are they."

"Maeve and Nimue became friends at Dun Rowans," Myrdden nodded toward them, "so I hope Gwyndenvere and Fiona will also become good friends with her. Like them, she is a warrior. Believe me, if there is another war, our backs will be well protected."

Arthur glanced to the ladies who were huddling to hear what the others were saying. He nodded. "Aye, and from the looks of it they seem to be doing just that. We are blessed to have both beauty and skill in our ladies. We are also blessed," he turned to them as he smiled, "to have a troupe of entertainers who will grace our board tonight. I was keeping it as a surprise from you, but they will be able to bring us news of what has been happening to our south. They have recently been in Cornwall and in the south of Cymru. I understand they were to our east before going to Cornwall, so may also have news of happenings in what is now called London."

His face became sober. "I understand from others that more Saecsens have been brought to this land by our friend Morrigan."

Myrdden nodded slowly. "That's what caused me to leave Tir na nOg." He said. "Oberon sent news to Kings Lir and Lugh about Morrigan's invitation to another group of Saecsen. She told them that there was unrest in the west and there could be an easy victory for them if they followed her instructions. I understand she sits on the throne next to the fellow called Marduch."

He smiled wryly, "One thing about Morrigan. She is probably one of the most beautiful women who ever existed. Unfortunately she uses that beauty to entice men into her traps. Once there they are like the fly caught in a spider's web. Like the spider she spins strong cords around them making them helpless to do anything but what she wants them to do. Unlike the spider her cords are invisible so she is able to make them believe what they do is their own decision.

"Morrigan is adept in her ability to manipulate. She attempted to entice me shortly after the destruction of Atlantis. Fortunately, as son of King Murdo, I had already been well trained in the arts of the mind. I received further training in Tir na nOg, as did Nimue, so now, with what I learned there, I should be the stronger of the two of us. Still, she is a very powerful opponent, and we must not underestimate her. She will induce Marduch into a war he thinks he wants, and once she finds out you have our presence to reinforce your resistance, there will be attempts on all our lives."

He shook his head, a sorrowful look on his face. "Unfortunately, Morrigan doesn't play by any rules but the ones she makes up as she goes along; and she's not above changing her own rules if they don't seem to be working. We must be careful."

Arthur motioned the servants for the food to be brought in. He nodded as he did so. "I know you are right, and I'm right glad to see you bring Kevin, Maeve, and their men with you. At the moment, though, Morrigan doesn't know you are here. If these entertainers decide to travel east when they leave here she will find out. If they go north it will take a bit longer for the news to get to her, but get to her it will. So, let us enjoy ourselves for the next fortnight as we have these entertainers with us. It will be a grand celebration of welcome to," he smiled happily as he lifted his glass of mead, "our royal guests and friends."

"If I might interrupt the festivities for a few minutes." Kevin turned to Arthur. "I have a duty to perform I feel I have neglected for too many years."

Arthur's face showed his curiosity." And what is that, pray tell?"

"I must honor Aione, Kyle and Finbar by giving them the gold arm bracelet to acknowledge them as Celtic warriors."

Arthur nodded. "That is a good idea. They are true warriors and deserve the honor. Do they know of it as yet?"

Kevin smiled and shook his head. "No. They do not. I wanted it to be a surprise. Do I have your leave to do this?"

"Of course you do. Why do you even bother to ask?"

"This is not my castle, so I ask the lord of the castle for this privilege."

"Granted. Now let's get on with the ceremony."

Kevin nodded to a nearby page. "Go tell Aione, Kyle and Finbar their king asks them to come to the Great Hall immediately." As the page left he turned to another. "Go to the library. On the table you will find three gold bracelets. Bring them and the bags of gold to me. Be back before my warriors arrive."

"Sire." Was spoken even as the page turned and ran toward the stairs leading to the next floor.

Shortly after three men in the livery of Dun Rowans came through the large doors and entered the hall. Kevin stood and called them forward. All three wore puzzled looks, wondering what they had done to deserve this – and would it be good or bad.

"Aione! Step forward to the table please." Aione did as he was commanded, his head held high and his shoulders thrown back. No one would accuse him of being a coward in case he was going to be censured. "Lieutenant Aione of the Royal Guard I commend you for the service you have performed for me, and thank you for the number of times you have saved my life. I hereby recognize your worth as a warrior and present you with this gold bracelet to be worn to show all of your status as an honored warrior. I also present you with this token of my appreciation."

Aione took the gold circlet and pushed it up onto his bicep as his face showed his emotion at this honor. He accepted the bag of gold as well, bowed his head to Kevin and muttered, "Thank you, my lord. It is an honor to serve you." The hall erupted with the sound of fists slamming down on the wooden tables to acknowledge the other's feelings toward the awards. Aione stepped back as Kyle was called forward to receive the same honor in the same way. Finally, after the hall had erupted with its acceptance of these men as warriors, they left to go back to their own meal and the evening's festivities began.

* * *

The Round Table was in its own room in Caer Maellot. The table itself measured twenty feet across. Seated at the table were the leading warriors of Arthur's army. Chairs had been added for Kevin and Myrdden as plans were made to anticipate the expected invasion of the Saecsen. Arthur leaned back in his chair, elbow on the armrest, chin resting in his left hand, forefinger across his mouth as Kevin presented his ideas. Of those at the table only

Myrdden, was aware of the fact of he and Tim being brought back from the future.

"Right now," Kevin explained, "our men are using two weapons; the sword and the pike. Both of these weapons are used in man-to-man fighting. This means the two armies are mingling with each other. Since both armies are generally dressed in similar fashion it becomes difficult to know whether the man opposing you is friend or foe. As you have noticed, my men are all dressed alike. When they fight they know they can attack anyone not wearing the same clothing they wear. In other words, they are uniform in their clothing. I suggest we do the same thing with the men under each of the kings here in Cymru.

"Also, I would suggest those of us who are leaders have banners with our arms blazoned on them, and perhaps a coat on which our arms are represented. The men in our commands would wear uniforms of the same colors in our arms so we could distinguish them quickly in the heat of battle.

"Another point I would like to make has to do with another weapon we might bring into battle with us. The bows we use are short and not very effective. There is a great deal of yew wood in the forests surrounding Caer Maellot. Here, let me show you my idea." Taking some of the rough paper that had been placed on the table Kevin took a piece of charcoal from the fire pit. He quickly drew a picture of a bow. "This bow is six feet long. Since each archer has a different draw length, we should make the arrows of a specific length. With practice each man would soon be able to judge from the position of the arrow on the rest whether his aim was true or not. Basically, this long bow is similar to those we now use. Its greater length, however, will give it a longer cast, and allow us to hit the enemy when they believe they are still out of range."

Lancelot smiled and shook his head. "Most of our archers are only five feet tall, or so." He said. "Their bows would be taller than them. The bottom limb would break when it hit the ground."

Kevin nodded assent. "True. But look where the handgrip is. It is a bit below the center of the bow. This means less than three feet of the bow will be below their shoulders, so there isn't any danger of the bottom limb hitting the ground."

"Let's give it a try." Gawain added. "Our bowyer can make one to the drawing Kevin made and the arrowsmith can make some arrows. Then we could have our best archer use the bow and let us know his opinion." He turned to Kevin. "How long would the arrows have to be?"

Kevin searched his memory for the length of the arrows the English had used in later wars. “I think a cloth yard would do, and we can fletch them with three feathers from the goose.”

Arthur nodded agreement. “I believe this is a good idea. If this proves out I would like to have a regiment of archers armed with the long bow. It might turn the tide of battle when the Saecsen army comes to invade us.” He paused then looked at Kevin thoughtfully. “Do you have any other ideas that might help, Sir Kevin, Sir Timothy?”

“I believe I do.” Tim took a piece of paper and drew a crude map of Cymru. “Here is the land in which we find ourselves. Here,” he put in a ragged line of mountains, “is the caer of Sir Ector. Here is Pembroke, Swansea, Bath, Cardiff, Harlech. Right now we have no means of getting news from here,” he pointed to Bath, “to here,” he pointed to Caer Maellot, “or here, here, here, and here.” With each ‘here’ he pointed to another of the villages where a king was located. “What we need is a means of rapid communication rather than relying on a man and a horse.

“Now, if we build a line of towers, all within sight of each other, and install a means of each signaling to another, we could pass word much more rapidly than a horse could travel between them.”

“How would they know what to signal?” Cai asked.

“Good question. We devise a system where a flag of a specific color in a specific position would indicate a direction, and perhaps an estimate of the size of an invading force. All the guards at each tower would need to know was what color indicated direction and size.”

Smiles spread across the faces of the men seated at the table. Lancelot nodded approval, “I believe the other kings will go along with this.” He said. “Getting an early warning means they can get their men assembled long before they could if they waited until a courier arrived. Having a better bow would also give them an edge over the enemy. Yes. I believe this might work. I hope we have enough time to get everything in order.”

Bagdemus looked at the crude drawing. He shook his head, a frown on his face. “I don’t see how the workmen of King Arthur’s can complete such a line of towers before the Saecsens attack. It would take an army of workers to do it before it is needed.”

“I don’t think it should be done with only Arthur’s workmen doing it.” Tim pointed back to the drawing. “It seems to me your workmen could build towers leading to your caer in Pembroke. Pelles workers would build towers leading to Cardiff. In other words each king sends a number of workers to build the towers that will alert them to danger." He looked up and smiled. "It only seems fair that the burden of building should lie on the shoulders of the king the towers are going to keep on their throne."

Accolon started to raise his hand in protest but put it down without saying a word. Tim waited patiently as the discussion took place. Those kings whose areas were not rich were protesting that it would cost them too much to undertake such a project. The kings whose fiefs were larger took the argument that they could not afford to do their own as well as the others.

In the end it was King Lot who banged his fist on the table. "Gentlemen." He roared out. "Cease this senseless palaver! All of you can afford to send workers enough to build three towers at a time, with an overseer to make sure they are in sight of each other. Once the first three are done they move to build three more. It won't take but a few months labor and a line of towers will extend from Caer Garda to your caer. I doubt Marduch will be in a position to attack us in the next three or four months. I, for one, would like to protect my throne and my lands from the cruelty we have seen the Saecsen commit when Vertigorm was leader. What say ye?"

The silence was almost palpable as the men looked at each other while Lot stood with a stern look on his face. Finally Ethelbert stood. His face was also stern, but he nodded. "Aye. Lot is right. I can afford to send enough workmen and overseers to build three towers at a time." He looked at the others. "And if I can do it, with one of the smallest fiefs of all of us, the rest of you can to. I'm with King Lot. I don't want to see my lands laid waste and my caer burned to the ground." He sat. In the end all agreed they could spare workers to build the requisite towers. Once it was decided the meeting was over.

Later, as Tim and Kevin were walking along the battlement surrounding the outer bailey, Tim stopped and looked out toward the Irish Sea. "Well." He smiled as he enjoyed the colorful display put on by the setting sun, "that's a start. I remember how the longbow played an important part in England's winning a number of wars down through the years. All we're doing is bringing it in a bit earlier than it first appeared."

"Aye. About five hundred years before the first records discuss it. Your idea of the signal towers was brilliant. I don't know why I didn't think of them myself."

Tim smiled. "Can't think of everything, can we? Anyway, I was remembering a couple books I read about the Napoleonic Wars and how there was a line of signal towers used that could pass the word rapidly. Like you, I just brought it in a bit earlier than it actually was used."

“I hope what we are doing will pass muster.” Kevin mused. “If we can get a peaceful future it would very nice.”

Tim suddenly turned sober. “If we get a peaceful future, and history is changed, does that mean we won’t have been born? After all, a lot of the reason we are here is because of the Irish famine, and England’s treatment of the Irish. If that doesn’t happen how will it affect us? Maybe, if things work out, we’ll just disappear and things will go back the way they were before we came.”

“You’ve been reading too much science fiction.” Kevin answered. “If what you say is true we would have disappeared already.”

Tim nodded thoughtfully as the rim of the sun dipped over the Irish coastline. “Perhaps. Or maybe we already live in an alternate universe. After all, who in our time ever went to Tir na nOg?”

chapter 2
London

If Morrigan was impatient she was controlling it very well. Her only reaction to the news of the visitors at Caer Maellot was a slight intake of breath and a quick raise of one eyebrow; an eyebrow that was just as quickly lowered. As the juggler moved his flaming torches through the air, catching them adroitly by the cool handles, she nodded her approval. When the bard sang his songs of the events in the north, of the walled city of Chester, and of a flood on the river Avon, her face was impassive. If she was seething inside no one at the table, and certainly not the entertainers, would ever guess, just as none would ever guess her true age. The time spent on the edges of Avalon and Tir na nOg had given her a slower aging process than other mortals. An aging process also acquired by her enemies, Myrdden, Nimue, and the rulers of Leinster. Morrigan still had the appearance of a woman of twenty, though it had been over nine hundred years since the destruction of Atlantis. She, like the others, would live an extraordinarily long life, unless it was cut short by a fatal accident.

No one could leave the table until Marduch had done so. Morrigan, who had Marduch in thrall, induced him to leave shortly after dinner was over and the entertainers left for their own meal. Marduch, wondering why she wished to call the evening's revelry to a halt so soon, rose, took her arm, and departed by the stairs in the corner of the room. Once in their room on the next floor he asked, "And why did we leave so early? The entertainers will be ready to give us more after they have eaten, and there is still much wine and ale to be consumed."

Morrigan nodded. "I know. You may go down again. I shall remain here for a little while. I must think where it is quiet, for they have brought news I had not wished to hear."

"What news is that?"

"They said Myrdden had returned to Caer Maellot. I believed I had gotten rid of him after the last battle. Too, he has returned with the king of Leinster, who is a gifted warrior, and his wife, who is no less gifted."

Marduch laughed as he shook his head at her foolish talk. "My dear, we have a well trained army at my command. The nobles and officers around my table are not only loyal; they are proven warriors. I have no doubt we can battle, and defeat, the paltry number of warriors this Arthur and his friends can send against us."

"You do not understand." Morrigan turned to him, a sneer on her lips. "Myrdden is a mighty wizard."

"So! You are a mighty wizard yourself. I have seen how you can make others do your bidding, and I have seen you turn arrows and spears in their flight. Surely he is not a match for you."

"Perhaps not." Morrigan said in a voice dripping syrup, "Still, it would be a hard fought battle," she turned away, "and I know not who would be the victor." She said so softly he couldn't hear. Turning back she added, "This MacMurrough is also one to be feared. While their army was not as great as that of Augustus and an Dragan, they were able to defeat our people. Remember well, the reason I invited you here was because the former captain took an oath never to return to this island. Since he was a man of honor I knew I couldn't get him back. You are here because of a defeat of the previous army. I want you to know whom you will fight now Arthur has been joined by these devils."

Marduch, who had seated himself as she talked, leaned back in the chair, placed his hands behind his head and said smugly, with a condescending smile, "My dear Morrigan. You worry too much. I am already a famous commander in the eyes of my people. I have many honors in battle and am considered a master of tactics. Do not trouble your beautiful head about such things as this. Leave the battles to one who knows what battle is like, and has already survived many. You just be the woman he wants to return to."

Morrigan shook her head in exasperation as she turned from him. "Go!" she said, "Go down to your entertainment and your men. One day you will see what I have said is true; and I hope it is not too late."

Marduch rose and put his arms around her. "Do not worry. We are well trained, and a surprise attack with your wizardry helping us will certainly win the battle. Once we have the south we can then move north until the entire island is under our control. I already have plans for our future as rulers. I have said it, and I will do it."

"Go downstairs, Marduch. Enjoy yourself while I make some plans regarding how to defeat them." She smiled wryly. "I will see what I can do about my wizardry."

"You do that, though I don't know why you won't come and enjoy the rest of tonight's entertainment. This is a very good troupe visiting us." As she nodded he left to go to the Great Hall. Morrigan began pacing the floor of the room, her face a picture of determination and thought.

* * *

Kevin sat on a stool in the courtyard near the stables as he applied a sharpening stone to the sword lying across his knees. Maeve, Fiona, and Nimue were riding in the countryside. Kyle and Bran rode with them. Duff, who was now assigned to watch over Nimue, rode with his friends. As Kevin worked on the sword edge Aione rounded a corner of the castle. When he saw Kevin he stopped and shook his head, a wry expression on his face. As with the others who had been to Tir na nOg he was aging slowly. He walked to his seated king. "Sir. What are you doing?" he asked.

Kevin looked up and smiled a welcome. "Why, I'm sharpening my sword. I thought it had lost a bit of its edge." He nodded to another stool, "Sit down, my friend, and join me."

Aione remained standing. "Sir. Do you trust me?"

Kevin's face was puzzled. "Trust you? Of course I trust you. You've been at my side for years, saved my life, shared food and drink. You are my Lieutenant of the Royal Guard. What makes you think I don't trust you?"

Aione looked at the sword. "If you trust me with your life why don't you trust me to sharpen your sword? Did you think I would do a poor job with it?"

Kevin shook his head as he looked from the sword in his lap to his lieutenant, a curious expression on his face. "I never gave it a thought." He answered. "I felt it needed sharpening so I came down here to do it. I guess I'm still in the habit of doing things for myself, as my former training taught me."

Aione nodded, pulled up another stool and sat down. He reached out his hand. "Would you allow me to sharpen your sword, Sir? I will do a very good job. That I promise."

Kevin lifted the sword and handed it, hilt first, to Aione. "I never doubted but what you would, my friend. I just never thought about it."

Aione took sword and stone, placed the sword across his own knees, and began the work of honing the edges. As he worked he commented. "Thank you, Sire, I feel it is my job to watch over your sword as well as you. Your life may depend on the edge, and I wouldn't want it to be dull." He gently moved the stone along the edge.

"Randall rode in from the east with his report. He says the line of signal towers has been completed from the first march near Bath to the various castles. One can easily see all of those nearest us, and each can see the next one down the line. Sir Timothy has devised a system so we can tell the direction and how many men might march against us." He smiled, "He also has a system so we can get early news of friendly visitors or entertainers at least half a day in advance of their arrival. Having all the workmen come from each of the kingdoms was a real help in completing the lines so fast."

Kevin nodded as he watched Aione's expert honing of the sword's blade. "Aye. Once they thought it over the other kings recognized the benefit an early warning system would give us. No enemy can make a sneak attack from the east. We will all be forewarned days in advance so we can assemble our men in the best locations to meet them. Sir Timothy had an excellent idea in the signal towers."

Aione pulled a hair from his beard and ran it along the edge of the blade. It was cut in two. He nodded approval. "That side is done. Now to sharpen the other side."

"If it comes out like the first I should be able to cut through the toughest leather armor any foe would wear. I have never gotten that blade that sharp. You do excellent work, Captain Aione."

"Captain?" Aione looked up, a startled look on his face.

"Aye, Captain. You deserve it. With it comes more responsibility, of course. You are now in charge of all my weapons, my armor, and me. You are also in charge of the others in your group. I have noticed they sometimes seem to lack leadership because all are of equal rank. Now, you will take the place you used to have before you joined me." He chuckled. "Though you don't look it you are older than them so your leadership is expected. You were their leader when you led them to me; you are their leader now. I trust you will serve all of us well."

Aione drew a deep breath and nodded. "I am honored, Sire. I didn't expect such an honor since there is already a Captain of the Guard back in Dun Rowans."

Kevin chuckled again. "Had you expected it you probably wouldn't have gotten it. You are right though, so you will be Captain of the Royal Guard and your men will automatically be the Royal Guard." He reached out and clapped Aione on the shoulder. "Your loyalty and friendship is something I treasure. I also notice you are not a braggart about your position with me. I can't say the same about your position with women, for I have heard some rather interesting tales regarding your use of your, uh, lance with the ladies, but with your men you are fair."

It was Aione's turn to laugh. He turned his attention back to the sword. "I'm afraid those days may be over, Sire. A lady in the court has caught my eye, and she doesn't approve of my being with others of her sex. She is cutting me very little slack in the noose she's tying around me." He looked up, staring into the distance, a half smile on his face. "I feel like a fly that has just landed in what looks like a lovely little net, only to find it is very sticky and my feet are caught. Now the spider comes and ties me up so thoroughly I can no longer escape."

Kevin nodded agreement. "I know exactly what you mean. I have been caught in the same web myself, and I've never been able to escape."

"Is that right, my dear husband?" A soft voice came from behind him. "And don't you ever think I'm going to allow you to escape." A gentle hand fell on his shoulder as he looked up into Maeve's smiling face. "I have you where I want you, and you'll never escape my web." She bent down and kissed him. "The trouble is, I'm caught in your web as well. I guess we are prisoners in each other's dungeon."

"I can live with that. After all, your dungeon is a place of great pleasure." He rose, took her arm, and began to leave, then turned and said to Aione, "I hope you are as lucky in your web as I am in mine."

* * *

In the Great Hall, as they watched the acrobats perform, Marduch noticed many of his nobles were already face down on the table. He took a seat next to his first captain. Out of the side of his mouth he whispered, "I tell you Claus, sometimes that woman acts as though she is demented. She is upstairs now planning a strategy to win a war against Arthur and his army." He shook his head in exasperation. "She is a pretty little wench, and very good in bed, but what gives her the idea she knows more of the tactics of warfare than I do? After all, she cannot be more than twenty years, while I have been fighting more years than she has been living." He laughed.

"Still, I have seen her use of her wizardry, and I will use it in our campaign to the west. Then, when she is older and has lost her looks, I shall lose her and choose another young wench. They are more fun than the older one's though, come to think of it, the older ones are very grateful after we have finished."

Claus wobbled his head to agree with his commander. “I think you have the right idea, Marduch.” His words were slurred as he looked, bleary eyed, at the performers. “Ash you shay, she ish a lovely thing. But what woman knows battle? I hear the women of the Celtic race fight alongside their men in battle. I hear they fight naked.” He smiled sloppily. “Now that I’d like to shee. I’d turn it into another type of battle before I pierced her with my dagger.” He laughed at his own joke, and took another drink of the ale before him.

“Aye, Claus, I’ve heard tales of the type of battle you prefer, though I understand it really isn’t much of a battle when you are involved. Nothing like what we will see when we fight Arthur. We must prepare to surprise him before he can rally his forces. For that reason I’ve devised a different type of battle plan. First, however, we must send in a spy. Do we have anyone in the slave pens who speaks their language and is willing to work for us?”

Claus thought for a moment, having difficulty in the process as the alcohol was clouding his mind. Finally he said, “I will have that matter looked into in the morning, Marduch. Right now I feel a bit sleepy.” With that he lay his head on the table and blubbery snores began to issue from his lips.

Marduch looked at him. “I should never have let you get so far ahead of me in your ale.” He murmured, taking another drink himself. “Now it will take me a while to catch up.” He turned his attention to the acrobats in the center of the floor.

chapter 3
Assignment: Assassination

Morrigan paced the room, her face a study in deep thought. Going to the window she threw open the shutters and looked out on the rooftops of London. Rain was falling vertically on streets already seas of mud. The only lights were those glimmering faintly from candle lanterns in several of the taverns offering ale and women for the night trade. Smoke clung to the rooftops like a wet blanket in the still, moisture-laden, air. A lone carriage plodded through the mire to some unknown destination while on the river a boatman slowly pushed a laden punt in the opposite direction. She studied the scene for a minute then a slow smile crept across her face. Turning from the window she picked up the small bell on the table.

"My lady." The last tinkle had hardly quieted before the maiden entered the room.

"Ashlee, is it?" The young maid nodded her head. "I wish to get some information from you. Please sit down."

"Yes lady." The girl seated herself next to the table. Morrigan seated herself across from her.

"Tell me, girl, do you know any assassins?"

The girl's eyes widened in surprise. "Assassins? Why, my lady, how would I know anyone who would do such a thing?"

Morrigan smiled cynically as she slowly shook her head. "Ashlee. Don't lie to me girl. I know you go into town, and I know you have friends in many of the taverns. If you continue to lie to me I shall have your nose bobbed and your cheeks slashed. Your ugliness will assure no man would look at you. Now," her voice was smooth as honey as she spoke; a pleasant smile on her face, "I wish to have some people disposed of and I want to know where I can find someone to do it. Do you understand me?"

"Yes lady." Ashlee licked her lower lip before answering nervously. "Bignose Roger and Fisheye Dick are both in town. I saw them at the Crown and Sword last eventide. They will do anything for hire."

Morrigan nodded; her eyes narrow slits in her face. She looked at the rough beams of the ceiling. "That is good. Perhaps they might take care of the men. Now tell me girl, do you know any of our sex who might be willing to do the same? Mind you, they must be comely. I wish no crones for this job. They must be able to pass as young girls wanting to work as maids," her smile was sweet, belying her harsh words, "for a queen."

"For a queen, lady? May I ask where? Since you are the only queen I know, and I don't think it is you, it must be someone else."

"Yes. In Cymru at Caer Maellot there are two ladies who I would have dead. There are three, actually, but the last is a witch and would be no match for a common person like you. The other two are normal and should be easily dispatched. The pay will be very handsome for the young girls you find. Do you know of any who might be willing to work as their maids and send them off while they sleep?"

Ashlee thought for a moment. "I have a friend, Peig. She is my age and quite pretty. She just started working as a girl for hire at the Wayfaring Stranger. She might be willing to work as a maid. I can find out."

"Good. I need two at least."

Ashlee thought for a moment, then smiled sweetly. "Would I do, lady?"

Morrigan's left eyebrow rose in surprise at the answer. She surveyed the girl, really looking at her for the first time. She saw a young blonde with a nice figure, a girl of about sixteen with a plain but comely face. She smiled as she nodded. "Yes. If your friend Peig is as comely as you I believe the two of you would do nicely. *Abair mo, un will gaylga agut*? (Tell me, do you speak gaelic)?"

The girl nodded. "*Ish mahy*. (Yes, I do)"

"*Agus tu cara*?" (And your friend?)

Again Ashlee nodded. "*Ish shi. Taimid an Eirrein*." (She does. We are from Ireland.)

"Good. Go find your friend and bring her to the castle."

"Now, lady?" Ashlee said, her surprise in her voice.

"Now! I wish her here before the sands in this glass are emptied." Morrigan turned an hourglass over. "Oh yes, If you can find the two villains of which you spoke, bring them with you. If you can't, leave word for them to contact me. Now, leave."

Ashlee curtsied, "Yes lady." She hurried out the door, darting a backward look at the sand slowly trickling from the top of the glass.

The hourglass still held a quarter of its sand when the two girls entered the room where Morrigan waited. Try as they might to keep their skirts from the clinging mud of London's roads, they could not succeed. The bottoms of both dresses were a shiny black mixed with the brown of the dung of horse droppings. Both girls were panting from the run back to the castle and the climb up the narrow stairs leading to this floor.

Morrigan glanced at the two girls, then at the glass. She nodded her approval. "Very well done. It shows your willingness to follow instructions. I presume you left instructions for the men to contact me." Ashlee nodded her answer, still too winded to speak. Morrigan nodded to two chairs now at the table. "Sit down while I discuss the situation with you."

Seating herself opposite the two Morrigan opened a drawer in the table and removed two daggers. With blades of six inches encased in a leather sheath, the knives looked innocuous enough. Morrigan withdrew one from its sheath, its steely brightness shining in the light of the wall sconces. "These are now yours." She said as she reseated the blade and pushed it across the table to Ashlee. Peig found herself in possession of the other.

"Now." She looked at Peig. "You are known as Peig?"

The girl nodded. "Aye, lady. Peigeen ni Molloy."

Morrigan mentally slapped herself for neglecting to learn Ashlee's name. Now she turned to the girl. "And your name, Ashlee?"

"Aislinn ni Flynn." She stated, giving her name the Irish pronunciation, which was very close to what Morrigan had already called her.

"And you are both from Eirrein?"

"Aye, lady. Loch Garmon, but our fathers brought us to Briton years ago. Then they died in the army and we were left on our own. Tis a wonderful opportunity you give us to better ourselves." Peig answered.

"Yes. I offer you a chance to make quite a bit of money, and if you succeed I will offer you good positions in this castle. Now, listen closely to me." As she spoke Morrigan looked deep into the eyes of each girl, knowing by doing so she would bend them to her will. Once she had them under her will they would do anything she commanded. Slowly their eyes closed under her spell until both chins rested on their chests. Morrigan smiled then commanded. "Raise your right hand and pat your hair in place." Both girls did as she commanded.

"When you wake up you will remember none of this. You will be sorry you fell asleep in my presence. You will believe you must leave London and travel to Cymru. There are positions for maids at Caer Maellot and you wish to return to your own people. You will remember deep in your mind what I now tell you.

"In Caer Maellot there are two ladies of high renown. One is Queen Maeve, the other is Princess Fiona. These two ladies are very evil. They are in league with the Prince of Earth and Darkness himself. Because of this you will be a blessing to the world if you use these knives to kill them as they sleep. You will act quite normally as you work your way into their confidence. Once they trust you completely you will be able to kill them. After you have killed them you will remember nothing of your part in their deaths, but will leave Caer Maellot and return here as soon as possible. If anyone asks why you leave you will say you received word your mother is ill and needs you. You will then come directly to me to report the success of your deed. You will remember none of this until the time comes to use it. Now, wake up."

Both girls stirred, their eyes opening slowly. They looked around, startled, then at Morrigan. "I'm sorry, lady. I didn't mean to sleep in your presence. It was that I was suddenly so sleepy I couldn't keep my eyes open." Ashlee said, looking around her in trepidation.

Morrigan laughed. "Do not worry, my dears. Sleep is a blessing all of us seek. I do appreciate your bringing Peig to see me, Ashlee. Now, what is it you wished to tell me before you fell asleep?"

Ashlee thought for a moment. "Oh…yes." She said as if suddenly remembering something important. "Peig and I wish to leave London and go to Cymru. Neither of us like city life, and we want to return to our own people where they speak our own language instead of this strange tongue of the Saecsens. I felt I should tell you and beg your permission to leave your employ."

Morrigan looked from one to the other. "Both of you are unhappy here and wish to go to the land of the Celts?" She asked. Both girls nodded. "All right. You have my blessings. You have been a good maid, Ashlee. The two of you may sleep here until morning. In the morning I will give you fresh linen, some money to tide you over, and an escort to the borders. I hope your journey will prove profitable."

"Thank you, lady. Perhaps we can do something for you sometime as well."

"This is quite possible. Time will tell. Where are you planning to go?"

"We thought we would go to Caer Maellot. We heard they need maids there, and we will make good maids. We hear King Arthur is a good king to work for."

"I have heard that as well. Sleep now; and blessings on your travel." Morrigan left the two, a smile on her face. Things were going well. She went to the Great Hall to join Marduch. Her plan was almost complete.

As she entered the Great Hall a wry smile touched her face. A bard was singing, but only to those of his troupe that were there, for Marduch had joined the rest of the nobles and officers. Heads resting on the table in front of them, or thrown back in the chair in which they sat, the occupants of the hall were asleep.

Morrigan looked at the bard who stopped singing at her glance. Having been with a troupe herself she well understood what had happened. "Well, sir bard, it would appear your lullaby has soothed all the savage breasts. Since no one is awake to hear your lovely songs I give you leave to find your own rest."

The bard bent his head in acknowledgement. "Thank you, my lady. It is greatly appreciated." As he and his troupe left the hall Morrigan picked up the tankard before her chair and drank. Putting it back on the table she patted Marduch's head. As he stirred and murmured drunkenly at her touch she said, "Sleep well, my lord. Worry not. I shall take care of things tonight."

As she left the hall a guard approached with two ruffians in tow. "My Lady." He said as he approached. "These two said you wished to see them. They said your maid told them to come here."

Morrigan eyed the two men up and down. It was apparent they had acquired their names honestly. The nose of the one called Roger was bulbous and veined in red. His hair was grizzled and stringy, while his cloak was grimy with the filth of many seasons. The other, as unkempt as his fellow, had a scar running from forehead to chin across his left eye. The eye itself was unable to close and of a blue/white color that indicated blindness. Both were very obviously from the lowest dregs of London's society. She shook her head in dismay and looked at the guard.

"I had told my maid to send me two warriors for a job I had. The job will require someone a bit more refined than these two. Give them each a piece of silver and send them on their way. They are certainly not fit for the positions I am trying to fill." Disgusted, Morrigan went to the stairs and returned to her rooms.

* * *

The port city of London drew the ships from many places. Roman, Phoenician, Greek, and Irish trading vessels were always present at the docks. Once their wares were safely in the houses lining the docks the seamen, thirsty and lusting for women after long and arduous days at sea, would head for the taverns lining the mole. What better place to find the type of men for the work Morrigan had in mind?

Morrigan was impatient. Marduch and his men slept drunkenly in the Great Hall, waiting until the morrow, and the end of their headaches, to begin planning their strategy. Taking her cloak and hood from its peg she fastened the tie at her throat and went down the stairs to the main door. Her ability to cloud the minds of the guards allowed her to leave without being seen. The rain had stopped, though the streets were still a mass of mud to which she paid no attention. She knew exactly what she wanted, and walked along the mole looking for a ship that had the rake of an Irish curragh. She knew when she found it the men would not be far away, for they would look for the nearest tavern to slake their thirst for ale, and their desire for women.

The docks along the mole held two vessels of Irish types. The tavern they would frequent was at the top of the dock. Morrigan threw back the hood to allow all to see the beauty of her face, opened the cloak to display her figure, and entered the public house. She walked to the bar. "I wish a room for the night." She said to the owner. "How much?"

The publican looked her over and smiled slyly. "For such a beauty as you, three pence for the night."

Morrigan gave him a scornful look. "Do you take me for a fool? I am willing to give you one pence for the night, and that is overpaying you."

"Are you trying to rob me of food for my children?" He threw up his hands in horror at the thought. "Two pence, and not a half pence less."

Morrigan showed her irritation by shrugging her shoulders and then nodded. "Two pence then, but I will want your best room for my business."

The innkeeper smiled and nodded. "The best room you shall have, for I know a lady of your beauty will do well tonight. With all these seamen you will be kept very busy, and make good money for your labors. You may use Room 1 at the top of the stairs."

Morrigan smiled and nodded. "You have my thanks. You may find a surprise awaits you at the end of the night." She turned back to the room as she began a survey of the men that would be available to her. She wanted the man young, comely, and strong. Her eyes quickly passed over those who were older, and those who had obviously seen too much sun and sea. She knew from experience that once she had bedded a man he was in her power for the rest of his life. Unlike the use of hypnotism, as she had used on Ashlee and Peig, the man in question would do her bidding long after he had left her side.

There were four young men she could see; young men of perhaps twenty years that would serve her purpose. She sidled up to the first and gave him a seductive glance. Her beauty was such no man could withstand her use of it given her dark powers. In only moments she was leading him by the hand to the stairs. When they came back she led him to a table, bought a tankard for him, and went to her next victim. Within two hours she had the four men for whom she sought. Approaching the table with the last young man in tow she said, "Come with me. I have work for you."

The small party walked up the mole and entered the castle grounds. Though they passed three guards they went unnoticed. Upstairs Morrigan seated them at a second table in the library. Nearby the two girls still slept under Morrigan's spell until she would awaken them in the morning. She had no worry about their hearing what she would say to the young men.

She spelled out her plans for their employ over the next hour. They would escort the two girls to Caer Maellot where all would ask for employment. The young men, all of them with Gaelic as their language would pass unnoticed as to their assignments, just as the girls would not be noticed for a strange way of speaking. When they had the opportunity they were to kill Arthur, Kevin, and Timothy. Once they had their orders and her strategy had been given Morrigan told them to sleep until she woke them. On the morrow they would begin their westward trek.

She felt very content with her success as she undressed, washed off the evidence of their lust, and went to bed. While they were not able to rid her of Myrdden she felt they would be able to rid her of the leaders of the caer. She slept well that night.

Chapter 4
A Sword Fit for a King

Before sending her select group on its way Morrigan decided to have them walk to Cymru. Too much unwanted attention would be attracted if six peasants rode while other peasants walked. A cold rain had begun as they left the castle, and continued for the four days it had taken to walk from London to the pass that would lead to Cymru. Though it had not been a hard rain it had left the roads little more than mud paths the entire distance.

Heads down to escape the wind that blew the sharp needles of rain into their faces, they moved through the pass and into the little town at the foot of the mountain. The money given them by Morrigan would bring food, lodging for the night in a rude inn, and a meal to send them on their way the following morning.

As they slept the storm broke and they woke to a day of clear sky, a warm sun, and a drying road. They had no suspicion their journey had already been marked by a signal tower on the heights above. There, a sharp-eyed servant of Sir Ector's saw the small party leave town. The flags he waved toward the tower on a hill ahead gave number and direction. Long before they would get to the coast their approach would have been noted, and news of their progress passed on to each tower on their way.

Morrigan's ability to control their thoughts through hypnotism had left them with the surface idea of obtaining employment at Caer Maellot. In the hour before she woke them she changed her mind about stabbing them. Concocting a poison she gave each of the girls a small vial with orders to put it in their ale once they had been able to get the women to trust them.

As the group walked the westward trail they discussed the opportunity that would face them if the two girls could become maids for the queens, and the men could become part of the guard there to protect the Irish king and his friends. No thought, or discussion, was given to the buried reasons for their leaving London for the west coast of the island. Instead, their youthful good humor led to much flirting, joking, and as they bedded for the night, coupling. This youthful behavior was transmitted as information as they passed without noticing the various wooden towers hidden by the rows of trees near the lane on which they traveled.

* * *

"It is difficult, nay, impossible to get into that castle in London." The voice came from near Myrdden's shoulder. It was the voice of Oberon. "I have sent Puck to do the spying. If anyone can get information it will be that lad. He's young, only about two thousand years, but he's a good devious head on his shoulders. Still, he says the castle itself is protected by some sort of spell the likes of which he's never seen before."

Myrdden was used to the way the fae operated when in the land of the mortals, so wasn't surprised when he couldn't see Oberon. The fae can become as small as small as insects when they so desire, or appear to be as large as mortals. Oberon was about the size of a butterfly as he sat on Myrdden's shoulder. "So he hasn't been able to get any information from there at all." Myrdden answered in a flat voice.

"Och, I didn't say that." Oberon said with a chuckle. "I merely said he can't get into the castle, so has no idea about plans of attack. Morrigan is not always as smart as she believes herself to be. She left the castle in a disguise a few nights ago. Puck reckoned she was up to no good, else why the disguise, so followed her. He was right in his thought. She went to a pub near the docks where the ships from Erin dock. She rented a room to which she enticed four young, strong, Irish seamen. She slept with them then took them to the castle with her. She used her powers to blind the guards to her exit, and to her return with the four. Then, five days ago, the four men and two young women left the castle and are on the way in this direction. You might check with the signal operators as to any news of them."

Myrdden nodded. "You are correct in that. If Morrigan slept with the young men she has some control over them. I know not whether her control lasts as they move away from either the time of their coming under her sorcery, or a distance away from her. If she sent them they are up to no good. I suspect the same of the women, though it would have to be another type of sorcery for them. I appreciate the warning. I will look into the matter right away. It sounds as though your Puck does have a good sense of what is going on."

"Oh yes. While he is a merry soul, given to horseplay, he does well when the situation warrants. He is still trying to find a way into the castle. Perhaps Morrigan has left one of the entrances unguarded."

"Possible, though in these circumstances I suspect she has tried to cover all ways in. I'll check the guards in the watchtower and see what information they might have on these six travelers."

"Oh yes," Oberon added, "Tenedril was assigned to follow them when they left London. She reports they are all talking of getting employment with the kings here at Caer Maellot. The two women wish to be lady's in waiting, the four men apparently wish to be guards."

Myrdden nodded, a wry smile on his face. "Good warning, Oberon. If I know Morrigan she has assassination on her mind. Did they talk of anything like that?"

"Tenedril says the only thing they talk about, besides bedding each other, is employment here. Those seem to be the only things on their minds."

"From what you say they are young and lusty."

Oberon laughed. "Young and very lusty, from all reports. I will keep you informed if any more information comes out of London."

"Thank you for your help in this. I fear Marduch will attempt a campaign before too long, and I think Morrigan is trying to make sure the opposition doesn't have much of a chance." He chuckled. "I believe she may be in for a surprise."

* * *

The dingle by the river was quiet as Myrdden and Nimue walked, hand in hand, along a path near a small waterfall. Myrdden stopped and pulled her down beside him on a mossy embankment. He knew, after the years together, she was what many would call fae, a dark one, a seer, and one who would much later be termed a psychic. He looked into her dark green eyes, eyes that could flash from being a seductress to a seanachie to fae all in seconds. "Tell me, acushla, what do you see in the future with these young people?"

Nimue smiled slyly, "Ah, Myrdden love, sure what would you do without me?"

Myrdden shook his head. "Without you? I don't even want to think of being without you. You mean everything to me."

Nimue nodded. "Aye. That is true. Together we make a whole. Separate we are only a part of a person. Each has talents the other lacks." She sighed and closed her eyes. "I can see two young ladies who do not know they have been sent to kill the two Irish women. They have been given a potion to be slipped into the wine, a potion that will cause them to become as stone. While they will appear to be dead they will only be without their conscious self, their bodies rigid and seemingly not breathing. They will be buried and not wake until two days after they are entombed. It will then become a horrible death they will have." She opened her eyes and looked into Myrdden's. "You are stronger than Morrigan, love, and can undo what she had done."

"What has she done?"

Nimue's forehead furrowed in thought. "She has placed them under a spell. She took over their minds and has given them thoughts she buried deep. They do not know these thoughts, and are of the belief the potion is one that will help the two live a longer life. They will not even realize it was what they did that caused their deaths."

"And I can stop them from this?"

Nimue nodded. "Aye. You must take control of their minds, as Morrigan has done, go deep inside and root out the idea of putting the potion in their wine." She paused. "Better yet. Get the potion from them so they do not have it any more. Once it is no longer in their possession they will forget about it and become trustworthy help."

"And what of the men with them?"

"As Oberon told you, they are to kill the kings and Timothy. As you know, she has a power over anyone who has sex with her. I am uncertain right now how you might be able to overcome her power. I won't know until I see them, talk to them, and touch them what might be done outside of their deaths, to prevent their attempts to take the lives of our friends."

"I believe, my dear, we must have a talk with Morrigan."

"The protective circle?"

"Aye. The protective circle. While it will only be her spirit that comes to us, that spirit will be visible and powerful. We must protect ourselves until we can find some way in which we can send her to a place where she can do no harm for a long time. She will live long, as all of us who have been in the environs of Tir na nOg will. She must not succeed in her desire to rule all of Briton, and after that the world."

"I will meet with these men after they arrive. Meanwhile, Arthur must be protected, as must the others. What will you do?"

Myrdden shrugged. "I must see the Lady of the Lake and obtain her advice. I believe she has a desire to see Briton free from the oppressive boots of a conquering force of strangers."

Nimue closed her eyes again. When she opened them she smiled. "I believe that is the right choice. Much good will come of it." She smiled coyly. "We are alone and will be for some time. Isn't there something else we would rather do than talk?"

* * *

They sat at the round table, leaning back in their chairs, their crest emblazoned on the table before them and a banner with their coat of arms hanging on the wall behind them. Myrdden was the one who spoke first as Arthur and the others listened carefully. "We have a group of six travelers, peasants from their wearing of the gray cloth, made up of two young women and four young men. They are all from your province of Leinster, Kevin, if I'm not mistaken. Oberon tells me they have come to seek employment with us. The two women wish to become maids to Maeve and Fiona. Nimue informs me they come to assassinate them." These two raised their eyebrows and listened more closely. "I believe you may also be in danger, Gwyndenvere, for I believe they have been sent by Morrigan."

He turned his attention to the men. "There are four young men who are coming to seek employ in the Royal Guard. From what Oberon said they are all from Irish trading ships. Morrigan went to the docks to search for young, lusty, men she could seduce, and thus compel them to do her bidding. When she beds a man he becomes her thrall, for how long I do not know. Until now she has been in constant contact with those she has bedded, and since she sleeps with them near every night the spell has no time in which to wear off. These men have now been a week since they were ensorcelled, and have bedded the girls during that time. That being the case I have many questions regarding Morrigan's power after men leave her side for a period of time."

Myrdden paused, his gaze fixed on Kevin's banner. Then, his words slow and thoughtful, he said. "I have no idea as yet whether she spins a lifetime spell, or one that wears off in a short time if the man is away from her bed. I will find out once they arrive. Be it known, as far as we can find out, the purpose behind all of them is assassination. Morrigan is once again attempting the conquest of Briton, and she knows it will be much more certain if all of you are dead before the battle begins. I doubt Marduch knows of this treachery, for his is a warrior's heart, and he would wish to win the victory on the battlefield, not in the bedroom." Myrdden leaned back in his chair as he finished.

Silence filled the room as his audience digested the news. "What do you suggest we do?" Kevin asked quietly.

Myrdden shrugged, a half smile on his face. "I suggest you hire them in the positions they wish. I do not believe their assignments will be carried out quickly. After all, in order to do this thing they must be near you, and they will only be near you when they have gained your trust, and the trust of your guardians." He spoke to the women as he said this. "Just be on your guard with them. Since you sleep with your husbands I doubt they would risk death at his hands if they attempted this thing at night. I would suggest, however, you sleep with your swords near at hand."

He thought for a moment more then nodded. "Aye, but this is Morrigan. Nimue says the young ladies are meant to use a potion on you. The potion would be more her manner of doing you in for if the girls stabbed you they would be quickly caught. Be careful what you eat or drink when they are near. Meanwhile, before they have a chance to do any harm, I will see what I can do to stop this nonsense before it can start."

He turned to Kevin, Tim, and Arthur. "As for you three, you have your captains of the guard. I know Aione is going to be leery of these four from the start. He will let nothing happen to Kevin. The same goes for Finbar and Tim. Your captain is also loyal, Arthur, so tell him to be careful how he uses the one you may assign to your guard." He turned to Lancelot, Galahad, and Cai. "You can help as well. Very discretely inform those men under you, men you can trust to hold their tongues, to take care and be watchful of the actions of these men. Arthur, I have told Eamon and Duff to guard you at all times. My own powers, and those of Nimue, will protect us now more than their prowess at arms. Meanwhile, once here and hired I will have a discussion with each of them." He nodded sagely, the half smile returning to his face. "I also have another plan that will take a bit of time to bring to a head, but I believe it will accomplish more than any battle ever could."

Arthur looked at him quizzically. "And what is that plan, Myrdden?"

Myrdden shook his head. "You really do not want to know, Arthur, for it involves a bit of what you would call ... wizardry."

Arthur nodded. "So I wouldn't understand even if told, eh? A wizard against a witch, eh? I certainly hope you are stronger than she is."

Myrdden sighed. "So do I. Though I believe I am." He shrugged. "She does have a powerful ally, though. Yes. We shall see." Myrdden rose from his seat and began pacing the room. All eyes were on him as he walked back and forth, hands behind his back, his face stony as he thought. No one interrupted his thoughts, knowing when he had figured it out they would be told. Finally he stopped behind Galahad's chair. His gaze rested on the silver shield of Arthur, silver with a red dragon rampant.

"Unfortunately Morrigan is not the least of our worries. We know Marduch has a larger army than ours at the moment. While I may be able to thwart her plans to assassinate the rulers here in Caer Maellot by overcoming her power over the six she has sent, we still have to face the Saecsen army when Marduch finally decides to attack."

His gaze lowered from the shield to Arthur's face. "That means, Arthur, you must call on the other kings, and Ygraine, to send their armies to swell our ranks. Perhaps first, a sweetening of the honey jar by inviting all of them to a grand banquet here at Caer Maellot. While entertaining them…er…royally you might point out the danger we all face if the Saecsen armies win over ours. We would become their slaves. And given their bent for violence and cruelty," his face took on a crooked smile, "a gift to them from the Romans perhaps, none of us would escape beheading; at a minimum. That would come after a period of torture to wear our spirits down."

Arthur looked around the table, an unasked question on his face. As he looked at each member of the Table Round he received a slight nod of approval. Finally he himself nodded. "Yes, Myrdden, an excellent idea." His sigh was one of resignation. "I suppose I must invite Ygraine, she is my mother, after all. I wonder, though, if she has forgiven me for being the son of Uther as well. When last we met we parted on terms that were not too happy."

Myrdden nodded. "This is true. Yet there have been four years pass since the last time, and time can heal many wounds. Because she commands the armies of Tintagel she must needs be invited. Since there will be so many kings in attendance we must also have the best of the bards in the country attend for their entertainment. Perhaps you could send messengers to find Wamda the Green and his troupe. You must spare no expense to win them over. You must prove your right to be high king."

"I thought I already had when I pulled the sword from the stone."

Myrdden shook his head. "Then, yes, you did. Unfortunately one must prove oneself each time one faces a challenge. There are many who would come against you to overthrow you if they felt you were not living up to the duties of high king." He paused and there was a silence no one wished to break. "I must obtain a sword that is fit for a high king." He murmured to himself.

"I still have the sword from the stone, and another given me by Gwendenvere on our marriage."

"Aye, that you do, but that is not the finest sword in the kingdom. The one was placed with a spell by the Lady of the Lake. It is a rather ordinary sword, special only because you are the sole person with the ability to remove it. Some of the other kings have finer swords than that. The only reason they wanted it was because it would mean they would occupy the seat of High King.

"The marriage sword is better than that of the other kings, but it is still one made by mortal hands. We must obtain a sword that will let them know you are the one blessed and chosen to lead. I will see to it."

Myrdden looked at Arthur. "Now, with your permission, I must see what information the watchmen have regarding these six travelers. Do not send out the invitation until I am sure of having the sword. That should take only two days."

"Perhaps we should just tell them we need no new help and send them on their way." Lancelot opined.

Myrdden shook his head. "No. If we do that she will conclude we have some method to spy on her plans. Best we hire them, and watch them. I should not be gone longer than two days. By that time they will have arrived here. I will talk to each of them separately, but not in such a way as to raise their suspicions. We want nothing to get back to Morrigan. I presume she got her previous information from the bards that were entertaining us when Kevin and Maeve arrived."

"But we will have bards, and other entertainers, if we have a banquet for the other kings." Arthur said. "Once they leave they could go directly to London and in their entertainment there let her know what is happening here."

Myrdden nodded. "I know. We will have to be very careful about what is said and done while they are here. We want nothing to get back to Morrigan until it is too late for her to act on her knowledge."

"All right. You will handle things your way, and I have noticed that your way is usually right." Arthur turned to the others. "I believe we can go about our normal business. Be watchful: and especially watchful for the safety of our visitors from Ireland once these travelers arrive. I would not wish to be the one to send unhappy tidings back to Leinster regarding their king."

* * *

The guard on the ramparts of Caer Maellot was bored as he leaned on the parapet and watched a ship enter the harbor and prepare to dock. Nothing had happened on the watch, and now a ship was landing at the foot of the cliff. Leaning over the parapet he watched as the ship, Irish from the cut of her sail, warped slowly toward the quay. The crew spilled the wind and the sail dropped. The small ship slowed rapidly as the pilot moved the tiller to bring her side to the edge of the pier. Then, with the ship dead in the water, the sailors threw lines to the men waiting on the pier. Heaving on the lines the men began pulling the ship toward the dock. Once safely alongside they tied the lines to the wooden bits of the pier.

As he watched he saw a white haired man in the green and gold livery of the Province of Leinster wait for the gangplank to be lowered. By his side was a huge Irish wolfhound. The dog looked around, and though the guard couldn't see it, there was a sad expression on its face. The man began walking up the road that led to the gate of the castle. The dog followed obediently at his heels. The guard moved to the inner portion of the wall to watch as man and dog entered the inner bailey. Once inside the gate the dog lifted its head and sniffed the air. As it did so its entire demeanor changed. The head rose, the eyes lit up, and breaking away from its keeper it raced toward the back of the bailey as the man ran clumsily behind it.

Kevin was entirely unprepared for the attack as the dog rounded a corner, saw him, raced toward him and leaped. Both paws landed on Kevin's chest as, off balance, he went backwards. The dog's paws remained on his chest and the huge head came down, a red tongue came out, and Kevin's face was thoroughly washed. Laughing, he hugged the dog. "Beog." He said, "I'm glad to see you too." From his position on the ground he looked up as the Castellan of Dun Rowan came to his side. "Och, Michael. To what do I owe this honor?"

Michael looked at the two forms lying on the ground. "Wasn't Beog pining away at Dun Rowans because he missed you? And didn't I think if he couldn't find you he might just die? So didn't I think the best thing I could do was to bring him over here to see you were all right?"

"Aye." Kevin struggled to his feet as Beog tried to keep him in the reclining position. "'Tis good to see you." He looked at the happy wolfhound standing at his side, "So himself missed me, eh? 'Tis good to see both of you. Beog, go greet Aione. You'll be helping him guard me." The dog turned its head toward where Aione was standing, but didn't leave Kevin's side.

Four years earlier, on a hunt in the province, Kevin's party had come across a wolfhound puppy in the forest. The mother had apparently been killed by a wild boar, but the puppy was still near and, small as it was, trying to protect her. Kevin took the snarling bundle of fur, petted it and soothed it.

Since it was so small he named it Beog, which means Little in Gaelic. The name stuck even though Beog was now a very large dog, and one that generally wanted to be near Kevin wherever he went.

"What is that?" Tim asked as he came around the corner of the keep and spied Beog by Kevin's side.

"This is Beog." Kevin answered, his hand on the dog's head. "Beog. This is Tim, and he is a friend. Treat him like a friend." The dog looked up as Kevin spoke then looked at Tim.

"Is Beog some kind of pun?" Tim asked as he approached, holding out the back of his hand for Beog to smell. "The name sounds like a word we used to use in English to mean large. Looks like you have a double pun in his name."

Kevin shrugged. "When I found him he deserved the name. When he grew he sort of outgrew the name as well, but it was too late. Just remember though. I used to have a dog I named Kitty, just to make the neighbors shake their heads when I called for Kitty and a golden retriever ran up."

Tim shook his head as he patted Beog's head, scratched behind his ears, and in general began making friends with him. With Kevin by his side Beog allowed Tim's ministrations, and since there were no threats to Kevin, began to accept him. "I think you should show Maeve he has arrived." Tim finally said as Beog began licking his hand to show his acceptance. "Unless, she doesn't know you have a dog here."

"You're right. I think she has missed Beog as well. Come on boy, let's find your mistress." The two walked off followed discreetly by Aione.

* * *

On Myrdden's return he went directly to the Great Hall where Arthur was just having the noon meal served. "Come! Sit! It is good to see you back." He motioned for those to his right to move down a seat to make room. "The travelers have arrived, and as you advised, have been hired. We are being watchful of them. The four men have become men at arms and are eating with their contingent in the warrior's mess." He threw the remnants of a pork chop to the dogs waiting behind the table.

"That is good. I shall talk to them when we return." Myrdden stabbed a piece of roast beef he had just cut from the large round and placed it on his plate. He then spooned a large portion of mashed turnips yellow with melted butter, and some greenery that was on another dish. "Right now I'm hungry." He added as he began to demolish the food on his plate. "It was an interesting journey." He added between mouthfuls.

"You said, when we return. What do you mean by 'we'?"

Myrdden smiled as he chewed a bite of meat. Finally he said, "Just what I said. You and I are going to go to the Lady of the Lake and see if she will surrender a sword to you; a sword whose name means 'cut steel'. In the language of the fae it is called Excalibur."

Arthur's eyebrow lifted. "A sword of the fae? They are very reluctant to give mortals any of their workmanship. What if she says 'Nay!'?"

Myrdden shrugged. "Then we shall have tried. I have a feeling obtaining the sword is a possibility, but only you can ask. She demands to see you, talk to you, and judge you for herself. Once she has done so she will make up her mind."

Arthur nodded. "This is a good sword?"

Myrdden laughed aloud. "Good? My dear High King, this is a sword that is far above all other swords. It is a sword that was once worn by the leader of the Tuatha de Danaan and later won by the High King of the Milesians. The Fae, remnants of the Tuatha de Danaan finally won it back and have been keeping it since in their away places." He nodded. "Yes. This is a good sword."

"When do we leave?"

"If you have finished your meal as I have finished mine, we leave immediately."

Arthur motioned a servant over. "Have my horse saddled, and provisions made for a two day journey." He ordered. "And make sure Myrdden's steed is also saddled and provisioned."

"Aye, my lord. It is done." The servant bowed, touched his forehead, and left.

"I must change to traveling clothes." Arthur said as he rose. "I shall be with you in a quarter glass. Since you are still in your traveling clothes I shall meet you at the gate."

* * *

"This is the lake?" Arthur asked as they came to a large basin formed as the river filled in a large, low, area on its way to the sea.

Myrdden nodded. "Aye. This is the lake, and here is the Lady of the Lake."

Arthur turned to see a young woman dressed in a swirling, diaphanous, light blue gown. Her face was composed, her eyes were deep blue, and her hair seemed to blow about though there was no wind. The slim circlet of gold around her head indicated her station in her own land. Arthur bowed before her. "I am honored to meet you, Your Highness."

She nodded, and then spoke in a voice that resembled the sound of water as it flowed over the stones of the river. "Myrdden has informed me of a boon you would ask."

Arthur nodded. "Yes My Lady. He informed me of a sword, a sword named Excalibur, that you might allow me to use in my defense of this land."

"You say, 'In defense of this land.' What do you mean by that?"

"There is a woman from Atlantis who is guiding the Saecsen invaders in an attempt to conquer Briton. I would defend against them then bring the entire island under one rule that we might be stronger than any invading force. To do this I must needs have a sword other kings will recognize as belonging to one who deserves their respect, and whom they will allow to be their leader."

The Lady of the Lake lifted her hand and placed it on his head as she closed her eyes. When she opened them again she said, "You speak well and it would seem your motives are pure." She beckoned to the lake where a pale hand rose above the waves holding a sword and its sheath. "There is your sword. Go and take it. Use it well."

Arthur looked at the expanse of lake before him. "But I have no way to get to the sword." He said.

She smiled. "Then take my boat." Arthur looked at the lake and there was a boat that had not been there before. It had no oars, nor oarlocks. He looked back at her. "Get in." She commanded. Arthur did so and the boat moved of its own power toward the hand and sword. Once there it stopped, he took the sword still encased in its sheath, and the hand slowly moved out of sight beneath the surface. As it disappeared the boat moved back to shore of its own accord. Only Myrdden awaited him.

Arthur scrambled onto shore the sword and sheath in his hand. Standing before Myrdden he unsheathed the sword and admired its beauty, as well as its balance and heft. "This is a handsome sword." He breathed. The hilt was of ebon circled around with gold wire. The guard seemed also of gold, though it was not soft, as gold would be, but seemed harder than iron. Along the side of the blade in the alphabet of the Fae, its name was etched. He turned to look at the lake. The boat was no longer there and the lake was calm as the surface of a mirror.

Myrdden smiled. "She judged you." He said. "And came to the conclusion you were honest in your desires. Now, which do you like the most, the sword or the sheath?"

Arthur looked at both. He swung the sword in an arc before him. "Ah, the sword is extraordinary. Yes. The sword is what I choose."

Myrdden nodded. "The words of a warrior. The sword is important for anyone it strikes will receive a death blow. Yet it is the sheath that is the more valuable of the two. When the sheath is firmly attached to the belt, and the belt is around your waist, you cannot bleed no matter how many cuts you receive. Never sheath that sword in other than the one in your hand. Now put it about your waist and we will return to Caer Maellot. We have much work to do."

As they rode Arthur turned to Myrdden and asked. "Of what use is not bleeding if I have many cuts?"

Myrdden shook his head in amazement. "Because, my dear Arthur, if you do not bleed you do not lose blood. If you do not lose blood you retain your strength for fighting. Once the fighting is over you will be able to go to the surgeon and have your wounds repaired so when you do remove the sheath and belt you will only bleed a little, and will heal more rapidly. That is the value of the sheath."

Arthur nodded wisely as he slapped a hand to the sword at his side. "Cut Steel and a protective sheath. Och, that is a good combination for what we may find coming our way in the near future."

* * *

"Ah." Myrdden said as he came upon one of the new girls. "You are new, I take it, and your name is?"

The young girl smiled as she curtsied. "I am Peigeen, your honor, Peigeen ni Molloy. Yes. I am new and am now a maid to Princess Fiona."

"Good." Myrdden's voice was jovial as he motioned to the library they were passing. "Would you mind sitting for a moment with me? I would ask you a question or two."

Peig's brow furrowed. "A question, Sire? About what?"

"I understand you and your friend have just come from London and I would enjoy hearing the news from there."

Peig smiled in understanding. "Yes, Sire, I'll gladly give you the latest news from there." She entered the library and waited as Myrdden seated himself. He waved her to a chair, and she gingerly sat down at the table. "Is this all right?" She asked nervously.

Myrdden nodded. "Quite all right." He sat down opposite her and caught her eyes with his electric gaze. He spoke soothingly as he brought her mind under his. "Close your eyes and rest. It has been a difficult trek to Caer

Maellot and you are tired." He smiled as Peig's eyes closed and her breathing deepened. "Now look into that part of you that has been hidden since you left London. What do you see?"

Peig's voice was almost a monotone as she answered. "I see Ashlee finding me and taking me to the castle. She said the queen had work for us."

"You met with the queen?"

"I met with the queen."

"Her name?"

"Queen Morrigan."

Myrdden nodded as a wry smile touched his lips. "And what did Queen Morrigan do and say while she talked with the two of you?"

"She asked if we spoke Gaelge. When she found we did she told us to come here to work as maids to two evil women."

"Who are these evil women?"

"Queen Maeve and Princess Fiona."

"Why did she want you to work for them?"

"To gain their trust. Queen Morrigan gave us a potion to place in their wine. At first she gave us knives, but then thought the potion would be better. She wanted us to kill them at first, but then told us the potion would overcome their evil and change them into good people. Once we have done that, and they are changed, we are to leave Caer Maellot, and return to London where she will use us as maids."

"Peigeen ni Molloy. Listen carefully to me. I am Myrdden. I order you to open your mind to mine, and especially the part that Queen Morrigan closed off."

Peig's face furrowed as she struggled to do his bidding. Then she shook her head. "It is not for me to have the strength to open that door. It is shut very tight."

"Will you let me help you?"

"Oh, yes. I wish to open it but I need someone stronger to help me."

Now Myrdden's eyes closed as he moved to Peig's mental side and began pushing on the door Morrigan had locked. In his mind he saw the lock and the bolt holding that door shut. As he stared at the lock he mentally forced it to unclasp. It came reluctantly open as Morrigan's power, strong as it was, succumbed to his. The lock opened and dropped to the floor. Now they pulled the bolt, pushed, and the door swung open.

"Is the door opened, and are you ready to open that room to me?"

"Peig nodded. "I am open and ready. What do you wish?"

"You have been given bad information. You have discovered Queen Maeve and Princess Fiona are not evil. They are good." He paused. "Erase the suggestion and belief they are wicked. Replace it with the knowledge they are good women who treat you kindly and do not harm you in any way. Because they are good you will enjoy working for them. If you like it here you do not have to return to London. Do you understand?"

Peig's face was calm as she nodded her head. "I understand. Queen Maeve and Princess Fiona are good women. They do not ask too much of us or beat us as other mistresses have in the past."

A smile touched Myrdden's lips. Nimue was right, as usual. His ability to capture their minds was more powerful than that of Morrigan. "What do you think of Princess Fiona? Do you enjoy working for her?" He asked.

Peig smiled. "Oh yes. Princess Fiona has been kind to me. I was surprised she was so polite in asking me to do things for her instead of ordering me to do them. I think she is a very good lady, and I am going to enjoy working for her."

Myrdden nodded, a satisfied smile on his face. "Good. You will remember our meeting here as a talk of the news of London, and you will retain the belief in the goodness of your employers. When we are through you will go to your room, get the potion Queen Morrigan gave you, and bring it to me. You may now awake, and you are finishing a talk of the news of your trip."

Peig opened her eyes. "…then we saw the walls of Caer Maellot. It is such a lovely castle. I am glad we were hired. Is that all you wish to know, Sire?"

Myrdden nodded. "Thank you, Peigeen ni Molloy. You have given me some interesting news. Did Aislinn work in a different place than you?"

"Oh, yes Sire. She worked for the queen herself. She has much other news you might like to hear. Would you want me to send her to you?"

"I would appreciate it, if you know where she can be found."

"Oh, I do Sire. If I might leave I will find her and have her come to see you. Do you want her to come to the library?"

"Yes. Send her here. I'll wait for her coming."

Once Peig had departed Myrdden sat at the table. *So Morrigan is up to some new tricks, eh? Her powers have grown; no doubt of that. I'll straighten Aislinn out, make sure she gives me her potion, and get the latest news from the castle.* He sat for a moment longer. *Ill have to check out the four men as well. Nimue is probably correct in saying they are assassins. I must try to overcome that power she has over them, but how? Once I get all the information I had best have a talk with Morrigan.*

chapter 5
Assassins

"Now, Sir Kevin, I have the yew blank ready to be made into a bow. I don't quite understand how you wish this done." He shot a nervous glance at Beog, lying on the floor of the workroom near where Aione stood watching Kevin and the bowyer discuss the new weapon.

Kevin walked to the table, picked up a piece of charcoal, and said, "Here, let me draw you a picture of what I would like. The upper limb of the bow should be slightly longer than the lower limb, so the riser will go here with the hand grip here." As he spoke he was making a rough drawing of the bow he had in mind. "The riser should be carved so as to fit the hand of the user. So I would make an indent here where the web between thumb and forefinger would go. Now, looking at it from the archer's viewpoint there should be a window carved just above the grip, with a shelf on which the arrow rests. This keeps the hand from being cut by the fletching on the arrow when it is released."

The bowyer looked over the rough drawing. After digesting the picture he nodded. "I see. The notches for the string should be about an inch below the top and bottom of the bow. How high above the riser should the string be when the bow is fully drawn?"

Kevin placed the side of his fist on the table and lifted his thumb straight up. "I believe this should give the right distance between riser and string." He thought for a moment. "Still, I believe once it is done we should make a number of strings of different lengths and see which of the heights gives the better cast." He smiled and shrugged his shoulders. "After all, we've never made a bow quite like this before so we have to do a bit of experimenting with it. When do you think you can have it done?"

"I'll get to work on it right away." His face puckered in thought. "I believe I might be ready to test the first one in two days. Once we know what we are doing we," he indicated his helpers, "can probably do at least two a day."

"That's good." Kevin rose from the chair. "Let me know when this one is finished and we'll have an archer test it out. Meanwhile, have one of your men make a number of strings, each about a fingernail's length shorter than the other. Then we can find out what the correct fistmiel will be and make the others accordingly."

"Aye, Sir Kevin. I'll let you know." He touched his hand to his brow then took up a shaver to begin working the wood. Kevin and Aione, who had watched the doings with interest, headed toward the keep. As they left the room Beog gave the bowyer a last glance, and trotted at the heels of the two men.

"Aione." Myrdden called as Kevin entered the keep. Aione turned to look at him, cast a watchful eye on Kevin's retreating back, Beog at his heels, then motioned Kyle to take his place as Kevin's bodyguard.

"Aye, Sir." He answered as he walked to Myrdden.

"Come with me for a moment. I won't keep you long. I just need some information, and wish to give you some as well." They moved to one of the benches near the wall of the keep. "What think you of these four who have joined us?"

Aione gazed in the direction of the barracks where the four should be at the moment. He let out a sigh of frustration. "To be honest, I am torn in my thoughts of these. They are braw men and will make good warriors." His face twisted into a grimace. "Yet there is the possibility of their being sent here to kill my king. I would they were evil to the bone so I could kill them myself, but they aren't. They are good men of Eire who came here to find a good job. I don't know what happened to turn them into assassins, and I don't care because if they try anything they are going to be dead before they can accomplish it."

Myrdden nodded. "I know how you feel. What happened was they all lay with Morrigan. There is something about her that when she has lain with a man he becomes thrall to her and will do her bidding. I know not how long this slavery lasts, but I hope to find out. I believe it is diminishing; yet I'm not sure. Just make sure your men are on constant guard until I can overcome her allure over them. From my observation the desire to be with her again is a major part of her power." He paused. "It has been a month now, how much are they trusted by others in the keep?"

"Too much, in my way of thinking." Aione answered. "Not all know of their intent, and since they are braw, likeable, men in all other ways everyone has taken to them. They have the run of the keep, as far as I know, and it is that freedom that gives me pause." He looked toward the entrance to the keep. "If you don't mind, Sir Myrdden, I'd like to get back to my duty. I trust Kyle like I'd trust my own brother, but I feel better when I'm at his back."

Myrdden smiled and nodded. "I understand, Aione, and I commend you on your loyalty. Go back to your duties. I'll try to see you when Kevin is abed." He chuckled. "I know you aren't that close when he's abed with the queen."

Aione gave him a queer look, then headed toward the entrance to catch up with his liege. In the foyer Kyle was flirting with Aislinn, and didn't hear Aione's approach. Aione tapped him on the shoulder and said, "I thought I told you to guard Sir Kevin."

"I did." Kyle answered. "But when he went up to the library with Beog I though it was safe to leave him."

Aione went up the winding stairs two at a time. Beog, lying out of sight near the door looked up at his entrance, recognized him, and lay his head down on his paws. Aione moved to the other side of the door and sat on a chair that was also hidden from anyone entering the room.

Time passed with only the sounds of Kevin's writing on the parchment with the goose quill pen. He was recording the earlier events with the bowyer, and what he hoped to accomplish once the bows were in the hands of competent archers. As he wrote, his mind fully occupied with his task, he didn't notice as Beog raised his head and looked toward the open door. A man dressed in the gold and green uniform of Kevin's guard entered the room slowly. His eyes were fixed on Kevin's back as Beog's head came off his paws. His eyes now were fixed on this interloper he didn't yet know.

Unknown to the intruder there was another pair of eyes fastened on him as well. Both Beog and Aione watched as the man quietly approached Kevin's back. When he was an arm's length away he slowly drew his scian. The small knife was all that would be necessary to dispatch the unknowing Kevin. At the appearance of the scian two things happened so rapidly as to be one move. Beog was out from under the table as he leaped for the man's throat, and Aione's own scian was buried in the man's back before he could even raise his own to kill Kevin. Kevin leaped to his feet and turned to see the soldier's body, the throat torn out, lying in a pool of his own blood.

"Off, Beog! Good boy." He said as he patted the dog's head. Looking at Aione he smiled. "Thank you also, my friend. With the two good bodyguards

I have I should be safe from anything." He looked down at the body. "This is one of those sent my Morrigan, isn't it?"

"Aye, Sir." Aione looked at the body and nudged it with his foot. "It looks like her spell lasts a bit longer than Sir Myrdden thought. If you don't mind, Sir Kevin, I'll get a servant to clean this mess. I'll also send one of my other men to watch while I let Sir Myrdden know what has happened. I shan't be gone long."

Kevin gave a half smile. "Aye, Aione. Go let Myrdden know so he can talk to the others of this group. Perhaps her spell isn't as strong in them, or perhaps they will have to be sent to one of the other kings until it wears off. I would rather not have them killed if they can be rescued from her spell. And, yes, have some of the servants' dispose of the body and clean up the mess. Meanwhile Beog and I will go to the Great Hall and inform Arthur of this event."

* * *

Myrdden shook his head in disgust. "I must find some way of countering the spell Morrigan has over the other three men. Except for the fact they are sent to be assassins they are good men. The fact the spell is unknown to them is another thing. They are supposed to kill the kings and don't even realize that is what they are to do. It must be something in her blood that gets into them and causes them to come under her spell."

Nimue listened to his musings, and his frustration, as they walked in the garden outside the walls of Caer Maellot. She was silent, thinking her own thoughts as Myrdden expressed his. They walked in silence for a bit as she mulled his words over in her mind. "Perhaps you have the cause without knowing it." She said.

They stopped in the middle of the path as Myrdden looked at her, a puzzled expression on his face. "What do you mean?" He asked.

A half smile touched Nimue's lips. "Perhaps," she said as an eyebrow lifted, "it is not her blood, but other of her fluids that are absorbed."

Myrdden shook his head, the puzzled look still covering his face. "I don't understand."

"You say she lays with them and after they have lain with her they are in her thrall." Myrdden nodded assent. "Then perhaps it is other of her fluids that bring about that compulsion to do her bidding."

Myrdden's expression changed as he understood the point she was trying to get across to him. "I see what you mean." He shook his head sadly, "But I have no means at my disposal to counter that type of charm."

Nimue laughed. "Of course not, but I may be able to do something about it."

"No. I do not want you to lay with them."

Nimue laughed merrily. "I don't mean to lay with them, m'acushla, but I do mean to mix a potion that we can give them that may counter hers. You are more powerful than she, as we have seen when you were able to break her spell over the two young women she sent to kill Maeve and Fiona. Perhaps I am more powerful than she in other ways. Tonight I will make a potion we can put in their ale tomorrow. We will then see if I am more powerful than she in this use of our fluids to bring men to do our will."

"Do you believe yourself to have that power?"

Again Nimue laughed as she lifted her head and kissed Myrdden's cheek. "M'acushla," she whispered, "I get you to do my will, don't I?"

Myrdden laughed, "Aye that you do, but that is because of the love I have for you."

She looked at him archly, "Are you sure that is the only reason? I have you under my spell. The trouble is, I am also under your spell so I do what you wish also. Go tell Arthur what we are doing, and I will bring the potion to you later." She reached up and kissed him again. "Don't be too far away, acushla." She smiled archly. "I will need you to help me obtain the fluids."

* * *

Marduch marched into the Great Hall and stood before the dais and throne he had installed. A servant came up and helped him remove the helm, thick leather breastplate, and arm protection. Once these were removed he unbuckled the sword belt and greaves. "Ah," Marduch breathed, "in a way it feels good to have those things removed, in another way I would desire to keep them on that I may march westward with my armies." He shook his head, a puzzled look on his face. "I can't understand why Steiner has not yet come with more reinforcements. I shall have to send another messenger to let him know of my displeasure."

Morrigan nodded agreement. "Aye, my lord, and when he arrives you will have to share the glory of the conquest of the island with him. Which of you, pray, will be High King and which will be vassal?" She cocked her head to one side and gave him a long, sultry glance. "Och. That is the question, is it not? How went the campaign to the north?"

"Very well! Very well! We took our army into the fen country. They have been giving us trouble for some time. They have raided some outposts to obtain arms and food. We know not which of the villes were conducting these raids, so we decided to teach some a lesson. Not wishing to kill all in all the villes we selected two, surrounded them, and marched in. There was a bit of combat, but we quickly subdued the men and herded them to one side. Then my men had their way with the women as the men watched, and as they still watched, we killed the women as we finished with them. Then we killed the men."

"And the children?"

Marduch smiled broadly. "You should have been there. It was great fun. We took the children and had two of my good captains throw them in the air. The game was for the soldiers to catch them on their spears as they fell. The ones who were able to center their spears on the body were given special rations. Those who were not so accurate were made to parade with their spears for the space of a full glass. That will teach them to have better focus as they aim at the enemy to the west."

"So none of the children lived, eh?"

"None. The villes are now deserted of people, though not of the blood of the people. We buried none so that the other villes would see our mettle and our focus. That will bring them to our cause if nothing else will."

Morrigan raised an eyebrow as she tilted her head to one side. She shook her head, a sad look on her face, but said nothing further. *What is done is done*, she thought, *there is no use pointing out the fact that killing the children will further their resentment, rather than bring them to our cause. Once we have won the day I shall have to do something about him... and his army. I want the people on my side, but that means I must win their trust after I rid myself of this braggart. Those that don't come to me will, of course, deserve death.*

To the north, in the fen country a lone boy of ten years rose from the carnage in a ruined ville. He looked around at the bodies of his family and friends. For a while he wept over those of his family who lay in the cold hands of death. When the weeping was over he tore strips of cloth from the hem of his mother's garment and used it to bind his own wound. It was painful, but even at the age of ten he knew the spear thrust in his side was not fatal. Then, drawing a deep breath, he turned his gaze to the west. His face was set, his blue eyes cold steel slits, as he found a small punt and began rowing along the narrow waterways that made the fen a maze. He knew the maze, and he knew how to keep himself hidden from the soldiers who might be patrolling various areas within the fen.

Once out of the waterways and on hard ground the boy moved quickly and quietly through the forests and glens as he snuck by outposts of Marduch's men. At first food was stolen from the stores of the sleeping soldiers. As he moved further west food was obtained from peasants along the way who listened to the story he told. When he continued his trek he left them with faces hardened by the tale. Neither Marduch nor Morrigan would find allies in these people. Nightfall found him sleeping under the thatch of one of the houses, miles from the previous one. It would be days before he reached his destination, but he was not deterred.

He might be too small to do much about what had happened, but he had heard Marduch talking of the reinforcements he had sent for, of the coming battles between his armies and those of Arthur, and his plans for future conquests. Arthur would be warned that there would be another army besides that of Marduch that would be coming against him.

* * *

As the various kings began to arrive at Caer Maellot Myrdden found Aione. He beckoned him to a private area where he dug into the pouch at his waist. He brought out three small vials stoppered with wax. "After what happened in the library Nimue and I felt it would be best if we could find a potion to counter Morrigan's power over these men. These vials hold that potion. We worked most of the night to obtain the necessary fluids to make them, but we feel they will counter her spell." He handed them to Aione. "Take these three to the pub and buy them a pint or two." He smiled sardonically, "When they are somewhat stupefied pour one of these vials into their drink. It will cause them to sleep, but also should counter the spell."

Aione took the vials and place them in the sash at his waist. "I understand, Sir. If you don't mind I'd like to attend to this right away. I know where the three are and they are off duty. A pint or two at the pub would be welcome."

"A pint or two for them, Aione, and charge it to the castle. It would behoove you to make sure you are not caught addle witted."

"Only in appearance, Sir, only in appearance. My wits will be sharp throughout. After all, I was there when their friend attempted Sir Kevin's life. I don't want anyone to succeed in that."

"Good." Myrdden turned to leave, paused, and then turned back. "Let me know when it has been accomplished. When they wake I will wish to ask them a few questions to see if our potion has worked."

Myrdden went back to the keep and the Great Hall where the leaders of Cymru were beginning to assemble. All would be here by the morrow, but tonight there would be the first of the feasts that would mark every night of their visit. Feasts, and the entertainment of the most famous of the poets, would assure the continued interest of the guests. Arthur had made sure to send for the cream of bards and poets. Simon of Locklear, Liam of Glastonbury, and Michael of Llannfirr were men who were allowed to wear seven colors in their clothing. Their rank was the equal of that of the kings whom they entertained. They would be well received.

* * *

After the noon feast Arthur rose from his seat in the Great Hall. "Let us adjourn to the room of the Table Round," he said, "for we must make plans to defend ourselves against the possible attack from the east." Heads nodded assent as the guests rose and moved toward the great doors. Leaving the Great Hall they walked down the corridor to the room where the table was found. The servants had been busy for all around the room were now the coat of arms of the participants.

After finding their seats beneath the shields bearing their arms Arthur, seated at their level, began the meeting. "Word has reached us from the east that this Saecsen, Marduch, is preparing an army to come against Cymru in the near future. The witch Morrigan, at least some call her a witch, has sent assassins to Caer Maellot to murder King Kevin of Leinster, Sir Timothy Mac Egan, myself, and our wives. One attempt has already been made. The assassin's head is now on a pike at the entrance to the castle, as you may have seen when you arrived. The threat is real, though as yet his army is not ready. The question is this: should we march eastward and catch him unaware or should we wait and form our lines of defense here, in Cymru?"

"Are you very sure of his plans?" The question came from Ygraine of Tintagel, Arthur's mother.

Arthur nodded. "Yes, Queen Ygraine, the information we have is quite good. What we do not have is any information as to when he plans his attack."

"Is not your army sufficient to win the battle against him? After all, he cannot have too many men in place and ready to go to war."

"It depends on the size of his army. King Balin of Bath has the latest information." He turned to where Balin was seated.

Balin nodded wisely. "Aye. My spies in London have brought information to me that the Saecsen armies now number ten thousand or so.

Marduch has sent a message to the continent to bring another army and another commander to help him. As yet, I believe, he has received no answer. Of this I am not sure for much might have occurred in the four days I was enroute here."

Ygraine arched an eyebrow at Arthur. "So, the question remains, can your army win over an army of ten thousand?"

Arthur sighed, shrugged his shoulders, and said, "I don't know for sure. I know we have some new weapons King Kevin will demonstra…" An interruption came as a loud knock sounded on the door to the room. Arthur turned toward it, annoyance showing on his face. "Enter!" he called. The guard came in, pushing a small boy ahead of him.

"Sire." He said. "This lad just arrived from the fen country north of London. He was half starving when he arrived. We fed him and as he ate he told us his story."

"So?" Arthur said, his voice cold.

"We believe, my mates and I, all in this room should hear it."

"It has to do with what we are discussing here?"

The guard nodded. "Aye, Sire. It does that."

Arthur beckoned the boy over to him. "Come here boy." As the boy approached he asked. "What is your name?"

"I hight Robert of Cardis, Sire."

"Well, Robert of Cardis, what brings you to Caer Maellot?" The boy stood trembling before King Arthur then looked nervously around the room at all of the other kings and warriors there assembled. "Speak boy. No one here will harm you. You are among friends."

Robert began the story of what had happened at his village. As he spoke his voice broke when he came to the murder of his parents and his brother and sister. The four queens in the room moved to comfort him. As the tears and trembling subsided the boy continued with the tale of his near escape from death, his desire to come to Caer Maellot to get help to avenge his family, and the way in which he had finally got there.

"Thank you, Robert of Cardis, for I believe you have made up my mind for me." To the guard he said, "Take the boy out and make sure he has a bed. From this time on he is part of this castle." Then he raised his head and looked each of the other kings in the eye. All four queens had wept with Robert as he told of his family's death, and their eyes had become steel hard when they heard of the killing of the young children. As Robert of Cardis left their eyes were hard and faces set in stern lines. The men had also been touched by the tale. "Well, my lords, what is your desire?"

There was a babble of comments as each tried to speak and whatever they had to say was covered by the talk of the others. Arthur finally restored order. "Now, let us speak one at a time." He said. Turning to Ygraine he asked, "Has your question been answered?"

Ygraine nodded. "Aye. It has been answered. I will send my army to join yours on my arrival at Tintagel."

"Thank you." He turned to the others. "And you, my lords, what is your answer?"

This time there was no babble. Each in turn answered with the same words. "My army will join yours within a fortnight."

"Attack or wait?" Arthur asked.

The answer was again unanimous. "Attack!"

Then another question came up. "There was talk of a new weapon before the boy appeared. What type of weapon is this?"

Kevin rose and went to the door. "Bring me the bow." He said to the guard. Once it was placed in his hands he moved to the center of the room to demonstrate its use. Later he would have a better demonstration by one of the archers who would shoot it from the battlements. All knew the die had been cast, however. The war would begin within a month, and hopefully the reinforcements would not have arrived by that time.

* * *

"Remember the field archery courses we had when we were learning how to shoot a bow?" Tim asked Kevin as they walked the battlement of the bailey. "Two courses of fourteen targets at various distances laid out through the woods. There were shots across ravines, off a cliff face on one course, up a hill, down a hill, and all that just to get a medal or a trophy for our prowess. It did teach us how to aim at various distances and elevations."

Kevin nodded. "I remember the fun we had when we went to those tournaments. What's your point?"

"These are new bows and the archers are not familiar with their use. They are longer than the old ones and all arrows are now the same length. Because each archer's draw is a different length, they are going to have to learn their aiming points all over again. We had our arrows cut to our draw. I remember mine were twenty-eight inches long and yours were closer to twenty-nine. These are all going to be a yard long, so there will be six to ten inches extending in front of the bow. They need practice, a field course or two, and a few tournaments with prizes for the best shots. A contest among them might be a good thing to have."

Kevin leaned over the balustrade and gazed at the ships in port. He nodded. "That's a good idea Tim. Let's get on it right away. That way when the bows are finished and the archers from the other kingdoms arrive we will be able to have tournaments between the various kingdoms. We'll also find the best archers that way as well."

"We had better have some of our artisans make targets while we have some of the servants work to build a course in the woods around the caer. We can go out and walk off a course or two, mark each shooting stand, and where the targets will be in relation to the stands. Once we have the course laid out a team of workers can clear the shooting paths. While they do that the carpenters can build the bases for the target butts." He smiled broadly. "It's going to be interesting to see how rapidly these archers can adjust to their new bows."

* * *

"As you know, it is not lawful for our kind to meddle in the affairs of humans. It must be done by another human." The voice came without preamble as Myrdden sat at the table in the library writing an account of the events of the past few days. He smiled, shook his head at the humor of the situation, and without turning said. "Hello Brian. It is good to hear your voice again."

Brian Connor came around the table and sat opposite Myrdden. His smile was mischievous as, with twinkling eyes, he said, "Hello Myrdden. Good to see you."

Myrdden leaned back in the chair and placed the quill in its receptacle. "And what brings you from Ireland to Briton?"

Brian's face lost its smile. "News from London has come to us by way of Oberon. While his people cannot broach the palace, they can listen in on the talk among the officers of Marduch's army." He smiled sardonically. "It would seem Marduch has little to say lately about what he wants to do. Morrigan is able to control him through what seem like soft suggestions, but are really velvet wrapped around iron orders. There is some apparent jealousy between him and the commander he desired to come from the continent, so he hasn't heard from that source as yet. His armies, to keep their appetite for killing whetted, have made a number of raids to the north of London, and Morrigan seems to have approved of the killings that have occurred."

Myrdden sighed and nodded understanding. "It seems the longer Morrigan is here, and the older she gets, the greater her desire to kill and conquer. She seems to believe the way to get people to follow her is to force them with a spear or sword. More flies are caught with honey than with vinegar, but she doesn't seem to understand how that works. What is on your mind that you tell me things I already know?"

"Morrigan must be eliminated from this situation."

"I know. The question is how? Nimue and I were going to call her with the white circle, confront her, and see if we could best her at her own game."

Brian shook his head. "No. Don't even attempt it. The Fallen One who backs her power is far more powerful than the two of you. If you tried it you might well be killed."

"We would be protected by the circle."

Brian sighed. "The circle works against those of our kind who have little power. It doesn't work against one who was created to occupy the high place from which he fell when he rebelled. No. That won't work, so don't try it."

"Then what will work?"

"Lyonnesse is descending more quickly than it was before. Soon it will have been completely inundated and lands end will be nothing but a steep, rocky, coast with few inlets. Lir and Lugh have much power, and they have talked things over with the one who took the Fallen One's place. There is a prison prepared on Lyonnesse, a prison with shackles not made of iron, but made in the eleventh dimension. The lock is also made there. It is only this that can keep the one who has fallen from being able to rescue her. You and Nimue do have a duty, but it is in a much more powerful circle than the pebbles that hold our kind captive."

"All right. You know I will obey Lir and Lugh. What is it we must do?"

There is a place south of Bath called Stanhengue. It is an ancient circle of large stones, some call it the hanging stones, erected long before the druids came to power. It is lost in the antiquity of time as to the built it. The upright stones are massive, as are the stones forming a lintel over those huge stones. These will be a protection for you not because of their size, but because of the power they possess for good when used for that purpose. You must be ready to travel there, summon Morrigan when told, and the higher powers will then transport her to Lyonnesse and her new home. I will come to you when the holding area is finished so you might make the journey."

"This will prevent her from doing what she wishes to do?"

Brian nodded. "Aye. Lir has used the Stone of Seeing and finds without her Marduch will lose, Arthur will kill him, and his army will retreat across the channel. Arthur will then be able to consolidate this entire island under the rule of Caer Maellot. He will have to conquer Alba, but by might and diplomacy it will be done. Once done there will be a long period of peace as the country grows and becomes united as a strong people. Under his rule the peasants will be educated as well as those who sit in power. From the way Lir describes it there will be a golden age."

"If Marduch wins he will conquer and kill, Morrigan will have him killed and become queen of this island, and her desire for conquest will expand until it extends around the world. These will be the dark ages for education even of those who she allows to sit in power. She must be stopped."

"I agree. You may tell Kings Lir and Lugh I await their bidding."

Brian nodded and disappeared. Myrdden laughed at the quickness of his departure. "*Slan go foill* to you, too." He murmured.

"*Slan agat*! The word came from behind him, and he knew he was alone. Picking up the quill he again addressed the parchment before him. New information was added to bring it up to date.

chapter 6
Stanhengue

"It is a far different thing to fight armed warriors than to fight unarmed villages of old men, women, and children." Morrigan's face held a crooked smile as she paced the throne room. "Besides, you are killing off our future subjects."

Marduch waved a hand to dismiss her objections. "My dear young lady," He said in a condescending voice. "it matters not if they die. They would die anyway when I have finished with Arthur's army. When the time comes we will merely bring my people over from Saecsony and we will repopulate this island with our own. Please, don't worry your pretty head about what I'm doing. I want to make sure my troops are blooded so when they do go to war they will not be afraid of those they face." He turned to look out the window.

"After all, I've been a warrior for half my life, and all of yours, I know how these things go. Believe me, when we are done I will give you Caer Maellot on a silver platter so you can do what you wish within it." He didn't see the raised eyebrow, or sardonic nod given the back of his head.

"I would suggest you attack soon, then, so I might have my prize." Her voice was honeyed as she spoke. "I would start pulling my army together if I were you."

"That is a good idea." Marduch said as he turned. "I think the time is ripe to begin preparations. We should be ready to move before the first snow falls."

"That is good. I'm looking forward to being mistress of Caer Maellot in place of Queen Gwendenvere. Since she is a warrior queen she will probably be killed in battle, if she is not dead already."

Marduch's face puckered into a frown. "Why would she be dead already? She is not much older than you."

Morrigan caught herself. She shook her head and shrugged her shoulders. "Oh, no reason, no reason at all: just wishful thinking on my part."

Mollified, Marduch nodded. "I understand. I wish Arthur and his friends dead as well, but as yet I have heard nothing like that from the west." He laughed shortly. "I guess I'll have to take care of that bit of business myself." He patted his sword. "And here is the blade that will do it."

* * *

Arthur looked out over the plain surrounding Caer Maellot. He turned to Kevin and Myrdden, waved his arm in a gesture taking in all the plain from the cliff at the back to where it began on the other side. The plain was filled with tents with the banners of the various kings showing where their men were billeted. "Young Robert's story did more than I could ever have accomplished." He said. "The armies are assembled. What do we do now, attack?"

Kevin shook his head. "No. The time is not ripe. The archers must become acquainted with their new bows and arrows, and the yeomen must learn how to work together as a unit with their allies. This next month will be spent on training. The yeomen will do mock combat on the fields we have prepared while the archers will have a series of tournaments on the archery courses. All must learn to work as a team rather than as individuals."

Arthur nodded understanding. "I see. Yes, it is best they become well acquainted. To that end should we not integrate the way in which each kingdom is set up with their tents? Then the men could mingle with each other."

"Oh, they will mingle." Kevin answered. "They will mingle in the pubs over their flagons. More importantly they will mingle on the practice fields and in the tourneys we are going to have. Tomorrow we begin."

The archers assembled on the green where a tent had been set up. Groups of four were sent out. Each group consisted of one archer from each of four different kingdoms. Each group had a clerk who would keep each archer's score. As they grew accustomed to their new weapons those who were the best would come to the fore. Once the best from the first flight had been determined they would be pitted against each other. This would continue until the best from each kingdom had been found. The reward would be to become captains of their own groups. Meanwhile, archers not in these tourneys would continue to practice and compete until all had become proficient in the use of these bows.

On the other fields the yeomen were intent with their own combat experience. With blunted swords and cushioned pikes they practiced the tactics of parrying their opponents thrusts, sidestepping so a pike would pass harmlessly by rather than impaling them, and other tactics of both dodging and of stepping into the opponent to deliver a deciding blow. Throughout all of this on both archery course and field the men of the Round Table mingled with the various armies. The four queens helped train the women warriors as well as through their presence they showed they were in this fight along with the men they would command. With all the activity the month passed quickly.

* * *

"So the army marched west yesterday." Morrigan commented as Marduch buckled his sword around his waist. "Where is your armor, my lord?"

"Armor I won't need for another week when we go into battle. My sutler has placed it on the horse carrying my tent and personal equipment. I won't really need this," he patted the sword, "until battle, but I feel undressed without it. Besides, my men expect it of me when I ride to them."

"You leave for the west today?"

"Aye. I will ride to catch up with my army and lead them on to a glorious victory once we enter the area of Cymru governed by this upstart Arthur."

"Thus far your armies have had little fortune when they faced him or his father. Why do you expect success where others have failed?"

Marduch eyed her, allowing his eyes to travel over her lovely figure. "Because, my dear Morrigan, I believe you will witch my sword and the swords of my army so we will be able to conquer these followers of the new god. I know you are in league with a powerful god yourself, and your prayers to him will reap benefits for all of us. You have told me before he is on our side. Now is the time for him to prove it."

"I will do my best to assure you of victory, my lord Marduch. After all, I do wish to sit on the throne of Caer Maellot for I understand that castle is far more pleasant than this one. I look forward to your victory. To do so I must go to a place of power. I understand there is such a place near Salis. It is called Stanhengue. There a circle of great boulders is placed in a powerful form. I will go there for there is great magic in that place."

Marduch nodded and smiled his agreement. "Good. I have heard of this ancient place. I am sure you will be able to marshal your powers to assure our victory." He walked to her and kissed her. "For luck…my luck." He said and strode from the room.

Morrigan watched from the window of her room as Marduch, head held high as he looked on the citizens of London with disdain, rode to meet his men. As she watched she called her lady in waiting. "Pack my things and tell Stanislaus to ready the palace guard to accompany me. I feel I must go to a place of power to accomplish my ends. We will go near the ville of Salis where there is a place called Stanhengue. It is a place of great power, and we will need that power to conquer Arthur."

As was always the case when Morrigan left the castle, except those times when she did not wish to have anyone know of her activities, she was accompanied by a number of armed warriors. Most of the palace guard, with no one to guard at the palace, looked on the jaunt to Stanhengue as an enjoyable excursion. There would be no danger from the enemy to the west, and surely the lovely Morrigan would allow them to be entertained while she went about her business. Still, because of their precious charge, they were watchful as they rode through the day to the west –and Stanhengue.

Tents were set up for the night as Morrigan's cook prepared the meal for her and her servants while the guard cooked from their own provisions. The great stone circle was a hundred yards away and toward the east were the barrows where, it was believed, the bodies of those who built the circle were buried. It was a place of mystery, it was a place commanding awe, and the merriment of the guards on the way dissipated as nightfall came. The great circle, still perfect after all the years, stood with all its pillars capped with large, roughly rectangular, stones that formed many doorways leading into the interior. There was almost a reverent silence that pervaded the camp that night for the sense of the power of the Otherworld was very evident even away from the circle.

Morrigan relied on perceptions not possessed except by those of Atlantis: perceptions that would allow her to know when the battle was about to begin. When she knew Marduch was within a day's march of Caer Maellot, and had set up his own camp, she ordered the guard to stay in camp and, alone, walked to the circle and slipped between two of the upright pillars. She turned to orient herself then went to the altar stone where she began the ritual that she knew would call the spirit others called The Fallen One.

She had scarcely begun when she heard a familiar voice behind her. "Greetings Morrigan, or Lilith, or Morgan, or whatever you wish to be called tonight."

Morrigan turned quickly. Myrdden and Nimue were standing in the center of the circle of stones. Her face hardened and she stared at them icily. "What are you two doing here?" She asked. "I was under the impression you two were helping Arthur and his friends in the coming battle."

"Oh, but we are." Nimue answered sweetly. "We are helping him by making sure you are no longer able to use the dark powers to aid the Saecsen."

Morrigans smile was cruel as she lifted an eyebrow and sneered. "You know not the powers I have at my command. My Great Lord will cast you down and together we will assure a Saecsen win. Then I will become queen of the country and be able to work my will over all."

"There is no doubt your great lord has much power." Myrdden answered. "I believe, though, the powers behind us are even greater. King Lir and King Lugh have joined with higher powers to take you to a place where you can no longer interfere with the destiny of the men of this island."

Morrigan shook her head angrily. "No! Even with the help of those two you will find me stronger." She smiled cruelly as she lifted her arm, held her hand before her, and pointed at the two. "You are in the same circle as me now. Were I outside I could not do this, but I am inside." It seemed a bolt of lightning lashed out of her hand toward the two. Taken by surprise Myrdden's gesture was slow, slow enough the force of energy threw he and Nimue back to the stone pillars behind them. A second surge lashed out, but better prepared the two fended it off.

The power of the unleashed forces both sides were using threw some of the stones of the lintel falling to the ground as the deflected energy bolts struck them. Others of the pillars were toppled as the three exchanged blasts of energy they would not normally possess. Myrdden and Nimue were able to prevail as Morrigan's protective force began to weaken. Finally, in the now ruined circle of Stanhengue Morrigan slumped to the ground. Her gown hung in tatters from energy she hadn't been able to divert. "What will happen to me now?" She asked weakly.

In answer to her question the forms of Kings Lir and Lugh materialized. "Now, Morrigan, we return you to Lyonnesse and a prison forged in the lands of the eleventh dimension. I understand you will eventually escape, but it will not be for many hundreds of years in the future."

The two grabbed her arms and Lugh slipped a pair of bracelets on her wrists. They nodded to Myrdden and Nimue. "Thank you for a job well done. We will see her to her prison now." With those words all three disappeared.

Nimue sighed deeply as she looked at the ruins of Stanhengue. "It was a place of great power, for good in this instance, but she was going to use it for evil."

Myrdden nodded as he also surveyed the damage. "It still is a place of great power, though it has been weakened because the circle has been broken. I wonder what the future will think of this place." He took her hand. "Come, let us return to where we belong. I doubt her minions will investigate this before morning." With one last look at the circle they slipped out to where their horses were guarded by Eamon, Duff, and the three new warriors. The only light was that of the full moon as it shone down on the empty ruins.

* * *

The semaphores not only warned Caer Maellot of the approach of Marduch's forces, they were also instrumental in protecting the returning party from the ruins of Stanhengue. As Marduch set up his camp in a valley ten miles east of Caer Maellot, not suspecting his approach had been known shortly after he left the plains and hills around Bath, the warriors at the caer were preparing for the approaching battle. Tents were struck and the men moved into quarters that had been built into the walls of the outer bailey.

Each archer was now issued a full quiver of arrows, and caches of arrows were placed on wagons that would follow their advance. The yeomen would march forward ahead of the archers. As they approached within bowshot they would stop, stoop down, and the line of archers would send volley after volley into the lines of the Saecsen army.

After training on the field courses the archers had practiced shooting, pulling an arrow from their quiver and nocking it on the string. They had become so adept at this the best could shoot three arrows in less than a minute with great accuracy. Waves of arrows would kill or wound many of the foe before the yeomen would advance. After the arrows had done their work the yeomen would march forward for hand to hand combat. Once the hand to hand combat had begun the archers would stand back and act as snipers, picking off individual members of the Saecsen army as they fought. Kevin had planned the attack so the battle would begin with archers lined up on the ridge above the valley. The actual fighting would take place in the valley. Given the high ground the armies of Cymru should prevail.

As Arthur, Kevin, Tim, and Myrdden rode out, each leading what would later be known as a regiment of combined yeomen and archers, Marduch was still setting up his camp. He expected to march the last ten miles to Caer Maellot, place a siege before it, and starve his enemy into submission without a major battle. His men had been adept at the killing of untrained villagers, had felt the excitement of the kill, and were anxious to face what they expected to be a much smaller army. At nightfall he met with his captains. “Tell your men to sleep well tonight. We will break camp before dawn and march to Caer Maellot in the early morning hours.”

He allowed himself a cruel smile. “They will be unsuspecting of our coming so the victory should be easy. Tell the men they must kill the kings, and they may do with the women what they will. Steiphos, you will command the northern front. Claus, you will take the southern front. I will command the center and be first to enter the castle. Good luck to you and your warriors.” He lifted a glass of the ale he had brought. The others lifted theirs in answer. “Prosit! To a quick victory, but if needs be, to a quick siege.” They drank, the captains saluted Marduch, and left to talk to their men. Marduch glanced at his servant. He smiled happily. “Tomorrow we will command all of the southern part of this island.” He stomped the floor in his excitement. “It will be a great victory, and I shall be a hero to my people when I bring them over to replace these Celts. Join me in a toast to that victory, Jens, then to bed.”

In the early morning the camp awoke, the cooking fires were lit, and the aroma of the meats and bread that would break their fast filled the camp. The yeomen began the work of dressing in their battle gear, honing their swords a final time, and preparing for the march west. As they were finishing their meal the sun began peeking over the hills to the east, and the sound of trumpets sounded from north to south along the crest of the ridges to their west. Unprepared as they were they looked up in surprise as the first rain of arrows filled the sky over the hillside, darkening the sky and slashing into the huddled men in the valley below. As they ran for their shields the second volley flew after the first.

As Claus left his tent an arrow, addressed ‘To Whom it May Concern’ caught him in the neck. He looked at the blood spurting out onto his leather cuirass, looked up at the hillside, and collapsed. The last thing he saw was an expanding pool of blood staining the ground in front of him.

Marduch’s eyes were wide with surprise as he rushed out at the cries of the men around his tent. The entire camp was chaos as men desperately tried to run from the wave of arrows raining down on the camp. There was no place where they could escape. Some hid behind trees to await the end of the barrage. They were used to hand to hand combat: not being targets for arrows. “Morrigan, my witch woman, you must help me now. You promised!” Marduch shouted as he tried to get his men into some semblance of order so they would face the enemy.

While the Saecsens were veterans of combat in other places, the tactics of Marduch had been to surprise the enemy and make victory quick and easy. These men were not used to being surprised, and while blooded with that of innocents, it had been over a year since they had seen real combat. It was difficult to get them back into their decimated ranks.

The barrage of arrows was over and the ranks of Celtic yeomen now ran down the hillside toward the camp of Marduch yelling and clashing their swords on their shields as they ran. Again Marduch was surprised. Instead of the small army he felt Arthur commanded he was facing the combined armies of all of the kings of Cymru under the command of their High King. Arthur, riding a white horse, rode down in their center as Kevin to the south and Tim to the north followed suit. Myrdden, leading another band came in from the west while an even larger band with Maeve at its head had circled the valley and came from the east. These were the yeomen of Queen Ygraine of Tintagel. No matter where he looked there were yeomen clanging their shields and shouting as they came.

Marduch bellowed, "Attack! Attack!" drew his sword and ran forward. Arthur dismounted as Marduch ran toward him, drew Excalibur, and prepared to engage the Saecsen chief. Marduch, enraged as much as surprised, had become a berserker: a warrior so entrenched in blood lust that nothing would stop him except his own death. As he ran toward Arthur he hacked at the men standing between them caring not whether they were his own or the enemy. Raising his sword high he prepared to give a chopping cut to cleave Arthur's head in two. Excalibur caught the downward stroke and cut Marduch's sword in two. Recovering quickly, Arthur stabbed forward to catch Marduch's shoulder on Excalibur's point.

Undaunted, Marduch grabbed the sword of a fallen warrior and began slashing strokes in an attempt to disembowel his enemy. Arthur remained calm as he caught the majority of the strokes before they could harm him. Some cuts appeared on his arms and sides as he fought, but there was no flow of blood from the wounds.

Marduch, crazed by Arthur's ability to parry his blows, raised his sword high over his head exposing his entire chest. Arthur drove forward. The point struck Marduch to the left of the sternum, entered, and slid completely through his body. Arthur tugged at the sword. It seemed caught. He raised his foot and placed it on Marduch's chest to push as he pulled the sword back. Marduch took two steps backward, sword still held high, then toppled to the ground as it fell from his lifeless hand.

From the Saecsen warriors around his body the cry went up. "Marduch is dead! Marduch is dead!" They dropped their weapons as they raised their hands to indicate their surrender. In a spreading circle the combat ceased as the word reached the forces Marduch had commanded. With him dead there was no desire to continue to battle for a cause that was now as dead as their leader. Weapons dropped, arms raised, the Saecsen were herded into a number of groups in what was left of their camp. The armies of Arthur surrounded them.

Steiphos, the only commander left sought out Arthur. He handed his sword over as a token of surrender of the entire army. "We are yours to do with as you will. With our leader dead there is no hope left for us in this country."

Arthur looked at him. "I should have you and your men all killed for what you did in the villages north of London." He said. "The killing of innocents, and we know what happened from the lips of one you thought dead. We do not take it lightly." He looked around at the field where the battle had been fought. Few of his men had died. Over three quarters of the army of Marduch were dead, dying, or badly wounded. Their cries and groans rose from the field as friends tore arrows from the bodies of the wounded and attempted to staunch the flow of blood.

Arthur shook his head sadly. "You have lost many men. Many of these who live now will not be alive by nightfall. You may tend to your wounded and bury your dead. You must leave this island and not return. Nor must any of your people come to this island again. That is the decree of the High King of Briton. Our shores will be guarded while we move to make all on the island one people. Your life is spared so you may take this message back to your people. Anyone, or any army, will immediately die without trial if any attempt to come to this land. Is that understood?"

Steiphos nodded, a glum expression on his face. "Aye, it is understood."

"Will it be obeyed?"

"I will attempt to assure its being obeyed. I cannot answer for any but myself and my men."

Arthur nodded. "Perhaps, knowing they must come in small ships, and they must land separately, and anyone from any ship will immediately be killed, might be a deterrent. Don't you believe that to be true?"

Steiphos half smiled and nodded. "Aye. It is a good argument you make about not attempting an invasion. The order will be passed on to my leaders."

"Good. Arthur smiled wryly. "While I trust you at this point, I will leave men to guard your camp and to watch you on your way."

Steiphos also smiled wryly. "That is what I would do if I were you. There will be nothing to disturb their watchfulness, believe me." He looked around at the tattered remnants of his army. "After all, we have few warriors left to return to Saecsony. I don't understand how you knew of our coming. It is always Marduch who has surprised the enemy. Never has he been surprised."

Arthur looked to where Marduch's body lay. "There is a first time for everything, isn't there Captain? He will never surprise his enemy again, nor be surprised himself. You may leave as soon as you are able." He returned to his horse. "Liam. He called to his captain. "Post a guard to make sure they leave as soon as they have buried their dead and taken care of their wounded. See them safely to London and on ships back where they belong. Then make sure London is a safe place for our people and send word back to me it is ours. You will then be governor of the Province of London. Once we have control you and your men may take your wives and families to live there."

Liam nodded and smiled broadly. "Thank you, Sire. It shall be as you wish. Thank you for your trust."

"You deserve it or you would not have it." Arthur turned and beckoned the other leaders who had led their men into combat. "Come, let us return to Caer Maellot." He turned to Kevin and Maeve. "I realize now that the battle is won you must return to your own kingdom in Eire. I hope I can persuade you to remain a while longer to advise me on setting things up." He looked at Tim. "And what of you, Sir Timothy, will you stay or will you go with your king?"

Tim looked around him, then at Kevin. "Ive been with Kevin pretty much all my life. I guess I'll return to Eire with him. We will be ready to answer your call if you need us. But I suspect Myrdden will be with you for quite a while longer."

Arthur looked at Myrdden, an eyebrow lifted as a question mark. Myrdden nodded. "Aye, Arthur. I will be with you most of the time, but I will find time to visit Kevin, and Tir na nOg. I'll be there when I am needed."

"Good. Then, if you will stay a day or two longer, Kevin, you might help me in getting a government organized for the southern part of this island. I must begin uniting it so we find a peaceful solution to our problems. I presume I might call on you if I find I need help."

Kevin reached over and clapped Arthur on the shoulder. "Tim, Maeve, and I will always be there if you really need us. Right now I have to get Beog back to familiar surroundings. I think he's getting homesick for Dun Rowans."

Their laughter echoed behind them as they spurred their horses toward Caer Maellot.

LaVergne, TN USA
27 November 2009
165417LV00002B/23/A